TABOR'S TRINKET

TABOR'S TRINKET

JANET LANE

FIVE STAR

An imprint of Thomson Gale, a part of The Thomson Corporation

THOMSON

✳ ™

GALE

Detroit • New York • San Francisco • New Haven, Conn. • Waterville, Maine • London

LIBRARY OF CONGRESS CATALOGING-IN-PUBLICATION DATA

Lane, Janet.
    Tabor's trinket / Janet Lane. — 1st ed.
      p. cm.
    ISBN 1-59414-542-3 (hardcover : alk. paper) 1. England, Southern—Fiction. 2. Fifteenth century—Fiction. 3. Vendetta—Fiction. 4. Nobility—Fiction. I. Title.
PS3612.A5498T33 2006
813'.6—dc22   2006022294

U.S. Hardcover:
ISBN 13: 978-1-59414-542-1
ISBN 10: 1-59414-542-3

First Edition. First Printing: November 2006.

Published in 2006 in conjunction with Tekno Books.

Printed in the United States of America on permanent paper
10 9 8 7 6 5 4 3 2 1

DEDICATION

I dedicate this, my first published fiction novel, to John Penaligon, my husband of twenty-one years. He put up with me when I dragged our family through Somerset, looking for obscure towns and landmarks, and through all the late-night keyboard sessions and challenges, he gave unflagging support to my writing dreams.

I'm not sure he would eat a spell cake, but with his charm, sense of humor and adventure, John has helped make my life the stuff of dreams.

ACKNOWLEDGMENTS

When John and I married I gained a husband and a new family. Thanks to Dot and Nancy for reading those early versions, and to Jack, Carol, and all the Penaligons for their support. Thanks to my incredible daughters, Jessica and Jalena, for sharing their enthusiasm and their many talents, including editing and graphic design. Thanks to my mother, Mary, and my twin siblings, JoAnne and John, for the love and laughter. Thanks to Pam, Rose, Laura, Jan, and Carol for their treasured friendship and encouragement.

I appreciate the help of my friends at Rocky Mountain Fiction Writers, especially to the members of my Kay Bergstrom critique group, Kay, Peggy, Robin, Sue, Sharon, Alice, Leslee, and Teresa; and to my Alphas, Jim, Karen, Margaret, Vicki, Bonnie, Lawdon, Michael, Heidi, Rosita, Christine, Gail, Shannon, and Tony. Thanks to Pam and my Celestial Sisters; my Story Magic plotters, Karen, Diane, Kay, and Jasmine; to Margie Lawson and my KaizenWriter motivational group friends.

Thanks to the research librarians at Bemis, Jefferson County, Denver Public Library and the University of Denver.

Thanks to Geraldine Buchanan of the Winchester Museums Service for maps of the St. Giles Fair, and to the Winchester City Council for information on trade routes and medieval-minted coins.

Acknowledgments

Thanks to Jessie Wulf and Susan Mackay Smith for their tireless efforts with the Rocky Mountain Fiction Writers Colorado Gold contest. Thanks to historical author Denee Cody for her helpful input, and to Denise Dietz, who saw the potential in this story. Thanks to John Helfers, to Alja Collar for her patience and help, and to my editor, Alice Duncan, for her enthusiasm and keen eye to detail. After all input, any errors with historical fact are mine.

CHAPTER ONE

Marseilles, France, 1426

The sound of strangers' voices woke Sharai. Ropes binding her feet, she stumbled to standing and stood lifted on tiptoe to see outside the forecastle at the bow of the ship. A slave ship. Dawn. Seagulls called, circling the limp sail that flapped around the main mast. Below that, the dead body of the slave, Zameel, draped over a coil of ropes, his forehead white with maggots and his neck black with grotesque knots.

Sharai's mother stirred, her eyelids red and swollen. "*Ves' tacha,*" she rasped in Romani. *My beloved.* "What is it, my little *Faerie?*"

"Shh." Sharai put her fingers gently to her mother's lips.

". . . and touch nothing!" A man's voice commanded from outside the ship on the port side. Heavy footsteps sounded as men jumped on board. "If anyone still lives, kill them."

Fresh terror seized her chest. All the crew and slaves had died, all but Sharai, her mother, and the captain, who lay still at her feet. He had been delirious these last few days, but still able to navigate to Marseilles where he had planned to sell forty healthy slaves.

Sharai checked the captain but he didn't stir, nor did he breathe. He must have died during the night. She pulled his dagger from a sheath at his side. Its blade had been recently sharpened and its ivory handle had been delicately carved with a bird in flight. She gripped it tightly.

9

Footsteps sounded on deck and she knelt by her mother. "Feign dead," Sharai whispered. Not a hard task, for they were close to it. The bug-ridden biscuits had run out days ago, and they had been living on ale, wine, and rancid meat.

"Mother of God," exclaimed a man. "Slaves. Gypsy slaves, dozens of them."

"There's more below deck," said another. "What stench!" He gagged and retched, and the dull splashing of vomit followed.

Sharai's throat constricted in reaction to the sound, and a cockroach crawled up her neck, but she willed herself to remain still.

"See the lumps. Plague!"

"Get off the ship! Burn it!"

Liquid splattered on the deck, followed by a whooshing sound. The rope ladder creaked and the men's voices diminished.

Sharai risked checking. "They have gone." Using the captain's fine dagger she severed the ropes that bound her and her mother's feet. "The shoreline is but a hundred yards away. We must swim to safety."

"Curse Murat," her mother said of Sharai's uncle, who had betrayed them. "I cannot swim, Faerie," she said. "I have no strength. Go without me."

"Never!" She lifted her mother's chin. "I will help you."

"You are but eight summers. I will drown you. Go!"

Sharai half-carried, half-dragged her mother down the ladder from the forecastle to the main deck. She grabbed a small wine barrel and dumped it, and the stale, musty odor of tainted wine filled the air. "I cannot leave you here," she told her mother, and handed her the empty barrel. "Hold onto this and you will stay afloat."

A gust of wind whipped the smell of burning death and the heat of hell into their faces. Hurrying past the flames, they climbed over the railing. Sharai slashed the last remnant of rope from her ankles and dove into the water, imploring the helpful spirits for safety.

Hampshire, England, August 1430

His chest wound throbbing, Richard Ellingham, younger brother of William, Baron Tabor, leaned against the metal gate leading into the armory. The smell of blood and burned hair blended with the odor of rusting metal. Coin Forest Castle was under siege, and uncertainty burned into his flesh as surely as the pitch-laden arrows had. He fought the darkness that came in waves and threatened to carry him away.

Cyrill, his knight, fell against Richard, his lined face creased in pain. "The Hungerford knights have breached the curtain. God's blood, and your father barely cold in his grave."

Richard steadied him. "Their claim is false, but their swords are not."

Richard's brother, William, lord of the castle, hurried down the steps to join them, his expression lacking all traces of his customary confidence. At twenty-one, he was short but able-bodied, a fitting lord of the castle. "All is lost."

Richard rested a hand on his brother's armored shoulder. "We did our best. We must leave. To the tunnel," he said. "Make haste."

"We can't," William replied, backing against the stone wall. "They've cut us off."

"Then the armory." Richard opened the gate. "Come on!"

William rushed ahead and a dozen of their men hurried into the armory, the sight of their gold and green livery reassuring.

Aurora, his brother's wife, ran to Richard, grabbing his arm. Her red hair tangled past her shoulders and fear glittered in her eyes. "They've taken the keep!"

A rush of forbidden love pulsed to the surface. Richard

wanted to wrap his arms around her, shield her from the fear. As always, though, he controlled his emotions. He took her arm to guide her. "You must hide." Despite her protests, he pushed her behind a shelf of broken back plates, stuffing the folds of her skirt behind the wood.

She struggled out again. "Let me go!"

"We're outnumbered. Stay here, and be silent."

Across the chamber, Cyrill and his men swung the gate shut.

Behind them the enemy's footfalls echoed in the stairwell as they clambered down from the great hall. One knight slipped on the stairs, made wet from the rains. The knave recovered and joined the rest of them, a wall of black and white liveried knights. They turned their shoulders against the gate, ramming it to keep Richard's men from homing the lock. The black and white broke through, pushing forward, and the gate collapsed. Grunts and shouts of pain from both sides echoed in the damp chamber.

Three of the attackers advanced into the armory, downing four of the defending knights, leaving less than a dozen to hold the castle.

From the adjoining, smaller chamber William appeared, driven backward by Rauf, Hungerford's son. The enemy. Metal clanged and Rauf's sword struck William's flesh with a wet thud. William's armor broke free at the shoulder and exposed his hauberk, glistening with blood, and a second knight advanced on him.

A primitive shout filled the chamber. Richard recognized it as his own. He ran to aid his brother and drew his sword, but the narrow doorway offered no room to swing it. He shoved his sword sideways, blocking the tall knight's attack on William.

Richard drew his dagger and cleaved it into the tall knight's neck.

The Hungerford knight froze. His sword, poised to strike

William, dropped from his hand and he fell.

The meaty-faced Rauf swung at and missed William.

William smashed an armored fist into Rauf's face, driving him back. "Thanks, brother." William lunged forward, following the press of enemy knights to the fireplace.

Richard saw movement out of the corner of his eye. He turned and a swinging mace rushed toward his face.

He ducked.

The mace grazed his face.

The blow shook his skull. Richard slipped into a dull senselessness, vaguely aware of his careening sense of balance. He tried to find his feet, and warm liquid pumped down his face. He fell, and the stone floor punished him, cold and unyielding. Death would come to him, too, on this day. Blackness overwhelmed him.

A firm hand pulled at him. "Richard. We must away."

Richard strained to obey Cyrill's plea. He managed to lift one eyelid. His limbs, frozen as a winter frost, struggled to move, but he was still alive.

He listened, hearing no more clanging of armor. Torches hissed, and somewhere nearby metal scraped on stone. The sick-sweet smell of blood mixed with the stench of sweat, and pain throbbed like devil's fire in his ears and teeth.

The fighting had stopped. Gingerly touching his left eye, he found it swollen shut. Only Cyrill was there, to his left. Black and white clad bodies littered the floor, but there was one, a stout one, in gold and green. One of theirs. Richard crawled to his side. His brother, William.

"Nay!" He gestured to Cyrill. "Give me light!" He raised his brother's head, but William's gaze was unseeing. A part of him had hated William for taking Aurora from him, but Richard loved his brother. Gone in his arms. Sweet Mary. Richard closed his eyes to stop the pain.

"Help me." Aurora's voice was tight with pain.

Richard gently rested William's head on the floor and hurried to the skirted form on the floor in the corner.

Aurora rolled to her side. Her hair pressed against her neck, matted with blood. In the torchlight he caught the muted green in her eyes, framed with a sheen of tears.

He propped her with his left arm. He moved her hand from her side, saw her life's blood pumping down her bodice.

Fresh pain sliced through him. *Not her. No.*

She shook her head. "I'm sorry."

"No. No apologies." Despite his love for her, she had chosen William instead of him.

She offered her hand and he took it. A tremulous sigh slipped between her parted lips. Her head dropped, and her hand relaxed in his.

He felt love slipping away, and his breath caught. "No!"

Her suffering over, she sank back on his arm.

Richard tried to swallow the pain that stuck in his throat like a sharp rock. He smoothed Aurora's curls back from her face and closed her eyes, laying her head gently on the stone floor. He took a breath so deep it caused his chest to throb again.

He looked around the keep, at the blood-soaked bodies and fallen swords. Could he have prevented this slaughter? He'd sensed trouble coming from that pig Hungerford and had tried to warn his brother. "I should have been more insistent that William increase the guards. I should have kept after him."

Footsteps clamored on the stairwell above. More men coming.

"Don't blame yourself again," Cyrill said. "We must go."

"I cannot leave her."

"You must. Hungerford's men were called above, but they'll be back soon. We can access the tunnel now."

Richard stumbled down the circular steps, past the storehouse and treasury and into the dungeon.

The remaining handful of his men were waiting there.

Richard gestured toward a small, inconspicuous hallway. "Follow me." The hall led to an inner chamber. Aided by the knights, Richard moved the stone that blocked the doorway. He met the loyal gazes of his four remaining men, their brows glistening with sweat and blood beneath their armor. "Go."

They squeezed past the stone, their torches flickering in the revealed passageway. Behind them, they pushed the stone shut, closing the entranceway.

The low tunnel smelled of wet earth and mildew, and a chill brushed his face with each step.

Cyrill stabbed the torch into the darkness.

Spiderwebs clutched at Richard's face. He brushed them off, moaning from the pain of touching his burned skin. He stumbled again, and sharp stones tore at his shoulder. "My eyes." Even his good one had swollen shut.

Cyrill placed Richard's hand on his shoulder. "Hold on."

One foot in front of another. Uneven steps, slippery footing, floor muddied from the heavy summer rains.

Occasional drips of water, the light splattering sounds of scurrying rats.

"The passageway is narrowing. Take care," Cyrill warned.

Richard fought the dizziness. Through the pounding of his head he sensed the tunnel dropping steeply.

Cyrill halted. "Bloody pox."

Richard pulled his eyelid open to see. Ahead of them, water sparkled off the torch's light. "God's bones. The rains have flooded the passage."

"We're trapped." Cyrill walked knee deep into the water. " 'Tis a steep bank down."

Richard looked back the way they had come. "Hungerford's men are closing in. There's no going back." Richard removed his damaged breastplate, then his helm and leg guards. He nodded to Cyrill and the others to do the same.

Shed of their armor, they stood facing the lazy sparkle of light that wriggled, mesmerizing, on the black water's surface.

Cyrill's breath came in shallow puffs. "How long before the path rises again so we can breathe?"

Richard stared at their inky obstacle, dark, swirling, taunting him for his hesitation. "I don't remember."

The youngest knight, John, stepped forward, his yellow hair matted with blood and sweat. "Don't try. William's gone, so you're Lord of Coin Forest now, Richard. We can't lose you, too."

Cyrill stepped forward. "He's right, my lord. You're the last son, the last hope." His knight rested his hand on his shoulder. "Richard, Baron of Tabor. Lord Tabor."

Tabor. Richard nodded, feeling of a sudden older than his nineteen years. "If we don't escape soon, we'll be dead and in a place where titles don't matter."

His greying eyebrows furrowed, Cyrill looked to him for a decision.

The sound of clanging armor echoed in the darkness from which they'd come. Enemy knights swarmed closer, thick as hounds on a downed boar. To remain would be suicide.

Torchlight danced across the water, a winking surface that masked the perils that might lie beneath. Guards routinely checked the tunnel, but they had never reported flooding. The skies had spilled rain for more than a sennight, and now this. He regarded his sword, the curved handle, crafted for his large hands, the fine blade. "This will weigh me down." He placed it in a niche above the rough stones and hoped to reclaim it someday.

He gave what he hoped was a reassuring smile to his knights. "Time for baptism, men." Taking a deep, painful breath, he dove into the dark water.

At next morning's first light, Cyrill showed Tabor to a bed in a large storage tent near the Gypsy dancers' wagons at St. Giles' Fair. Three knights had refused to swim the flooded tunnel and stayed back to fight to their deaths. Tabor, Cyrill, and John made it through the tunnel to safety and then traveled through the night to Winchester and nearby St. Giles, a large fair where desperate men could disappear amid the crowds of buyers, sellers, and thieves.

Cyrill pulled the blanket from the bed and gestured to Tabor to lie down. "Rest now." At thirty and five, grey had claimed Cyrill's temples and brows, but his eyes reflected strength. And raw worry.

Though the ceiling tarp dripped and the ground had been muddied from the rains, the tent was spacious, with a small fire pit in the middle of the floor. Crude ropes strung at eye level sagged with the burden of colorful fabrics. A half-dozen chests cluttered the corner, apparently moved to make room for the bed that awaited him by the far wall. The air smelled of wet wood and the faded evening's ashes.

"I can't rest. Hungerford's men are at Coin Forest," Tabor protested. "We must purge them."

"Stay you still." Cyrill prodded the hole in Tabor's chest.

Pain shot up his throat, and Tabor drew a sharp breath.

" 'Tis deep. How would it be to tell your mother you died, as well?"

"But the king . . . ," Tabor paused, as all men did. England's king was but eight years old. "Well, the Regent, Bedford, must be notified, but he and the king are away at Rouen." England's war with France plodded on with none of the success it had enjoyed before Henry V's death.

"We'll get word to Gloucester, the Protector. In a few days

you can return and we'll rout the vermin."

"Thanks be my mother is at Fritham," Tabor said. "But William." Memories of his brother formed in Tabor's mind—William's arrogance, prancing his horse after winning at tournament. The time they scared the Hawkridge girls by bursting pig bladders when they were in the garderobe. Fresh grief ripped through him. "Hungerford will pay."

"But what of the three knights left behind?" Tabor's gut wrenched. Secrets spilled under the pressure of torture, even with the most loyal. "The treasury—"

"They won't find it." The hesitancy in Cyrill's eyes betrayed his words. He squeezed Tabor's arm in sympathy, bade a hasty goodbye and left.

A woman entered the tent. Etti, his friend, leader of the dancers. Her black hair fell well past her shoulders, brushing his hand. She nudged Tabor onto the bed, forcing him to lie down. "Fie! Tabor, your face." She shuddered.

Above high cheekbones, her ebony eyes flashed. Lines clustered at the corners of her eyes and mouth, leading Tabor to believe she had lived at least forty summers.

"Thank you for safe harbor. I'm in your debt."

She laughed. "Ah, now I have a landed noble in my service. Music to my ears." She produced a small vial, forced his eyes open, and splashed a liquid in them.

It stung. "Agh! What is it?"

"Just eyebright and ground ivy." She removed the crude bandages on his chest and gasped softly. She sprinkled liquid on linen and dabbed gently at his chest wound. "I'll be back to stitch this closed." She poulticed it and handed him a small blue flask. "Here. Swallow this for the pain. And spare me your thoughts on the taste."

"I need to go."

"Ha! You'll stay until you can travel." From a chest she pulled an armload of crude, torn linen. "With that face, no one will know you, but your clothes will draw attention. Here." She held up a shift of russet cloth and helped him change. "There. You'll be taken for a commoner now, Lord Tabor." She winked in that playful way her people possessed, and then she tended to a fire. Etti was one of the dark-skinned souls who came from a place called Little Egypt.

She'd called him Lord Tabor. Hearing his new title reminded him of his loss, and fresh pain stabbed him, a pain no tincture or bandage could heal. His brother, William, was dead. And Aurora. In the quiet that followed, Tabor thought of her. Like the sensation of inhaling smoke from a torch's fire, a sharp pain burned in his chest, below the gaping wound. He turned his head toward the wall. She had never been his. She'd only played with him, used him to get close to William, heir to the title and castle. Though she sought only station and wealth, his love had been real. He heard a soft moan—his own—and then sleep overwhelmed him.

A clicking sound awoke him. The herbs Etti had given him made his mind blur. How long had he been sleeping?

A woman knelt in front of a chest of clothes. No, a child; a girl not yet upon her womanhood. She hummed a hymn, her voice a light velvet, her tone as sure as the monk singers at Winchester. Her arms were thin, her skin lighter than Etti's but still swarthy, like a ripe walnut. She twisted her long black hair into perfect rolls then slipped into a formal headdress, using a polished metal mirror in the chest lid to adjust the veil.

"Ooh," a tiny voice purred, and pudgy fingers grabbed the edge of the chest. The golden curls of a child's head appeared and a hand reached upward, short fingers grasping for the veil. "Mine. Mine!"

The older girl laughed and handed the child the veil. "Be

gentle, Kadriya." Scooting a bucket to the overhead lines of clothes, the older girl pulled down a smock, slipped into it then pulled on a gown and tied the laces. Standing on the stool she had gained enough height for the flowing skirt, though the bodice sagged on her flat chest. Tabor smiled at her slightly believable illusion.

Kadriya squealed and placed the large veil over her head like a blanket.

"Lovely, Lady Kadriya." The older one straightened her back, lifting her nose toward the tent top. The movement made the lace of her veil dip past her tailbone. Tabor caught a glimpse of her silhouette and her raised eyebrows. Too entertained to interrupt, he remained silent.

She held a rag in her hand and waved it like a fine kerchief. "You fancy my necklace, do you? 'Tis a family heirloom." Her tongue twisted around the phrase, leading him to believe she may have just learned the words. 'Twas a gift from the king himself." She turned a few degrees and dusted the air with her rag. With great flourish she offered her hand to the tiny girl. "Come, Duchess. Sit with me in the great hall and we shall have a feast." She shrank from an imaginary enemy. "Away with you. Such a knave you are, and me a fine lady. Guards, protect us. Take him away." She turned from her imaginary knave, leaving him in the custody of her equally fanciful guards.

She spun too quickly and the long skirts caught under her foot. Her arms swung in big circles and she tilted out of balance. With a cry she stumbled off the bucket, landing in an inglorious heap on the hay-strewn floor.

Kadriya gave an audible gasp and covered her mouth.

Laughter bubbled up in Tabor's throat, but the effort brought sharp pain to his ribs. He groaned.

She gasped and stood, clutching the dress to her chest.

Kadriya scrambled behind the girl's skirts.

The older one approached. "What are you doing here?"

Tabor held out his hand in a gesture of peace. "I crave your pardon. I should have spoken up. I enjoyed your singing."

Her hair fell free from the left bun and her brows drew with suspicion. "Indeed." Her gaze dropped to his chest, then back to his face. "Even your hair is burned. You have tangled with the devil, I see."

"Forsooth. I'm sorry to have startled you. Etti invited me to stay."

Her frown diminished. "Etti knows you?" She loosed the other bun and her hair fell free, shining and black as ink.

"We're friends. I'll be here for a few days."

Her eyes widened, and she approached him.

Her oval face featured high cheekbones, and the curve of her face reminded him of the soft line of a willow branch bending in a summer breeze. Her nose was thin and straight, perched neatly above a generous mouth that was parted in curiosity. Her eyes were dark brown, astonishingly direct and framed by thick lashes.

Tabor blinked. Realizing he had been holding his breath, he exhaled. In a few years she would become a beautiful woman.

"What is thy name?"

"Arthur," he lied.

She moved closer, lifted the blanket and appraised his clothing from neck to feet. "You're poor."

Surprised at her boldness, he found his voice. "Aye. But I will find a way to repay Etti for her kindness."

"Good. Mayhap you can be put to work on the stage. 'Tis creaking so badly that the dancers cannot hear the music."

Concerned that she thought him a commoner, capable only of low labor, he teased her. "And what is thy name, my *lady?*"

"I am Sharai."

Sharai. It rhymed with "Dare I" and the sound rolled off her tongue as easily as fresh berries from a plate.

"I am laundress to the dancers." She thrust her chin out. "But not for long. Soon I will leave here and live in a grand castle. You shall see me in finery. Come, Kadriya." She lifted herself tall again and glided out of the tent.

Kadriya followed like a dainty golden shadow, her large eyes fixed on Tabor until the tent flap closed.

Silence fell around him. The tent seemed smaller, the air less charged without Sharai's presence. He shrugged the feeling aside. She was just a child with giddy dreams.

The next morning it hurt to breathe, but his eye was healing, and he would travel on the morrow before his face lost its swelling, which would put him at risk of being recognized by Hungerford's knights.

He needed to return home. The treasury—sweet saints, if they found it, 'twould be almost as good as stealing the castle. The tapestries—he shook his head. Best to forget that, but he would need assets from the treasury to replace the horses and stock, the buttery and wardrobes, at the minimum, to get Coin Forest through harvest.

He flexed his arm muscles, testing them, and struggled to a sitting position. Swinging his legs over the side of the cot, he struggled to sit upright. He needed to regain his strength, join Cyrill, and oust Hungerford.

The colorful fabrics blurred, and a pattern of black dots filled his vision. He grasped the bed linen and eased himself back onto the bed. God's teeth, he couldn't even sit upright. He rested, welcoming the clarity that returned when his head remained on the pillow.

He looked toward the tent flap. No sound had alerted him, but he sensed a presence.

Tabor grabbed his dagger and closed his eyes enough to appear sleeping yet still track the prowler's progress.

Greaves protected the man's massive calves. Tabor could look as high as the intruder's chest without revealing that he was in fact awake. The man wore a padded hauberk, equipment marking him as a knight, but no armor. *Friend, or foe?*

"Tabor." A familiar voice.

God's bones! Rauf, Hungerford's son. His bulbous nose was swollen, bruised and broken from William's blow. Rauf, the swine who'd killed his brother. "How did you—"

"Find you? Rats leave droppings. The dark-skinned hag is washing bloody linens in the river, and this is her tent." He grunted. "I see your garments now reflect your true station. Peasant." He raised his sword and lunged.

Tabor rolled toward him, stabbing Rauf's thigh.

Roaring, Rauf pulled his sword from the mattress and grabbed his thigh. "Devil's whelp." He raised his sword again.

Tabor thrust his dagger, slicing Rauf's arm. "Rot in hell."

Rauf's sword pierced Tabor in the side.

Pain seared through Tabor, and red flashed behind his eyes. Pinholes of blackness gathered, clouding his vision, and he fell back on the bed.

Rauf bellowed again.

Tabor heard Sharai's shriek followed by a string of unfamiliar words, punctuated with a cry of *"Chut! Chut! Chut!"*

Women's voices joined Sharai's, and, swinging their baskets and pails at Rauf, they raised a large chorus of the strange chant. Sharai pulled a heavy kettle from the dead fire. Using her lower body strength to swing it, she made clumsy connection with the side of Rauf's head.

Rauf fell.

Sharai dropped the kettle and pounced on him, her dagger flashing. With a wild cry she drove it into Rauf's back.

Rauf moaned from the floor, then became silent.

Sharai stood, her small chest heaving beneath the thin fabric of her soiled smock.

Etti appeared. "Take what's left of him to the marshal."

The gravity of his situation struck him. By the saints, he had been saved by a handful of women. Heat crept up his neck. Saved by women!

Sharai placed a small hand on his forehead. "Fie. He's torn your stitches. Etti will need to sew you again."

Etti offered him a vial. He drank the potion and fell into a welcome darkness where pain and its gnawing tentacles could no longer reach him.

When Tabor awoke, the tent glowed with the horizontal light of evening, and the rains had stopped. Heat from the fire warmed his bones. Moving with care, he raised his hand to examine his body and noted new bandages on his side.

And the girl, Sharai, stood above him. She wore the same short, soiled smock over a stained blue skirt, and bare feet. Her ebony hair fell past her shoulders. "I brought you some ale."

"Thank you, my *lady*."

She sat cross-legged atop the nearest chest. "Stop teasing me."

He attempted a smile through the pain. "I mean no harm." He thought of her courage. "You saved my life."

"Low-class sod, he was, attacking a wounded man."

"Such language from a lady."

" 'Tis true," she sniffed. Her eyes narrowed. "Be you a murderer?"

"Nay." He thought of the women dragging Rauf from the tent. "What did you tell the Fair marshal?"

"That he attacked us." She patted her leg. "I'm quick with my dagger." Her wide brown eyes seemed to reach into his mind. "Why did he wish to kill you? What did you do?"

"Naught." He would not attempt to explain the long-standing

feud between Rauf's family and his or the intricacies of their
claim to his family's properties, but Tabor appreciated her
mettle. "I'm no thief, and I promise you, Sharai, that I'll
remember your help this day." He reached for her hand and
squeezed it. "Thank you."

She looked so young to him. Her innocence was beguiling,
and her strength and skill with a dagger exceptional.

He released her hand. "Where are you from?"

A brief flicker of pain shadowed her eyes, then she recovered.
"Little Egypt."

That story again. He'd heard it first from the growing
numbers of dark-skinned people in France, and now a handful
of them were here in England. They claimed to be of noble
blood, disinherited of their lands and on some manner of
pilgrimage. Some of the dancers, he'd learned, were skilled in
the carnal arts. He found them charming, though strange in
their nomadic ways. This little one was most intriguing. "How
old are you?"

She stood taller. "Ten and two."

He wondered what this dream-filled girl would say of her
background. "Are you a noble, then?"

"I am."

"And someone has stolen your finery?"

Her eyes darkened. "All has been stolen, but I will regain it."

"How so?"

"I have it all planned. I shall snare me a noble to wed."

Her words shattered the glow of charm that had surrounded
her, and Tabor pulled back. Snare a man, would she? As some
hunter would trap a witless rabbit.

Her dream was impossible. She'd saved his life, so he'd help
her see the error of her plan. "Never. I know of Gypsies from
my travels in France. There your people are known as heathens.
Palm readers. Potion makers. King Henry and his royal advisers

will never allow it. If a noble weds you, he'll be dispossessed of his lands and turned out like a beggar. Then you'll be in worse shape than you are now."

"Your king does not recognize royalty from other lands?"

"Yes, but—"

"I am a princess. And a Christian. I attend church. I have been baptized by a priest from St. Giles Church." She gestured toward the church tower just ten stone throws away. "Would your king call me a heathen, then?"

"No, but surely you—"

"Then you're mistaken. I forgive you."

Mayhap she had no choice in the matter. "To wed a man for station alone—there are cruel men, like Rauf, the man who attacked me. He's a noble. Would you wed such a man?"

She seemed to think about that problem.

"Your parents have chosen this path for you?" Tabor asked.

"My parents are dead. I choose it for myself."

It may be the practical way of things, he knew, but Tabor had seen men and women in love, had read stories of marital passion, and he wanted nothing less than that for himself.

He would explain it to her and set her on a better path. "With no family duty, you need not look at station when you choose your husband. You're free to follow your heart."

"I shall follow my hand, thank you, right to my mouth and the mouth of my babes."

Her eyes, so round and earnest. She'd likely seen her share of misfortune, felt more than her share of hunger and fear. He tried to dismiss the bleak thoughts of Aurora's betrothal but could not. "Nobility involves duty. Sacrifice." He said it as much to himself as to her.

She gave a short laugh. "You, in your well-worn rags. What would you know of nobles?"

Her words of dismissal jabbed at his pride. " 'Tis plain by

your dress you're no lady. Nor do you speak as one. However can you hope to rise to such a level?"

A knowing look came into her dark eyes, a cynicism beyond her years. "Mannerisms of the nobility are easy to learn. I watch the women. After worship. They hold their hands low, in front of them, and they move in short, slow footfalls." She stood and took mincing steps across the tent, as if she were walking on quails' eggs. "They hold a trencher thus." She mimed sliding meat off a server, bending her little finger. "They drink in this manner." Elbow high, she lifted an imaginary goblet.

On behalf of his birthright and his mother's grace at court, he took offense at her mocking summary. "You may parrot a lady's movements, but what of letters? Embroidery? Courtly etiquette?"

"I know some letters. The St. Giles priest trusts me to launder their finest ceremonial linens. In return he teaches me to read." A radiance in her eyes revealed her determination.

Her fortitude angered Tabor, but he held his tongue, refusing to speak of the stories that kindled his own imagination, tales of pure love, untainted by greed. She was too self-absorbed, even at her young age, to fathom such. "And what of honor?"

"Honor? You yourself pointed out that oaf who stabbed you was a noble. I've seen your other English nobles, too, here at St. Giles and at Stourbridge, seen the cruel ways they treat their retainers. They have less regard for them than slaves. Nobles use the poor." She gave a crooked smile. "And I plan to return the favor."

Her disdain stung as a personal insult. "Such a lovely face, but what a cold heart. Should you find him, I pity your sorry noble."

"You know not what I've endured." Her voice wavered with emotion. She composed herself, reclaiming her lofty aura. "Enjoy your sad lot in life, poor Arthur," she said, lifting her tattered skirt from the ground. "And I shall take my path." She stalked to the door, her bare feet smacking in the mud.

CHAPTER TWO

Five Years Later—August 1435

Tabor reined his horse to the crest of the hill. There in the meadow, overshadowed in the distance by the imposing Winchester cathedral, sprawled St. Giles Fair. Late afternoon sunshine slanted on the checkerboard of tents lining the river. Boasting flags of their owners' colors, they sprouted on the bank like so many errant wildflowers.

Tabor looked for the weed among them, Hungerford's black-and-white coat of arms. Not there. Good. Neither he nor his loutish son, Rauf, were here. The fair was free of vermin.

It was here that Tabor had sought refuge in Etti's tent five years ago, and it was here that Tabor would now buy horses and books for his scribe. And locate a seamstress for his mother.

He breathed deeply, taking in the aroma of pork roasting in spits and the bustling of mummers, gamblers, and merchants. He would see old friends. Enjoy the wenches. Laugh.

He checked the purse hooked on his belt, felt the modest bulge of coin, and reality dulled his excitement. He had regained his castle, but the crown continued to founder in chaos, affecting Tabor's legal recourse against Hungerford.

The war with France limped on, and the child King Henry played with toy swords while his uncles clashed with legal weapons for control. Tabor's petition to remedy Hungerford's siege was met with a terse note demanding that Tabor "keep the peace."

29

Cyrill and the young knight, John, shifted on their horses beside him. Cyrill spat. "Cursed long ride. My back is torturing me."

Excitement shone on John's thin face. Shorter than Tabor by three inches, he kept his yellow hair bowl cut high above his eyebrows. At ten and eight years he was eager to gamble. "Is there time for games before dinner?"

Tabor laughed. "A fool and his money, John."

"I'll do better this time."

"Avoid the dice tables and you'll keep company with your coins a bit longer."

They dismounted, passed the fair gates, paid their toll, and set their horses to grazing.

Tabor glanced past the bend in the river ahead, where the low, grey dancers' tents huddled together.

She came to his mind then.

In the five years since he had last seen the Gypsy girl, he sought her out each time he visited here but found neither her nor any Gypsy. It was as if the dark-skinned people had vanished.

Sharai. Her name whispered in his memory like yielding summer grasses in the wind.

She had been pleasant, but she had also been strong, felling Rauf, stabbing him. He hadn't died, after all. Afraid Rauf would bring others to finish Tabor, Etti smuggled him from the fair, hidden beneath bolts of fabric. And Rauf had been so embarrassed at having been bested by a girl that he spoke naught of it to the fair marshal.

Where is she now?

He turned away, putting the tents behind him. She was doubtless with some wealthy merchant, wearing finery as she'd predicted. She was but a passing memory, a dash of inspiration best left to the angels. *Or devils,* he thought, remembering her schemes.

Cyrill moved into his vision. "We know not who is in attendance here."

"Be at ease. Curtis, the marshal, keeps the peace. Note how many reeves he hires to enforce it."

"Aye, they crawl the grounds like spring rabbits. Yet as one who was almost murdered on these same grounds, you speak lightly of danger."

"I'm not wounded now." Tabor's jaw tightened. "Rauf dares not challenge me to a fair fight."

They approached several large casks of mead stored in the shade of ancient willows at the river's edge, its honey sweetness tingeing the air.

Cyrill signaled to the mead master and thrust his leather flask out, and the vendor filled it. "Welcome, Lord Tabor, Sir Cyrill. 'Tis been a while."

Tabor waved away the offered mead. "Later, thanks." He must be sharp for the games. "Are we too late for amusements?"

"Nay, milord. Tables are open, if you feel lucky with dice, or target practice." He raised his eyebrows. "Or archery."

Tabor's blood pumped a little faster. He turned to Cyrill. "Join me?"

"Not against you." Cyrill moved closer and spoke in a growling whisper. "My lord, with all due respect, if you simply gave up the Burley manor you could afford your purchases—"

"I will not."

"—instead of trying to gamble your way back to solvency."

A sense of inadequacy gripped Tabor. He struggled to keep Coin Forest afloat. Plague had stripped the region of hale souls to harvest the crops, and many who'd survived were leaving for the cities. He sent a prayer to his patron saint Monica. He'd test his skills again and he must win. "I'll not break up my father's holdings. Not one piece will fall."

Cyrill nodded and pulled out of the huddle. "As you wish. I'll inspect the horses and get settled."

They entered the archery arena. Competition had already begun, led by burly farmers, mostly, their muscular forearms bulging from holding the plough, their skin deeply etched and sun-leathered.

The games judge, a pinch-faced rooster of a man, eyed a dark-skinned man just past his prime, leaning against a wagon. Despite the day's warmth, he wore a fine red cloak.

The skin, the dark eyes. *A Gypsy. They've returned.*

Tabor's blood pulsed faster, and he searched the arena for a perfect oval face with bold, brown eyes. He found none.

"Shower shooting's next," the games judge said. "The wager's now two shillings. The prize?" He paused for effect. "One pound."

At hearing the stakes, the crowd murmured.

A fair, curly-haired wench approached Tabor. "Win for me, Lord Tabor." She winked. "And I'll devote *all* my pounds . . . to your pleasure."

Diana had caught his fancy in London last spring, and she had proven most capable at pleasuring. He gave her a lusty kiss, and the crowd cheered.

The Gypsy appraised his competitors, lingering on Tabor. Shrugging the elegant cloak off his shoulders, he handed it to a friend, dipped into his purse and with an easy sweep tossed his coins into the hat.

Tabor deposited his wager.

"One target, one minute," the judge yelled. "Ready now. Brace. Draw. Loose."

Tabor released his first arrow then pulled the next one from the ground where he'd positioned them. Nock, string, pull, sight, release. The secret lay in making the arrows available without his ever having to drop focus from the string.

The sky had become thick with arrows, arcing to form a tunnel of slender fingers of wood and sparkling blades.

At the judge's command, all shooting ceased.

Tabor strode to the target. With each step, the prize amount rang in his ears. *One pound. One pound.* It would buy him a badly needed suit of upper body armor.

He reached the butt. Red and green fletched arrows crowded the blazon, his and the Gypsy's.

The judge nodded to Tabor and pointed to the target. "Eighteen, two on the blazon is four, twenty-two points."

The crowd cheered and Tabor raised his fist, smiling.

"Count Aydin, sixteen, three on the blazon for six, twenty-two points. A tie. You'll split the winnings."

"Too bad, Tabor." Diana brushed against him and joined other women headed toward the dice games.

Tabor saw his new armor vanishing in the Gypsy's triumphant brown eyes, but he had won fairly, so Tabor shook his hand. "Congratulations, sir. Your name?"

His smile revealed even, white teeth. "Count Aydin." He pronounced his name carefully, as if he were a herald giving accolades at a tourney.

"From Little Egypt?"

"Aye."

Tabor kept his voice casual. "Would you know of a young laundress named Sharai?"

The Gypsy's eyes darkened. "We have no laundress by that name," he said, and spun away.

"Lord Tabor." The fair master approached.

Tabor nodded. "Good eve, Curtis."

Curtis's head squatted on his barrel-like body, his face punctuated with piercing grey eyes that begged challenge. Tabor suspected that, when his mother first offered her breast to him as an infant, Curtis looked twice and selected the other one. Just in case. Perennially suspicious, he never let down his guard. Over all, fine qualities in a fair marshal.

"Hungerford's not here yet, but he's due," Curtis said. "Have you settled your quarrel with him?"

Heat seared Tabor's gut. "The man murdered my brother and his wife and plundered Coin Forest."

"I hear he has claim to your estates."

"Nay. His claim is groundless. My family is of noble blood, lineally descended over centuries. Hungerford whispers perjuries in the king's court."

"And the King doesn't intervene?"

"At thirteen? He's too young to rule. The council leaves us to settle it."

Curtis nodded. "So be it. But mark my words, Tabor."

Tabor winced at the lack of title. It burned into his skin, an echo of Hungerford's claim that his ancestors were peasants, making Tabor and his family undeserving of the king's grant of Coin Forest.

"There will be no incidents between you and Hungerford. Not at my fair."

"When is he due?"

"Three days hence."

Curtis left, and John rushed to Tabor's side. "What did he say?"

Tabor slapped his back. "That you're poor with dice, and would we join him for a wager at noontide."

John's eyes widened. "Really?"

"Aye. And he'll be bringing his own dice box."

After a moment's hesitation, John laughed. "Loaded. I follow."

Hours later, Tabor pursed his winnings, left the chess tables, and released two carrier pigeons to Coin Forest, summoning six knights to guard his purchases during the return trip home. He walked along the riverbank, dimly lit by a new moon veiled in a thin haze of clouds. Tabor watched them hover, moody and transparent, like the threat that loomed over his head since his brother's death. Tabor would buy horses and re-crew harvest laborers, then he would petition Humphrey, Duke of Gloucester, peacekeeper and Chief Councillor, to cure the Hungerford problem.

And he would avenge his brother's and Aurora's deaths, ere another full moon passed.

Sharai cried out and caught the offending fragment of needle in her teeth, pulling it from the tender flesh on the side of her finger. Blood beaded and rolled, dropping on the table.

Kadriya, lit by a sliver of early morning light from the tent's fire vent, looked up from the pet dove she'd been cuddling. She perched the bird and ran to Sharai. "Is it bad?"

"Nay. Cursed things. They've been breaking at the eye. The merchants shall hear about this." She sucked her finger and wound a remnant strip of linen around the wound.

Kadriya's small hands encircled Sharai's wrist. "I'll get some comfrey syrup to be safe."

"I'm fine, Sprig." Sharai used her pet name for her seven-year-old charge and stroked her light brown hair. Kadriya's father was a *Gorgio*, a white nobleman from Southampton who had wooed and abandoned her Gypsy mother. Months after Kadriya's birth, her mother died, and Sharai, ten at the time, had cared for Kadriya since then. Both without parents, home, or family, they shared much in common, and Sharai could not have loved Kadriya more if she were of her own blood.

A mile away the grand cathedral bells chimed, signaling Lauds. "Gather you your basket, and let us to the river for your lessons," Sharai said.

"*Then* can we go to the main gate?"

Sharai laughed. Merchants from Douai had arrived at the fair yester eve with ten pack mules and four wagons filled with bolts of fine draperies and weavings. Kadriya thought the colors brighter than any rainbow. "Would you have us haunt the front gate the day long, until they settle in their stalls?" She tickled Kadriya's neck. "Come. Show me how much you've learned."

They walked down to the riverside, to a place not far from the fair tollbooth where the willows grew. "Let's go there." She selected a lone willow clear of any shrubs where someone might lurk. "We will have privacy, yet be heard by the Marshal if need be."

Sharai wove her way through the sighing branches, threading the slender green tendrils through the uninjured fingers on her left hand, enjoying the cool brush of the leaves against her skin. "Get busy, then. Hold your basket. Pretend I'm a big knave browsing the stalls. You will approach me—"

"I know, I know," Kadriya interrupted. "I'm selling purses. You'll try to pull me away."

Wearing her strictest expression, Sharai glared at her. "This is serious. You're small. Barely five stones. There are bad men here, bad man who will—"

"Steal me, sell me, hurt me," Kadriya recited, tapping her foot in impatience.

Had Sharai impressed her sufficiently with the dangers? "I want you to be safe while you work," she said.

"Aye. So I see you. You're a big oaf. 'Silk purses for your ladyship, my lord,' I ask." Kadriya offered an imaginary purse.

Sharai smiled and slipped into the lesson. "Why, thank you, child. Bring it closer so I may see it." Sharai put her hand out as if to take the purse, then lunged forward, grabbing Kadriya's right arm.

"I turn to keep my right hand free." Kadriya tugged, trying

to pull away, but Sharai maintained a solid hold. "Let go. Let me go!"

Sharai pulled her off balance and dragged her along the grass on her knees. "Bad child. You'll come with me, now."

Kadriya scrambled, positioning her feet under her body, and regained her balance. She swung her basket at Sharai's face and pushed hard, jamming the stiff handle at her throat. She kicked Sharai in the shins and grabbed her forearm, sinking her teeth into Sharai's flesh.

"Ouch. Sprig, too hard." Sharai released her arm.

Scooping a handful of dirt, Kadriya threw it in Sharai's face, then stood back, reached for the leather strap at her calf and pulled a tidy three-inch dagger, slicing the air and backing away, her small chest heaving.

"You bit me too hard."

Kadriya lowered her dagger. "I didn't break the skin, that was the only rule. I did well, then, didn't I?"

Sharai laughed, spitting dirt and rubbing the red welt of teeth marks on her right forearm. "Aye. You need no more lessons. You're strong enough to sell alone. But only before noontide, never after. Any rogues who were heavy in the cups the night before will still be abed then."

Kadriya's smile faded and her large, green-flecked brown eyes grew serious. "Thank you for the dagger."

"You're old enough now. Never use it unless you have to."

Kadriya turned it in her hand, tracing the pattern of the bird in flight carved on its ivory handle. "Who gave it to you?"

"It was an unintentional gift."

"Good score. 'Tis fine."

" 'Twas no lift. I claimed it from a dead man's belt." She averted her eyes from the handle, which brought back memories of the ship. The plague, the stench of death. And the fear.

And the dark waters of Marseilles that stole her mother from her. "I was as young as you then." She brushed the remaining dirt from her arm, wishing she could whisk the memory away.

"In Wallachia?"

"My home? No. In Marseilles, where I met Etti. She brought me here."

Kadriya touched her face. "Be not sad."

Sharai attempted a laugh, but it came out a strangled sob. She wrapped her arms around Kadriya.

They sat in silence, and the sun broke free from the clouds.

Kadriya wriggled out of Sharai's embrace. "Can we go to the main gate now? To see the Douai fabrics?"

This time, laughter came easier. "Sweet Sprig. How can I be sad with you?"

"Sharai?" A rough masculine voice sounded from the trail to the tollhouse.

She drew her dagger.

" 'Tis me. Count Aydin." He approached, wearing a brown doublet and a scarlet cloak trimmed at the sleeves in fox. She should know. She sewed it to his precise specifications, making several alterations to suit his fancy. He wanted the length almost at the knees to reveal his muscular calves, and extra padding in the doublet at the chest, though he hardly needed it. Still, he wore it well.

As he should. He instructed her to make it of such quality that it would equal that worn by the finest noble. He was Romani—Gypsy—like her. He had proclaimed himself their tribal king two summers ago, and, to appease the English nobility and garner alms, he dubbed himself a pilgrim and a count.

Count Aydin held no real title. No power, either, at least not with her. Sharai may have stumbled with men at first, but now she would control her own fate. She bowed slightly. "Your Grace."

"Don't mock me. I worry for you."

Sharai knew what Aydin worried about. What all men concerned themselves with, their belly, their purse, and their bed. "Kadriya and I can take care of ourselves."

"Sadly, no. Your unfortunate incident two years ago proves that."

Memories of the dark incident flashed before her.

"You know how I feel about you."

"I appreciate your concern, but we're capable. Really. Of taking care of ourselves."

"As tribal king, I feel I must ask you . . ." He stopped and looked at Kadriya.

Sharai turned to her. "Sprig, go you to the river now, and catch us some frogs for dinner. Get some extra for Etti; they're her favorite."

Kadriya hesitated.

Sharai pulled her left earring, their private signal that she didn't feel threatened.

Kadriya pulled hers in answer, signaling she'd stay close by.

After a second glance at Count Aydin, Kadriya retrieved her basket and walked down the bank, just out of sight.

Sharai tucked her smock, pulled loose from her tussle with Kadriya, into her skirt waistband. "Speak your mind, Count."

"Very well. I've waited for you. Been patient, and watched over you. When I found the nobleman, I ordered him killed, and it was so done."

The nobleman, Fletcher. She remembered his gentle smile, a gold necklace and a sweet kiss, then a choking grasp, the sound of tearing fabric, invasion, and pain. "I never asked for his death."

"He deserved it. And after my devotion, I deserve you, Sharai."

Sharai braced herself. "We've discussed this. You are *corturari*. I am *vatrasi*." Though they were both Romani, the terms split

39

them as decisively as russet and silk. Corturari were traveling Gypsies. Except when wintering over, the count never stayed in one spot longer than a moon's passing. Sharai came from a tribe of Gypsies who settled. She had known the serenity of a permanent home, and yearned for one again.

"But we're both Romani, and I am your king. You're seventeen now, of the age to marry. I can offer you a large wagon. The best horses. A fine tent."

"Yes, but—"

"Gold." He touched her cheek. "For your fingers. For your ears." His gaze fell to her chest. "To wear about your neck."

He thought she could be lured by a fancy wagon and baubles. To Sharai's shame, she had been lured, with Lord Fletcher. That she could ever have been so young and thick-skulled brought a fresh rush of anger at herself, and at Count Aydin. "So you up the offer? I'm a fine specimen so you raise the bid." She brushed his hand away. "This is not a horse auction."

"Be not daft. You're a treasure, and I will treat you as such. I will lavish gifts on you. I own papers of protection for all of England and France. I'll make you my wife, and no one can hurt you again." He drew her to him. "Break the tile with me, Sharai."

His breath was hot on her face, and she smelled that odor again, faint but still detectable, a trace of an odd, decaying kind of smell. The count's teeth were white and healthy, unlikely the problem. It seemed to come from deep in his throat.

He controlled her tribe. He was persuasive. Handsome to many, mayhap, but that scent, and an unsettling darkness about him she couldn't define, repelled her. Unable to tolerate his closeness, she pushed him away.

"I don't want you." She covered her mouth, but too late. The words had to be said, but they could have been kinder.

A dark gleam entered his eyes, a look of power and determination.

"I rule the tribe. By virtue of your association with Etti, you and Kadriya are part of it. Deny me, after all I have done for you. . . ." He paused and took a deep breath. "You look at no other, so I know you're mine. 'Tis time you put your . . . ," he paused, searching for the word—". . . misfortune, behind you. I shall see you tonight. I so enjoy watching you." He gave her a tight smile and then turned and strode the narrow path back to the fair.

CHAPTER THREE

Tabor sat in his tent, bent over his financial books. After a day of gambling, he'd fattened his purse by thirty pounds, three crowns, twelve shillings.

Cyrill pushed the tent flap aside and entered. His short, grey hair neatly framed his face over friendly grey eyes. "I trust you won enough to buy six horses?"

Tabor felt the familiar pressure, squeezing his throat. His mother depended on him. The people of Coin Forest and his other holdings depended on him. He ran his hands through his hair. "Barely enough to buy two. And I still have incidentals to purchase."

"Tourneys would bring more income."

"You know my thoughts. With Hungerford about, we can ill afford to travel for extended periods. We need supplies now, for harvest. We can't wait for the next big tourney. On the morrow, we'll lure the goldsmiths into high wagers."

Tabor tapped his finger on the numbers, willing them to look more promising. "I'll find a way."

Cyrill raised a brow. "Those numbers will not change for the staring at them. Come to the stage before the show is over."

He lifted the tent flap, and Tabor heard more clearly the strains of music, lilting flute tones and drums. The music, the dancers' bawdy jokes and easy passion—a welcome diversion. Tabor rolled his papers, stored them, and grabbed his money pouch. "I'm ready."

At the dancers' grounds, John's yellow head stood out in the large crowd. Seated close to the stage, he waved them over. "By gad, you two owe me a favor for holding these seats. I all but lost my head a time or two."

Indeed, most seats were filled. Even Count Aydin, the Gypsy with the red cloak and fine aim, was forced to stand at the sidelines. "Thanks, John." Tabor settled in.

On stage, a dancer swayed to the beat of the drum. The drummer, a small fellow with a foxhead cap, increased the tempo, and her hips responded. Above them, her ample breasts swayed in opposing circles. She wore a gauzy yellow gown, pulled tightly below her breasts to accent them, and cinched again at the hips. Being of a fair volume, she resembled three short links of sausage, all undulating in different directions.

"Such full moons," John's voice sounded mellow and husky, and from the crowd, several whoops and raucous invitations arose.

On stage, she flashed white, even teeth and encouraged them.

Her dance ended and she bent forward, giving the men a last gasping glimpse at the size of her breasts.

Cyril strained forward. "More. More!"

She pulled the outer hem of her gown upward, creating a fabric trough. John rushed ahead, tossing farthings into her skirt. Other men followed suit. A man balanced with one hand on the stage and grabbed upward to cup her buttocks.

A burly guard appeared, his torn left eyelid and shoulder-length, wiry hair giving him a rough countenance. He stomped on the man's hand. "Down, you dogs." He glared at the others. "All of you."

She exited through the curtain, blowing kisses at her admirers.

Moments of quiet stilled the crowd, then the foxhead Gypsy began beating the drum again, a slow, even tempo.

Six dancers appeared and formed a circle in the middle of the stage. The music stopped and the dancers left the stage one by one, revealing a new dancer who stood alone.

The men had been rowdy through the previous dancer's performances, but they grew quiet then, and Tabor leaned sideways to see past the stocky man in front of him.

Though small in frame and cloaked in yards of silk, the woman's curves were apparent. Her face was veiled, her eyes cast demurely downward. Her bound hair swayed behind her, and she wore layers of different colored fabrics, soft blue, and shades of red vibrant as rubies in the flickering torchlight.

She strode to the front of the stage, her steps deliberate, almost as if in challenge.

Tabor rose to see her better.

A flutist played light, liquid notes, matching the movement of the fabric that breezed against her legs. She turned her back to the men, placed her hands on her hips, and froze.

Beside him, Cyrill growled, "We don't want to see her backside."

The bearded man turned and growled back. "Shut your hatch."

Swaying softly, she moved to the music and lifted her hands in the air.

Her fingers curled like perfect fans, as if casting magic high, then drawing it back down upon herself. She untied the red scarf on her head and, reaching wide, stretched the fabric from hand to hand.

The drums beat faster and with a flip of her wrist the scarf jumped from her left hand, sailing into the air like a mist.

Such fluid movement and timing. Tabor likened her motions to those of a huntress, waiting for prey and releasing an arrow quietly and surely to the target. Beneath all the grace and allure, this woman possessed patience and purpose.

The drummer stopped and her hair, freed from the confines of the scarf, tumbled past the small of her back. Black as a moonless night and shiny with rich waves, it shimmered in the torchlights, swaying in invitation.

A strong urge rose in Tabor to feel the weight of that hair in his hands, experience it brushing his arms, his chest.

Bending sideways, she tied something on her ankles and the shimmering fabric of her gown seemed to glow.

The musicians stopped and the men, having fallen under her spell, remained silent, waiting.

She resumed dancing and a tiny melody tinkled from small chains of bells that graced her ankles. Her movement stopped, silencing the bells and, in a flourishing sweep of her left hand, she pulled her veil free.

Her oval face held high cheekbones, with round, thick-lashed eyes, dark and challenging. Her lips, full and upturned on the right side, taunted Tabor, drawing him closer.

His heart faltered. He remembered those eyes, that smile.

Sharai.

A shiver coursed through him. It was the girl who had saved his life. She had also become every bit as beautiful as he had anticipated. And she was here, not with her rich noble.

She spun, dancing her bare feet over the stage.

The floorboards didn't squeak. He remembered her suggestion, five years ago, that he help Etti by fixing the stage boards. He heard no squeak, only the melodic ring of her bells. Who had fixed the floor for her, he wondered.

The silk covering her legs parted slightly, affording a tantalizing glimpse of her thighs and her smooth, flawless skin. Her finely toned muscles flexed with the movement of her dance.

She possessed the breasts she had yearned for earlier, not full moons like the previous dancer, but firm mounds swelling the top of her costume.

Coins sparkled in her hair near the temples, and she wore a gold necklace that caught the torchlights, bright and dazzling.

"Sharai," he murmured.

A man stood on the bench, blocking Tabor's view.

Tabor fought his way around him to the front.

Sharai lilted across the stage, her movements delicate. She tipped her shoulder and slowly raised her lashes, taking them all in, innocent but suggestive.

Shouting their appreciation, the men banged empty mugs on their sword hilts, creating a clamor.

She withdrew to the back of the stage and bowed primly, signaling the end of her performance.

Tabor took advantage of her bow and flipped a coin, arcing it low, and it slipped neatly down the bodice of her gown.

Instinctively her hand rushed to her breast and extracted the coin. Looking from the coin to Tabor, she gave him a trace of a smile and held his gaze.

His heart stirred in a way it had not in years.

She left then, and the stage lost its color and mystery, reverting to a basic square of frayed ropes and rain-rotted lumber.

Tabor stood in the afterglow of the spell she had woven.

Coins continued to sprinkle the stage, and the men called for more. The wiry-haired brute with the torn left eyelid reappeared on stage. "Show's over." He directed a young boy to clear the floor of Sharai's coins. He waited, legs spread and arms folded, blocking the stage door, until all were collected.

From the right of the stage four more guards appeared, prepared to keep order. Discouraged, the men turned away from the stage and elbowed their way to the mead barrels.

Cyrill tapped him on the chest. "What ails you, Tabor? Close thy mouth, and let us away."

Tabor's gaze remained on the stage. The man had taken Sharai's coins. Who was he?

Sharai slipped into the dancers' area, a simple wooden storeroom that housed merchant signs and served as the performers' dressing room.

The guard, Wilson, handed her the coins.

"My thanks, Wilson." She disliked the coarse men who grabbed at her, as intent on impressing the other men with their brashness as they were at feeling a woman's flesh. She would never have agreed to do it had Etti not assured her she would always have a guard, and had it not been for the income.

The coins the men tossed often totaled thirty pence or more, enabling her to make in less than a bell's time what it would usually take a week to do. It would help her repay Etti, at least regarding finances. She could never fully return the favor Etti extended when she saved Sharai's life ten summers ago.

Wilson resumed his position at the side door.

Several dancers stood by the dressing table and mirror, but two, Diana and Codi, peeked through the curtains at the men.

Codi turned to Sharai. Her thick eyebrows were arched high. "Sharai. Your handsome admirer, Tabor, refuses to leave. Count Aydin's talking to the reeves. They're approaching Tabor, but still he pushes forward."

Loud voices and the sound of curses and fists on jaws came through the curtain.

Sharai peeked. Tabor had broken free and was picking something up from the stage floor. One of her ankle bells.

His dark hair brushed his collar and framed a strong nose and cheekbones. She admired the clean lines of his face, his smooth, healthy skin, and his jaw line, framing full sensual lips. His eyes held a burning, determined interest. A shiver of excitement bolted through her.

47

Such feelings brought disaster. She tamped them down and turned away.

Codi stayed at the curtain. "The reeves have taken him. Poor Tabor. By the saints, he is a handsome devil."

"That's *Lord* Tabor," corrected Diana, her voice rich and throaty. Her tight blond curls bounced with each turn of her head.

Codi laughed. "He just punched the reeve a good one. I remember those large hands."

Diana laughed. "He knows just how to use them, too."

Sharai held her arms to her body. "Prithee keep your pleasuring details to yourself." Diana and Codi were *Gorgio*, non-Romani, and entertained the men with private pleasures.

Codi nodded. "He has lover's hands. You should try them, Sharai. I enjoyed him in London." She grinned. "And 'tis not just his hands that are large."

"I don't share your thoughts about men."

"Oh, you'd like him well enough, Sharai," Diana purred. "He knew just where to put that coin, now, did he not?"

Sharai turned the coin in her hand and blinked. He had tossed her a crown.

"Aha, my girl. You blush. You do like him." She strode forward in triumph, linking her arm in Sharai's. "He can take you straight to heaven with those hands. I felt guilty taking his money. 'Tis almost that I should have paid him. If all men could be so—"

"Diana." Etti appeared from behind the hanging clothes, her dark eyes flashing. "Leave Sharai in peace. You know what happened to her. If she wanted a chronicle of your customers, she'd ask you."

Diana straightened. "I saw the way she looked at him. Believe you me, I know yearning, and yearning is what passed between those two. I saw it."

Etti frowned. "Leave her be."

Diana laughed, a deep, self-indulgent rumbling that made Sharai wonder how Diana had become so womanly that even her laugh sounded sultry. "You must break out of your cage some time."

"I'm in no cage. I lost my purity, nothing more nor less. And in my mind nothing . . ."—she glared at Diana for emphasis and repeated it—". . . *nothing* about the activity bears repeating."

Codi put her arm around Sharai's shoulders. "Try this, pet— just share a kiss with him," she whispered. "Innocent enough. Just one, and I wager you'll believe us, then."

"Never."

"Just one."

"Cease."

Codi laughed. "You're afraid. Afraid we might be right."

"Men are barbarians. I'll suffer this foolishness no longer." Sharai slipped the coin into her waistband and spun away from them toward the door.

"Sharai, wait." Jennamine, the voluptuous dancer who preceded her on stage, approached, her round face pinched in worry. "Prithee help me. My seam has split again." She turned to show the yellow fabric, strained and torn with a gaping three-inch hole in the side seam.

"By the saints, Jennamine, again?"

She grimaced. "I know, but you're so skilled with the needle, you can fix it, can't you? Say you will or Etti will have me quartered. She warned me twice now about my weight." She patted her hips and waist as if willing the inches away.

" 'Tis not your weight Etti worries about, but your girth. Fabric is costly." Sharai pulled her behind a row of trunks. Leaning close, she whispered. "Breathe out and hold it. We'll get you out of your gown, and I'll see if I can add an inch or two."

Jennamine peeled the fabric away from her ample curves. "You're our best seamstress ever, Sharai. All the girls say so." She handed the gown to Sharai. "Many thanks." She leaned closer. "Don't be angry with Diana and Codi. They mean well, and pleasures with a man *can* be good." She lowered her voice to a whisper. "I enjoy them with Wilson."

Wilson? The guard, with his wild hair and ragged eye? "Jennamine! Etti will have him flogged." She thought of Kadriya. "And what if you get with child?"

"Shh. She won't find out, and I take the herbs so I shan't be singing lullabies." She lowered her voice, "Wilson has knowing hands like this Lord Tabor." She left with a light giggle.

Sharai set to work on the split seam. Wilson stayed, waiting to escort her safely to her tent.

His face and hair made him look like the losing rival in a cockfight, but his body appeared fit and clean. She dared a glimpse of his hands and then looked up.

He met her glance, smiled in a self-satisfied manner, and performed a perfunctory check at the door.

Her neck heated, and she cleared her throat. "Just a couple more stitches, Wilson, and I'll be done."

"Aye. The ale is dwindling, I fear," he hinted.

He's eager to be with Jennamine. What did they all know that she did not? She remembered the noble's rough hands, tearing her skirt, the pain, the bruises. Mating was a coarse, savage act, and she'd kill the man who tried to touch her.

She stitched nimbly, closing the seam, and the yellow fabric blurred. She saw him again in her memory, the handsome Lord Tabor. Tabor. It sounded clean and sharp, like the angles of his face beneath his thick, dark hair. Tall, just enough muscle to be strong but not so much as to resemble a bull. He moved with a cat's grace. Were it not for his pale skin and height, she would think him a Gypsy, too.

Mayhap he was not like the others.

Something about him seemed familiar, yet so beguiling; surely she would have remembered meeting him before. So bold, the way he flipped the coin down her neckline, and the intimacy of his glance caused her breath to come with difficulty, as if the forest faeries had cast magic upon her. The vulgar men with their lewd gestures and suggestive grins faded, and she could see only Tabor's eyes. . . .

"Ouch!" She sucked her finger, tasting blood. "Cursed needles."

"Here, milord. A fresh towel for your jaw."

Tabor placed the soothing cloth on his face, which still ached from yester eve's bashing at the Gypsy stage. "My thanks, Cyrill."

"Have you broken your fast?"

"Aye, the reeves tossed me a slab of bacon and bread."

"So, how was your night in the tollbooth?"

"You've spent your share of nights in such places. You know well how it was. Cold dirt floor. Mice. Bugs. I simply wanted to talk to her. A pox on Curtis for holding me."

"You did seem, um, determined."

"Merely to talk."

Cyrill laughed. "Shall I send for her?"

"Nay. I would visit with her in my own time." He tossed the wet towel on the table. "Now I must find a seamstress for Lady Anne. For the harvest festival."

Brushing his mustache, Cyrill stopped mid-stroke. "Your mother insists on holding the festival, even with the alarming shortage of funds?"

"Appearances. She craves acceptance. After Hungerford's

slurs on our ancestors, I can sympathize. First he stole our treasury, then our dignity."

"Sweet misery, Tabor."

"No lectures. I'm capable. I shall prove it to my mother and all at Coin Forest."

"But such waste—"

"My mother must look her best for the festival. I'm off to find a seamstress. We meet at two bells for bowls. *Au revoir.*"

At ten bells, Tabor crossed the fair grounds, entering the livestock and market area. The grey morning was filled with the smell of manure and fresh straw and the noise of squawking geese and pigs. Men hustled, pulling tarps, still wet with dew, from their booths. The air itself seemed rich with life and hope, for income from this fair would take these farmers through the coming winter.

Tabor reached the cloth merchants and, after making some inquiries about a reliable seamstress, learned of the best one at the fair.

Sharai. Again she surprised him.

On inquiry, Curtis advised that Sharai was creative and skilled with the needle, but warned that she would not take an outside commission due to her loyalty to Etti.

Tabor would find out for himself.

He approached Sharai's tent, deciding he would not tell her about his deception as the wounded peasant, Arthur, five years ago when he sought refuge in Etti's tent. Or that he knew of her failed plan to marry a noble.

It would embarrass her and she would never accept his offer of employment.

Then there was the issue of her competence. He would have her sew a gown and see for himself her level of proficiency.

He caught his first glimpse of her in the tent. Her braid hung over her shoulder, past her waist. He remembered her on stage, her hair loose and flowing, and his body responded. He chided himself. She was just that skinny, scrappy little girl, grown up. Five years ago she saved his life. He would be pleased now to offer her honorable employment, a chance to leave that tawdry stage and stay decently clothed, by gad.

Kadriya ran from her dove's cage in the far corner of the tent. "He's here."

"Quick, Sprig. Go you out for a bit. I'll be fine."

"All right. But I'll stay close by."

Sharai shooed her and took a position behind a stack of fabric bolts, her hand buried in her pocket, stroking the markings on the crown. *I will never be sold again.* If he wanted more than a dance, she would return his coin. She would sell baskets and dances, but not herself.

He entered the open tent, the top of his head brushing the ceiling until he neared the center poles. His dark hair, cut short at the sides, fell to his collar in the back, and a bruise decorated his freshly shaven face at the jaw line.

His form-fitting green doublet revealed a trim body and strong shoulders, but the lining did not lie smooth at the neckline. She could do much better. The tailoring flaw was counterbalanced, though, by his brown tights and elegant girdle, from which a money pouch and handsome, jeweled dagger hung. The bulging moneybag reminded her of his position, and her own.

She raised her chin and faced him, eye to eye. "Good morn, Lord Tabor."

His lips curved in an inviting smile. "And to you, Sharai. You know me, then?"

Against her will her eyes strayed to his large hands. "Your reputation precedes you."

"Aye, as does yours." He knelt down to examine one of the lower bolts of brown wool. "Your skills as a seamstress come highly recommended."

He'd come on business. Though sewing paid little compared to the dancing, Sharai needed every coin she could gather for Etti.

She assumed her business manner and let the crown drop to the bottom of her pocket. Needing support, she rested her hand on the top bolt. "What do you need?" She regretted her choice of words even as they passed her lips.

He lowered his head to hide a smile and then raised his lashes, looking up at her.

The skin at her throat awakened, tingling down to her breasts.

"I seek your services on behalf of my mother, Lady Anne. She would like a houppelande with matching headdress. Silk." He browsed the fabric bolts. "Blue." He rose to standing. "The same hue as the gown you wore yester eve."

She met his eyes and a trembling struck her chest, as if her drummer held his drum before her and pounded hard. His brown eyes betrayed his calm features, for there burned a fire inside them, and she heard the echo of Diana's husky voice mocking her, "Yearning. I saw yearning."

She turned away, realizing too late from his expression that she had revealed the same to him.

Sharai fussed with the selvage on the black wool. "Do you have a style in mind?"

"I have a drawing." He produced a sketch on paper.

Accepting the paper, she extended her hand too far and their hands touched.

Heat whispered on her skin and she jerked her hand back. The sketch was primitive, but clear. His mother wanted the newer styled, wider sleeves. "Excuse me. I think I have the perfect bolt of blue for her."

She ducked behind a worktable. *Gather your wits, Sharai. He's a noble. Noble, noble, noble. You're naught but a hunk of bear meat to him. He's comely, but at heart like all the others.* Clutching the blue silk, she breathed deeply and marched out to show it to him.

She dropped it on the table. "Will this do?" She piled another bolt, a deeper blue, on top. "And this for trim. Or would you prefer an ivory?"

"Let me see." He pulled the bottom blue bolt free and unwound the fabric, letting it drape in folds on the table. "The color is good. It will bring out her eyes."

Surprised, Sharai stepped back. Women might inspect the fabrics, but men generally pointed at a color, stood for measurements and left.

He unwound at least three ells of it. "May I? Just to see how it falls." Careful to not let it brush on the ground, he draped it over her shoulders, letting the fabric slide through his fingers. "Nice weight." He focused on her eyes, then followed the drape line from her shoulders to her toes. "Perfection. And I must say, your performance last night was such, as well. You're beautiful."

She collected the fabric and took it from him. "I trow not your intentions. You doubtless have no mother named Lady Anne, and you need no houppelande."

"Certes I do. I'm in need of any and all of your skills."

"And pray what does that mean?"

"Your dance is bewitching. You have skills with a needle, and I should like to hire you to sew for me. And if you have skills in pleasuring, which I daresay you must, given the way you dance," he said, his voice caressingly suggestive, "then I should like to negotiate with your manager. The wild one with the torn eye."

Egad, he thought Wilson arranged . . . she gestured the insult away like a horse fly. He was like all the rest. Why had she let down her defenses? "Get you gone." She slapped the crown in his hand. "And take your money with you. It cannot buy that which you seek."

He stroked his bruised jaw and smiled. "You've changed."

What did he find so cursed amusing? "You speak in riddles. Be gone."

"As you wish. I'll need it in two days."

His grin stirred her to new anger. "What?"

"My mother's dress. Blue is perfect. She's this much shorter than me," he gestured, "and she weighs ten stones, but don't let on to her I told you."

"Two days? And no measurements? I cannot—"

"I'll make it worth your while. You do sell your tailoring skills, do you not?" He gave her an innocent smile. "See you on the stage." He pulled something from his pouch and tossed it high in the air.

Instinctively, she caught it and opened her hand. Her ankle bell.

She looked up, but he'd already left.

CHAPTER FOUR

Well past Sharai's tent, Tabor slowed his steps. He wished to go back and unspeak the words that had upset her. Should not a woman who craved silver above all else be pleased to be offered silver? Like Aurora, his mother—forsooth all women; they said one thing and meant another.

Now he'd stirred her anger and risked his chances of hiring her as his mother's seamstress.

Curse his impulsiveness. Time and again his father had chided him about it, held William up as the example of calm thought, while Tabor . . . well, Tabor's brain always responded one step behind his fist. Or mouth. "You have no self-restraint, Richard," his father would say. And then he'd look at William and sigh and wonder where he had erred in rearing his second son.

So now Tabor might never hold those long, dark curls in his hands.

The flap-lidded man did not manage her. Could they be lovers? Nay. He refused to believe it. Sharai was beautiful enough to catch the eye of any craftsman at the fair. Even the goldsmiths. Aye, they would be at the stage tonight and see her.

He shook his head. *What am I thinking? She's just a dancer. A Gypsy.* No need for him to meddle. He would control this strange impulse he had to carry her home. The little temptress would be naught but trouble.

But why did she return my coin?

Pain stabbed his middle back. He turned, protecting his face.

A Gypsy girl of six or seven summers stood, her hands loaded with stones and braced for another throw. Her eyes flashed in anger, and her brown hair shone with golden highlights.

"Stop it. Who are you?"

"Kadriya."

The little girl from five years ago.

" 'Tis true what they say about nobles," she said.

"And what pray tell is that?"

"Your skull is as thick as tree bark. She was happy to see you. Then you hurt her."

"I offered her employment."

"Sharai does not pleasure. Why do you not know?"

"I—"

"Do not hurt her like the other noble." She narrowed her eyes. "Or I will cut you with my dagger."

Tabor approached cautiously. "I understand. She's fortunate to have you for a friend. I have no plans to hurt her."

"She wants the count to leave her alone, and she wants you. . . ." Her words trailed off, and two lines of puzzlement appeared between her eyes.

"What does she want from me?"

She shrugged, gave him a final glare, and ran away.

At three bells, Tabor strode, pleased, from the bowling courts. With precious metals the goldsmiths were sure of hand, but with the subtle bumps and valleys in which the bowling stones must roll to the feather, they were not as skilled. Earlier, Tabor had placed modest wagers against the clock-makers to familiarize himself with the courts before taking on the goldsmiths. Time well spent, he thought, patting his money pouch.

His gaming had netted him horses, armor, barrels, and pitch. To celebrate, he stopped at the food booths and bought an egg-shaped marchpane, a French confection. Savoring the sweet, he approached the monks' booth, where three wooden cases of books rested, sheltered under an awning from the rain. Tabor hoped one of them was an adventure or a new King Arthur tale. If so, he would rent one for his scribe to copy.

A crashing sound, followed by Sharai's voice, drew his attention.

The monk's booth was located just to the south of the Gypsy stage. Tabor turned in that direction.

Sharai said something, short. He couldn't understand the language, but her inflection, usually strong, was weakened by fear, or uncertainty.

A man spoke, the voice dry, the words crisp. Count Aydin. Whatever he said was curtly stated. A command.

Sharai said something about dancing.

Aydin lowered his voice. Whatever he was saying, he didn't like having to say it, and it sounded like a complaint.

Sharai answered decisively.

Tabor cursed his ignorance of their language. Clearly an argument, but—

The count issued another command, his anger increasing, his speech becoming staccato.

Silence.

The count asked a question.

Sharai answered, more control in her voice.

The count spoke again and, though the words were incomprehensible, the message was clear. He mentioned dancing again, and the word "king," and Kadriya's name. He was threatening her.

Sharai responded with a plea, her voice suddenly vulnerable, and she mentioned Etti's name.

Another edict from the count.

Tabor caught a glimpse of him, stalking toward the ale barrels, his red cloak unfurling.

An urge rose in Tabor to step on that cape and cause the count to choke himself. His appetite gone, Tabor tossed the remainder of his marchpane to a roving dog and hastily selected his books. Sharai may be shallow and wild, but she had saved his life five years ago, and now it was Tabor's turn to help her. He'd see Etti and get some answers.

He found Etti with a silversmith, being fitted for rings. Her braided black hair rested on her red smock, worn over a green skirt. An ivory shawl draped across her shoulders. She sat, straight and proud as a queen at court, and Tabor was struck again at how these landless wanderers could possess such elegance. Outside they owned naught, were even beggars, yet inside their hearts they were serene and confident.

Etti carried no official title within her tribe, but she enjoyed considerable business success with her dancers, which bode well for the Gypsy tribe as a whole, because marshals from the larger fairs welcomed them—so long as they camped a distance from the church and established merchants, and agreed to break camp before the bishop arrived.

Etti had been Tabor's friend ever since she'd read his palm many summers past, when she traced his lifeline and saw strength and good fortune.

She greeted him with a smile, slipped a bold silver ring on her finger, and they walked along the crest of the hill overlooking Winchester's great cathedral.

"Count Aydin's been with us two years," she responded in answer to his question. "He's a good leader. After we found the English fairs, Aydin discovered ways to learn the schedules in advance, learned which divisions of goods were to be offered during the fair run. That helped us know when the most valuable goods—and most wealthy patrons—would be there.

"He's done the same for us at Troyes and Reims."

Tabor nodded grudgingly. Those were the largest fairs in

France. That explained why he'd missed seeing Etti and Sharai in St. Giles the last several years. "I served in Calais. Fought in Normandy with the Duke of Bedford. It's dangerous there."

"Which is why we're here. You English may have burned Joan of Arc, but the French still whisper her name and hold her in their hearts. When you dragged your boy king to Paris and crowned him King of France, they were fit to kill. The French will crown their dauphin. They're far from being defeated, mark my words." Etti stopped walking. "But you didn't come to talk politics. What troubles you?"

"The count's power. What is his role with the Gypsies? From what I overheard today, he is a . . . king?"

"Aye. Whether we're in France or England we rule our own, separate from the king's or church's courts."

"He controls legal issues?"

"Aye, and any quarrels."

"So he has absolute power in your tribe?"

She raised an eyebrow, her eyes bright with mischief. "Nothing is absolute, is it, Tabor? But yes, his orders must be obeyed."

"Or?"

"Or he can fine, punish, or throw out those who defy him."

"What of Sharai?"

"Ah, Sharai. She has grown into a beautiful woman, no?"

"I could see it five years ago, but I never dreamt she would be so captivating. What happened to her parents?"

"Both dead before I met her. She comes from Lipscani, in Wallachia. I met her in Marseilles. She was eight and just a heartbeat from death." A gentle smile curved her lips. "She's a strong girl."

"No family whatsoever?"

"No."

Tabor recalled Sharai's words years ago. "All has been lost," she had said. Guilt needled him over his hasty judgment.

"So, no," Etti continued. "No family."

"Except Kadriya?"

"Kadriya's only half Gypsy. Father ran off before he knew he'd become one. Kadriya was a baby when Sharai took her in. After the mother died."

Tabor stopped walking. Impetuous and grasping as she was, Sharai had opened her heart—and purse strings—to an orphan. The count had threatened Sharai about Kadriya. "Why does she dance?"

"That should be plain to you, who struggles with his coin. We all have to live somehow. Sharai uses her gifts."

"Of course. But can the Count stop her from dancing?"

"Where did you hear this?" A sharp edge formed in her voice, and Tabor wondered if it came from fear for Sharai, or concern over lost income.

"They argued loudly on the stage. He threatened her."

"Fie! He wants Sharai to wife. She must decide."

To wife. He'd thought of Sharai with a rich nobleman, but the thought was vague, it had no face or personality. A sensation passed through Tabor, one he couldn't name, but it left a feeling of unease and a need to act. "I think she has decided. She doesn't want him." He hesitated. "Does she refuse the count because of the flap-lidded man who collects her coins?"

Etti raised both her brows. "Wilson? He guards the dancers and is forbidden to touch them."

Relieved, he continued. "She saved my life. I want to repay her, and there is a way we can help each other. I need a seamstress to prepare for the Feast of St. Michael."

"That's more than a month away. We leave for France before then."

"It could become a permanent position." The offer spilled out of his mouth, surprising him. "Aydin is trying to break her will. I may not understand their language, but I heard the possessiveness and the threats in his voice. I would save her from that fate."

"Why?"

"She saved my life. I am indebted."

"So you wish to buy her services through September. Or longer?"

"Until Michaelmas at the earliest. 'Twould seem like a good exchange for both parties. My mother will have fine clothes for her festival, and the count cannot force himself on Sharai."

"So you are prepared to make an offer, then."

Tabor hesitated. If Curtis, the fair marshal, spoke the truth, Sharai gave most of her earnings to Etti. Likely Sharai felt obliged to pay Etti in return for taking her in at Marseilles. More proof of her honor—at least toward women. Tabor estimated what Sharai might earn with her dancing. He would offer half.

"No bargains," Etti warned.

"I'm taxed for funds, as you well know." Tabor spoke carefully. He had witnessed the shrewd negotiating powers of the Gypsies firsthand, at horse fairs and at the markets. If he showed weakness, she would turn him in his own grease for the roasting.

"She will surpass your hopes," Etti promised, beginning the negotiations. "Sharai's the best seamstress I've seen outside of London. She's a treasure."

"You know my position, Etti. Hungerford has—"

"I know, I know. You struggle." She pointed at his money pouch. "Your winnings today?"

Instinct brought his hand to his coins. "Aye."

"Sharai is a very special woman."

"Aye, but I think not of her in that way. I am obliged to her because she saved my life. For that, I wish to protect her."

"She craves security, and respect."

"Respect I can give her." He thought of his land woes. "Security is not so easy for any of us, I am afeared."

"Will she be safe with you?"

"She saved my life. I swear by my patron saint Monica, I will protect her."

She opened the ornate basket she carried and held it out. "Then count me your coins."

"What mean you?"

"You can have Sharai's services through your Harvest Festival for the precise amount in your money pouch, now."

Tabor winced. He had let her get the upper hand.

"You hesitate."

"Indeed. I still need implements for the harvest."

"Good things come dear," Etti countered.

"I cannot."

"Very well."

They walked in silence. Tabor tried shrugging it off. He'd done the best he could, but the woman's demands were impossible. He had debts. Responsibilities.

Sharai. Sharai. Her name sounded in his head with each step he took. Etti was grasping and unreasonable.

He must help her. Tabor shook his head, abandoning any hopes for a reasonable deal, and poured his coins and notes into her basket.

Etti smiled and riffled through his winnings. "Twenty-two pounds in notes, eight crowns for two pounds more, fourteen shillings and three pence." She regarded him with a smile. "Not enough."

He raised his eyebrows. "Not enough? God's bones, woman, 'tis all."

She eyed his pouch. "I see another coin in there."

Gypsies. Tabor shook his head and retrieved the last coin. "You would take my last farthing?"

"Aye. She'll be worth every jot."

"But how can I cheap the fabric for Sharai to sew the gowns? Thanks to you, I haven't a single farthing left."

"I grant you credit on ten bolts, your choice of fabric and color. That should dress your mother and a small army for your fine affair. Oh, and Tabor, one more thing."

"What?"

"I told her of Arthur, that it was you, five summers ago. She knows now of your debt to her."

Harry, Baron of Hungerford, passed the fair gate and proceeded to the tollhouse. He dismounted, giving the reins to his first knight.

Thick-necked Curtis, the fair marshal, approached. "Good afternoon, Lord Hungerford, and welcome. You look well."

Hungerford scoffed. *Liar. I look like what I am, a man broken by illness.*

Curtis gave an enthusiastic smile, doubtless trying to match the generosity of Hungerford's earlier, private donation. "We didn't expect you until the morrow."

"My business proceeded more smoothly than I had predicted." In reality, Hungerford had arrived at precisely the right time because the land usurper's son, Tabor, was still here. Blinking from a raindrop. he regarded the skies. "Rather grey day for a fair. Do you have sheltered diversions?"

Curtis nodded. "Chips tables are covered, my lord. It so happens the young Tabor is there, trying his luck."

Hungerford gave him an approving nod.

His knights staked their tents, set up the cots, and raised his black-and-white flag.

Hungerford removed his cloak and rested on the cot, his muscles shaking from the day's effort. At the least his cloak concealed his thin frame. He supposed he should feel fortunate to make it to forty and five in spite of his wretched muscles, which wasted away on his very bones. His condition worsened every day, and he wondered how long it would be before he could no longer stand. The sickness he contracted ten years ago had whitened his hair and slowly eroded his strength, and neither a physic nor any amount of rest, prayer, or church endowments improved it.

He felt time slipping away from him, yet the heir to the Tabors, those filthy thieves, still held Coin Forest Castle.

His son, Rauf, entered. Beneath his doublet Rauf's chest spread, tight with muscle, his legs sturdy and strong. Hungerford used to feel the warmth of pride that any father would experience, but it had dulled over the years into fear. His son's instincts were mired in violence.

"Mayhap you should rest. Your color is not good."

The ride had taxed him sorely, and Hungerford rose with effort. "Nay. Tabor's knights have arrived, and his party will leave at dawn. I need a public disturbance to report to the king."

"All this intrigue, for what? Why not kill him outright? His throat will slit cleanly, and that'll be the end of it."

Lord Hungerford's jaw tightened, and he wondered at the air between his son's ears. "So Tabor can be killed without effort, can he? You've had two chances to do so and failed. Remember the Gypsy women? Stabbed by a little girl. And he's evaded your traps since then."

An angry red crept up Rauf's neck. "I was injured, and a half dozen of them—"

"All women. Which sad outcome demonstrates the wisdom of my approach. I let you try your way when you stormed the castle."

"Aye, and we took it, did we not? And you still use the proceeds from his treasury to soften the king."

In an obtuse sort of way Rauf was right, but admitting it

would only inflame his arrogance. "Our attacking the castle reflected poorly on us. I've spent the last years regaining our dignity. Petitioning the king. Courting my cousin's good will. Pursuing our legal rights."

Rauf scowled. "Dead, he has no rights."

"Think of your aunt's disgrace." He would never forget the look of disbelief in Margaret's eyes when she was pulled from Coin Forest Castle and placed in prison for practicing sorcery. Her brief marriage to Tabor's father had been annulled, and Margaret had languished in prison for three years.

"Tabor's father stole the castle from her. We must take it back, but legally. He must be dispossessed, Rauf, as our family has been dispossessed. I have legal proof of Tabor's unworthiness to own it."

"Is it? Legitimate proof, I mean."

"Do not split hairs. It's acceptable legal proof, enough to sway the king's council, and that's all that counts. Now I need only taint his reputation with a public arrest, and we can make our case." He grabbed his walking stick, elaborately carved and painted in black and white. "Let us go to the games tables. We shall see how hot the young Tabor can burn."

Sharai passed the archery butts and bowling courts on her way to the covered games tables. The day was almost gone, and she had not yet made a sale because of the rain. If the customers would not circulate in the open air of the market booths, she would bring her wares to them.

Straightening the oiled cloth over her basket again, she made sure it shielded the silk purses from the rain. No matter how small, Sharai saved every remnant from the costumes she made for the dancers. She cut the scraps into pleasing patterns and stitched them together to make the purses. At three pence, they sold well as a gift or memento of the fair.

Since discovering that chess bystanders would purchase small items just to have her gone so they could return their attention to the match, the chess area was her favorite place to sell her purses.

She could not believe it when she first saw men such as these, tossing their hard-earned coins so casually onto a table, knowing there was a good chance they would lose them. And what would they receive in return? A thin thrill that rides on the whisper of fear, fear they would lose it, and a logic-defying hope that they would double their coin without honest toil.

These men, whose wealth was generated from the sweating backs of their servants, willing to risk their wealth because it was somehow . . . amusing.

A bearded merchant boldly threw coins on the table in a wager, then quibbled with Sharai over having to pay three pennies for a purse for his wife. She noted in dark fascination that he did not even know how the bishop could move on the board.

The covered games area was filled to capacity. Circulating among the bystanders, she waved her purses high, praising their beauty and value. She sold three, and then moved on to the next table.

Knights she had not seen at the fair before were seated there, wearing green and gold livery, Lord Tabor's colors.

Hungerford spotted him first, in the games tables shelter. Tabor, the tall, dark-haired sod he would humble.

Tabor and another man were in the final stages of chips. They had stacked small wooden tiles of varying lengths over sixteen inches high, a delicate tower that seemed to teeter just from the weight of the attention it received from the fascinated group of onlookers.

Three of Tabor's knights sat at the chess tables, and four more watched the chips competition.

Nearby, a sturdy Gypsy man in a red cape leaned against a side support pole.

Resting his right elbow in the palm of his left hand, Tabor raised his chip with the slowness of sunrise to the top of the precarious stack. The crowd mumbled softly, falling silent as he placed it cautiously on the top.

His hands were sure. The stack held.

The crowd released a collective breath.

Tabor grinned at his opponent and shuffled his two remaining tiles in his hands.

What arrogance, Hungerford thought. *I'll delight in seeing him fall.*

Tabor's opponent regarded his three remaining chips with a grimace. He reached to the top, but his hand shook with nerves, and fear flickered in his eyes. He would topple the tower and lose.

Hungerford nudged closer. "Beware, goldsmith. You play against Lord Tabor. When he cannot earn it, he gambles. When he cannot win, he cheats."

Tabor turned like a cat, with swiftness and a grace sufficient to avoid disturbing the delicate tower. "Lord Hungerford? Methought the air smelled foul."

"As if you would know, having been blessed with only a commoner's nose."

Hungerford jerked forward to topple the chips.

Tabor blocked him before he could nudge the table.

Hungerford swung his walking stick, hitting the table leg soundly.

The tower of chips faltered, then fell.

"You bloody sod!" Tabor launched toward Hungerford, ready to strike. With visible effort he stopped himself. "Get you away from me before I forget that you cannot fight man to man."

Rauf stepped forward. "You call yourself a man, fleeing your castle in fear and leaving your brother to die?" He grinned at the Hungerford knights. "What a fine 'man.' "

Tabor's veins appeared in his neck, pulsing, and his mouth twisted to an angry grimace. "By the saints, he died before I found him. Slain by you."

Hungerford signaled to Curtis, who stood at the ready. Tabor would attack Rauf. Curtis would allow Tabor to mark Rauf with violence, and he could press the matter in court.

The sounds of mumbling grew as news of the disturbance filtered through the game rooms.

Rauf kept goading. "You flee. You lie. You cheat."

"Rauf. Rauf, is that you? I thought I recognized your voice." A woman's voice cut through the low din, her tone taunting, compelling.

Silence fell and heads turned toward the woman, short, dark-skinned, with a thick braid of raven hair that reached to her waist. Egyptians, they were called, but some people shortened it to simply *Gypsy*. They were known for their music, dancing, and equestrian skills. This one was not yet twenty, and her round eyes contemplated his son with disdain.

Rauf dismissed her. "Be gone, woman."

But Rauf's shoulders had dropped, and her interruption had dissipated the heat of a fight.

"Use your ears, woman." Hungerford waved her away. "This is a matter between men. Be you gone."

"Can you fight, man to man, Rauf?" Her lips curved in a taunting smile. "I have not seen you do so."

A Hungerford knight reached for her.

She spun nimbly away from him.

Glancing nervously at the sturdy Gypsy with the red cloak, Curtis strode in front of the Hungerford knight, blocking his access to the Gypsy woman. "Leave her."

The woman advanced within an arm's reach of Rauf. "Think,

Rauf. You must remember me. I was but twelve years old at the time."

Rauf studied her, and his face blanched.

Egad, it must be the little girl who had stabbed Rauf years ago, now grown into a woman. Hungerford pitied Rauf and cursed the timing. How unfortunate that she showed up here, now.

She made a sweeping gesture of the large area. "Mayhap these fine men would like to hear my tale."

Rauf's eyes widened. He hesitated, glanced at Hungerford, then backed away from Tabor.

Hungerford regarded the young woman. If she revealed to this crowd how she, naught but a girl, had defeated his son, he would be made a laughingstock.

Something shone on her face, unusual for a woman.

She showed no fear.

She would not back down, and his son already had. Hungerford's jaw tightened at this missed opportunity. Mayhap he would have to resort to his son's more direct approach, after all.

And this woman would have to be silenced.

"Sharai?" Tabor called from outside her tent.

Inside, Sharai stoked the fire for light against the growing darkness and considered whether to answer. Her face flamed again, remembering what Etti told her, that the handsome Lord Tabor was Arthur, the poor wounded man to whom she had shared her childish dreams all those years ago. It had been less than an hour after the incident at the chips tables. Count Aydin had escorted Sharai to her tent and ordered Wilson to guard her, in case Rauf's men came 'round. Tabor's voice brought a new wave of anger, and she made no effort to conceal it. "What do you want?"

"I would speak with you. Please."

Wilson stood by the door, wild hair framing his questioning eyes.

She nodded. "Let him in."

Tabor entered, regarding her with gratitude. "Thank you for interrupting at the chips tables."

"I must say, I wondered at your restraint. From what I've seen, your nature is to brawl."

" 'Tis a struggle."

"The old Hungerford colludes with Curtis."

"I suspected such."

"Then why did you allow yourself to be trapped?"

"Hungerford was not due to arrive until the morrow."

"Who says this?"

He nodded. "Curtis." He paused. "I've been distracted." The look in his brown eyes simmered, making it clear how he had been distracted, and it made her heart skip. He was devastatingly handsome, to a fault.

She noticed, then, the scar above his left brow and at the temple, and remembered those days, five years ago, and his lies. "They baited you like a bear. Why?"

" 'Tis a long story, Sharai, I—"

"Oh, come now, *Arthur*." She burdened the name with sarcasm and paced toward him in swaggering steps. "Do you not want to tell me about your peasant life, and how difficult it is, wearing these *rags*?" She pulled on his silk collar, grinding out the words.

"Forgive me. I should have told you sooner."

"Instead you use trickery and deceit to amuse yourself at my expense."

"I was never amused by your dark plans to use someone just for his financial station."

"Be not daft. I was twelve years old. You, with your silk and velvet and finery. You come here, throwing your silver around, gambling on a whim and tossing me a crown. A crown! On the stage."

He looked honestly confused. "You performed well. You deserved it."

"You think money will solve your problems."

He laughed. "You, of all people, to utter such. Aren't you riding the high horse."

"You have no notion of hunger, or the cry of a child in need. You're arrogant."

"You're calculating."

"Irresponsible."

His brown eyes blazed with sudden anger. "Manipulating."

"You and your silver reek."

He stiffened as though she had struck him. "Really? My silver is good enough to buy you."

"Never."

"I already have." He stuck his chin out and raised an eyebrow, his charm fading into an air of privilege and self-indulgence. "With my last farthing. Etti strikes a hard bargain, but we agreed on a price. You leave with me on the morrow."

Her hand flew to her neck. Memories of Lipscani and Marseilles fell over her, standing, her eight-year-old body naked, in the middle of a ring of buyers, men with small, assessing eyes, poking and prodding her like a goat at market, and her chest squeezed in panic. "You cannot buy me."

CHAPTER FIVE

Sharai burst into Etti's tent, where Etti sat under candlelight on an elaborate wooden casket. "Tell me it's not true. Tell me you didn't sell me to Lord Tabor."

Etti's expression was unreadable. "Not you, *Pen*," she said, using a term of affection. "Just your services."

Sharai's throat constricted. "How dare you make a contract without asking me?"

" 'Tis a boon to all parties." She rose, smiling. "I got a nice bundle from Tabor. Big enough that your debt to me is paid." Her voice softened. "We're even, Sharai. You're free—and Kadriya gets to go with you."

"But—"

Etti waved her objection aside. "Tabor gets your fine skills with a needle and you, my dear," she said, fluffing her hair and shaking it around her shoulders, "you get your chance at a handsome, unwed noble."

"That was folly, a stupid dream when I was but a child."

She nodded. "I thought so at first, but seeing his concern for you—he is concerned, my dear—and he wants to repay his debt to you. You can't fault him for that."

"What debt?"

"You saved his life. Now he wishes to spare you from Count Aydin." She gave Sharai a look of reprimand. "You didn't tell me the count ordered you to stop dancing. You weren't going to, were you? In spite of his threat?"

Sharai thought of his hands, squeezing her arms in anger, and shuddered. "He has no right."

"He does. Do you wish to wed the count?"

Sharai's throat constricted at the thought. "Nay, but Lord Tabor is selfish, wasteful with his coin."

Etti laughed. "His purse is empty only because of you."

"But he's a nobleman." The word stung on her skin like a hot summer rash. Another nobleman, Fletcher, Baron of Chantbury, had looked with longing upon her, kissed her, led her to believe that he cared for her, and Sharai had dared hope he'd provide a life for her and Kadriya. But he'd wanted only her flesh.

"One does not sew golden threads in burlap," she told Etti. "He's too fine to consider a woman like me."

"He's honorable."

"He's full of lust, and full of himself. I won't go with him."

Etti's gaze captured her with a look of affection tempered by determination. "It's done, and you will go."

Sharai felt her lifelines being ripped away. "Etti!"

"I know him, better than he knows himself. He is not Fletcher. Lord Tabor's a good man, and the way he looks at you?" She raised her eyebrows suggestively. "Pack your clothes and sewing basket, and take Kadriya." Etti squeezed her hand. "This is your chance."

Tabor wedged Kadriya's dove cage between the side of the wagon and a crate of spices. "It fits, my girl," he said to Kadriya. He gestured to an open spot in the wagon. "Here's a place for you and Sharai."

Sharai rubbed the early morning chill from her arms and settled into the soft seat of fabric bolts covered with a greased canvas, helping Kadriya in behind her. "Thank you, Lord Tabor." Though she had little choice, she would be civil. A spot of red flashed from behind the tollbooth, and Count Aydin appeared. Seeing Sharai and Kadriya in the wagon, his expression clouded in anger. Cursing, he approached Tabor and grabbed his arm. "*Choro!*"

"What?" Sharai exclaimed, stunned at his gall. "He is no thief, and I am not some property to steal or recover."

He released Tabor's arm and grabbed hers. "Get out of the wagon."

Sharai resisted. "Nay."

Tabor circled the count's neck with his arm and wedged his forearm against his throat, pulling him away. "Let go of her."

"Stop, both of you." Etti rushed to the scene. "Count Aydin, don't pull that dagger. Tabor, release him. See this contract, Count?" She held a parchment. "An agreement, between Lord Tabor and myself, for Sharai's services. She's to be seamstress to Lady Tabor, Lord Tabor's mother."

Tabor released him, and the count pulled his arm free. "I am your king. You have no right to enter into contracts." His eyes narrowed. "Further, you cannot read."

Etti shot him a warning glance. "But the Baron can," she said, reminding him of Tabor's status.

At the sound of his title, Tabor raised his chin in barely suppressed arrogance, he who thought he could buy her affections as well as her sewing skills.

"You never forbade it, Count," Etti continued. "It's legal. Isn't that right, Curtis?"

The fair marshal approached, made a show of taking the contract and examining it, and handed it back to Etti. "It's proper, aye."

The count bared his teeth at Lord Tabor and his big chest rose and fell as if he had been running uphill. He grabbed the parchment, shaking it at Etti. "How long is she bound?"

Etti didn't flinch or shrink, and in spite of her meddling,

Sharai admired the strong, clever woman who had cared for her for nine years.

Etti calmly plucked the contract from the count's hand. "Until Michaelmas."

Count Aydin cast a look of raw longing at Sharai. His brown eyes seemed to glow, as if a spell had been cast with a special light only he could see, stripping him of reason and restraint. He turned to Tabor. "Your contract is with Sharai. Kadriya must stay with her tribe."

Sharai's heart seized, and she put her forehead to Kadriya's to still her speeding heart. She would die before she let him take Kadriya.

Tabor mounted his horse and positioned himself between them and Count Aydin. "I'm sorry, Count, but I bought them together, as a pair. Etti will tell you."

Etti nodded. "Yes, I included Kadriya."

Tabor nodded to his knights. "It's settled then. Time to go."

The wagon lurched forward, moving from its spot near the river. Sagging willow branches, wet with morning dew, brushed Sharai's face, and they rode toward a village. His village.

Nestled on the fabric bolts, Kadriya slept in a compact curl, unaware of the sharp turn their lives had taken.

Three more wagons lumbered behind them, laden with goods and several fine horses hitched to the back. Lord Tabor and Sir Cyrill rode ahead. Two knights flanked the wagons, with two more in back. All wore armor, and the clanking created an ominous song in the damp morning air.

They traveled north and west from Winchester, in an area unfamiliar to her. The clouds eventually lifted and barley fields, shorn of their bounty, lay naked and cropped in the late August sun. Like the fields, Sharai had been left exposed and vulnerable. Doubts swirled in her mind. What if Etti had misread

Tabor? What if he craved the flesh but not the woman beneath it? *Why fret? Is this not what you wanted? A rich noble to care for you?*

Years ago, yes, but she was no longer a stupid, dreaming girl. Emotions warred within her. Tabor had freed her from Count Aydin and prevented him from taking Kadriya from her. Tears stung her eyes. By that deed alone, he'd repaid his debt to her tenfold.

But scheming with Etti, tempting her with coin until she could no longer resist, so arrogant, buying her like a sack of eggs at market. He'd been helpful, but insulting, leaving little doubt what he thought of her: someone worth helping, because she'd saved his life, but also someone of little worth, someone with no free will. *Like a slave.* For that she wanted to strike him, to give back some of the hurt his words had caused.

She was obligated to him until Michaelmas, a little over a month away. When her obligation to Lord Tabor was fulfilled, what then? She saw Count Aydin's eyes in her memory. She could not return to St. Giles.

The wagon slipped into a large rut and tilted awkwardly. Sharai leaned right to keep the wagon's uphill wheel on the road. She cursed the loose, twelve-year-old tongue that had started this turmoil. *Never tell secrets to strangers.* She would add that bit of wisdom to her life rules.

Kadriya stirred. "Why so vexed, Sharai?"

Because I'm hurt and afraid, and I'm not even sure of what. "I'm angry. They negotiate for me as if I have no say in the matter."

Kadriya reached in her dove's cage, stroking the white bird's feathers. "Aye, but Tabor paid Etti well, and he let me come with you." Kadriya hugged her. "And he saved you from Count Aydin."

"I could have handled him in my own way." Yet a shadow of fear clouded the back of her mind. He would have taken Kadriya from her if she didn't sway to his wishes. Tabor's contract had given them a chance to stay together.

Sharai impulsively hugged the young girl who had no more home than she, the one who represented Sharai's only family. At the least, Tabor had given her that.

She would fulfill her commitment to him, which would complete her commitment to Etti. She would be free by Michaelmas, still time to return to France and find a new tribe that would accept them. Traveling was perilous for unescorted women, but if they traveled only in early morn and stayed on the pilgrim routes . . . well, she had no choice in the matter. She would not be owned. She and Kadriya would find a new tribe, one without Count Aydin.

"Sharai, wake up."

Roused from her nap, Sharai propped herself on an elbow so she could see over the top of the wagon. Their journey had taken a day and a half, judging by the height of the sun, which had warmed her into slumber. They rolled to a stop at the crest of a hill.

Kadriya stood over her, jumping in excitement. "Up, up, and look."

Sharai blinked and stood, following Kadriya's gaze. In the distance a golden-stoned castle perched like a jewel on the breast of the land. Set at the base of a series of gently rolling hills, the castle shone amid tilled meadows spread like a green velvet skirt around her. 'Twas not so grand as the cathedral, but nestled as it was in the valley, it spoke of strength and security and beauty.

"It's so fine," Kadriya said. "Lord Tabor, you're a king."

Ahead, Tabor laughed. "Not quite, Kadriya."

Vaguely reminiscent of the castles Sharai had seen near Troyes, it echoed the continental style, a tall, rectangular castle with a drum tower at each corner and roofed like a French chateau.

A village nestled in front of the castle, and a small church sat to the left, built near a narrow river.

To the distant right a forest grew, the sunlight disappearing into the tall, dense growth, whispering danger and mystery.

Lord Tabor stopped by Sharai, contemplating the view. " 'Tis my home. Coin Forest Castle."

His features had softened with pride and a quiet passion that made her heart skip, and she wondered at the thought of owning something so lovely as this castle, with all its bounty and wealth.

The shelter of wealth. To her it was as if the nobles floated in the clouds, far above the threat of midnight attack, or hunger and suffering.

Bosh, Sharai. You're like a kitten chasing a golden thread. Stay you far from such thoughts.

Wealth. Luxury.

Security.

Near as grand as a church, it was, and all Tabor's.

Baron Tabor, she reminded herself, shurgging the spell away. A nobleman. She had no right to such privilege, even in her dreams. Why did she continue to covet such possessions when they were far beyond her grasp? But is was only in the secret places in her mind that these yearnings dwelled. Easy enough to keep them safely hidden. She shrugged off the yearning. Riches would never sway her, ever again. "How grand," she said to Tabor. "You must be very proud."

As if realizing his guard had dropped, he thanked her and urged his horse forward, leading the procession once again.

Cyrill blew his horn, signaling their arrival.

From the castle, an answering signal sounded.

A party of knights rode out, escorting them down the narrow

village street, and Sharai was drawn into the bustling excitement of the village, and the villagers' pleasure at Lord Tabor's return. Their smiles and shouts of welcome made clear their affection for him.

Green and gold flags flew from the castle towers. Visible through the rooftop crenellations, sentries held their posts.

A wide moat flanked the castle. From shore's edge, a few dozen people gathered, delivering boxes of noisy chickens and geese, a squealing pig, firewood, flour, and bales of wool.

The knight named John approached, his hair the color of ripe wheat.

"What goes here," Sharai asked him.

"Tenants, delivering their rent," he explained.

Heavy chains clanked as, link by link, the drawbridge descended.

Several children appeared from inside the castle. They climbed to the top of the drawbridge, shouting with delight. Dangling their legs over the side, they played a game of mettle to see who could leave them there the longest before succumbing to fear when the drawbridge met the walkway to the shore. A dozen dogs romped behind them, barking, scratching their way up the lowering drawbridge and then sliding back down.

The heavy timbers let down further, nearing the partial bridge that spanned the moat, which seemed at least three rods wide. One boy, a brown-haired rascal of about ten summers, left his legs dangling long after all the others had lost their courage.

Sharai closed her eyes, not daring to look, but anxiety made her peek. The rascally boy had finally pulled his legs to safety. He scrambled up, his short hair revealing big ears red with excitement, and raced forward to Sir Cyrill, banging the knight's armor excitedly.

Sir Cyrill gave the boy a scathing look. "Master Thomas." His voice cut with reprimand. "Godspeed," he said, reminding him of his duty.

Thomas winced, then straightened. "Godspeed, Sir Cyrill." He offered his hands.

Sir Cyrill dismounted, handed Thomas his reins and removed his helm, handing it to a taller, more mature boy, likely his squire.

Beside Sharai, John laughed. "Cyrill's bad luck of the draw, getting young Tommy as page. He's a wild one, that." John dismounted, handed his reins and helm to his squire then proceeded across the drawbridge.

A woman approached from the castle side, dressed in an outdated green damask surcoat over a white under-tunic. The flesh at her waistline strained against the confines of the fabric, and her hemline was at the least two inches too short. Sharai lingered not on the hemline lest she embarrass her, but checked the pulled seams again, fearing they would surrender to the tension as Jennamine's seams often did.

The woman's face was old but pleasant. She had the same coloring as Tabor, but not his height. Her features were softer, her nose gently sloping, cheekbones less prominent, same strong chin, but her eyes were vivid blue. *Tabor's mother. Forsooth. She exists.* From behind her short, veiled headdress, her drastically plucked brows were furrowed, but she managed a smile. "Tabor. Thank the saints you're safe."

Tabor dismounted, and his mother patted his shoulder awkwardly. Taking her hand, he led her to the wagon. "Sharai, this is my mother, the Lady Anne."

Sharai nodded, as she had seen the noblewomen do at church services. "My lady."

"And Mother, may I present Princess Sharai." He gestured toward Sharai, giving her a wink.

More arrogance and humor at her expense. Sharai glared at him.

"From Little Egypt," Tabor continued. "She's the best seamstress outside of London, here to serve you as such from now until your Michaelmas festival."

Lady Anne's smile grew wide with pleasure. "Lovely. Oh, Tabor, how could you be so charming as to bring me a foreign servant?"

Sharai bristled. "Thank you, my lady, but I am a merchant and craftswoman, not a servant."

"A craftswoman." Anne's laughter bubbled like a pebbled brook in springtide. "My dear, you are but a woman. And lovely. Just look at you." She held Sharai's hands out, examining her as if she were one of the small, exotic dolls offered at the French fairs.

"Red skirt, all those fine yards of linen." She touched Sharai's skirt, raised her thin, ribbon-like brows and corrected herself. "Lawn, rather, I should say. Very fine." Her gaze traveled upward. "Dark skin, enchanting eyes, all this finery." She fingered Sharai's bracelet and gold earrings. "Welcome to Coin Forest, my dear." She linked her arm with Sharai's and led her to the drawbridge. "Well done, Tabor. You have excelled for a change."

Tabor's smile faded. "Prithee give Sharai her own room, Mother. Near yours, for your convenience."

The tension between mother and son chilled the air. Sharai gestured to Kadriya. "Come, Sprig."

Lady Anne scrutinized Kadriya's light hair and dark skin. "Your daughter? But her coloring . . ."

"My adopted sister," Sharai explained.

"Well, then, come along. Sprig?"

Sharai smiled. "Her nickname. Her name is Kadriya."

"Kadriya. Lovely. Very foreign," she said, her tongue embracing the word. "By all means she shall be known as Kadriya."

The sound of lapping water on boats came from below the drawbridge. An unhappy pig stumbled from one of the boats to dry land, grunting in relief.

Lady Anne covered her bulging waistband with her arm. "Doubtless you noticed my gown. I'm in desperate need of well-tailored clothes. Most were pillaged during the siege and I've struggled finding a competent seamstress. Little Egypt. So far away. I must hear all about it."

You would not wish to hear of my travels. "Living in such a beautiful place as this, I can't imagine leaving it."

"Thank you, Share-eye," Lady Anne said, stretching the syllables of her name.

They passed through the outer curtain, patched here and there with a lighter colored stone, and entered the crowded bailey.

The castle was guarded by great towers and many knights, and secured with a sturdy portcullis. Men would have great trouble breaking in, as they had in her small home years ago. The walls of stone brought a comforting sense of security.

Curious eyes raked Sharai as thoroughly as Lady Anne's had, and self-consciousness made her tighten her scarf.

Lady Anne shooed the chickens and geese aside and pressed past the people.

In the great hall, ivory linen draped the high table, a fire burned in the massive fireplace, and a rich tapestry of deer hung on the wall, just like in the stories she'd heard.

Kadriya's mouth gaped.

Sharai gestured for her to shut it. Later she would praise her for keeping quiet.

They ascended the circular staircase, Lady Anne huffing from the climb.

"Your chamber, Sharai. Yours and Kadriya's."

My chamber. Sharai had never had her own chamber. She'd once shared a small room with her cousins. Dazzled with the thought, she passed through the heavy doorway.

Inside, an untended fireplace held fresh wood, waiting to be lit to drive away the impending evening chill. A large bed loomed to the left, covered by ornate woodwork from which curtains of forest green linen hung. Sharai approached the bed and ran her hands along the covering. Down, cool, smooth as poured cream and soft as a sigh. She glanced at Sprig.

Sprig, focused on twitching the canopy tassels, didn't notice.

Sharai smiled. " 'Tis lovely, my lady. Thank you."

Lady Anne pulled a bell suspended by a rope near the bed. "I offer my best, and I trust you will give me yours." She opened a shutter, and a cross-shaped loophole in the stone cast a narrow shaft of sunlight onto the fine rug beneath her bed.

An old woman entered the room. Her thin, greying hair peeked out from her hood. Her gown was of coarse, undyed linen. The sun highlighted her skin, ravaged by pox, but her grey eyes were kind.

"Britta, this is Princess Sharai from Little Egypt. She will be my seamstress for the festival. And her sister, Kadriya. Fetch fresh water for her basin so she may prepare for supper."

Britta gave Sharai the same intense head-to-foot examination, but she did it swiftly and less conspicuously. "Aye, my lady."

Lady Anne clapped her hands in excitement. "You will give me a hand reading after dinner, my dear, will you not?"

"I beg your pardon?"

Lady Anne made a waving gesture with her hand. "You Little Egypt people are skilled at that, I've heard. You will read my palm and tell my fortune tonight."

Tabor entered his mother's chamber and found her adjusting

the pin she wore, their coat-of-arms, a horizontal sword threading three silver circles. His father had given it to her shortly before his death.

"You look well, Mother."

Her hands fluttered to her veil. "I'm so pleased with Princess Sharai. She will read my palm tonight."

He blinked back a vision of Sharai's gleaming curls in the stage light. "She has many talents."

Lady Anne gave him a knowing smile. "As you might rightly know. Besides snaring me my exotic seamstress, how was your trip to St. Giles?"

"Lucrative. We have new armor and eight good horses." He never disclosed his method of raising funds. But then, Lady Anne had never shown an interest in such things.

"And blue silk?"

"The perfect shade. I brought ten bolts for your fancy."

"You're doing better."

The barb stung. He rounded his right shoulder, trying to dislodge it. "We must speak of finances. I spied the new carpets. We agreed before I left that now was the time to preserve our funds."

"How can we have the Lords Bromley, Frodesham, and Hardgrove here with bare floors, Tabor? Really. And the bishop. Surely you see."

He knew well the names of his neighbors, guild leaders of the All Saints Parish of Hampshire. Five generations of his family had been guild leaders. Still, he must tie his mother's loose purse strings. "You try my patience."

"Did you see Lord Hungerford?"

"Aye, and Rauf."

"That they roam the countryside freely is pure outrage. Did you speak?"

"Nothing civil."

She gave him a look of pity, as if she preferred not being bothered by him, but he was her last living son and, like a bad case of dysentery, she must deal with it. "He killed your brother and Aurora, and still he walks freely, tainting your father's name. Why can you not kill him?"

"Shall I defy a royal order? I can not very well protect you from the confines of a dungeon, Mother."

"As I see it, you can not very well protect me from the freedom of your current location."

He slammed his fist on the table and her wine tipped, landing with a clank and a splash on the floor, just free of one of the new carpets. "Always you needle. Do you think I care not that Coin Forest is threatened? I've served the king well. Almost lost my arm in Normandy, yet here I am, hands tied."

" 'Tis all in your mind."

" 'You've heard the whispers. Did you not complain to me of it afore I left for Winchester? We were the most respected family in Hampshire. Now Hungerford's slurs besmirch the purity of our bloodlines. God's bones. What are we, if not noble? Mere peasants." He shuddered at the nakedness of the word.

"Our properties are at stake. The king has ordered me to keep the peace. Cast no more shadows on my skills." He picked up the goblet, slamming it on the table. "Spare me any further public insults."

She covered his hand. "Wait. I have news." Her smile grew wide, and her eyes had a telltale sparkle. "I received a response yesterday from Lord Marmyl. He answered my counter for Lady Emilyne's dowry."

His mother and Lord and Lady Marmyl were well advanced in wedding negotiations for Emilyne and Tabor. "Good news?"

"Very. Better than we thought."

"Tell me."

She settled on the chair, preening the folds of her skirt, her grin forcing dimples in her cheeks.

"Mother."

Her eyes glistened. "One . . . thousand . . . pounds."

A massive log collapsed into the fire, sending sparks flying in the great hall's fireplace.

The heat felt welcome to Sharai, the sturdy walls comforting. With the exception of an occasional night at a monastery or church, she hadn't spent an evening in a permanent building in years, and never in one so grand as this.

She sat at the left end of the high table nearest the fire. Next to her sat the priest, Father Bernard; then Sir John, Lady Anne, Lord Tabor, and Sir Cyrill.

Dinner had been an unending spectacle of excess. First, fine silver ewers of water to clean their hands; then boar's meat with a tangy mustard sauce, eel, minced chicken, and baked fish with tantalizing spices. Fine red wine in more silver goblets, and a sweet confection that had melted in her mouth. Sharai savored every bite, to the point she could hardly breathe. She pulled at her tight waistband with a new appreciation for Lady Anne's strained side seams.

Something tugged on Sharai's skirt. She jerked her legs back with a gasp and looked under the table.

Kadriya's disheveled curls came into view. "Kadriya, nay," she whispered. "Go you back to the lower tables."

"That Tommy boy plagues me. He keeps pulling my hair. I want to sit with you."

Sharai glanced toward Lady Anne, who continued to pick at her food, even after all the courses had been served. "High table is reserved for important people," Sharai explained, talking into her lap.

"So why are *you* sitting here?"

Sharai muffled her laugh. "I have no illusions. Lady Anne

thinks me an unusual ornament. She will have me read her palm. As to Tommy, did I not teach you how to defend thyself?"

"Then I may slog him?"

"Quietly."

"Sharai." Lady Anne's voice interrupted them.

"My lady?"

"Be you possessed, talking to yourself? Prithee come, and read my palm."

Tabor placed a set of pouldrons on the high shelf, adding it to the growing collection of armor. He handed a helm to Cyrill. "This needs repair. And this cuirass, too."

They placed the pieces on the armorer's worktable. The room smelled of metal and wood and sweat.

Cyrill added the helm, and it clanged against the other pieces. "Good to be home." He patted his stomach. "Dinner last night, what a fine meal." He measured Tabor with his grey eyes. "What troubles thee, milord?"

"This shelf." Tabor ran his hands along a storage shelf behind the anvil. " 'Tis where I hid Aurora. During the siege."

"Aye. You tried to save her."

"But failed."

Cyrill sighed in exasperation. "Ignore your mother's criticisms. She's never pleased, my lord."

"Lord Marmyl has met her demands."

Cyrill smiled, his grey mustache rising. "Excellent news. The treasury will be replenished. And her father an earl. That should shore up your standing with the parish, and the king." His grey brows creased. "You're not sure of the Lady Emilyne? She's a handsome woman. And strong. She should give you healthy heirs."

"Aye." The Lady Emilyne stood tall, possessed strong bones, long brown hair, clear green eyes, and a cool disposition.

"She's also above reproach. Exemplary. You could not make a better match. In this your mother has been faithful."

"Sooth, I know this."

"Aurora toyed with you. 'Twas misery you felt, my lord, not love." He paused. "I see you rented more books at St. Giles. I took the liberty of reading the titles." He frowned and met Tabor's gaze. "I would that you cease reading those Arthurian legends. 'Tis all fiction, tall tales. And Chaucer's yarn of knights?" He shook his head in disapproval. "Stay you grounded in reality, milord. Lady Emilyne will be good for you. For Coin Forest."

"Forsooth." Tabor clapped his hands together, dusting them off. "Please finish the inventory. I must tend to my birds."

Tabor climbed the circular stairwell, following its upward curve. His muscles responded with strength, and his blood pumped sure in his chest, but strange, disquieting thoughts came to him. The girl, Sharai, the look of greed in her eyes when she spoke of her rich noble. The Lady Anne, the same look in her eyes when she spoke of the thousand pounds.

He couldn't reconcile the joy of love he read about in his books to the cold reality of marriage. When he was younger, he was certain he could find the love he'd felt for Aurora, with another woman. She would be lovely and warm and come from a good family, with a good dowry—or fair; it needn't be large. Love was more important.

Then the siege, the stripped treasury, and Hungerford's insidious claims about questionable nobility, and they'd watched their standing among their peers—and in London—sink to the point of alarm. His notions of love were only fond dreams. His mother's delight at Emilyne's dowry was based on need. Sharai's childish dreams were based on simple greed.

Sharai, free as a butterfly, fealty to none. She had no estates, no honor to salvage. Mayhap women craved the comforts of wealth, but a man had a duty to his people. Tabor governed his properties in peace and fairness, while Rauf ruled with force and terror. Tabor would spare them from Rauf, and Tabor would save his estates for his heirs, all more noble causes than simple female creature comforts.

Dowries, negotiations. 'Twas the way of the world. And Lady Emilyne was a very good match. He should be pleased.

CHAPTER SIX

The next morning, Tabor exited the church, quickening his stride to catch up with Sharai, who was some fifteen yards ahead, walking toward the village. The post-dawn air was crisp; dew gleamed in the grass, and the sky shone blue, free of clouds. All signs promised a banner day.

A perfect day to clear the air between them. She'd been frosty with him since they left Winchester. He'd find a way to make peace with her.

Her tightly braided hair, still damp from washing, fell almost to her waist. Instead of her Gypsy skirt she wore a high-necked houppelande and black cloak. His mother must have given her more appropriate clothes.

"Good morn, Sharai." He braced himself for her dark look and dismissal. " 'Twas a pleasant surprise to see you at Lauds."

She stopped walking and cast him a dark look. "Oh? Surprised that I could rise so early, or surprised that I attended?"

"I've heard that Gypsies . . ."

He hesitated to detail what he knew, that Gypsies were heathens, dipping into the world of magic with palm readings and spells.

". . . are pagans," she finished for him. "Things are not always as they seem, Lord Tabor. Like knights. I've always heard they're chivalrous. Kindly."

He straightened. "I subscribe to the codes of knightly honor."

She stopped, regarding him with raised eyebrows. "And you demonstrate it by buying women, against their will?"

He studied his thumbnail. "I spoke those words in anger, in response to your insults. I bought your services, not you. Please forgive me."

He waited for her acceptance and apology. After all, she had condemned him as irresponsible.

She continued walking in silence.

"Your sustained anger is puzzling, Sharai. Is it not obvious I did you a favor? Tell me you do not enjoy your respite here, far from the count's threats and the humiliation of the stage."

Her eyes grew wide. "Respite? Your mother's list of gowns grows by the day. She's invited friends to see my work and they arrive in just two days."

"You're being paid well."

"Thank you, though since I was rudely excluded from negotiations on my *own contract*, I can't speak to the price. And what of the stage? The mere word furrows your brow. So you wish to take me off the stage, too? The stage is nothing. I use my dancing to earn a living. 'Tis more honest than your gambling. Should I save you from your gambling, then, as you spared me from the stage?"

There was a fire in her eyes, a glow of injury. Still, her argument pulled him into an arena so compelling that he could not leave it. "You compare your dancing—enticing men to look at you—to my gambling? What you were doing was sinful. Women should not reveal their legs, nor move like that in the presence of strange men."

They advanced to the opened drawbridge, and she pulled away. " 'Tis unseemly to continue this conversation," she whispered, nodding to the sentries and several people walking the bridge to the castle.

He lowered his voice and guided her over the drawbridge to

the fishponds "You've engaged me in debate and you cannot escape so easily. 'Tis daylight. Let us take a walk, in plain view, and explore this topic."

She smiled unconvincingly, as if she had just stepped on a bug with new shoes. "I attract men to my stage with music and colorful costumes. I work hard with my performance. I give what they need and take what I need. A fair exchange."

"Hedonism. You dare compare that to my gaming?"

She laughed. "So self-righteous. Can you not see that you risk the wealth your people here earned for you," she said, gesturing to the farmers and villagers at the gate. "And what of knighthood, and service to your king in times of war? Don't you see the similarities? Men are given physical strength, women, physical beauty. When you use your God-given assets for profit, 'tis a manly, honorable thing. Yet when women use their God-given assets for profit, it's unacceptable and you condemn it."

A light breeze whispered through the grass. Tabor wanted to poke holes in her argument—he knew there were several—but he couldn't.

"So you lure men to the gambling arena—the archery butts, the bowling courts, and such. You offer them the fantasy of beating you and winning large amounts of money. With your skill, you win, and take their silver."

"I don't cheat."

"You have some integrity. Yet gambling is not so fair an exchange as my dancing, because they never receive their fantasy."

He allowed himself the luxury of a knowing smile. "I did not receive my fantasy from you."

She returned his smile with an even more dangerous one. "I fill some fantasies. I cannot fill all."

He guided her down the small path to the mill. "Oh, I think you can," he said, a deliberately playful note in his voice.

She ignored his tone. "I already did. If you were honest, you'd admit it. Why else would you toss me a crown?"

"You impugn my honesty and dare say that your dancing is more forthright than my gaming."

"I do." The power of her conviction shone in her eyes. "I've seen the many sides of a man's thoughts, and I understand them."

"Highly unlikely."

"The problem for you is that you presume my thoughts to be similar to other women's thoughts."

"They are. You revealed your plan to me five years ago. You want to use a man for his wealth. Far from unique thoughts, Sharai. You are predictably female in your goals and schemes. And you can spout all you wish about the stage, but you and I both know what you're selling when you dance."

"I promise no more than fantasy. Whether they find it depends on their imaginations."

"What I saw with my own eyes was not my imagination," he protested.

"What did you see?" She tipped her head to the side, and new challenge sparkled in her dark eyes. "Men are most imaginative. For some, the lifting of my veil is their favorite part. Others enjoy the bell dance. Some, as you point out, like to see glimpses of my legs. Some like my hair." She flipped a long braid behind her shoulder. "Which did you like, Lord Tabor?"

His vision seemed to have blurred for all images but that of her face, flawlessly oval, and her eyes, wide set, a rich mink brown, thickly lashed. Power shone in them, a feminine power so compelling. . . .

He swallowed. "It's merely a performance. Not reality."

Not reality. Cyrill's words, too. Nay, Tabor refused to believe passion was only imagined. He remembered the look in her eyes when she retrieved his crown and saw him. "The power that passed between us that night was real. As it is now." She would acknowledge the womanly charms she possessed, and admit how she clouded his judgment with them. Impulsively he reached for her, pulled her to him.

She gasped, then twisted to the side and pushed a dagger to his throat.

The blade's point pricked his skin like a rose's thorn.

Her simmering femininity was gone, replaced with a dark violence that narrowed her eyes and hardened her mouth. "Make no mistake, Lord Tabor. I've been sold at auction like a slab of meat. I've been starved, insulted, beaten, and I have survived. At one time I thought I was nothing to anyone but a tradable commodity, and I wanted nothing more than top price.

"But then I realized the real price for trading myself. It's too high, but I'll trade any of my skills. You need laundering? I'm thorough. Sewing? I excel. Dance? I do it well. I increase my worth to others with my skills, but you cannot buy me. And I will slit your throat before you force me." Her voice was coarse with the primitive threat.

Near the drawbridge, Cyrill saw the dagger and drew his sword, rushing forward.

Tabor stilled him with a gesture. He froze, moving neither closer to nor more distant from her. He held her gaze, waiting for the fury to pass.

The tip of the blade remained pressed to his neck. Her anger was fierce, but just a thin veil over sheer fright. He felt the trembling of it, saw it in her eyes. And then he looked past the womanly curves and flirtations, past the prickly exterior and saw the little girl with a dream, a little girl in a hazardous world of dangerous men. Someone had hurt her. Violated her.

He wished he had been able to spare her, but the scars were

there, it was too late for that. He tried to tell her, with his eyes, that he cared.

She released pressure on the blade and withdrew it.

He felt her heat through his doublet, her softness and the clean smell of her hair. He raised his left hand, tracing the handle of the dagger, down her fingers, closing gently around her hand, never leaving her eyes. "By my patron saint Monica, and by every saint who has lived and died, Sharai, I will never force you."

She made her way to the castle, patting her chest to settle the storm swirling in her chest. She should not be alone with him. Kadriya would not again talk her way out of Lauds. From now on Sharai would rouse her lazy bum out of bed and force her to go with her, every day.

He had come so close to her. She thought he might kiss her, and something inside made her want him to do so.

Remember, Sharai. Nobles want pleasure. Only pleasure.

She supposed they could not help themselves. Men had needs.

But not all of them were bad, were they? She thought about the men she'd known in her life. Her father. She saw him in her mind's eye, strong, handsome, an intense man, covering his quail cages, his talking bird perched on his turban. But he'd left them, only to die on the road out of town at the hands of thieves. Damir, the pottery maker who wooed her mother, then betrayed them. Count Aydin, whose kindness carried a dear price: no permanent home and life with a man who repulsed her.

But Father Robert at St. Giles Church was kindly. The priests seemed to overcome their preoccupation with the physical and act in a truly noble way. Good men, she thought, must struggle with their urges. Women were not afflicted thus, thanks be to God.

A sham as false as a summer breeze in autumn, Sharai. You felt it, too. She did not wish to be like Diana and Codi, but she didn't want the life of a nun, either. Codi's voice echoed. "Just one kiss."

Ridiculous. Never.

Take a chance, Etti had urged. Sharai closed her eyes, remembering his touch, how it had traced fire on her skin. She put a finger to her lips, wondering.

Tabor found Sir Cyrill at the quintain, waiting for him to begin daily exercises with the squires. Cyrill wore his padded hauberk and a no-nonsense expression on his face that should have warned the squires that hard work was in order. The squires, if they saw it, were deliberately oblivious. They thwacked each other on the butt and played keep-away with their battered helms, their pouldrons slipping haphazardly on their bony shoulders.

Cyrill looked relieved to see him. "You would do well to consider taking the Gypsy girl's dagger. What stirred her to such anger, my lord?"

Tabor shook his head. "I was merely seeking logic in a whirlpool."

He felt weak from his efforts to retain self-control. It had happened again with her, a heady desire stronger even than with Aurora, but something more, like a . . . He struggled to find the word.

"My lord?"

"Connection. Some manner of connection."

"What say you?"

Tabor made a sweeping gesture with his right hand, touching the small surface cut her blade had left on his neck. "Never mind."

He caught a flying helm, and the squires stumbled over themselves to stop. Their grins vanished, and they hurriedly settled the helms on their heads and stood at attention in the warm sunshine. "Good day, my lord," they mumbled.

"And to you," Tabor said. "Now, fetch your lances and get to work."

Sharai watched the attendants clear the high table of the last of the pigeon and sweet pastries. Another night's feast. Kadriya had joined some children for a game of hoodman's blind, and Lady Anne, pleased with the fortune Sharai had ventured in her hand, had retired for the eve.

The great hall was mostly cleared, save for Sharai and Tabor, the attendants, the dogs, and a few knights who gathered at the fireplace, deep in their cups and tales of valor.

The harpist still lingered, her fingers dancing over the strings like gleeful spiders after a windstorm. The music sounded clear and pure. The melody lilted, striking chords that lightened her heart.

Sharai followed the notes, drifting in a moment of freedom, when she could allow her thoughts to fly far from daily demands. The music swelled, receded, and then ended.

"That was lovely. Thank you." At Tabor's signal the harpist bowed, stored her harp, and left the hall.

Tabor placed his hand on the table, palm up. "Be you ready to read my fortune, Sharai?"

Sharai smiled to herself, careful to not let him see any evidence of her amusement. Even a big, powerful man like Lord Tabor held curiosity about his future. As if he needed to be told that he would be prosperous and live a long life, sheltered in this fine castle, eating this superior food, his wish a command to any within earshot.

Ordinarily Sharai did not *dukker the vast* but she had witnessed enough palm readings to know the procedure. She had given Lady Anne three satisfying readings so far.

She studied the big hand he offered. Large enough for her to place both of her hands in his one, it was calloused from his sword, but clean. His skin felt warm to the touch, the pulse strong.

Heat raced up her arms, speeding the beating of her heart. She concentrated on keeping her breathing even.

"Heart line." She spoke aloud to quell the faeries that fluttered in her chest. "See, 'tis the line that runs from under your little finger across your palm." She traced it with her fingernail.

He jumped visibly.

He's sensitive.

She tuned out the thought. "This line curves upward. When it comes to your love life, you can be extremely demanding. You tend to get jealous easily, and you crave constant attention."

His brown eyes met hers. "You're still angry." He paused, as if contemplating whether he should continue. "Forsooth, I brought you here to save you from the count's advances."

His gaze was direct and sincere. She felt surprising relief at his admission. She pressed for more. "And?"

A shadow of irritation crossed his face. "And yes, I needed a seamstress, so we've helped each other."

"Thank you." She returned to the lines in his hand. "You are also extremely close with your family, and if given the choice, you would like to be near them as much as possible."

Pain filled his eyes.

"You lost your father and brother. I'm sorry." She rushed on. "This line, from under your index finger across your palm, is your Head Line." His was straight, indicating a lack of self-confidence, but she would not say that. "You're comfortable with order and structure. Strength in numbers."

He nodded. "True."

"Now let's look at your bracelets." She pushed his big paw backward, revealing a series of lines where hand met wrist. "You have several bracelets. You will enjoy many years of happiness."

She looked at his lifeline. "Something unexpected will come into your life." She noted the sudden change in direction of his line, its abrupt ending, and cold settled in her stomach. His life would end violently, and soon. Her heart skipped in alarm, for him and for her. She found him exciting and looked forward to seeing him, being near him. . . .

His brows wrinkled in question. "What else?"

She could not tell him he would die. "But you will find a way to conquer the challenge," she finished hastily.

"That's all?"

She released his hand. "You have a strong will, Tabor, and will enjoy much happiness." She knew naught of palm readings, she told herself, dismissing the fatal sign. She'd probably confused the lines.

A probing query entered his eyes. "You're unsettled."

She fluttered the linen at her neckline. "Nay, just a bit warm, from the fire."

"Thank you for the reading. Allow me to repay you by escorting you for a walk in the night air."

"Nay, 'tis not necessary—"

"But worthwhile," he said with a wink.

Her insides fluttered in spite of herself. Knowing she shouldn't, she could not resist smiling and accepting his hand.

Outside, the air still held the warmth of summer. The earth released its musky scents, and a gentle breeze touched her face.

They walked along the interior moat shoreline. The water shone, sparkling in the moonlight, the surface broken occasionally by swirling fish, the silence interrupted by frog tunes.

" 'Tis a very wide moat."

"Widest in Wiltshire and Hampshire." Pride rang in his voice.

The image of his severed lifeline interrupted the peaceful

moment. He was overbearing, but he had shown her kindness and hospitality.

"You shiver." He offered her the cloak he'd insisted on bringing. He draped it gently on her shoulders and tied the front. A velvet cloak of protection seemed to embrace her, a caring feeling so sweet but elusive, just beyond her grasp; she was like a poor man savoring untold riches but knowing he only transported them to another. Such dreams would not come true, she had learned, but she could not dispel the fleeting joy of his tenderness.

She touched his hand, and his eyes connected with hers.

She felt a rushing in her ears, and the air hummed between them. She could feel his breath on her skin, and his masculine scent, touched with a hint of apple wine, filled her senses.

He came no closer, keeping his promise to not force her. She would need to move to him.

Her whole being became overwhelmed with waiting, waiting, and an insistent yearning.

His gaze was soft as a caress, inviting her.

"Just a kiss. No more." She heard a husky voice scarcely recognizable as her own.

"As you wish, Sharai."

She followed the roar of her heart and moved toward him. *Take a chance, Sharai.*

His lips felt soft against hers.

He deepened the kiss, his mouth sliding gently across hers.

The rush in her ears became a pounding, drawing her closer.

His tongue entered her mouth, and she felt flickers of heat in her stomach. She didn't know desire could be so pleasant.

She met his tongue and heard a strange sound escape from her throat. She recognized the sound of desire in her own voice. Surprised, she drew back.

He buried his face in her neck.

"Sweet Sharai, you make me your slave with your kisses. Come you to my chamber tonight. I will please you, I vow."

She pushed him away. "I am not your slave."

"I only meant I'd do anything for you. I'm sorry."

She turned from him. "Forgive me. I must go."

Sharai thrashed in her bed, lost in dreams.

She was eight, back in her native Lipscani. Damir, a family friend, had been courting her mother, and was there that night.

Just before dawn several men broke the small door with their heavy boots and ripped the shutters from their windows, smashing her mother's clay pots and flowers. "Come with me," Damir had said, and he smuggled Sharai, her mother, cousin, aunt, and uncle to a field in a valley not far from their home, and they huddled in the cover of dairy cows in a pen adjacent to the barns. Riders approached.

"Stay still," Sharai's mother, Reena whispered. They hugged the ground.

The men opened the gates and rode in, scattering the cows. "There. See them."

Sharai and her family jumped the fence, running into the fields.

Run, Sharai!

The men followed on horseback.

Sharai's uncle and aunt fell, and the sound of clubs hitting their bodies filled the air.

Sharai and her mother ran for the cover of trees.

A man neared them and struck Reena on the shoulders.

With a groan, she fell.

Terror seized Sharai. She could not leave her mother. She ran to her, tried to pull her up.

They were dragged back to the cow pen, their hands and feet tied.

In the early light of dawn she saw Damir, visiting with the evil people who had captured them.

"Romani?" they asked Damir.

"Aye. Strong. Healthy." He accepted a small bag from them.

Damir met Sharai's gaze. He cast his eyes downward and then left on horseback, never looking back.

Sharai's hands formed into fists, and she shook them at Damir. "*Choro!*" she screamed. "Thief! May the *mulla dudia* haunt your every step." She fell on the ground, pounding the grass.

"There, now, There. 'Tis all right. Just a dream, is all."

Sharai felt a tapping on her shoulder. She blinked, saw her comforter.

Kadriya knelt in front of Britta, Lady Anne's maid, who held a candle. Kadriya put her small hand on Sharai's shoulder, steadying her. "It's all right, Sharai."

Britta lit a torch to chase the morning gloom and filled the basin with warm water.

Sharai rose. Kadriya's side of the bed was empty. She must have already dressed and gone. "You needn't help me, Britta. I can do that."

Britta wore a hood over her greying hair, and the small fan of wrinkles around her eyes were evident in the light. "I worry for you."

The nightmare. "I'm sorry to have awakened you."

Britta placed the basin and towel by the fire. "Will you be washing your hair again this morn?"

Sharai sat close to the fire and submerged the fresh linen. "It's late. Just a quick bath today." She washed her face and neck, moving down the right side of her body, covering it to ward off the chill, then washing the left side. She cherished this luxury of having a morning fire and a snug roof over her head, under which she could clean to start her day. She swabbed her teeth with sage leaves, rinsing with mint tea.

Britta watched the morning rituals with great interest. Sharai supposed it was her curiosity that kept her close by. Hers, or Lady Anne's, she thought with a smile. "Thank you for your help, Britta, but I can tend to my own water in the morning."

"Odd that you wash every day, if you ask me. You'll likely be stricken, getting your head wet like that."

"It has never made me ill. Washing makes it easier to braid my hair," she explained to Britta. "My friends use oil, but I prefer water. It makes neat braids without leaving a hot feeling on my scalp all the day."

Sharai slipped into her red linen gown, an ill-fitting garment Lady Anne had given her. When she found a moment, she would alter the dress.

She thought of Tabor, and something tugged in her stomach again. She'd kissed men before, but never felt incendiary passions like those he kindled in her. Had she gone to his chamber last night, she would have been in his arms when the dreams came.

She dropped her comb. *What are you thinking, Sharai? He is a noble.* She folded and re-folded her towel. *Aye, but not like the rest.*

She noticed Britta staring at her. "Thank you for soothing me last night."

"Must have been unpleasant," Britta ventured, eyes widened with fresh curiosity.

"Aye. Memories best forgotten," Sharai answered quickly before she could ask pointed questions. "So what do you suppose Lady Anne has in store for us today," she asked, changing the subject.

"More sewing. Now that negotiations with Lord and Lady Marmyl proceed so smoothly, I expect they shall visit soon.

He's an earl, you know. Think of it. An earl's daughter, here in Coin Forest. Their shield is blue wings on silver, you know. Mayhap you could sew a blue tablecloth in their honor.

Egad, another project. "What shade of blue?"

"Like the sky."

That was Lady Anne's gown material. "I doubt we will have enough of that color for the head table. Mayhap flowers instead," she suggested.

"Yes. Oh, my lady is so excited for their arrival. And who could fault her? Tongues are wagging, and I hear her dowry is a fortune."

Sharai's body stiffened. "Dowry?"

"Aye, from the Lady Emilyne to Lord Tabor. They will be wed, and Lady Emilyne's dowry—" Britta glanced toward the door and leaned forward, lowering her voice. "I hear tell 'tis one thousand pounds."

Tabor crossed the bailey, enjoying the warmth of the sun on his face. Cyrill and he had worked the devil out of the squires again, and they had learned the penalty of an inaccurate aim. Now, he would like to enjoy some of this fine day. A ride in the woodlands would please him.

A ride with Sharai. She filled his senses, and he wished nothing more than to be with her. She was more than he had ever hoped for. Fantasy be dashed. Sharai was real.

His steps were light, and he couldn't get there quickly enough. He would rescue Sharai from Lady Anne's ambitious projects and show her the woodlands. He would hold her in his arms, taste her kisses, and this time, she would not wish to stop.

He climbed above-stairs to the solar, a withdrawing room where the women sewed. The windows there afforded more light for their tasks.

In the solar Lady Anne held fabric at various points on a

dress form, while Sharai slipped pins into the silk. Britta bent over a table, cutting material, and Kadriya waxed thread and rolled it on a spool.

Tabor approached. "Hello, ladies. How goes your progress?"

"Good," Lady Anne replied. "Sharai is every bit the seamstress you promised."

"But we must not work her to exhaustion. You have been holed up here all morn with your fabrics. I'm taking a ride to the woodlands, and I would show it to her."

Lady Anne shot him a dark glance. "We need to continue. There'll be plenty of time for rides."

"Just two hours, Mother. It will give you time to balance records with the butler, and we'll be back before you notice our absence."

Sharai's hair was confined in a tidy braid again, disappearing behind her proud shoulders, and her temptingly curved lips stole his breath as if he had jumped off the cliffs in Southampton. He met her gaze. "Come and I'll show you the meadow of the Coin Forest Legend."

"Yes."

The word, and the breathless way she uttered it, made his heart beat faster.

"Kadriya, too. Kadriya and I would join you."

Tabor nodded. Not the more personal time with her that he'd hoped for, but still she would be with him.

Sharai and Kadriya approached the stables. They had changed from their English gowns and were wearing their usual fair garb, short smocks over voluminous, flowing skirts.

Tabor mounted Bolt, his destrier, and the groom, Charles, brought Sharai a horse, Spirit, one of Tabor's best.

She stroked Spirit's muzzle and nodded to Charles. "Please remove the saddles for Kadriya and me."

Tabor blocked the groom's hand. "Nay. They will ride properly." He lowered his voice. " 'Tis the lady's way of riding, Sharai. Surely you would want to appear the lady." He stressed the last word.

She laughed, but it rang with a bitter edge. "Years ago, yes, but you and I both know I am not."

By the saints she was ill-tempered this morn. "I meant no harm, Sharai, I merely wished to point out—"

"Cease." She released the saddle straps with startling agility and lugged the saddle to a surprised Charles. "I know full well what you think of me, Lord Tabor. I may change my language and my dress, but inside I will always be Gypsy." She swung fluidly onto Spirit's bare back.

Next to her, Kadriya mounted Prince, her pony. With a sideways glance at Sharai, Kadriya mimicked her perfect posture, right down to the proud tilt of her head.

Sharai's gaze challenged him. "We're ready."

Learning nothing from her dark expression, he led them by the pastures north of the castle.

Sharai nodded toward a herd of dairy cows. "They look fat and happy. Your sheep, too. I see a few have lambed late."

"Yes." They passed the west fields, flush with oats, and through a break in the hedgerows between the north and east fields. Once in the open, he urged Bolt into an easy canter.

They crossed a stream and approached a stand of trees, soaring tall in the sky, taller than most cathedrals, save for Salisbury's pinnacle.

He stopped Bolt and covered his shoulders with his cloak, thinking of the previous night, how he'd covered her shoulders, how warm she'd been. Then.

The women donned their cloaks.

He wound through the trees, his eyes adjusting to the shadows of the green canopy. Cold, wet air chilled his face, and the rich, rotting smell of leaves and decaying wood filled his nostrils.

In a high branch above, a blue tit sang its variety of calls.

Sharai's palfrey broke a branch. It snapped loudly and fell.

Kadriya reined closer to him. "How far is it?"

"Just past the mushroom tree."

They rode on in a silence broken only by the soft hoof falls on the forest floor, and by the occasional snort of the horses.

The sun scattered fingers of light through the green canopy of leaves that covered the tall linden and oak trees, the yews and the shorter chequers. His land, his forest. It flowed through his veins as surely as his blood, and he would die defending it.

They reached a clearing where an ancient oak felled by lightning sprawled across the middle of it. "This fell when I was but a boy," Tabor said. By falling, its hundred-foot height had become a hundred-foot length, atop which moss, plants, and a profusion of brown mushrooms grew. "According to the legends, we follow the same route Roman soldiers took one day, over a thousand years ago. This trail leads to the site of the Coin Forest Legend."

Kadriya turned her pony sideways. "Pray tell us the legend, Tabor." Her brown eyes, flecked with green, grew wide with excitement.

Encouraged, Tabor continued, hoping Sharai shared Kadriya's interest in local lore. "A small band of Roman soldiers, cut off from their troops by a band of Picts, were pursued from Southampton to this region, where they struggled to reach the safety of Salisbury. They carried with them a military map to be delivered to the emperor, Magnus Maximus. The Picts craved the soldiers' map, but they lusted even more for their cargo: Gold. A fortune in Roman coins, which was to be distributed as salary for the Roman Legions."

"The forest provided cover, but the soldiers, having no reference point in the darkness, became lost and the Picts continued to gain on them.

"When capture appeared inevitable, the soldiers buried their coins and separated."

"Did they come back for their coins?" Kadriya asked.

"Be patient, Sprig," Tabor said, using Sharai's nickname for the young girl.

They had entered another meadow, divided by a cheerful stream. Just past the meadow, a well-worn trail led to the right.

Tabor followed it, guiding Bolt up a large hill. Tall trees soared in the dark canopy, and one, a badly deformed oak tree, stood out, even in the gloom. Thirty feet from the ground, the tree suddenly expanded, its straight trunk becoming a large bubble then, higher up, it reverted to its normal trunk size again. Tabor pointed at it. "Note you that tree."

Sharai spotted it. "How odd."

"It looks like it is with child."

"Kadriya."

"Well, it does. See, like she carries it low, 'twill be a boy."

"Enough. Ladies do not talk thus," Sharai scolded.

Kadriya lowered her head, her lower lip thrust out. "You tell me to speak the truth. Fine, then. It looks like a giant gourd."

Tabor cleared his throat to clear the air. "Only one soldier made it to Salisbury alive. He could not retrace his path to the coins. Thenceforward, the village of Tabor became known as Coin Forest."

Tabor dismounted, grabbed a dead branch and pointed it at the base of the misshapen tree. "Fifty years ago, on this ground, four Roman coins were found in bear scat. The forest was combed for months with no further clue."

He made a sweeping gesture with his arm, encompassing the trees and the vegetation strewn forest floor. "Somewhere in the shadows of this forest lies a fortune in Roman coins."

"Oh," Kadriya crooned, apparently caught up in the magic of the story. "I shall find the treasure."

Tabor gave her a stern look. "You are welcome to look, but you are never to come without escort to the forest, Kadriya. But Sharai must needs return to her work, and I to mine. Next time I'll tell you of the nightingales and take you to the southwest forest, and another legend, Dragon's Green."

Kadriya urged her pony forward. "And I shall tell you a Gypsy story, Lord Tabor, about the Forest Faeries."

"Never you mind, Sprig. Lord Tabor's head is full enough of tales. He needs no more." She urged Spirit forward to pass him.

Tabor grabbed the reins and held her back, waiting until the others moved further ahead. "What mean you by that comment? You've been cold to me this afternoon. Why?"

"Because I was foolish enough to trust you. To believe what you say." She laughed. "The hot-tempered, judgmental Lord Tabor, high on his horse of truth and honor." She slapped his hands with the reins.

Surprised, he released them.

"I have a word for you, and you won't like it, but I should have read it in your eyes, long before now. I shan't make the mistake again."

"What word is that?"

She paused and turned to face him. "It's a word used at the fairs when people present their wares for more than they are. Deceitful."

"I suspected it before, but now I know. You *are* mad. It's a legend. How can the Coin Forest Legend be deceitful?"

" 'Tis not about the legend, though it seems well suited to you with your preoccupation with money. And after all those lofty speeches, Tabor."

"I cannot continue this conversation."

She reined Spirit sharply, and he backed up. "Yes, I suppose you wish not to talk with me. I have no thousand pounds with which to buy you." She grit the last two words out and urged Spirit into a full run back to the castle.

CHAPTER SEVEN

Tabor crossed the drawbridge, heading for the church. He pulled his cloak close to ward off the morning chill. Sharai would be there for Lauds, he knew. She hadn't missed a morning in the two weeks she'd been here. Since their visit to Coin Forest, she had uttered only the most necessary of words to him. Her anger over his pending betrothal seemed to have spent itself, and all that was left in her eyes was a minimal civility.

He missed their conversations. Just seeing her scattered his thoughts and reminded him of his longing. The soft swell of her breasts from her breathing after climbing the stairs. The way her hand went to her heart when pleased, to the back of her neck when provoked. Kadriya frequently encouraged the hand to heart movements. He had so far managed to inspire only the gestures of annoyance.

He wanted her to trust him, but he must admit he did not trust her, either. And the issue of Lady Emilyne's dowry disturbed her beyond reason.

Mayhap, being a Gypsy, she had no knowledge of marriage contracts. Yet she claimed nobility in Little Egypt, so surely she understood the concept of bloodlines. What had driven a girl of nobility from her country to a state of near starvation in France? Mayhap her father had been found guilty of treason or refused to support his king financially or militarily and had forfeited all lands and titles.

He shook his head, trying to get her out of it.

He could not deny his obligation to complete wedding negotiations with the Marmyls. One thousand pounds. He must face his political realities. The Tabors had offered the king military support—his father fought with valor at Agincourt, and Tabor himself fought with Bedford in Normandy. Yet from the way the king had responded to Hungerford, loyalty meant less to him than financial gifts. Wealth was the new sword that would sway Gloucester by bolstering the war-ravaged treasury. Wealth would protect Tabor's family and estates from political threats.

Hungerford had alliances—his cousin in the king's council, a significant advantage. And he had wealth. He had stolen Tabor's treasury, using it these years to buy favor in the courts. Emilyne's dowry provided the chance to even the score. Everything, Tabor supposed, had a price.

His mother had negotiated a fine contract, and he would wed Lady Emilyne and accept her dowry. With a thousand pounds, he could secure legal favor, regain his stature with the parish, increase the security of his knights, repair the village curtain, re-roof the church, hire workers to bring in the harvest—the list was too long to deny. His family, his village—both needed that dowry.

Approaching the church, Tabor noted the crowd milling in front of the building. None had entered. Even Father Bernard, his elderly priest, stood before the door, shifting his weight from foot to foot. Anticipating trouble, Tabor's muscles tensed.

Sir John strode toward him, his yellow hair bouncing from the energy in his step. "A message on the door, my lord," he said, his words rushed.

The villagers frequently used the church door to post notices of meetings, contests, or to share simple messages. What was posted there?

Bracing himself for bad news, Tabor hastened to the church door. A gruesome message had been nailed to the heavy wooden door: one of Tabor's own carrier pigeons, blood still dripping. Tabor's gut knotted. He scanned the crowd, searching for an expression of guilt among the men's faces, but found none.

The note attached to the bird slipped easily from the nail. It was written on fine paper. Tabor read the message through the spatters of blood.

Thief. You continue your father's sin of stealing from women to fatten your coffers. Death will visit Coin Forest again. Will Lady Emilyne see you through that, "Lord" Tabor?

Sharai appeared in the crowd and sent him a worried glance.

Tabor lifted the dead bird's leg and unwrapped the message that had been removed once already, intercepted before it could be delivered. He unfolded the small piece of parchment.

To the Right Worshipful Lord and Lady Marmyl, I extend greetings. May this letter find you hale. I am most pleased with your acceptance of dowry terms. We joyfully anticipate your Thursday arrival at Coin Forest. Until then, may Almighty Jesus preserve you, both body and soul, &tc. . . . The Right Honorable Lady Tabor.

So like his mother, Tabor thought. So formal, yet lavish, ever the contrasts. Tabor pocketed his mother's note and scanned the bloodied one. Tabor could see the beefy, taunting face, as if he were there, before him. "Rauf." His vision blurred, and a pressure built behind his eyes.

Sharai worked her way through the crowd, followed by Kadriya. "Did he sign it thus?" She spoke softly so only he could hear.

"Nay." He turned to his knight. "Sir John, clear the door so Father Bernard can celebrate Prime."

Kadriya stared, wide-eyed, at the dead bird.

Sharai grabbed her shoulders and turned her away. "Go you to the solar, Kadriya, and prepare your thread. I'll join you soon."

Tabor crumpled the note in his hands. God's bones! Hungerford was hunting him, playing with him as a cat plays with his prey. Entering his own stronghold. Anger drove him to decision. "Cyrill," he shouted.

Cyrill hastened to his side. "Milord."

"Gather provisions and armor up. We shall meet the Hungerfords head-on."

"On the road, my lord? Or at Hungerford?"

"Engage knights. Archers, as well. Bring scaling ladders. Crowbars."

Cyrill's brows shot up. "A siege?"

"Hatchets. And pitch." Tabor would end this standoff and clear the shadow that had hung over his family since before his birth.

Sir Cyrill barked orders, designating men to organize the horses, food, and wagons, and the knights hurried away. The peasants not called for archery duty shuffled uneasily into the church.

He felt a pressure on his arm.

Sharai's hand, a look of concern in her eyes. "The note is unsigned. How do you know Rauf sent it, and not Lord Hungerford? Or someone else?"

He pulled his arm free and stalked toward the castle. "No one else would write this. My family has no enemies but them."

She hurried to catch up. "Where will you go?"

"Bishops Road to Hungerford. Due south. A two-day ride with wagons."

"And?"

"I shall finish what the blackguard started in St. Giles when he accused me of leaving my brother to die, the bloody sod." He walked faster, his blood pumping hot. "My estates are in good shape now. I have strong knights. Mercenaries, yes, but trained, and ready for battle."

She seemed quiet, thoughtful. "I heard at the fair that Hungerford claims your father stole Coin Forest from his family."

"Drivel. His aunt tried to kill my father with a potion. He barely survived and lived thereafter with a nervous tic on the left side of his face. She was tried and found guilty of witchcraft. Imprisoned. And my father's marriage to her was annulled."

"Why is there still a problem, then?"

"Hungerford petitions the king trying to regain Coin Forest."

"Regain? So Coin Forest was a Hungerford holding."

"These matters should not trouble you, but I will tell you nonetheless. My father did not steal Coin Forest. It was given to him, and I will die before I let those vermin have it. Now I must needs prepare for battle."

He turned from her and strode to the castle. He collected his armor and returned to the bailey.

Lady Anne met him at the doorway. Her eyes shining, she squeezed his arm. "Take care of it, Tabor. Finish them."

Loading a wagon with filled quivers, Sir Cyrill greeted him with a slow, somber nod, but hesitation in his eyes.

"You think I should wait."

"The king's order, my lord," Cyrill said, reminding him of King Henry's message to maintain the peace. "What will be gained by force?"

"Peace," Tabor growled. "Waiting has proven futile. If anything, Rauf becomes more bold."

Later, Tabor walked with Sir Cyrill, taking final inventory of the loaded wagons. Tabor nodded to the ten and two knights who would accompany them to battle, along with their squires and the archers. "I must pray, and then we shall be off."

He entered the church, and his eyes adjusted to the dim light. The stained glass in the east window depicted a bishop kneeling before the Virgin. The red and yellow glass made colored shafts of light on the reed-strewn floor. A single figure stood before the rood screen. "Sharai."

She turned. Her dark eyes appeared liquid, her face serene, framed by a few black curls that escaped her braid. She held prayer beads in her hands. He covered her small hands with his, then lifted her beads to the light. At closer glance, he saw that it was made not of beads, but of globes of red-colored silk and six large ovals of black silk, sewn so deftly that no stitches were visible.

A treasure from scraps. She could make so much from so little. Where had she developed such patience and resourcefulness, he wondered.

"Please forgive me, Sharai. I interrupted your prayers."

She shook her head. "No mind. I'm glad to talk with you before you leave on this . . . battle. I have no family, but I have Kadriya. And Etti. And you have shown me kindness, and—" She hesitated, then frowned. "And I care for you." Her eyes blinked as if revealing the information pained her.

Her unexpected affection brought a quiet warmth. "I care for you, too, Sharai."

She kept looking at his hand.

He turned it over. "What did you see there?"

"Forsooth, I cannot be sure. I have learned much about you, though. You have a short temper and react quickly, ofttimes too quickly. Mayhap this is a time to resist your impulses, to abstain from doing the first thing you think of. Mayhap this time you would do the *second* thing you think of."

"What know you of battle?"

"I know of survival." She lowered her lashes, but the furrow in her brows revealed her pain. "I know the penalties of misjudgment. That is what I would wish to spare you."

He recalled Rauf's attack and how Sharai had come, with her dagger and women, to his rescue, and his face grew warm. "You saved me once, Sharai. 'Tis sufficient for one lifetime."

"We help each other, don't we?" She paused. "What will the

king think of you if you lay siege to Hungerford's manor, and fail?" She folded the silk beads and slipped them into a fold of her skirt. "What will the king think of you if you're successful?"

A vision rested in Tabor's brain, but it did not involve the king. It involved Rauf's neck in his own hands, squeezing tighter until Tabor finally stilled Rauf's murdering hands and forever silenced his perverse mouth. He did not respond.

"So you have no plan. You merely react to Rauf's message."

Her dark eyes met his, warm, lacking their usual fire. She placed something in his hand and closed it. "Godspeed. Keep this round your neck. It will protect you."

He touched her cheek with his free hand. With a last gaze, he left the church.

Outside, he opened his hand, revealing a pale blue vial about the size of a spoon's bowl, with a black string. *I care for you.* Her words embraced him like a strong fire on a winter's night. And she had given him this gift. Enchanted, he pulled the flat cork free and scraped a dab of the salve, putting it to his tongue. His mouth squeezed into a grimace, and he spat. It tasted like rancid fat and smelled of worms.

Tabor and his knights followed the old Roman road known as Bishops Trail. They'd been traveling for two hours, the supply wagons tilting right and left from the stone path, which had settled crooked from centuries of rains, the bobbing heads of the archers on foot, arrows rattling in their quivers. First Tabor and his knights, Cyrill and John, followed by the wagons, flanked by mercenary knights.

The sky frowned on them, rumpled, grey, threatening rain. He slipped the disgusting amulet Sharai had given him under his hauberk, and her words echoed in his mind. What will King Henry think if he kills the Hungerfords? Or if he fails?

I will not fail. His jaw tightened, his muscles straining to act, to finally send his enemies to the netherworld.

He'd sent for reinforcements from his manor in Fritham, located a full day's ride northwest of Hungerford. They would bring more men and materials and rendezvous just before Hungerford.

How long before they took the manor? Not long. Hungerford had not received license to crenellate, so they would not be assaulted from the rooftop. Though stately, the manor lacked a moat, and the curtain was reported to be in ill repair.

Yet after leaving the note on his church door, they would be expecting him. No matter how stealthy their approach, the Hungerfords would have assembled a formidable welcoming party.

He stopped his horse. Of course, Rauf would be expecting him to come galloping to their door in two-fisted fury.

Don't do the first thing you think of, Tabor. Hatred worked up his throat like a sickness. How could he not? He urged Bolt forward.

Tabor kicked the small fire, scattering the flames. His Fritham men had joined them and they were camped outside Hungerford Village's perimeter. He glared at three of his knights. "A fire announces our presence. We leave to reconnoiter. Wait for my signal."

Tabor mounted Bolt and nodded to Cyrill. Though Tabor wanted to shout a rally cry to vanquish the Hungerfords, he would use caution this time.

They rode forward, steering clear of the small village, and approached the manor. Three stories tall, it perched on a high hill and sprawled in three directions. Spies had advised that as a security measure, they had covered the hill with a layer of loose rocks—useful information, for this could not be seen in the quarter moon's light.

The horses stepped soundlessly in the moist grass, allowing

them quiet approach.

Tabor reined to a stop. "The drawbridge is down." He would have expected it to be up, at least partially.

Cyrill made a troubled sound. "And minimal guards. Look you at the bastions."

The bastions were vacant save one lone guard. Laughter and the musical notes of lutes and clapping drifted down to them.

The Hungerfords would not be making merry if they expected his attack. Yet here he was, army and weapons at the ready. Hairs rose on the back of Tabor's neck. *Something is amiss.* He signaled to Cyrill. " 'Tis a trap. We're going back to the camp."

At camp, Tabor and Cyrill met with John at the supply wagon. "Where are their men?"

"Most curious," John said. "They're all inside. The hall is packed, and they are at leisure."

"It makes no sense. Cyrill, we must retreat. Quietly. And you must return to protect Coin Forest."

"And you?" Cyrill asked.

Tabor could not leave without solving this mystery. "I'll stay."

Cyrill shook his head. "Not alone."

John stepped forward. "I shall stay with you, milord."

"With that butter-top head of yours? You will be recognized at first blush."

John lifted the oiled canvas covering the wagon bed and put his hand inside, then wiped a thin film of pitch on his yellow hair, blackening it. "Not now."

Tabor used a rag to rub the tar evenly on John's hair. "You'll have a devil of a time washing this out, but it works."

Tabor looked at the sliver of the moon. Midnight would come soon. "Sir Cyrill, take our horses and have the Fritham men wait for us just past the Druid stones. Fetch us two linen tunics from the archers. I'll wear the hood forward and stay clear of the manor." The thought of dressing as a peasant in Hungerford's estate made him cringe, but it might help him learn more about Hungerford's plans.

Tabor sat alone in the corner of a Hungerford alehouse. Some forty souls crowded onto the slab benches, deep in their cups, many gnawing on roast chicken. A group of four pilgrims and a lone tinker occupied the table next to Tabor. The small village was situated on the way to Salisbury, a popular pilgrimage destination, and from there a good road led east to the grand Cathedral of Winchester.

At the opposite end of the alehouse, John flirted with the prostitutes, most of them older than Tabor, hard women with broken teeth and muscle enough to pressure any patron who refused to pay. One was young, though. Built strong, like the others, but mayhap just ten and four, with teeth intact, though her red hair and grey gown were deeply soiled. She knew several men, and she occasionally pulled the top of her dress down, affording brief glimpses of her large breasts.

The men close to her laughed and reached out to grab them, but she was faster than they and covered them before they could.

John bobbed his neck like a chicken, keeping her in his sights.

To John's right a young cripple had crawled close to the fire to beg, dragging his useless legs close to the wall to avoid being stepped on. Above him, a stout lad turned chickens on the spit.

One guest's voice traveled over all the others, a bragging fellow named George of Wooten. A small man with grey, thinning hair, George was on pilgrimage to St. Swithun's shrine for a chest ailment. George had appraised Tabor with his small eyes, taken in his coarse linen tunic and dirtied hair, and calmly turned his back to him.

Tabor swirled the thin ale in his flask. He felt the absence of his sword, but peasants invited arrest if they carried one, so both he and John each carried only a dagger.

The tavern master's eyes held no respect for Tabor, had looked past him, in fact, to the well-dressed pilgrims, serving them first. Tabor's disguise had worked to diminish his standing, but the victory brought with it a sense of inferiority, making him feel less powerful, more vulnerable.

George kicked a begging dog away and leaned toward another man at his table. "I saw them march here, bringing their beds and baggage. My brother worries for his sheep. By the time they left Lord Hardgrove's manor, his larders were stripped bare."

His friend, better dressed than George, emptied his mug. His face showed scabs from a bad shave, and he missed a front tooth. " 'Tis their right, by gad. Watch your words."

"Could it be a call to arms?"

Tabor strained to hear more. Did they speak of his men? Had Sir Cyrill been intercepted? Or his Fritham men, waiting for him at the Druid stones?

The friend laughed. "Where would we fight? We've lost all but Normandy and Calais."

"Bloody French. The war has cost us. And the coronation took our last penny."

"How know you this?" another said.

George straightened. "My brother is a clerk in the Exchequer. And mark this: the king himself was short two thousand pounds last year in covering his personal expenses."

"Sweet misery. Then England is defeated. At Southampton I heard the bishop of Winchester's going to France to negotiate peace."

George jerked his head around, confronting Tabor. "Boy."

Thinking he referred to the boy cooking the chickens, Tabor looked behind him.

"Nay. You, peasant," George said, poking his shoulder. "You with the brown hood. Your ears are large. Be you a spy?"

Tabor shook his head.

"Curiosity kills the cat, you know. What's your business here?"

"Waiting for a friend, sir."

George pushed his tankard forward. "Refill my mug, then, peasant. I'll give you a couple of farthings so you can buy a bigger hood to hold those ears."

George guffawed, and his friend joined in.

Tabor's neck warmed unpleasantly, but he responded, approaching the tavern master at the barrels. "A refill, prithee, for George of Wooten."

The tavern master nodded, filled the mug from the barrel tap, and handed it back to him.

Tabor passed John and lowered his voice. "Hear anything?"

"Gloucester," John said.

Humphrey, Duke of Gloucester, the king's uncle and Chancellor of England during the king's minority. "What about Gloucester?"

"He's here," John whispered. "At Hungerford's manor."

God's teeth! As if rising from the depths and breaking the surface of the water, Tabor saw it now. Hungerford invited Gloucester, then taunted Tabor with the bird and note. Tabor, in his temper, had responded just as Hungerford had anticipated.

Except Tabor had not attacked. For once he'd reined in his initial instinct. Tabor swallowed. But if he were caught here, it could be construed that he had defied the king's order to keep the peace. He grabbed John's arm. "We must leave."

Just then the tavern door opened. A gust of night air swept the room and two guards entered, followed by a large, burly nobleman.

Tabor dropped his head so the hood would cover his face.

It was Rauf.

CHAPTER EIGHT

At Rauf's appearance, the tavern became quiet. He stepped into the room, his sheer size demanding attention. Dressed for ceremony, he wore a red velvet doublet with black hose.

He stationed one of his guards at the front door and the other at the side door, leaving just the bolted window for escape. He gave his guards pointed looks. "No one leaves."

Tabor caught John's eye and gestured with a thumb to the side door, then moved a step closer to the fireplace, looking for a weapon. He spied only cooking tools, but they might work. He spied some cooking tools hanging there.

Rauf pointed at the tavern master. "An ale."

The tavern master handed a full tankard to the young, red-haired wench.

Her hands shaking, she passed it to Rauf and bowed. "My lord."

Rauf spied the cripple at the wall and strode to him. "Worm. Did I not forbid you to enter?" He kicked the cripple in the side.

The young cripple groaned and tried to shrink further into the wall. "Sorry, my lord. I did not beg, you see?" He held his empty hands out. " 'Tis cold tonight, and by your grace, I wish only to warm myself."

The cords in Rauf's neck tightened and he shuddered with dread. Rauf splashed his tankard of ale into the cripple's face. "Get away from me. Get out."

The cripple gasped but kept his hands held upward in a plea for mercy.

The pilgrims shrank to the far side of the tavern.

Tabor started toward Rauf, but saw the guard looking for someone who might defend the crippled man and stopped.

The cripple tried to cover his legs, normal down to the knees, where they withered away to fatty sacs of flesh reminiscent of a turkey's wattle.

Rauf shivered and his expression distorted into one of loathing. "The devil's work. I told you, you abomination, we do not . . ." He kicked the cripple in the ribs.

"Give . . ." He kicked him again.

"Alms." He struck him a third time.

The red-haired wench rushed to Rauf, touching his shoulder. "Please, my lord. I'll take him out. I beg your pardon—"

Rauf backhanded her.

She reeled and was caught in the arms of the crowd.

Tabor roared and lunged toward Rauf, tackling him, and together they tumbled onto a table.

Tabor's hands squeezed around Rauf's neck. Months of frustration surged through him and he bellowed again, letting it loose.

Tabor saw movement, the flash of a sword drawn high.

He rolled off the table.

The front door guard rushed forward, sword drawn, looking for a clean target.

Buffered by the table, Tabor retreated to the fireplace. He grabbed a long handled spoon out of the young cook's hand and retrieved a pan of hot fat drippings from its hook.

Rauf eyed the bubbling grease in Tabor's hand and stopped.

Tabor gestured to the cripple. "Get him out of here."

The red-haired wench stooped to lift him, but Rauf pulled his sword and bent down, his lip curled in disgust. "Return to the hell from whence you came." He ran the young boy through.

The wench screamed.

The cripple grunted softly and looked to the wench. Blood pooled on the floor, and his head dropped on his arm.

"You cutthroat," Tabor said.

Rauf turned slightly toward his knight but kept his eye on Tabor. "Do not kill this one." Rauf swung, slashing his sword at Tabor's arm.

Tabor threw the bubbling grease at Rauf.

It splashed onto Rauf's sleeve, sinking into the skin. Rauf roared in pain.

Tabor dropped the pan and dodged Rauf's sword. Grabbing a hefty mug from the mantle, he pitched it at Rauf's head.

Rauf ducked and the mug struck the guard's shoulder.

Tabor withdrew to the corner and the guard ran around the table, sword swinging.

Tabor dipped and the sword passed him. It penetrated the fireplace beam with a large "thwock."

Rauf saw the knight's sword rendered useless in the small space and pulled his dagger.

Now they were even. Almost. Tabor pulled off his hood, tossing it over the guard's head, then rammed his fist into his face.

The guard reeled backward.

Rauf pulled Tabor off the guard and pounded his fist into Tabor's jaw.

A jolt of pain filled him and Tabor fell. He feigned unconsciousness.

Rauf pulled him up by his left arm.

Tabor smashed a clean shot at Rauf, and he fell backward. He chopped Rauf's wrist, ridding him of his dagger. A new, hot strength coursed through Tabor, and he punched Rauf between the eyes and straddled him. He hammered his fist into Rauf's face, again and again. Each punch purged something dark and oppressive from within. Blood sprayed, punctuating each blow, covering his hands.

Someone grabbed Tabor's arms, pulling them behind his back.

Tabor saw the hilt of the guard's sword heading for his face.

Then darkness.

The sun winked behind the banner as it waved in the gentle morning breeze, making a muffled whipping sound. Standing near the blacksmith stall, Sharai watched it flutter in the sunlight, bright and new.

She had walked in this bailey, slept in her snug chamber, and been nourished with regular, hearty meals for three weeks now. She'd observed the flow of the days, activity in the stables, the buttery maids, the knights, Father Bernard and his services. It gave her a sense of security, being under Tabor's protection in this fortress, defended by well-armed knights.

The banner snapped straight, revealing Tabor's coat of arms, a horizontal silver sword threading three gold circles against a green background. Sharai had thought his coat of arms would include coins, for Coin Forest, but the Tabor coat of arms originated hundreds of years ago, long before the family acquired this castle.

Sharai yearned for such stability. What would it be like, she wondered, to follow the seasons in one place, to plant seeds in the spring and tend the growing plants, and harvest the food come autumn, to sleep, warmed by the same hearth, year after year, to watch her babes grow into children and fine sons and daughters, to become familiar with the trees and paths and rivers?

She crossed the bailey and gave a critical eye to another banner that flew at the northeast watchtower. The banner was made of durable linen, but she had selected the more easily worked satin for the detail. The fabric had bunched a bit at the point of the sword on this one, but she'd been able to fix it.

She'd sewn the new flags on impulse after noticing the drab banners that hung, limp and tattered, at the keep and watchtowers. The guards raised the fresh ones just yesterday. When he returned from Hungerford he would see the new banners and know she was thinking about him.

Worrying about him. He'd left three days ago and his knights had returned, without him, yester eve. Now Thursday, and still no word. She swallowed hard. She prayed she was wrong about his palm.

She must be, because she'd crossed a thin line and could never return to where she was before she met the handsome Richard, Baron of Tabor. When had it happened? When had her feelings sneaked past the shield she'd held so close to her heart? She shook her head. 'Twas reckless folly. There was an army of reasons they could not be together as she so foolishly hoped in the secret moments of night, just before dawn. No other man could bring her happiness now, and, hopeless as their situation was, she still yearned to be with him.

Looking skyward, she sent another prayer to keep him safe.

"Come, Sharai." Kadriya, her round face framed with golden-brown curls and painted the picture of impatience, tugged her arm. "Tommy is ready. Hurry."

Sharai let Kadriya pull her, and together they ran across the bailey, skirts flying, to the north curtain by the garden.

Tommy, the little daredevil who annoyed Kadriya in every way possible, waved at them. He wore a wool tunic, the weave so coarse that his skin showed through. His hair resembled the grass in the pigsty, trampled and dirty, but his freckled face wore a sunny grin that forgave it. "Here they are," he said, pointing at the slender wooden poles leaning against the curtain. "Come on. I'll help you up."

He propped the tall poles against the stone curtain that enclosed the bailey and protected the castle from attack. The poles seemed to Sharai as tall as a tree, with a wooden wedge nailed into the side in the middle of its length.

"What are they called again?"

"Stilts," Tommy answered. "They lift you high in the air, and you walk on them. Men use them to walk in the marshes. My da saw them in Southampton when he delivered wool there and he made some for me." He stacked three crates one on the other and gestured to Kadriya. "You first."

Kadriya backed away. "Nay. Sharai, you first."

Challenged, Sharai climbed onto the crates.

Tommy pointed to the wooden wedges nailed to the sides. "Put your feet there, on the footholds."

Sharai inched her left foot past the right stilt and found her footing on the left foothold, then the right, leaning against the stone curtain for balance. She looked down, a mistake. Her feet were even with the top of Kadriya's head. Sharai had climbed many a tree before, but they had been rooted, not a tottering pair of unwieldy sticks.

Tommy positioned another pair of stilts to the right of the stacked boxes and mounted them. He gripped the stilts high, near the top, pushed off, and started walking.

Sharai mustered her courage and pushed off until she was standing. She wobbled there like a crane that had just been stoned in the head.

Tommy gestured, urging her forward. "Walk. Just walk, that's the trick. If you only stand there, you'll fall over."

Her earrings banged against her neck and the rough wood grated against her hands. Sharai worried she might get a splinter. Dizziness overcame her and she faltered. She lifted her right stilt, taking a step forward.

"Do not lift it so high," Tommy warned.

Her foot came down but slipped off the foothold. She teetered on the left stilt. Her right foot fished for the foothold and found it, but too late. She sagged to the right and dropped like a felled tree, landing with her skirts askew.

She struggled upright, rubbing her hip.

Tommy and Kadriya laughed. Kadriya mounted her stilts and took tentative steps toward her, following Tommy's suggestion not to lift the stilts too high. She took a few wobbling steps, eventually smoothing her steps as her confidence grew. "See, Sharai? 'Tis easy."

Sharai straightened her skirts and sent her an "I am your elder" look, but Kadriya deflected it with an expression of delight at having conquered the tall sticks.

Sharai propped her stilts against the curtain. "No sticks of wood will defeat me." She mounted them again and lifted the stilts more gently, taking shorter steps this time. It worked. She staggered across the bailey once, then gained control.

Laughter tickled in her throat and she let it out, adding a whoop of excitement. "I'm doing it. I'm walking!" How exciting, as if she were flying. The ground rose gradually into a hill, and from her high perch on the stilts she could see beyond the curtain, the twelve-foot stone wall that surrounded the bailey. The forest loomed before her on the left, the rolling meadows with sheep and cows, the neatly cultivated fields of oats and wheat to the right, and dozens of peasants, tending the rows.

And she saw, on the road in the distance to the east, a large party approaching.

Her heart skipped. Tabor. He'd returned, safe. Her amulet had overpowered the tragic lifeline on his palm. Relief swept through her, and she let out a little shriek of joy.

Four wagons and several knights on horseback advanced, bearing an unfamiliar coat of arms. As they advanced, the banners became recognizable. One blew open in the breeze.

Blue wings on a silver background.

She dropped from her lofty stilts, landing hard on the ground.

Kadriya dropped from her stilts and rushed to her. "Are you all right, Sharai?"

Slivers needled into her hands and she winced from the pain. "I'm fine." Reality dug like the rough wood in her fingers, and she cursed herself for letting her feelings get away from her. Of course, it would be the Marmyl entourage. Tabor's wealthy bride-to-be had just arrived.

Sharai and Kadriya scurried down the steps, dressed in their hastily donned houppelandes. Sharai wore the red one she'd altered to fit, and Kadriya wore a drab brown frock that Britta had given her, dull but acceptable.

"Make haste." Sharai urged Kadriya forward, their footfalls creating a noisy echo in the circular staircase. "If luck is with us, we shall be seated before they enter."

Lady Anne met them at the base of the stairs, breathless and rushed, wearing her blue gown. She'd netted and veiled her dark hair. Looking at Sharai's gown, her soft features wrinkled into a sharp frown of reproach. "You fool." She gestured impatiently to them, sending them above-stairs. "Don you your Egyptian costumes, both of you. Be swift now."

Sharai turned back up the stairs, steering Kadriya with her. "Come, let us slip into our skirts."

"And remember your bracelets and necklaces," Anne shouted after them.

"How dare she insult you," Kadriya grumbled.

"Did you not see her eyes? She's nervous."

"Of what? She is in charge. She's . . . ," Kadriya hesitated, "What's that word?"

"Chatelaine," said Sharai.

"Aye, that. She rules the castle when Lord Tabor's away."

"She wants to make a good impression." Sharai climbed the last step and caught her breath. "She wants to show us off. Like she draws attention to her fancy rugs by tapping her foot on them. Or the way the merchants display goods at the fair. Hurry now."

They changed and rushed to the great hall, where the head table was draped in fresh white and green linen. From the hearth a fire burned, casting a flickering light in the dark corners of the hall where the sunlight couldn't reach.

They approached the dais, where the head table was already occupied. An older couple dressed in finery, seated in the place of honor; Lady Anne, Sir Cyrill, and Father Bernard, who looked aged enough to have seen the Crusades firsthand. And a tall, lovely young woman Sharai had never seen before. *Lady Emilyne.*

The hall grew silent.

Lady Anne crooked her finger at Sharai. "Kadriya, be seated with Britta. Sharai, come you here."

Sharai felt the unpleasant sting of many eyes upon her. She had performed on stage, but to strangers, in a simple game of fantasy. Titles mattered not in entertainment. Here, rank was clear, and she was far from being a star on this stage. Here, Lady Emilyne reigned, the woman who possessed enough wealth and power to buy Tabor.

With each step forward, Sharai donned another heavy cloak of humility. They weighted her down like chain mail, like the time in the dusty streets of Marseilles, where she was humiliated and degraded.

But she'd sought nobility, she thought ruefully, and now she must follow its rules. Executing the slow, graceful bow she had seen the noblewomen offer each other at Winchester's grand cathedral, Sharai greeted Lady Anne. "My lady."

Two seats to Anne's right sat a tall man of considerable

volume, his brown hair assaulted by grey. His round nose dominated his clean-shaven face, which had seen at least fifty summers. Lady Emilyne's father, no doubt, the Earl of Marmyl. *An earl.*

An older woman sat between the earl and Lady Anne, likely Emilyne's mother, the countess. Her light brown hair peeked out from her white veil, which draped around her ample bosom, held in uncertain captivity by taut red damask.

Tabor's bride-to-be wore her light brown hair netted and veiled in white. She had alert green eyes and clear skin, and wore a green velvet gown that enhanced her eyes. She looked to be over twenty summers, but Sharai could spy no wrinkles.

Lady Anne clapped her hands, a small gesture Sharai had come to recognize as a sign of great pleasure. "This is my servant, Sharai." Lady Anne drew out each syllable of her name. "She is from Little Egypt."

Sharai cringed inwardly at being referred to as a servant, but kept her head held high.

Lady Emilyne examined her, her expression a mixture of interest and aversion. "What a curiosity. I have heard these 'Gypsies' have dark powers with animals."

Anne had the decency to share a glimpse of embarrassment with Sharai before she turned to the older woman to her right. "Sharai is a princess in her homeland of Little Egypt, and she sews my gowns."

Emilyne put fingers to Lady Anne's sleeve hem, checking the stitches. "Excellent work. Mayhap she could sew my wedding gown? I would enjoy her services."

Sharai's muscles tensed. *They speak of me as if I were not here.*

"Forgive me, Lady Emilyne," Sharai said, "but I have several gowns to finish for Lady Anne before my contract expires in a fortnight." Sharai would ride a one-wheeled wagon to Rome before she would sew Emilyne a wedding gown. A gown in which to wed Tabor. Sharai's stomach turned in distress.

Lady Anne laughed too loudly. "A trifling detail, Sharai. We shall extend your contract to accommodate Lady Emilyne." She nodded to Lady Emilyne as if that settled the matter.

"Psst."

Sharai turned to learn the source of the sound and saw Britta, making a space at the lower table, just behind her.

Sharai retreated to the lower table, sliding in next to Kadriya.

Though delicately seasoned, the steamed eels stuck in Sharai's throat. She tried to avoid looking at Lady Emilyne, and became angry with herself when she could not do so.

Emilyne's mouth, though small, was well formed. She appeared to have no breasts, then Sharai noted her sloped shoulders and realized that Lady Emilyne was a tall woman and self-conscious about it.

Britta made a clucking sound, and her pox-ridden skin stretched into a smile. "A fine one, ain't she? Her da, the Earl, was great in his time. Captured over a hundred Frenchmen at Agincourt and King Harry gave him more than ten properties afore he died."

Sharai started. "Ten castles?"

"Two. The rest manors. All large. And he serves in the king's high court. Imagine." She twisted a long strand of her grey hair back under her hood. "Lord Tabor's moved hisself up nicely with Emilyne, he has. Emilyne's worth a dozen of Aurora, by gad."

"Aurora? Wasn't she William's wife? The one who died in the Hungerford siege?"

"Aye. Tabor was sweet on her, but Aurora was no fool." Britta lowered her voice. "William was the better man, you know. Everyone said so, even old Lord Tabor. Besides, William was the older son and heir, so why would she choose Tabor?"

"But if Tabor loved her—"

"Bosh. What would any woman with good sense do? Wed a second born and wear wool, or wed the heir to Coin Forest and wear silk and fur?" She laughed.

A green-liveried squire rushed to the dais, and the hall quieted.

The squire bowed before Lady Anne. "My lady, one of our Fritham pigeons just arrived. A message." He offered her something small.

Lady Anne accepted it, carefully unfolding the paper. She squinted at the message, then dropped her face into her hand.

Lady Marmyl touched her elbow. "What is it, dear?"

"Tabor. Lord Hungerford has imprisoned him."

In the solar, Sharai wove the needle deftly through the light silk, turning the tiny hem with invisible stitches. It pierced through the delicate weave, in and out, drawing the fine white thread Kadriya had prepared for her.

Worry stilled her hands. Her reading of Tabor's palm had been accurate. Tabor was held captive by a man who had already tried twice to kill him. Tabor would die, if he had not done so already. Her amulet had not protected him.

But it should have. She'd followed her mother's formula, using seasoned bacon fat. She had ground the rain worms and spiders and collected their oil, just as she had learned.

All for naught.

She envisioned the sharp angles of Tabor's face, the proud set of his jaw. The way his brown eyes would widen ever so slightly when he looked at her, and the passion that darkened them when they kissed.

He'd been generous with her, and gentle. And kept his promise never to force her, though she knew he'd been tempted.

How ridiculous, Sharai, she scolded herself. She ached with a loss of something she had never possessed. If he'd lived, he would have been Lady Emilyne's, bought and legally contracted. She was merely a servant in his castle, well fed and sheltered, paid generously for her services. Yet in his presence she felt . . .

She pierced a few more stitches, then stopped.

With him, she felt valued.

A stream of affection and loss rose to her eyes, blurring her vision. Rauf's nature was dark. Had he tortured Tabor before killing him?

Rauf. His eyes had held pure hatred for her when she intervened between Rauf and Tabor at the fair. Fear rose in her belly. Rauf would come here to claim the castle. He would finish Lady Anne as he had William and Aurora and Tabor, and Rauf would find her here. With Kadriya.

Sweet Sprig. Sharai must protect her.

She studied the grand chamber, spacious and sturdy with its stone, a comfortable room in a secure castle. But Sharai had learned long ago that security could be but an illusion. With Tabor gone, the castle was vulnerable, and so were they. She and Kadriya must leave.

CHAPTER NINE

Father Bernard gave the blessing and dismissed the congregation into the dawn. Sharai left with Kadriya, and they pulled their hoods forward to keep out the light rain.

Halfway to the castle, Sharai sent Kadriya on and returned to the church. As long-standing priest, Father Bernard must know the region and could help her select a safe route away from Coin Forest.

She found him in the scriptorium. "May I see you, Father?"

He turned from his tall desk. The old priest's eyebrows had become white and wild over the years, like a crop of dried wheat after a gale, but his eyes were a kind, pale blue. "Of course, Sharai. What is it?"

"I seek your advice. It's about the bad tidings from Fritham."

He nodded. "I pray for Lord Tabor's safety."

"As do I, Father, but what chance can he have, alone in his enemy's dungeon?" She hesitated. "I fear for our safety, as well, should Rauf return to seize Coin Forest."

"Don't dismiss Tabor. Despite his mother's criticisms, he's clever and resourceful, and the situation is not simple."

"From what I've heard, it does not make much sense. What claim do the Hungerfords have on Coin Forest?"

Father Bernard returned to his desk. "These hostilities must be confusing, especially since you do not know what's come before." He hesitated, as if weighing whether to say more. "The Tabors and Hungerfords were allied at one time. Come." He walked back to his tall desk. "Look at this."

A large parchment filled the desk, a paper streaked with lines and cross lines. Like a giant spider web it stretched vertically and horizontally to cover the entire sheet.

"I'm researching Lord Tabor's bloodline back a hundred years," the priest said. "See, here's Tabor's father, Carswell, Baron Tabor. Here," he pointed to a line that ended, "is Lady Tabor, Margaret." He turned to her. "Lord Hungerford's sister."

Her name seemed to bounce off the parchment. "Tabor's father married a Hungerford?" Lady Anne's name appeared beneath Margaret's, with new lines joining Carswell and Anne and, beneath them, William and Richard. Death dates were recorded for Carswell and William, 1430. Sharai pointed to Margaret's name, which had no such date. "She still lives?"

"Aye. Matters of estate can be untidy. The king granted Coin Forest to Lord Hungerford's father, following the Siege of Harfleur, but years later there was talk of duplicity, some political betrayal by Hungerford. Carswell, Tabor's father, saved the king's nephew at Agincourt, and proved extremely loyal. When the opportunity presented itself, the king arrested the elderly Hungerford, pulled the grant and gave Coin Forest to Tabor's father."

"But what happened to Margaret?"

"Sorcery. I was here when he was stricken from her potion." He shuddered. "He never fully recovered. Later, Margaret was imprisoned, the marriage annulled."

"If the king gave Coin Forest to the Tabor family, why not just settle it in the king's court and be done with it?"

"The king is just fourteen, not ready to rule, and his two uncles, when they're not dealing with the war, fight over the throne. They have bigger problems to solve than bickering nobles and land disputes.

"And Hungerford's done his best to make this problem look

more complicated than it is."

"You met Tabor just after the siege. Carswell had just died, the king was in France, and Gloucester, his uncle, was Regent, but he was away in Scotland. Tabor reclaimed it by force, but now Rauf's father is trying to take it legally by challenging him on a test of unfreedom. It's an issue of the Tabor family line, and frankly, Gloucester has bigger problems, so it's been ignored."

"In London they fight like dogs for control, and the war with France drags on. They're too distracted to care about local land disputes."

He walked her to the door, signaling the end of their visit. "So you see, Hungerford yearns for something he cannot have. Coin Forest passed from his hands long before he could ever inherit it. He's too old to see it, perhaps, or too tormented with its loss to accept the reality of it."

The facts swam in Sharai's head like too many minnows in a bucket. The rich, secure noblemen were in fact no better than Gypsies, fighting for the biggest purse. For the Gypsy, the prize was a pilfered sheep or wild turkey. Or a fine Arabian after a slightly leveraged horse race. For the nobility, the prize was a castle, and power. "So there's nothing to stop Hungerford from attacking. Nothing to stop him from killing Tabor and marching back to reclaim this castle."

"Fret not, my child. We have a fortified castle and a garrison of strong knights to defend us. And an earl in residence," he added, tipping his head in the direction of Lord Marmyl's banner, which flew with Lord Tabor's at the keep. "You and Kadriya are safe."

His reassurances rang empty. With Tabor dead, Marmyl, earl or not, had no claim to Coin Forest. He would leave, and with him would go the protection. "We must go, but not to St. Giles. Can you help us arrange safe passage to Southampton so we can return to our people?"

His reassuring smile disappeared, and his blue eyes filled with concern. "You will not leave Coin Forest."

"My stay has been temporary from the beginning, Father."

His features grew stern. "You cannot leave."

She thought of the bandits that infested the countryside. "I understand. The roads are unsafe. Perhaps we can join other travelers at a nearby monastery?"

His wild brows drew together in a frown, and his blue gaze impaled her. "Did not Father Robert baptize you in Winchester?"

"Aye, but—"

"And I baptized Kadriya. You have entered into a new spiritual life with Christ. You are both Christians now. You cannot return to those heathens." He spat out the word with loathing.

His grip squeezed the flesh of her hands, stinging the wounds from the stilt splinters, and his eyes flashed with a fire she'd never seen in them before. "You will not leave."

Tabor awoke in a room of grey. A damp cold had penetrated his bones, and his hands were numb. He raised an arm to check his face, felt a weight on his wrist and heard metal clanging. His right wrist was chained to a stone wall. He bolted upright. He was in a crude cell, a small U-shaped enclosure eight feet wide and half that deep. It opened into a larger room with similar cells. He sat in straw over damp earth that smelled of urine and sickness, and he shivered from the cold.

He struggled to a sitting position and leaned against the wall. Weak light filtered in from two small windows high above.

His ribs hurt with every breath, and his lip was so swollen he could see it. He felt for his dagger. Gone, as he expected, but he still had Sharai's amulet. It had protected him thus far. Mayhap he would have to eat the foul-tasting contents to ward off starvation in this hellhole.

"He's awake." A dark-haired man with a pinched mouth watched him from a cell across from him. He wore a wool doublet and had been imprisoned long enough for a scraggly beard to have grown. Everything about him was thin, his lips, his arms, even his fingers. Behind him, another man, white-haired and dressed in merchant's clothing, rested on a thin bed of hay.

Tabor dabbed at his swollen jaw. "How long have I been here?"

The dark-haired man pinched his thin mouth even tighter. "Since morning, and dinner was served two bells ago."

Tabor rubbed his swollen jaw.

"I'm Will, and this is Ben," he said, gesturing to the prone man. "And you?"

"Richard. Is John here? My friend. He was with me."

"No one here but we three. We've been rotting down here for over a fortnight."

Peering more closely, Tabor noted Will's fine fabric and the fashionable length of his doublet. "How did you come to be here?"

"I'm accused of thievery—"

"Not true, by gad," Ben interrupted.

"—but never did I approach Lord Hungerford's wardrobe without his orders."

"He stole nothing," said Ben. "I worked with Will in court, and Will is a loyal, trustworthy scribe," said Ben. "He's innocent, but we must get free to prove it."

In his legal duties as baron, Tabor had heard his share of innocence pleas but had never denied the accused a chance to gather witnesses or evidence. "Those who know the integrity of your character will surely speak up."

"We hope." Will regarded Tabor. "What brought you here?"

"Bad judgment," Tabor replied ruefully. "My friend, John, was with me at the alehouse."

Ben nudged Will's arm. "The tavern. I heard the guards speak of that. One escaped. Mayhap he got free."

The sound of jingling keys gained Tabor's attention. The gate opened, and three guards entered.

One, the guard from the alehouse, wore a collection of bruises and a dark expression of anger. He strode to Ben and Will's chamber pail and lifted it. After determining that Tabor grasped his intent, the guard flung the contents in Tabor's direction.

Tabor dodged it, but much of the vile liquid splashed on his hose and shoes. "You bloody bastard."

The guard walked almost nose-to-nose to him, daring him to strike. "Swine peasant." He showered Tabor's face with spittle.

Tabor lunged at him.

The guard backed up.

Tabor swung but he had reached the last few links of his chain. It snapped taut, and Tabor's arm jerked to a stop. Pain shot through his elbow and shoulder, and he grunted in pain.

The other guard released Tabor's shackle from the wall and pulled him roughly out the door.

Behind him, Will raised his hands, waving to get Tabor's attention. "Please, Richard, tell Father Charles to get us out."

The guard turned to Will. "Wave that hand while you can, thief. We'll soon chop it off."

Will jerked his hand down, hiding it behind his back.

The guard tugged on Tabor's chain and kicked him forward.

Tabor gritted his teeth from the pain of each step. They emerged in the gatehouse, then crossed the bailey. The sun blinded Tabor, and he struggled to see.

As they approached the main door, a squire brought the guard a katch-polly, a catchpole or human prodding stick. He would be herded, like a common criminal, before the man who controlled the crown of England.

A pox on Hungerford! Tabor would die before bearing such indignity. He was an Ellingham, by gad, a knight with honor, which is more than could be said for the thieving Hungerfords.

Tabor leapt forward, jerking the katch-polly from the surprised squire's hands. He pushed the squire into the guard and ran toward the manor.

Two guards circled behind Tabor. "Get him."

Tabor worked his way closer to the stone entrance. With a final grunting effort he swung the katch-polly into the stone wall.

The metal head crashed into the stone, sending sparks. The wood splintered, and the damnable head device broke free from the stick, rendering it useless.

Grumbles and shouts filled the air, and the guards jumped Tabor, flattening him to the ground.

Lord Hungerford appeared in the doorway. The man was thin as a pikestaff, and his shoulders drooped as if he carried the burden of the world on them. "Fools. Bring him in."

They entered the grand hall and approached the dais, and Tabor's sense of victory quickly faded.

There, above the high table, was his father's bridal gift to his mother, a Venetian tapestry of a falcon hunt. Its real home was above the fireplace in Tabor's mother's bedchamber. Hungerford had stolen it, along with the other tapestries, after he murdered William during the plunder of Coin Forest.

Fury clamped Tabor's jaw until his teeth hurt. *Short temper. You react too quickly.* Sharai's words echoed, and he pushed the prized tapestry out of his mind. He would act on it later.

Rauf sat at the high table to the right of his father, Lord Hungerford, and then Bishop Garrew. *The Bishop.* Tabor wanted to slip into the cracks of the stone beneath his feet.

Rauf's face bore evidence of Tabor's blows, resembling a badly bruised apple. A gratifying sight. At the center of the high table sat Humphrey, Duke of Gloucester and chief counselor to the king, dressed in a resplendent purple silk doublet, cloaked in yards of black Douai velvet.

Tabor smelled his own stench, fresh feces and urine, sweat, dried blood, bruises and a tattered dignity that could fit in the eye of Sharai's needle. His tunic hung, torn and exposing half his chest, and his hair clung to his forehead, tousled and greasy from his disguise. His face was swollen from the tavern fight. Tabor approached Gloucester and bowed with as much dignity as he could muster. "Your Grace."

A handsome, fit man, Gloucester, just past thirty, had the same strong nose of his brother, King Henry the Fifth, with even features and keen eyes that missed little. Disbelief widened them now, and his thick brows were raised. "Lord Tabor? Is that you?"

Hot with shame, Tabor closed his eyes in an effort to stop the sick wave of failure that rose in his throat. As a child, he'd known the feeling well. At four and twenty, he thought it was just a nightmare of youth, but here he was again, falling short, once more, of others' expectations. Not his father this time, or his brother, but a member of the royal court and the most powerful man in England.

He met Gloucester's gaze. "Forgive my appearance, Your Grace, I've been imprisoned here against my will and—"

"A tall tale," Hungerford interrupted. "Tabor appears in the same clothes in which he was found, brawling in my alehouse. He came like a thief, unannounced, reveling with the whores."

"Visiting with pilgrims," said Tabor.

Gloucester cocked his head. "Dressed in this manner?" He sniffed and regarded Tabor with lips curled in revulsion. "Your father would experience the pain of death all over again if he were to see you thus. What say you?"

Tabor considered his response. Gloucester had to know of the siege; Tabor had reported it and it was most likely Gloucester behind the king's directive that Tabor keep the peace. He must risk Gloucester's ire by defending himself. "The Hungerfords attacked Coin Forest. Killed my brother, William, and his wife. Spread rumors about the integrity of the Ellingham bloodline, and two days ago they threatened my family's life once again."

"So you retaliate by dressing as a peasant and soiling yourself?"

Rauf rose. "Lies. We know nothing of pigeons—"

"Pigeons?" Tabor challenged him. "I said nothing of pigeons. You expose your guilt."

"And you can see by beholding him," Lord Hungerford continued, ignoring him, "that Lord Tabor creates his own questions about the . . ." He cleared his throat. "The integrity of his bloodline."

"Lord Hungerford, do you have adequate reason to question Lord Tabor's lineage?"

Hungerford cast a dark look at Tabor. "Aye, I have evidence, Your Grace."

"And Lord Tabor, you can present armorial bearings sufficient to defend your bloodline?"

"Aye. The Ellinghams are lineally descended over ten generations."

"And I imagine you don't have them on your person."
"No."

Gloucester signaled to his scribe. "Record this. That Harry, Baron Hungerford, and Richard, Baron Tabor, shall meet three weeks hence at King's Council. Bring your proof, present your case, and let us be done with this nonsense."

Gloucester rose, and all present followed suit.

"Lord Hungerford." A chill hung in the air on the edge of Gloucester's words. "London is recovering from yet another outbreak of plague. We lost men in parliament, the judiciary, and several in the treasury—even my own household.

"We are at war. I experience sufficient political intrigue in London and now Arras, as well. I do not expect it here, when taking air and rest in the countryside." Gloucester took a breath. "At your invitation."

Hungerford assumed a contrite expression. "Forgive me, Your Grace, I had nothing to do with—"

"And Lord Tabor. I expect your good father died too suddenly. You need to grow into your position. You dishonor your bloodline, your knighthood, and your king. I trust you will cease such boyhood pranks and that you will present yourself more appropriately when I next see you. At court."

Later that morning, Tabor stalked through the village of Hungerford. Daylight struggled through the stubborn layer of dark clouds, making the buildings appear even dingier than they were. Some faced the street with broken shutters, others with crumbling masonry. The market, half the size of Coin Forest's, was ill attended. The smoked fish looked good, but the peas, beans, and onions bore evidence of rot, a sign of improperly drained fields. George, the pilgrim, and his friends were there to buy provisions. They picked through the inferior offerings, their faces pinched in disappointment.

Rot or no, Tabor would have welcomed any of it. His stomach, empty since his last meal of dried meat yester eve, cramped from hunger. But he carried no silver, so he would find no meal here. He still reeked from the chamber pail and yearned for a bath and the comfortable weave of his own clothes instead of this scratchy, disgusting tunic.

From a distance the church bell rang a short, flat tone, ten times. He would arrive at the rendezvous point, the Druid stones, by dinnertime. He would meet John, enjoy a quick meal, bathe in the river, and change into his own clothes. At Coin Forest, Father Bernard would finish copying a graphical history of his armorial bearings so he could present it to the court. After that he would shove it down Hungerford's sneering mouth.

He had faced humiliation today, but he'd also emerged with a prize. He would have his voice in the king's court and end this long-standing ordeal.

He passed the town walls and entered the countryside, following a footpath that led past a group of trees. Nearing the thick grove, he noticed a slight movement of one of the lower branches and tensed. Hungry and weakened by the beatings, he also lacked even a dagger for defense. He wished Sir John would appear, leading Tabor's horse. He cursed the impulsiveness and lack of planning that had placed him in this predicament.

A movement to the right caught his eye. He turned.

The prostitute from the tavern. She glanced down the road he'd just traveled, then met his eyes. Her grey gown was even more soiled than before. Her red, braided hair had been pulled loose, and her face was covered in bruises. "I know who you are, Lord Tabor. Please come here so we may talk."

Tabor had no interest in entering a stand of trees unarmed. "I can hear you fine. What say you?"

She inched out from the tree, her closely set eyes stealing glances behind him. "His guards nigh caught me this morn. He will kill me."

"Who?"

"Rauf."

"I believe that. I'm sorry about your brother. What is your name?"

"Maud."

"I am sorry for you, Maud, but it is not safe to be out here, alone. Get you back to the village."

"I cannot," she sobbed. "Rauf will find me. He will cut out my tongue."

"Why?" Not that Rauf would need a reason.

"Because during the fight in the alehouse I warned your friend, the greasy-haired one, and he dodged the guard's sword and ran free." She tipped her head toward the road Tabor traveled. "You're leaving Hungerford. Please take me with you."

Maud had saved John's neck by helping him escape, but what if she lied now, to save her own? He studied her face. Her eyes were wet with fresh tears, swollen from many of them, and he could see fear in her trembling hands.

He looked to the sky and sighed. He could not leave her to Rauf's wrath. At the least, she was big and strong and might not slow him down too much. But she should know the risks of coming with him. "Rauf may want your tongue, but he wants my head. And I have no weapon, not even a dagger."

She smiled through her bruises and tears and lifted her skirt, revealing a stout leg laced with a leather strap that held a butcher knife, a short whip, and several daggers.

Tabor chose to travel on the open road.

"My lord?"

"Yes, Maud?"

She glanced nervously at a cluster of thick, unruly bushes. " 'Tis not mine to question you, but why are we traveling openly, when Rauf is about?"

"We can make better time." He felt at least temporarily protected by Gloucester's presence. "If Rauf plans an ambush, he won't do it on his own land. He'll wait until we're some distance from Hungerford so he'll look innocent. Once we gain distance, we'll seek cover."

★　★　★　★　★

They reached the Druid stones before dinnertime. Tabor walked to the center of the stones. "Where are they?"

Maud caught up with him. "Who?"

"Sir John, and my men from Fritham. They were to meet me here with my horse." He smelled his disgusting tunic. "And my clothes."

He paced the Druid stones, half again taller than he and spaced in a wide circle. Frustration gnawed at him, along with the pangs of hunger. "By the saints, can it get any worse?" He pounded a stone with his fist. "Where are they?"

"Lord Tabor." A slight young man, barely more than a boy, emerged from behind a tree, limping.

Adney. Tabor recognized him as a squire from Fritham.

"Godspeed, my lord." He pulled a set of reins and Bolt appeared, snorting imperiously.

Relieved to see his horse, Tabor breathed more easily. " 'Tis good to see you, Adney. Good, indeed."

The young man limped toward them and behind Tabor's horse followed an inferior hackney, presumably Adney's horse.

Tabor waited for others to emerge from the woods, but no one did.

"Where's Sir John?"

"In Fritham, my lord. Hungerford men were seen approaching, so Sir John took the knights there to defend it. He bade me inform you that he'll remain there to await your order. He left me with your horse and a pigeon."

"A Fritham pigeon?"

"Aye."

"But I need Sir John here. And bloody pox, I need a change of clothes." He eyed Adney's slight shoulders and short height.

Adney followed his gaze, glanced at his clothes, then at Tabor. "Sorry, my lord, but you're twice my size."

"Aye." He noticed the young boy stood on just one leg. "What happened to you?"

Adney looked down at his left foot. "Clumsy, my lord. I was mounting my horse and it startled. Wrenched my ankle in the stirrup."

"I need to get to Coin Forest, posthaste."

Adney glanced at Tabor, then Maud, and offered the hackney's reigns. "Worry not, my lord. I can walk."

Tabor paced the tall grass. God's bones. He couldn't leave Adney to walk, injured and alone, twenty miles to Fritham, and he had to get home.

And Maud. She could go to Fritham, but she was too heavy to ride the hackney, and Rauf was looking for her and he was near Fritham. "Bloody pox. My thanks for your generosity, Adney, but get you gone to Fritham and tend to that leg." He pulled a small paper, pen and ink vial from his travel bag. Using one of the short Druid stones as a table, he scribed a note to Sir John. *Stay in Fritham. Will send word from CF. Sending Adney home, midday Thursday.*

He remembered Will. *Ask Fr. Charles to free the scribe, Will, if innocent.*

He opened the pigeon cage, secured the note to the pigeon's leg, and released it to fly to Fritham.

Hefting the boy up on his hackney, Tabor sent him heading east.

Tabor settled into the saddle and helped Maud behind him. Her skirt reeked of sour ale, and she smelled gamey, as well. He pulled away from her as far as possible, breathing shallow bits of air, and urged Bolt north. "We must needs find a stream," he choked. "Soon."

"Sharai. Sharai." Tabor's hand glided over the cream-like smoothness of her skin.

She arched her body to him.

Her eagerness spurred fresh heat in his veins. He cupped her left breast, feeling the nipple harden in his hand. He noticed a coin between her breasts, where it had fallen when he tossed it down her neckline on stage. He lifted it, and stroked where it had lain on her skin.

He kissed her again and her mouth responded, wet and warm, against his lips. He twisted her long curls in his fingers, then, unable to resist the ebony tresses any longer, he buried his face in her hair.

"Sharai."

She pulled away, wrenching her hair from him so swiftly that it stung his face.

"Just do it if you please, but quit chewing my skirt."

A woman's voice, but not Sharai's. Tabor opened his eyes to an inky darkness. "What?"

"You said earlier you wouldn't be needing any, but that be fine if you do. Here." A big, firm bottom pressed against his groin.

He jerked upright. He no longer smelled the clean scent of Sharai's hair. Instead, the odor of spoiled ale and chamber slop met his nostrils, the stench that laundering in the stream hours ago had not removed. In the distance, a steady dripping broke the silence. *A cave.* He and Maud had taken shelter from the rainy night in a narrow cave. His small fire had dwindled to a single weak ember. *By the saints, I've been fondling Maud's skirt.* "Forgive me, Maud, 'twas just a dream."

"You keep asking me, 'Shall I? Shall I?' Well, 'tis spittin' clear you can, if you wish, Lord Tabor." She caressed his thigh, moving higher. "I'd be mortal proud to please you."

He pushed her hand away. "Nay, Maud. Forgive me for waking you. 'Twas just a dream."

She patted his arm. "If you go off dreamin' again and change your mind, I be right here, and I can make your little horn honk like a goose, I can." She poked him in the rib with her elbow. "And I'll wager 'tis not a wee horn, either, from what I heard." She laughed, a bawdy alehouse guffaw meant to entertain not one, but ten men.

Tabor gave a polite laugh and slid to the edge of the cave. He would forget the damp earth sapping the warmth from his bones, and he would rest. They would resume travel early the next morning, and come the morrow's eve he would sleep in his own bed at Coin Forest.

Tabor stopped his horse at the rise, which afforded a fine view of Coin Forest Castle. The setting sun cast a glow on the rolling meadows. Ripe with corn and healthy beans, the fields spread around the castle like a golden skirt of abundance. Harvest this year would be worthy of thanks and celebration. Provided they secured hands to harvest it, he reminded himself, making a note to meet with Edwin, his steward, to recrew and hire workers. "There it is, Maud. My home."

She said nothing.

Still distant, the castle stood in quiet splendor. Pride warmed him. This was his castle, his stake in the exclusive circle of nobility his father and brother had so gracefully occupied. He would reestablish his nobility in the king's court, and prove himself worthy of this inheritance. He would secure a place in that circle for himself and his heirs.

As they passed, a peasant rose from among the cornrows. He noted Tabor's clothes, and Maud, and his eyes widened in surprised recognition. "My lord. Good day."

Tabor touched the tunic he had come to loathe. It still reeked and, as if the timeworn, crude linen were not enough, the berries they had collected earlier for lunch had stained the sleeves purple. Tabor straightened, summoning a modicum of presence. "And to you."

Maud still had not spoken. "Maud?" He stopped his horse and put his hand on her shoulder. Her muscles were tense. "What is it?"

She turned to face him, her cheeks wet with tears. "My thanks to you for bringing me here, Lord Tabor. I care not what others may say about you. You are a good man, and I am in your debt."

He patted her awkwardly, remembering the cripple that was her brother. "You are a good woman, too, Maud. You're loyal, and you helped Sir John when you could."

She dabbed her eyes and smiled. "I'll be good use to you. I can scrub a floor to shine, and I can churn butter in half the time most maids can."

He noted her muscular arms and big wrists. "I have no doubt."

"And I have large breasts and skilled hands. I can make your guards smile. Why, in just one night I can—"

"Enough," Tabor said. "I saw the men in the alehouse. Their enthusiasm for you was apparent."

She beamed and batted her lashes. "Really?"

Tabor looked skyward. What was it about women that, when you paid them a compliment, they fished for more? "Aye. They were hungry for you."

"Thank you, Lord Tabor. Your men will be happy. I'll make you proud."

Humored, Tabor allowed a smile to form. "I wager they will find you immensely more interesting than a new shipment of armor."

She laughed her alehouse cackle. "And I know when to stop rubbing. Unlike armor, I do not chafe."

Tabor's smile grew to a grin. Erwin Watson's alehouse would never be the same. That was where he planned to deposit Maud, at least for now. Then he would procure the nearest merchant's clothes before arriving at the castle. He would not endure humiliation again for these God-rotting rags.

They approached the village, and the road turned, revealing the mill and a few people mingling just outside it. Their garments were fine, finer than merchant's garb. Tabor's muscles tensed, and he jerked his horse to a stop.

CHAPTER TEN

Cyrill handed Sharai one of the empty mill bags. Behind her, filled flour bags lined one wall of the mill, stacked waist high. Fine particles of broken wheat chaff floated in the slanting rays of sunset, and flour dust gritted his eyes. Lady Anne had brought the Marmyls to the mill, south of the castle and village, to show them the filters Tabor used to sort grades of flour. Sharai had come along, bringing her constant questions with her.

She was lovely, though too small-breasted for his taste—only a handful. And her curiosity. Cyrill had never met such a forward young woman, one who did not simply observe, but one who watched and absorbed. He had met older women, widows, who had worked alongside their late husbands and learned their crafts. They could manage the apprentices, buy the supplies, and not only make the barrels or breads but sell them as well. He knew widowed noblewomen like Lady Anne who, even though she spent to excess, had proven herself capable of managing a castle.

Sharai showed that type of awareness. She busied herself asking the miller about his fees and turning the flour bag inside out, inspecting the seams.

Small thing that she was, at St. Giles's Fair she had stared Rauf down, challenged him in front of his father and dozens of men. Cyrill respected her courage, yet she was dark. Strange.

She also held a keen interest in his Lord Tabor. She'd even fashioned a primitive amulet for him. Most unsettling, though, was their kiss by the moat and Tabor's subsequent behavior. He'd thenceforth lost concentration on critical details at which he was normally adept, notably anything that did not have to do with this odd Gypsy beauty.

Had Tabor been so distracted that he'd unwittingly fallen into a trap from which he could not escape? An image flashed into Cyrill's mind, one of Tabor's severed head being tossed over the castle curtain at sunrise. His stomach knotted. His sister in Fritham, widowed with eight children, depended on him to share the bounty from his fief, sixty-two acres of land abutting Lord Tabor's demesne, and he had hoped to wed again one day. With no land, he would be worthless.

He blew a clump of flour from his armored sleeve. He must protect his liege lord, but at the moment he could not. He had failed to do so five years ago, when Rauf killed William and had come close to killing Tabor. Cyrill had failed again when Rauf tried to kill Tabor at St. Giles. Cyrill should have been guarding him.

He should have insisted on staying in Hungerford with Tabor. Now Tabor was at Rauf's mercy, and Cyrill knew Rauf possessed none. He tried to push the dark thoughts from his mind.

The sound of several boys' excited voices distracted him.

"Lord Tabor. He's returned. Alive," the miller's son's voice shouted from outside.

Cyrill rushed out the door to see.

There on the back road to the mill sat Tabor on his destrier. Tabor's greasy hair hung over a bruised face, and he wore ragged peasant clothes. A tawdry whore sat behind him, breasts spilling like melted cheese out of her neckline and her face as battered as his.

"Lord Tabor." Cyrill rushed forward, helped Tabor off his horse and slapped him on the back.

" 'Tis good to see you, too, Cyrill. I worried for a time."

"Worried? By the saints, I thought you dead," Cyrill said. Then a putrid stench hit his nostrils, and he backed away. His lord smelled like a privy.

Holy Pope, and the Marmyls here. The earl huffed behind him, finally catching up. He was tall, but a back injury revealed a limp despite his strong legs. Sniffing to identify the odor, Lord Marmyl's smile of welcome faded.

Ladies Marmyl and Anne joined him, along with Lady Emilyne, her cool expression unchanging.

Lord Tabor looked about, as if to find escape. Exhaustion strained his eyes, making him look older than his five and twenty summers.

Sharai joined them, her brown eyes wide, her mouth curved in pleasure.

The red-haired whore scrambled off the destrier and bowed low, then backed up, staying close to the horse. She stood almost as tall as Tabor. Her hair glowed in the late sunlight, and freckles danced across her wide, bruised face.

Tabor gave a respectful bow to the earl. "Lord and Lady Marmyl. Mother. Lady Emilyne." He reached for her hand, but she pulled away.

The earl's greying eyebrows drew tight. Marmyl, Cyrill knew, was a man of power and considerable wealth, but few words. He offered a stiff smile. "Lord Tabor. We worried for you." He regarded the wench. "Obviously for naught."

A glimmer of anger lit Tabor's eyes, but he smiled it away. "Without Maud, here, I might not have returned. She helped Sir John escape, and he protected Fritham and kept Rauf engaged in battle so we could safely return."

Lady Emilyne's small mouth drooped at the corners, revealing her disapproval. "Well done, Maud. And you guarded him all the way back here. How good of you." Her blue eyes shone with revulsion.

Maud smiled broadly. "Thank you, my lady. I was hard pressed, and Lord Tabor needed a dagger." She lifted her skirt, revealing pleasant, muscular legs laced with a collection of knives and a small whip. "I had plenty, so we two made a good pair."

Only the bubbling stream and mill wheel broke the silence. Even the urchins seemed to hold their breath.

Maud's smile faded with uncertainty.

Sharai stepped past Cyrill, brushing him with her full skirt as she passed. She took Maud's hand in hers. "Thank you for helping Lord Tabor. 'Tis clear that you have both been in battle. These cuts above your brow should be tended by a physic, and you must be exhausted."

Maud beamed. "Thank you, my lady. You are very kind."

"You've earned it," Sharai said.

Tabor turned to Sharai, and his face transformed. His eyes softened, the worry line at his brow vanished, and he broke into an undisguised smile of welcome. He looked every bit like a man bewitched.

Cyrill stepped in. He would interrupt the spell before the Marmyls noticed. "My lord, you had best away to the castle now, to bathe and sup, and rest."

"Aye," Tabor responded, but he had eyes only for Sharai.

She met his gaze. "Lord Tabor." Her voice had turned silken, intimate.

Holy Pope.

Emilyne's eyes narrowed.

Tabor drew near and touched Sharai's cheek.

She covered her hand over his and closed her eyes. "Thank heaven, you're safe," she whispered.

Cyrill's heart dropped in his armor. *Slay the devil, Tabor is wreaking havoc with all our plans. We desperately need the Marmyl name and money, and here he is, giving sheep's eyes to a Gypsy woman.*

Sharai took his hand away and stepped back, raising a brow. "You have this habit of dressing like a peasant, Lord Tabor." She spoke loudly enough for all to hear.

Lady Emilyne's lips had thinned. "Does he?"

"Aye. When I first met him he was dressed thus. Though he smelled better, then." She laughed, and it seemed to Cyrill that she was trying to lighten the moment.

"Curious," Emilyne said. "He also appears to have the distressing habit of bringing home whores." She put her finger to her chin as though thinking and cast a deliberate look at the Gypsy. "Mayhap this one can sew, too, Sharai."

Eyes flashing with anger, Sharai spun to face her.

Maud stepped forward, her face animated. She touched Sharai's arm, distracting her from Emilyne. "Sharai?" Her blue eyes looked upward and to the left, as though retrieving a memory. "Sharai!" Maude cried, turning to Tabor. " 'Tis she you were calling in your sleep."

Lady Anne coughed. "You sleep with her?"

"Do you?" Lady Marmyl's voice rose an octave.

Sharai's brows lifted. "He called my name?"

"Aye. Sharai, he said." Maud talked quickly, apparently eager to please Sharai, the only one who'd welcomed her with kindness. "Over and over, plain as a pikestaff. 'Course in the dead of night I thought he said *shall* I, but laying eyes on you now, I can see how he would think of you, even in his dreams, when a man's most in touch with his—"

Tabor waved her back. "Silence, Maud."

Maud met his gaze, then looked toward the Marmyls and Lady Anne. Apparently realizing her error, she gasped. Lifting her skirts, she bolted down the road toward the village.

Lord Marmyl cleared his throat. "How inelegant, Lord Tabor.

You will explain later." His brows creased. "Privately." He took his wife on one arm and Lady Emilyne on the other, and they strode away.

Lady Anne approached Tabor, her eyes narrowed in anger. "You inept fool."

"What mean you? I do all in my power—"

Anne laughed. "Power? You look so imposing in your rags, Richard."

"—to save Coin Forest. While you perch in the castle like a fine bird, preening in your silk and new carpets."

"Silk and carpets? What about all those costly books you covet? Folly. I create respectability, and you—"

"A man has to fight. I sensed a trap in Hungerford. Withdrew and wore these clothes to conceal my identity, to gather information. I need welcome, but you give me insults."

"Look like a man and I shall treat you as such."

Tabor laughed, and it rang with an edge of bitterness. " 'Tis all appearance to you. And what were you doing at the mill at this time of day?"

"Showing the earl your method for sorting the flour. He was impressed with your land drainage methods, too. Then you show up dressed like a cur, dragging a filthy whore behind you." She regarded his tattered grass sandals, then met his gaze. "So you lust for Sharai, do you? Will you harbor a stable of whores after you wed Emilyne? 'Tis certain you've impressed them with your appetite."

A look of startled hurt crossed Sharai's features.

Anne threw a look of disgust toward the village, where Maud had run, and released a strangled sob. "How could you be so reckless?"

Tabor's face darkened. "Check your tongue, Mother."

"Why for? Would that William had not died. If only . . ."

She winced, and her words trailed off, but the thoughts

behind them had leaked into the air as sure as night was falling.

Tabor grabbed her arm. "You've harped the same song too long. William, William. He's dead and I'm not. Accept it."

She clamped her teeth together and jerked free from his grasp. "You've always been difficult." She turned on her heel and strode away.

To spare Tabor further embarrassment, Cyrill walked back to the mill. From the corner of his eye he saw Thomas and the urchins shift weight, then they backed away and broke into a full run. Tongues would be wagging through the night, he was sure.

Sharai's heart ached for him. Though shabbily clothed, wild-haired, bruised, and unshaven, he could still catch the eye of any maid, but Sharai could read nothing from his guarded features.

He turned from her and strode to a small grove of trees to the right of the large mill wheel.

She caught up with him and put her hand on his shoulder. His muscles were drawn tight under her fingertips, and he flinched from her touch.

Her chest was heavy with sorrow for him, for the wounds Lady Anne had unthinkingly inflicted. She wanted to help him, to ease the burden of his suffering.

She found the string around his neck and lifted it above the collar of his tunic. "I see my amulet worked."

He met her gaze. Pain shone in his eyes.

She smiled. "I'm so glad you're safe." Her voice broke as she tried to dispel Anne's shameful revelation about how little she felt for her second-born son.

He reached for her, then pulled back. "I am in no condition to be near you."

She came closer, wrapping her arms around his neck. The stench was unpleasant, but somewhere through all the odor was her very special man, a man who annoyed her, insulted her, and befriended her, a man she could never have, yet one for whom she cared deeply. "I shall hold my breath."

She touched her lips to his, the soft stubble of his beard tickling her face. She wanted to soothe him, to heal some of the raw wounds with her warmth and caring. His lips pressed gently against hers, and a soft flicker of heat streaked inside her.

His tongue slid over her lips and the fire deepened.

She welcomed him. Careless of the smell, she pulled him closer. He was alive. Alive. And he dreamed of her, called her name, Sharai, in his sleep. Desire swirled, making her warm and hungry.

The distant sound of children's laughter brought her back. They were not alone, and Tabor was not to be hers. He was spoken for, and his intended waited, just yards away. She felt the chill of loss penetrate her skin, settling deep inside. Wish as she might, it could not be dispelled. She ended the kiss. "You must go to your lady."

Tabor sat in the solar with Lord Marmyl, watching the fire, listening to the silence brood against the stone walls. Lord Marmyl placed great stock in strength, so Tabor resisted the strange urge he had to pace. It had been a painfully long day. Supper had been dismal, his mother avoiding him, Lady Emilyne glowering at him, and Sharai's absence chilling the great hall despite the roaring fire.

The clean, fine linen and soft leather shoes soothed him, but the comfort could not allay his injuries. His face throbbed, and the wine, though smooth and sweet, did not lessen the pain in his shoulder that came from jerking on the dungeon chains. He was near exhaustion, but summoned the energy to be wary. After his ignominious arrival earlier today, Lord Marmyl would have his say.

The earl rose. He wore a padded doublet of deep red velvet, featuring a high, standing collar that rose to his ears, the type of collar Tabor could not abide. Marmyl's hose were trussed to perfection with nary a wrinkle. He stood tall, and his brown hair, flecked with grey, precisely cut and combed, framed his small eyes and round nose. He approached the table and lifted three books, tilting their covers to the fire's light. "*A Knight's Tale. The Song of Diana. A Tale of Love.*" He read the titles aloud. "I recognize Chaucer, but these others? Obscure. I have seen such books burned. You prefer romantic myths over law, or history?"

"I find history useful. I own books of law, as well, but I find these stories fascinating."

"Wherever did you find them?"

"I rented them at St. Giles' Fair."

Lord Marmyl rose one eyebrow. "Oh. The same place you found the Little Egyptian," he said, referring to Sharai. "They claim nobility, you know."

"Aye."

" 'Tis total deception. They arrived in Paris when I served there. High on their horses they rode, and they dressed well. Called themselves counts. Princes. Even kings. But they lived in tents and camped at the rivers, drinking the very water they fouled. They lingered near the fairs and stole cheese, grain, especially sheep. They commune with the devil, you know. They can make bears dance, and they worship wood faeries."

Tabor recalled Kadriya's words: *I shall tell you a Gypsy story, Lord Tabor, about the Forest Faeries.* "The faeries are no more than stories, like our myths."

Marmyl put the books down on the table with a loud thud, and settled back into his chair. "They sell their women's flesh for coin, and have been known to sell their children as easily as a horse." Marmyl's brows furrowed in a stern expression. "The

Gypsy women dance at fairs. Bewitch young men. Distract them from their duties." He gave Tabor a pointed look. "Seduce them to their ruin."

"I have seen both Gypsy and Gentile dancers at the fair."

"They're heathens."

"Not Sharai and Kadriya. Sharai . . ." Tabor stopped before telling the earl, his future father-in-law, that at just twelve summers, Sharai had saved his life. The story would reveal weakness, and Tabor's face warmed with the mere thought of it. "Both have been baptized. Sharai used to attend the church in St. Giles, before they came here."

"Mark you the lessons learned in France. Where one appears, others follow. Hundreds. Then try as you might, you cannot rid yourself of them. They are devil's thieves, and the woman's presence here vexes Emilyne. She must needs leave."

"Father Bernard has forbidden her to leave because she is now a Christian."

"She can pray in any village. She need not linger here."

Tabor fell quiet. He'd learned from Cyrill that Sharai almost left before he returned, and the thought of her leaving had shaken him. He was thankful for Father Bernard's religious fervor.

Lord Marmyl rose, standing to his imposing height. He surpassed Tabor's height by an inch. "And Maud?"

Tabor stood, too, not allowing Marmyl to tower over him. "She saved my knight. I've promised her a home here in the village. I have no personal interest in Maud, I assure you."

"What you have not assured me is the more telling."

"About what?"

"Be not coy. Sharai. Hungerford. This whole issue of nobility and land."

"You question my nobility? How could you—"

"I question your competence." Marmyl's raised voice echoed.

"Come, Lord Tabor. Lower your hackles. We're on the same side. I fought with your father in France. Our families have been active in the same parish for generations. You're a second-born son, and frankly, your father neglected you. Let you wander with diversions like archery and books when you should have been fighting, and learning law and strategy. But you're strong and clever. You recovered well from the siege, and I've toured your fields. Crops are plentiful—you manage your lands well. And my daughter chose you."

He and Emilyne had played together as children, but had never been close. Ever since wedding negotiations had begun, Tabor had received nothing but frowns from her. "She seems not to like me."

"She requires wealth and dignity, and you've given her little reassurance in either area, I'm afraid."

"I am honorable, Lord Marmyl. I—"

"Then prove it. Until you do, we shall not tarry. We leave on the morrow."

"Leave? But I thought you'd stay until the harvest festival."

Marmyl's gaze was chillingly direct. " 'Tis Lady Emilyne's request to depart. She will only return once your Gypsy 'princess' has gone and you have secured your lands. I know of Gloucester's decision to hear your case," he added, speaking slowly to emphasize his words. "I will be there, too."

Tabor caught the subtle warning. Marmyl served on the king's council and was not only privy to his case, but could have an effect on its outcome.

"We go only to Wells to visit my brother. You may contact us there."

Tabor's stomach knotted. Marmyl's presence enhanced the safety of Coin Forest, as well as its stature. "I fail to see why Sharai's presence offends Lady Emilyne. She appreciates Sharai's skills with the needle, and has even had Sharai sew a dress for her."

"Whores are for play, Tabor, not to keep against the will of your betrothed."

"Sharai is not—"

"Lady Emilyne is a Marmyl, the daughter of an earl."

Tabor nodded, well aware of Marmyl's considerable stature.

"I will not have my daughter playing second to a heathen Gypsy."

Tabor's temper rose, and he took a step forward.

Marmyl waved his hand as if to stop him. "I can help you at council, Tabor." His voice lowered, becoming warmer, embracing Tabor like a concerned uncle, or even a father. "You're a proud young man, and thus far you've dealt well with adversity. You've displayed admirable strength and resourcefulness at saving Coin Forest, and I would be pleased to help you secure it for all time." He patted Tabor on the back. "And I would be proud to call you my son."

Proud to call me son. Tabor had craved those words from his father, and Marmyl offered it to him now. Tabor's throat constricted. The earl offered approval and acceptance.

Marmyl placed his hand on Tabor's shoulder. "We leave on the morrow, at first light. Do this, Tabor: settle with Hungerford. Prove your bloodline. And rid yourself of the cursed Gypsy."

CHAPTER ELEVEN

Tabor rested in his chamber. His bones ached from weariness, but sleep evaded him. The weak firelight cast pulsing jots of light on the shuttered window.

Out there, Coin Forest, the valley and gentle hills of his demesne. To the south, Fritham. Since William's death he'd salvaged the villages, but more repairs were needed. He yearned for the prosperity that William had enjoyed, and needed relief from the constant struggle to keep his holdings afloat.

Sharai. She entered his mind on a soft breeze. Now he knew the intense longing that Prince James spoke of in his *Tale of Love*. Tabor doubted anyone could pen the feeling that swept over him when he was near her. Sharai brought an excitement and a warmth in his chest that rendered breathing difficult. In Sharai's touch he found fire, but also . . . what? He paused and thought of it again. A special connection.

She could be just a scheming woman, as he had thought in the beginning. Mayhap she used her feminine ways to achieve her goal, and cared nothing for him.

No. She'd demonstrated her loyalty with Etti and Kadriya. He'd seen it in her eyes when he returned from Hungerford with Maud. All others judged him. Only Sharai welcomed him and cared for his safety.

He allowed a reckless hope to settle. Mayhap she cared for him as he did her. But what of Marmyl, and Tabor's obligations? With Emilyne, he could succeed, but he felt naught for her. She was attractive and intelligent, but he sensed no warmth or passion from her. She was honorable, well bred, and noble, all the qualities he'd admired and sought to sustain.

With Emilyne, he could succeed. He must try harder. Cyrill was right, his mother's advice sound, Marmyl's, too. Tabor might not love Emilyne, but he needed her. Marriage was not about love. That was just a notion found only in his books.

His family, his heirs, and the people of his villages depended on him. He could not abandon them to men like Rauf. He would take Sharai as his mistress. She wanted a noble's money, and with him she would have it, that and security for her and Kadriya. He would wed Emilyne to fulfill his obligations and strengthen his demesne, but he would not forfeit the love he had found with Sharai.

He needed to talk to Emilyne.

Tabor exited the castle and spied Lady Emilyne by the second tower. The predawn sky had lightened to silver, and men were loading the Marmyls' chests and mattresses into the lead wagon. If Tabor could not convince Emilyne to stay, they would leave. He must find the right words.

He straightened his doublet, a new one Sharai had sewn in green silk. Above the guard tower, his banner furled in a gentle breeze, and he smiled. Same material. He pushed the thought away. He needed all his wits to convince Emilyne that Sharai was innocent, not the dark threat that her father had described.

Tabor strode to the head wagon, where Emilyne was slipping a decorative red bag into a chest. She wore a tan gown trimmed in fox and tightly cinched, revealing a trim waist.

"Good morning, Lady Emilyne."

She straightened to her full height, which brought her almost to eye level with him. "And to you, Lord Tabor."

"I would speak with you."

She bowed formally. "As you wish."

He offered his arm and led her toward the stream, away from the wagons and the clanging racket in the blacksmith shed. "You look lovely this morn."

"Thank you."

" 'Tis my wish that you stay."

"My father talked with you. You know my wishes."

"Emilyne. You're young. Lovely, and the daughter of an earl."

"You should not forget that, Lord Tabor. Nor the large sum your mother insisted upon for my dowry."

"I appreciate your station, Emilyne."

"Then 'tis simple. Get rid of her and I will stay."

"Father Bernard has insisted Sharai stay. She's a Christian, you know."

Emilyne's upper lip contorted. "Gypsies. Father told me about what they did in France. They worship the devil. Commit sins with animals."

"Not Sharai."

"You would spite me with her, after my request? Offer a dark-skinned peasant your loyalty over me? And you wonder why I leave this morn." She freed her arm and spun away from him.

"Surely you're not worried about a poor seamstress and a seven-year-old girl. I brought them here as a kindness to my mother, and you've seen her skill with a needle."

"Fah! 'Tis her other skills that displease me."

"We've developed a friendship—"

"She is a whore, Tabor. A whore, same as Maud—"

"She is no whore—"

"—and you toss sheep's eyes at her. Publicly. In front of me." She cast her eyes down. "I'm not beautiful like her, Tabor, I know that."

Her humility made him pause. Tabor knew well the pain of being passed over. He took her hand in his, but felt naught but her smooth, warm skin. "If I so provoke you, why do you want me as your husband?"

She reclaimed her hand, twisted the gold pin at her cloak, and looked slightly past him. "I am twenty years old and must wed soon. I am healthy and capable. I can manage affairs when you're called to battle. I favor my father in his—height," she hesitated. "I told him that I will not look down on my husband. You are tall enough, pleasing to the eye and healthy, and from a good family."

'Tis hardly enough, Tabor thought. Her father doubtless saw political advantage in controlling Coin Forest, as well as Tabor's vote in Parliament. Still, an odd sensation passed through him, and he felt an urge to sit down. "You want me because I'm tall?"

Her delicate eyebrows tightened into a frown. "Be not daft, Tabor. Were you not pleased when you heard of our offer?"

Aye, Tabor thought. If he had been so enticed by money, how could he judge Emilyne for wanting a tall husband? "Yes, but—"

"The Gypsy whore is an insult, and you must get rid of her. If we are to wed, I will not tolerate her presence."

He thought of the twelve-year-old girl who risked her life to save him, who claimed and cared for a baby Kadriya, and worked hard to repay Etti for helping her in her time of need. "Sharai is an honorable woman. I will not have you slurring her name."

Her eyes narrowed. "So you have already decided."

Tabor stopped. The discussion had veered in a dangerous direction. "Nay. 'Tis not about you or her. I am pledged to you, Emilyne."

An expression crossed her face, one of annoyance and exasperated resignation. "You're confused, Tabor. My father can help you, but you must mind what he says, or you and your family will suffer ruin."

Her threat felt like a slap. "I have fought hard to keep my lands. Your father himself acknowledged that last night. Look at my fields. My knights are provisioned, my stables full, the larder well stocked."

"An illusion, Tabor, and I can see through it. I've heard the stories. You frequent the fairs, gambling like a desperate highwayman, rolling with whores and bringing them home. And fool me you will not. I have seen behind the rich carpets your mother laid to take our eyes from the want. You have many fine horses, but not enough saddles to ride them. Many knights, but outdated, inferior armor. Even your church leaks when it rains. You need my dowry, and I need you, but you will not touch it or me until you bend to my wishes." She turned to go. "And I shall tell her such this very moment."

He grabbed her arm. "You will not."

Her lips thinned with anger. "You prefer peasants and heathens over your own kind. Mayhap the stories Lord Hungerford tells are true and you aren't noble at all. At any rate, you're no longer my problem. You're a fool, and I will wed no fool."

Tabor climbed the steps to the solar. The Marmyls had been gone for nigh a sennight, and his wounds and bruises had healed. His mother no longer spoke civilly to Sharai, and begged Tabor daily to send her away and summon Emilyne.

Tabor had reminded his mother that Father Bernard had forbidden Sharai's departure, and Tabor forbade Lady Anne to do anything that would make Sharai feel unwelcome.

Still, he knew he must regain Emilyne's favor or forfeit the Marmyl family support at a time when his family and people desperately needed it. He had even penned a letter to Emilyne, asking her to return, but he could not find it in himself to send it, for the price of sending it would be the loss of Sharai.

A traveling caravan of tinkers and jewelers had arrived in the village, distracting all but the tower guards. The great hall was deserted, and the solar was empty of all but Sharai, who labored, still, at her craft.

She had spread a bolt of red silk on the table and was sewing pleats in the fabric. She hummed softly, a haunting, mournful tune that dipped in low notes with frequent sharps and flats.

He remained silent, savoring the look of her, the way her braids rested on her breasts, her stockinged feet free because she had, as usual, tossed off her shoes. Her rich, brown skin, and the ebony hair that escaped the braids at her temple, curling in twists that reminded him of how her hair fell when free.

She noticed him and stopped her haunting song. Her mouth curved in a gentle smile of welcome.

His heart faltered. His legs carried him of their own accord, and he was near her, feeling the heat from her body. "What is that tune?"

"A song about a young Gypsy girl," she said. A hint of cider from the midday meal lingered on her breath. "She chased a butterfly and became lost in the forest."

He traced the pleasing curve of her oval face. "She was found, though." He didn't know the story, but guessed.

"No. The faeries took pity on her and turned her into a deer, so she could live among the forest animals. 'Tis a song to remind young children to not wander off in the forests, for in the darkness it is so easy to become lost. I used to sing it to Kadriya."

He took her in his arms and pulled her close, and her breasts pressed against the thin silk of his doublet. "Am I a danger to you?"

Her breath hitched. "I cannot escape you. I close my eyes and I see you. You are always with me, yet I am alone. You can never be with me, but still you are there." A tear slid down her cheek, traveling to the curve in her lip.

A flash of sadness stabbed at him, and he brushed the tear

away. "I'll never leave you alone. You're with me, too." He tilted her chin and offered her a smile. "You're in my dreams, as, thanks to Maud, everyone in Coin Forest knows."

Her eyes seemed to glow with love, but in their depths, he saw a shadow of fear.

Hoping to erase it, he kissed her. Her lips were soft, wet with the salty tang of her tear. Her mouth and her small body fit perfectly to his. He deepened the kiss, savoring the apple sweetness of her mouth and the subtle movement of her legs, the unmistakable, delightful movement of desire as her thighs curved around one of his.

Her hands laced around his neck, and she pressed closer to him.

His loins heated, a sensation that filled him with a sense of being newly alive. With difficulty he pulled away. The solar offered no privacy, and he needed the luxury of time to purge her fear. "Come to my chamber."

Her face tensed and she withdrew.

He seethed. Would that he could crush the man who had ravaged her. He took her small hands in his and kissed her palms, his gaze never leaving hers. " 'Tis an invitation, not an order." He curled her fingers and brought her hands to his heart. "Bring your dagger, though you will not need it. I will do nothing that is not your wish. My chamber has a secret passage that leads to the hall. You can exit undetected." He kissed her again thoroughly, savoring the wet passion in her kiss. "Come to me tonight, and both of us will know 'tis of your own free will." He released her and walked with difficulty to his chamber.

Sharai rose from the bed, careful to not wake Kadriya. The candle on the hearthstone had burned to the bottom. She looked in the direction of Tabor's chamber, and her heart skipped in anticipation. Her body craved his closeness, and she yearned for the warmth of his arms around her, his big hands stroking her with such gentleness.

Fright stilled her legs before they reached the door, and she sighed, her breath escaping her body in a shudder. She feared Tabor was driven by lust, not love. She could ill afford to risk all for a simple night of passion, which would be, in the end, a simple, vulgar act. Had she not learned her lesson about men?

She returned to her bed and watched Kadriya in the weak candlelight, minding her even breathing, her golden hair tangled from playing, sticking out like an uncurried horse's mane on her pillow. Kadriya depended on her, and Sharai had promised she would always be there for her. Sharai would not find security bedding a betrothed man. She needed a husband, but she could no longer imagine leaving Tabor.

Frightened at the puzzle her life had become, she quietly slipped under the covers, trying to still the insistent humming in her body.

Four days later, Tabor studied the large parchment in the midday sunshine. Bold colors flashed across its surface, revealing the heraldic bearings that reached a century back in the past, summarizing his family's bloodline. He turned to Father Bernard. "Do you see anything questionable?"

The priest shook his head. " 'Tis a fine job, Father."

"Thank you." He smiled, wiping the sweat from his brow with a linen handkerchief. "Mustn't stain the parchment."

Tabor pulled the moist tunic from his chest. The last two days had been brutally hot, with heavy moisture in the air and nary a breeze.

Father Bernard pointed to the bottom left. "I need only to copy the Chivington line, and it will be ready for your trip to London."

Tabor would leave in two weeks for his hearing with Gloucester to prove the falsehood of Hungerford's claim. He nodded approvingly. "This will settle it."

"We do not need the earl's meddling." The priest had developed a keen dislike for the Marmyls. "You can manage your own estates."

"But the dowry."

"You'll manage."

He thought of Marmyl's power in the court and a pang of worry took the glow from Father Bernard's praise. "I hope so."

Tabor exited the church. Sharai would be taking her midday walk about now. It had been four days since he had waited in vain for her to come to his chamber, waited until the dawn's light vanquished all hope that she would trust him and come to him of her own free will. She'd been withdrawn since then, avoiding physical closeness, her withdrawal trying his patience. He must find a way to make her trust him.

He saw Sharai, but his mother was there with her by the well, and her words held a sharp edge. He hurried to them.

"Look me in the eye and tell me that this isn't the devil's work."

Sharai turned to Lady Anne, her back straight with defiance. "It's just—food."

Lady Anne lifted a handful of what appeared to be fine white sticks and shoved it in Sharai's face. "Is this typically your dinner, then, this collection of frog bones?"

Tabor waved Lady Anne to back away. "What goes here?"

Lady Anne turned to him. "Look at what this little sorceress has done. Britta saw her fiddling with a dead frog behind the stables last week, and cast your eyes on this. She cursed the frog and stripped its flesh and has spoken some spell upon it. You should never have brought these Egyptians here. They defile our family and land."

"But for my skin I'm Christian, same as you," Sharai said.

Father Bernard joined them. " 'Tis true, Lady Anne."

"She put a spell on that frog, and she chanted my son's name when she did it." Lady Anne hurled the bones into a patch of high weeds. Wiping her hands on her skirt, she glared at Tabor. "You scorn a dowry that could solve our woes, all for her. Do you not see?"

"I see you care more for your position than your son," Sharai said.

Lady Anne blanched and slapped Sharai.

Sharai glared at her then spun away and stalked toward the drawbridge.

Lady Anne turned to Father Bernard. "Explain these bone rituals."

Tabor followed Sharai, catching up with her at the turn to the mill.

"Forgive her. She's distraught about—"

"Losing that dowry. I know." She cast an angry look at him. "Are you going to ask about my sorcery?"

"I know you're no sorceress." He gave her a playful smile. "And since I'm still alive, your palm reading skills are suspect, as well."

"I never said your life was in danger."

"I'm better at reading faces than you are at reading palms." He smiled still, trying to make her see the humor. "I am curious about the frog, though."

Her chest heaved with frustration and anger. "I'll pay for what's due on my contract. Kadriya and I will find a tribe that welcomes us."

"I welcome you."

"You want me for pleasure. You're like the rest."

"How saintly would you like me to be? Did I burst into your chamber like a wild stag and take you against your will? Nay. I invited you. 'Twas not I that ravished you." He pounded his chest in frustration. "Not I!"

He took a deep breath and lowered his voice. "I would bleed before I harmed you." He stood in front of her to block her forward progress and swallowed hard. "I love you."

She hesitated, then grimaced. "Love, hah. Fancy words until you get that which you crave, and 'twill be the end. Think you I haven't learned the hard way?"

"How interesting. You're like my mother."

Her eyes flashed ebony anger. "What?"

"She judges all Gypsies by the actions of a few, as do you with men, judging all from the actions of one."

"You try to trick me with your words. I don't know your language well enough to spar with you."

He laughed. "Now there's a jest."

They had reached a low spot a half-mile past the mill, where the land dipped sharply and the stream cut a large crevice in the earth. There, just past a healthy stand of tall wheat, a patch of earth bloomed sweet with grass and flowers, shaded by a dense stand of willows.

He gestured to a shaded spot, just inches from the cool stream, sheltered from the sun. "The sun is insufferably hot. If we must argue, let's do so in the shade."

"It is hot," she agreed.

He claimed a lush spot on the grass, flattening the tall grass for her. "Now where were we? Oh, yes, I accused you of condemning all men based on the actions of a few."

She hesitated, then settled in the spot he had prepared for her. "Men have their strength and swords. Women have the softness of their bodies to sway men's minds. Once you know me, you will leave me."

"Is that all you think of yourself, Sharai? Or is that just how shallow you think me to be?"

She lowered her head.

"Tell me. I'm not ravishing your body, I'm just asking a simple question. What were you doing with the frog?"

She turned away from him, absently twisting a tall blade of cool grass around her finger. She could not tell him. He would laugh at her, and she had endured insults enough this day.

He rested his hand on her shoulder. "Is it about me?"

She sighed. " 'Tis all about you, Tabor."

He tilted her chin and kissed her, his lips soft and wet against hers. His hands slid down the sides of her neck in a possessive caress that wakened her skin. She raised her breasts to him without thinking, and a soft moan escaped his lips, sending a spike of desire to her lower body. Keeping his mouth on hers, he lifted her in his arms and settled on the grass with her in his lap.

He broke the kiss, and his big hands cradled her head. An errant lock of dark hair fell in front of his brown eyes. "I will stop whenever you wish."

His eyes were luminous with desire. She kissed him deeply, threading her fingers through his hair, savoring the coarse texture of the strands and the strength of his muscles under her fingertips. A waft of cool air from the stream gave relief from the heat.

He ended the kiss and lowered her, unlacing her gown, sliding it off her shoulders. His kissed her bare shoulder, trailing his fingers over the top of her breast. "Like velvet," he murmured. "Your skin is even more beautiful than in my dreams." He brushed his palm over her nipple, still covered by her gown.

She should stop him now, she knew, but like faeries making rings of magic, he awakened her skin, stirring her desire, stealing her resolution to resist.

Unable to bear it, she placed his hand firmly on her breast. His erection pushed against her, hard as stone.

Her breath caught.

"Relax, Sharai, and trust me."

Looking for reassurance, she saw his eyes, brimming with tenderness and passion. Tabor, who rescued her from Count Aydin, bore her refusal to come to his chamber, still sought her out. Tabor, who defied Lady Anne's will, stood steadfastly at her side, despite the penalties. The air humming in her ears, she nodded.

He bared her left breast, admiring it with a soft smile that sent a shock of heat to her middle. He lifted her to him and covered her nipple with his mouth.

A fluttering sigh reached her ears, and Sharai recognized a new quality in her voice, a sound she had never before uttered.

He moaned in return, sucking gently on her flesh, taking nips that made her want to crawl outside of her skin and jump into his.

He brushed his right hand over her belly, like a whisper that caused her to arch her body to him.

He met her gaze; his brown eyes a soft cinnamon in the sun, trance-like, so connected to her they seemed like reflections of her own. The corner of his mouth raised in smug pleasure. "You like that." His voice, low and sure, caressed her as surely as his hand. "How about this?"

His hand traveled up her skirt.

Breathless, she adjusted her leg, welcoming him.

He stroked her, touching her in new, unknown ways.

Her bones seemed to melt into something hot and liquid. Because it was Tabor, she pushed the fear aside, delighting in the sensations he drew from her.

His finger entered her slowly.

A sigh trembled out of her mouth.

His movements quickened.

Her breathing became ragged, and she felt as if she were ill and well and hot and needy. Desperation rose within her, and she pulled away.

He followed her. "Nay, Sharai. Stay with me, Sweetling. This is your time."

The movements were natural as breathing now, she could not escape, never wanted to leave his arms, his touch.

Something pooled inside her and she began falling, falling. Joy overwhelmed her, and she cried out. Waves of pleasure pulsed through her.

He kissed her hard.

Her body shuddered, then relaxed. She gasped for breath, threw her arms around his big shoulders and hung on.

He pulled her tight to his chest, rocking her gently in his lap. "You're free now, Sharai."

She melted into the warmth of his embrace. *No, Tabor,* she thought. *You have claimed my body and soul. I will never be free again.* Rejecting concerns for the future with a toss of her hair, she claimed the moment for her own, showering his face with kisses, savoring the salty tang of his skin under the hot summer sun.

Chapter Twelve

Sharai exited the great hall into the stifling midday heat and hurriedly crossed the uneven cobblestones of the yard to the empty kitchen. This time, the kitchen was finally deserted. The rotating spits stood empty; the overhead utensil hooks were filled with implements, and the enormous wooden tables cleaned of their flour and pans. The smell of bread lingered, bringing thoughts of childhood and her mother, and the safe feeling she enjoyed when in the circle of her arms. From the plaited rush mats on the floor, a faint smell of bacon grease rose, partially masked by sprinklings of lavender and mint. From a cage on a corner table several chickens clucked softly, oblivious of their fate.

Butterfly wings fluttered in her stomach. She had never before been inspired to make this love potion, and she wanted it to be perfect. She opened a small package and retrieved the frog bones she had painstakingly collected from the weeds. The ants had picked the bones spotlessly clean. Sliding a wooden mortar closer, she withdrew the pestle and deposited the bones. Grasping the top of the pestle, she broke the bones then ground in a circular motion, gently at first. Covering the top of the mortar with her left hand, she kept the bone fragments from flying out of the bowl as she worked.

She hummed a summer dancing melody and contemplated the new awareness of her body. She recalled her extraordinary experience by the stream with Tabor. 'Twas quite the greedy thing, this lust. It made her abandon all caution, forget all but desire.

Sweet wonder, Tabor had awakened her in ways she had never dreamed of.

He'd had his way with her. Or, had he? He waived his pleasure for hers. What did that mean? She could never endure the embarrassment of speaking of such matters with the pleasure dancers, so she still knew little of such things. By the saints, she missed her mother, who always had the right answers, and Etti was forever lost to her now because of Count Aydin. If a woman was pleasured but not the man, did it still make the woman a whore? Of course, the title itself meant nothing to her. She, who had been sold as a slave and raised in the Gypsy tents at regional fairs had been called much worse than that. She'd learned to ignore the condemnations; besides, each fair lasted but weeks and she could always move on.

But would she now? She no longer had a tribe, and she wanted to find a home. These weeks with Tabor had reminded her how desperately she wished to settle, to belong. Have, again, her own family.

Tabor was not meant to be hers. The pain of that thought rendered her weak, but she could not ignore it. She knew she must leave, but before she did she would know his love. At least she could then hold those memories of him, long after he had wed Emilyne and fulfilled his obligations.

She touched her fingers to her lips, blowing a kiss of wishes into the mortar, and in that moment she wanted nothing more in the world than to be in his arms.

She checked her progress. The bones had reached a state of fine powder. She pulled a small vial from her waistband and, measuring by eye, sprinkled a dash of dried bat's blood into the rounded vessel. She blended it, and then removed a small torte she had prepared earlier. Forming a small trough, she nestled her special ingredients in the middle and then folded it over three times for luck, sealing it shut. She slipped the concoction in the oven, still hot from the earlier bread-baking.

A pot clanged behind her.

Sharai jolted upright and turned around.

Maud, the cheerful whore from Hungerford, swung a huge pot into the fireplace, securing the handle on a hook above the fire pit. Her face now bruise-free, she wiped a tendril of red hair off her wet forehead and smiled. "Oh, 'tis good to see you again, miss." She focused on the oven and the small cake that baked there, her blue eyes sparkling with curiosity.

Sharai stood between Maud and the oven, blocking her view. Even Maud would laugh if she explained about the love potion. Laugh or, like Lady Anne, accuse her of sorcery. "Hello, Maud. What are you doing here?" She softened the question with a smile.

"Master Erwin had no need for more girls in his inn, so Lord Tabor brought me to serve in the kitchen. I'm strong enough to lift these pots without swooning in the heat, and I can fetch heavy loads from the buttery. Men have always said I'm good with my hands, and now the womenfolk will learn this, too."

Since Sharai had last seen her, Maud had acquired a light brown tunic the color of aged wood. It fit her stout frame and better contained her large breasts, and it provided a nice contrast to her fair skin. She broke pieces of kindling on her knee and stirred the coals, reviving the fire. "I told Lord Tabor I'd make him right proud."

Sharai sat on a stool near the fireplace. "I'm sure you will."

Maud blew on the fire and added wood. "Thank you for speaking so kindly to me that first day. I'd like to have swallowed my teeth in fear, what with that Lady Emilyne staring holes in me and her ma and Tabor's ma, ooh." She shivered. "I thought they was going to send me right back to Hungerford, and God knows, I'm afeared what Rauf will do if he ever spies me."

"Rauf?"

"Lord Hungerford's son." Her face darkened. "He killed my brother, Harry, a cripple, you know, no fault of his. Rauf thought his disease would rub off, but all Harry wanted was to stay warm by the fire."

"I'm sorry, Maud."

"I helped Sir John escape, and Rauf swore he'd cut out my tongue for it. 'Tis why Tabor brought me here, you know. He saved my life." She gave a little laugh. "Well, leastwise my tongue."

"I know Rauf. He has no honor. If it makes you feel better, Maud, he carries a scar from me."

Maud's eyes grew large. "You?"

"He tried to kill a gravely wounded man while he slept. I stopped him."

Maud nodded. "Just before I came here, he flogged my cousin because he startled Rauf's horse during a formal procession when the Good Duke came to stay."

"The Good Duke." She remembered Father Bernard's bewilderingly complex story about Humphrey, who ruled England for the child king. "Was the king with him?"

"Nay, but he brought enough others. Ooh-wee, were his men hungry and I don't mean for food. Old Lord Hungerford, he was all puffed up about the duke staying and all. We was all busy as fish at sunrise getting ready for his arrival, slaughtering pigs, sweeping the streets, brewing fresh ale."

"What was the purpose of his visit?" Sharai asked.

"I found out the real story from the men." She winked. "When Gloucester's men hit the pillow, they talked like the priest at Eastertide. There's this big meeting of the nobles called Parliament, some sort of royal business that sounds like begging. The king needs more money for war; the nobles give it to him. Gloucester runs these big meetings, and Lord Tabor attends them, too, right along with Lord Hungerford. Holy spitballs! Think of them two men in the same room."

"When did he arrive?"

"Two days before Lord Tabor."

She became concerned. "Did Tabor—Lord Tabor—meet with the duke?"

Maud fidgeted with her tunic. "Aye, and you know what he smelled like. Rauf's guards threw him in the dungeon, and they slopped a chamber pail on him and dragged him from the dungeon to the great hall, where the duke was breaking his fast."

Sharai's nose wrinkled from the memory of how Tabor stank, even two days after that. She thought of Tabor's pride, and she hurt for him.

She removed her cake from the oven.

"A little treat for Tabor?" Maud asked.

Sharai nodded. So the Hungerfords were that close to royalty. A sick feeling crept over Sharai. They were more powerful than she had thought. *And Father Bernard is more optimistic than he should be.*

"So how goes it with Lady Anne's dresses? For the harvest festival, I mean."

"They're done."

"Wait until the festival. There's music and games and—"

"Kadriya and I will leave before then."

"What?" Maud's voice rose in surprise. "Lord Tabor would not have you leave. He treasures you, my lady. It's in his eyes."

"The betrothal ceremonies will take place at the harvest festival. He is spoken for."

"But you're the woman of his heart. Surely he will take you as his mistress."

"To be his whore?"

"Whore, wife, mistress, what be the difference? All women are chattel. Is that not the word they use? My mother wed my father, but after she birthed Harry, he said her womb was foul and sold her to another man at market, like some goat or pig. What good came to her from being a wife?"

Sold at market. The phrase splashed panic on Sharai, and she could not form words for a response.

Maud gave Sharai a purposeful glance. "Men can spout and quote and preach and bequeath titles, but in the end, a man is guided by what lies between his ears—may be impressive or sad—and his legs, same story. My da, he had lots between his legs, little between his ears and even less in his heart."

She formed a basket with the fabric of her skirt and filled it with turnips. Snipping a green top off, she paused, knife in the air. "Folks here at Coin Forest are so much better off than at Hungerford, and I've heard from enough men to know why. Because of Lord Tabor. He's a good man. He can provide for you. All this, it will pass. He just needs some time to figure out how to beat Rauf at his own game. And now he has you, my lady."

"But I cannot—"

"I see it in your face. You're as smitten as he is."

Maud patted her hand. "You know Rauf. He must be stopped. Pray help Lord Tabor. He has lots up here. And here." She tapped her chest. "Pray don't leave him when he needs you most."

Sharai climbed the steps to the solar. She heard the murmur of Tabor's voice from above.

"Very well, then, quintain practice at first light. And be sure to rouse that rascal, Thomas." Tabor's voice sounded, low and resonant. It made her heart beat faster.

Sir Cyrill grunted. "The lad is a trial."

Tabor laughed.

She continued climbing. The glowing wall sconces became visible, then the top of Sir Cyrill's head. His grey hair revealed an indentation from wearing his helmet in the summer heat. The table where she sewed during the day had been cleared, and was covered now with candles and parchments. The two men stood at opposite sides of the tall table and Cyrill had backed up, as if concluding their conversation. Tabor rolled a parchment closed with his big hands, tying it with a leather strap. The candlelight cast a warm glow on his wide shoulders. He wore the green doublet she'd sewn for him. His hair gleamed, black as the night sky against his collar.

His gaze touched her, soft as a caress.

She no longer felt the pressure of her feet on the steps, and seemed to float to the solar level.

Cyrill cleared his throat. "I'll see to it then, my lord. Good eve." He nodded to Sharai and left.

Tabor's gaze never faltered. She had come here seeking his attention and indeed, his brown eyes burned, rich with a simmering sensuality that made each breath a trial. She could not decide whether to bolt or rush into his arms, and the thrill in the core of her body when he looked at her thus made her want to cry out.

He smiled. "Sharai. I missed you at the evening meal."

Struggling for air, she approached the table. "After Lady Anne's words of anger, I thought it best to avoid her." She placed a package on the table. "I made you a confection." Her fingers bumped into each other, presenting the small cake. "I hope you like it." She patted one side that had crumbled a bit in the unwrapping, and cursed her clumsiness. She had wanted it to be perfect. "I hope you like cherries and walnuts."

His big hand covered her wrist, stopping her fidgeting. He

lifted her hand, kissed it, then nestled it between the two of his.

Her insides jangled. "Won't you try it?"

"What are you offering?" An easy confidence touched his voice. He had learned the secrets of her body, and his eyes raked boldly over her, exposing the secrets of her heart, as well.

She shivered inside and withdrew her hand. "The cake," she answered simply, sliding it toward him.

"Cherries. Aye, I like cherries." He broke off a corner of the cake and popped it in his mouth. "Hmm, sweet." He broke off another chunk and chewed a bit more slowly. "Interesting texture."

His mouth moved rhythmically, transfixing her, and his tongue swept lazily across his upper lip to retrieve an errant crumb.

Faeries danced in her stomach, creating a soundless din that brought her close to swooning.

His chewing became audible. He'd reached the center of the cake. "Ow."

Her breath caught. "What?"

He struggled to speak. "Something sharp."

Her heart stopped. She hadn't sufficiently ground the bones.

His eyes grew large, and he explored his mouth with his tongue.

She grabbed his flagon. "Here, take a drink."

"Thank you." He swallowed some wine then coughed again.

She hoped for resolution. "Mayhap a cherry pit?"

He coughed again, harder. "Can't breathe." He stepped backward, seized in a convulsion, and sank to a chair, gasping for breath.

"Here." She pounded him on the back. "Does this help?"

He lunged forward, arms outstretched and eyes wide in distress. He collapsed on the rug and, with eyes closed, lay still and silent.

Sharai cried out. "Tabor, breathe!" She shook him, her heart racing. She'd been so careful. She moved him to his side, the dead weight difficult to budge, and pounded on his back with all her strength. She placed her hand under his nose and felt warm air. He was breathing. "Oh, blessed saints, you're alive."

He turned his head and smiled at her.

"What? Did you swallow it?"

His smile spread into a mischievous grin. "Poor frog. Though he died for a noble cause."

Realization made her scalp tingle. "How could you know—"

"Kadriya shed light on that mystery, though I admit, it cost me a trip to Coin Forest."

"I cannot believe she—"

He laughed. "Oh, be not so earnest about it, Sharai. I impressed upon her that I sought only to understand. And now I do. The cake is a . . . um, charm that will make me love you."

Appalled, she clutched her throat. He knew. She turned away from him.

He caught her at the waist. "Fret not, Sharai. I'm not angry."

She reached the table, grabbed a chunk of cake and threw it in his face. "Well, I am. You scared me half to death, laughing at my expense. Choke on it. 'Twould serve you right."

"Where's your sense of humor? I thought it was charming, and I want to tell our children this story some day."

He dodged her weapons of flour and sugar. " 'Tis a delicious, fine cake, my sweet, though your efforts are wasted."

"What mean you? I worked hours on this. . . ." She left the sentence unfinished, realizing whatever she called it could be her undoing.

"This spell?"

"I am no witch. 'Tis more like a potion, a special combination of ingredients mixed with hope, not sorcery."

His face lost all trace of humor, and his brow creased in

concern. "But some might call it such, and you must needs remember that and refrain from such practices in the future. I will not condemn you, though your skills in the kitchen are as suspect as your palm reading." His large hands framed her face, holding it gently. His eyes brimmed with tenderness. "I have loved you since you danced for me at St. Giles' Fair."

"I did not dance for you."

He touched her lips to silence her. "You did. You just did not know it at the time."

She recalled what passed between them that night, the power in his eyes, the desire. She had seen it, but didn't understand it. Until today, after the way he awakened her body, she understood. But remembering his patience, his gentleness, the way he sacrificed his satisfaction for hers, she knew that his love was real. There could be no other explanation for his behavior or his steadfast protection and concern since that night at the fair.

She gathered her composure and dusted the cake crumbs from his hair. "You liked the cake, then?"

He gave her an endearing smile that melted her heart. "Aye, and all the thought behind it." He lowered his voice. "And will you complete your love spell by coming to my chamber?"

She hesitated.

He walked behind her and nibbled her ear. "How else will you know if it worked?" His breath felt hot and moist, sending tingles down her neck. His hands traveled slowly down the curves of her body and her knees buckled.

His arms supported her, and she leaned into his chest, relying on his strength, savoring the rich chills of desire that rushed up her spine.

She wrapped her arms around him, safe in the warm circle of his arms, snug in his stone fortress. She twisted in his arms, pressing her body next to his, and laced her tongue around his earlobe.

He took a sharp, quick breath, his reaction stirring desire from deep within her.

She wove her fingers in his hair. "Leave thy door ajar. I shall be there in less than an inch of the candle."

She slipped her silk dancing gown on and tied the belt under her breasts. Lifting the end of her braids she untied them, releasing the full weight of her hair. A quick shake to set it free, then a firm twist to secure it high on her head with a large comb, and she was ready.

Almost.

To be presentable for her trip down the hall, she covered the seductively cut gown with a more modest one.

Hesitating, she returned to her clothes chest and retrieved, carefully in her palm lest she release their melody, her ankle bells.

With a last check on Kadriya, she walked to the door, closing it soundlessly behind her.

'Twas late, but it had taken time to be sure Kadriya was asleep, time to be certain Britta and the other maids slept, time to gather her courage. A rhythm of excitement pounded in her ears, and she knew her life would change when she completed the very path she took now, her bare feet finding their way down the midnight hall to Tabor's chamber.

Visions swirled in her mind's eye of her mother, alerting her to look out for herself because she could no longer be there to help her. "I will be your warning bell, *Faerie*," her mother had said. "I will speak to you in moments of decision. Be careful." Her mother's voice echoed urgently down the hall.

Lady Emilyne hovered, a woman most accustomed to having her way, a woman of wealth and power. She wanted Tabor, and Sharai doubted that Emilyne would let a penniless Gypsy girl stand in her way.

She saw Lady Anne, whose existence was threatened by a challenge from another noble. Lady Anne stood to lose all she held dear. Sharai could not blame her for her hostility toward her. Finally, she saw the Hungerfords, the old Lord, clever, member of Parliament, courting the Good Duke Gloucester, plotting to overtake Tabor's lands.

Why could it not be simple? In her heart it was. That was why she could walk past all these ghosts and touch the handle of Tabor's chamber door. Love made it all so simple. She'd found so little of it in her life, and to find it now, in such abundance, was heady and intoxicating, and she wanted to lose herself in it, savor and relish it this night. She would recover tomorrow and pay the price but, this night, she would love the man who loved her.

She held her breath and turned the handle. The door was heavy but well balanced, and it swung open noiselessly. She entered quickly and closed the door, lifting the heavy bolt and dropping it in place.

Candlelight warmed the chamber, along with a hearty fire. He was sitting in a chair by the bed, and his eyes reached out to her, called to her, claimed her. Her heart banged against her chest.

His cream silk tunic, laced loosely, revealed the muscles in his chest and made his big hands look almost as brown as her own skin. His dark hair fell past his collar in the back, and he had swept it away from the distinct angles of his face. His gaze pierced the distance between them.

Her breath caught in her chest.

He raised his arm, extended his hand.

Hungry for his touch, she drew close to him, fell into his arms, his kiss.

His tongue moved slow and easy, his touch gentle. He was a

marvelous lover and would not rush. A thrill of anticipation warmed her.

Then pride stayed her, and she pulled away. She might be inexperienced compared to him but she had a keen sense of her feminine power, of what he remembered so vividly from St. Giles' Fair.

She repositioned several candles to create an imaginary stage with lights. She turned to face him, saw the burning desire in his eyes, and faltered. He would think her childish, awkward. She avoided his eyes and slipped her outer gown off, revealing her dancing gown. Closing her eyes she summoned the memory of the sky, the white clouds, constantly shifting in their patterns. She slipped into the forest, with the swaying branches, their welcoming movements, and the wind, unpredictable and stormy, gentle and caressing. She became a faerie, bending, floating. She stopped to attach her anklets, deliberately bending before him to reveal the tops of her breasts as she did so, then danced to release the music of the bells. Their light melody filled the chamber.

She moved her hips to the beat of the song in her heart and raised her arms, splaying her fingers to touch the magic in the air. She twirled, extending her right leg so it could peek out from the layers of silk that fell to her ankles. Step, step, turn and sway, and the hunger and fascination in his eyes made her stomach tingle.

Tabor resisted blinking for fear of missing the images. His beautiful Sharai, moving in the rhythm of a woman in love, she danced before him, a silken fantasy from his dreams. Her gown wisped about her thighs, her movements revealing fluid muscles, the gentle curve of her calves.

Desire tightened his loins, an exquisite need that had been simmering and rising since his first glimpse of her.

When he thought he could absorb no more sensations, she

turned her back to him and released her hair, shaking it to create a shimmering black waterfall of curls. He wanted to close his eyes in ecstasy, but that would mean losing sight of this—this image of femininity that had haunted his dreams since that night at St. Giles.

His control vanished. Stepping round the candles, he reached for her, lifted her hair in his hands. Cool and silky, the tendrils curled around his fingers. He buried his face in it, then swept it aside, kissing the nape of her neck.

She had finally come to him.

CHAPTER THIRTEEN

She resumed her swaying dance, and he stroked her breasts, lightly at first then more firmly. He molded his hands over the gentle swell of her hips, and fitted her against him.

Her bottom pushed against his groin, increasing his desire.

She raised her arms and turned, jingling the small coins sewn in her comb. Her face shone in the firelight, and her eyes glowed with desire.

He kissed her, and her body melted against his. Her tongue moved greedily over his lips, seeking his tongue, finding it.

His breath caught, and he deepened the kiss.

He lifted her into his arms, wondered at how such a small body could incite such expansive feelings. He carried her to his bed, as he had imagined doing many times in his dreams, and laid her there. Her hair made an ebony spray on his pillow that reminded him of the midnight surf at Cornwall.

Once on the bed, she glanced uneasily about.

"Are you all right?"

"What?"

He gave her a playful smile. "Will your dagger be making a sudden appearance?"

"Don't make fun at my expense."

"Sorry. Are you nervous?"

Worry lines furrowed her brow. "Yes."

Desire pulsed insistently in his body, the pressure making him ache, but by his patron saint, Monica, he would not rush or frighten her. Just a while longer. "What say we simply lie down together, nothing more, and I'll hold you?"

She nodded, and he stretched his body out on the bed next to her, turned her away from him and wrapped his left arm lazily over her shoulder.

Her breathing evened out in the silence, and Tabor tried to do the same with his own, focusing his thoughts away from the curves of her body, concentrating on the candlelight dancing outside his bed curtain.

"That's it, then?"

He could no longer resist, and stroked her hair. "Whatever you wish, my love."

The candle flickered, the shadow of its flame licking the fringe at the top of the curtain.

"I would have you kiss me."

"That is your wish?"

"Aye." He heard the smile in her voice.

He stroked the gentle curve of her cheek. "Would you be wishing for a brotherly kiss, or a lover's kiss?"

She turned to him, all traces of fear vanished from her face. "I love you, Tabor, so it would be the latter."

The velvet darkness of her eyes caressed him, and warmth filled his chest. He had hoped, and become more certain when he learned of the frog cake, but her words sounded like music to him, bringing joy as delicate as her tinkling ankle bells, so strong he fought the urge to jump and blare like the red harts in autumn.

He pushed stray hairs from her face. He had never seen her look so vulnerable, or so trusting, and his heart swelled with the rest of him. "I love you." He kissed her, his tongue tracing the soft fullness of her lips. "I love your spirit. I love when you sing, and the look in your eyes when you regard me. I love *you*. And it has naught to do with the cake."

She laughed, then her smile vanished, and she touched his lips with her fingers. "I would have you love me now, Tabor." Her voice held a tinge of wonder.

He squeezed her hand. "Nothing has changed, my love. I will never force you." He kissed her leisurely, his hands skimming her body in a gesture of caress that held no hint of force or hurry.

She relaxed and returned his kiss, and heat spiraled back in her body.

Placing his hands on either side of her shoulders, he raised above her and lowered his head to her breasts, nibbling and teasing through the thin silk.

Pleasure hummed through her body, and she arched toward him.

He untied her belt and slowly removed her gown, covering her quickly with the comforter, all but her breasts. He took her nipple in his mouth and suckled, and his fingers moved lower, touching, stroking.

A shiver ran through her and she moved toward him, driven by her own passion. Her fingers curled around his arms, feeling their reassuring strength.

He smelled of plum wine and a pleasant musky scent, and she inhaled deeply, taking him into her senses.

He rolled onto his back and slipped out of his shirt and hose and slid under the covers. His large hands cupped her bottom, pulling her to him, and she felt the length of his naked body on hers.

Her heart beat loudly in her ears. The sensation of skin on skin, the feel of his desire, pulsing on her belly.

She tensed.

His brows wrinkled in concern, and he moved his hands to her shoulders, stilling them, question in his eyes.

"I'm fine," she said. It was right and wonderful with him. She caressed his back, feeling the strong muscles flexing beneath her fingertips. She rose to kiss him.

His hands resumed their movements, stroking her body, and the knowing touch of his hands on her, stimulating those new places, brought fresh heat to the surface.

She pushed her breasts against the hardness of his chest. Dizzy with desire, she wrapped a leg around him, inviting him.

He groaned, a surrendering moan that told her he would do her bidding. A pressure built between her legs, pushing into her, the sensation of hot, smooth, velvet skin entering her own. An exquisite fullness overwhelmed her.

He held her close, and his strength and his love surrounded her, giving joy and a sense of belonging.

They were one.

She was overcome with the simplicity of it.

He kissed her and withdrew, then reentered.

Delicious sensations streaked inside of her, and he moved again.

She moved with him, following his lead. His eyes were dark with passion, and as naked as his body, open and hungry and intimate. She welcomed the look and the man behind it.

He changed the rhythm, touching her again, stroking those places that made her hunger for him.

She gasped, clinging tightly, driven by needs he stirred in her.

They tossed, joined together, and she felt the weight of his body on hers, his moist skin, the male hardness of him, and the soft linen comforter below.

A new urgency built inside, one she recognized. Sweet saints, it was happening again, this marvelous feeling.

She answered his movements, urging him on. He stroked deep and fast, deep and hard.

She called his name and a groan of ecstasy escaped his lips. The magic quiverings caught her again and she surrendered to them, letting them build. She cried out and he was there, answering her, in her and around her, and the heat of his release pulsed inside her.

She held him close, feeling the unbridled beating of his heart next to hers. She had not thought it would be like this. No dream could have captured her in such trembling intensity. She had feared being used, pricked like a needle quickly in and out of the fabric of her body, not touching her soul, or, worse, insulting it with a lack of care.

He rolled over, twirling the strands of her hair and kissing them. Tabor had not taken, but had loved her with his body and with hers. She could make him tremble with desire; she could make him weak with need, and fill him with satisfaction, with joy.

"What are you smiling about," he asked.

"The potion," she said. "It works." She kissed him, sharing the magic. "Love me again."

Sharai moved the bed linen aside and reached across Tabor's large chest, scooping a fresh handful of berries. Dawn lightened the sky. They had spent another evening together. Sleep was nigh impossible because they kept touching each other, and touching led to more heat and passion, passion she relished in the arms of the man she loved.

She popped the fruit in her mouth, enjoying the tart sweetness as they burst in her mouth. By the saints, she was being so brazen. These last three nights had been a heavenly pursuit of delights, and Sharai couldn't get enough. She had delighted in each new discovery of the secrets of pleasuring, and with each new mastery, Tabor's smile had grown wider. She chewed another handful of berries, moaning with relish.

Tabor caressed her cheek. "You must cease with those sounds or I shall be forced to ravage your body again, and I'm not sure

I am up to the feat. I near fell asleep during practice yester morn. The men chuckle and make comments about my heavy eyes."

She laughed and dropped some of the small black treats into his open mouth. "Let them tease all they wish. Just so I have you."

He kissed her, his lips warm and gentle, and pulled her closer. "You do, indeed, my love. Why else would I be lying here with you, eating raw fruit?"

"You don't understand because you are *Gorgio,* not a Gypsy. *Gorgios* avoid raw fruit, but thank heaven you tried it. 'Tis a vast insult to refuse a Gypsy's food. Now I know there's hope for you."

"It's been said raw fruit causes fevers and indigestion."

"How so?"

"Black bile. Melancholy."

Sharai laughed and stroked his lower stomach, soft as a whisper, enjoying his obvious reaction. "Bosh. And do you feel melancholy now, my lord?"

He laughed and kissed her soundly. "Only because it's dawn, and not dusk."

She rested her head on his chest, enjoying the quiet and the gentle rise and fall of his breathing.

In the growing light she spied a small book on the table. She'd seen books in the monk's booth at St. Giles, and Father Bernard had allowed her to linger at the church and read the Bible. There were still so many words to learn. "May I see your book?"

Watching her intently, he handed it to her.

So he didn't believe she could read. Elated that she could pleasantly surprise him, she accepted the book. She would be forever grateful to Father Robert, who had taught her English and shared with her this potent access to knowledge.

201

The book was small. Covered in sturdy dark brown leather and bound with metal clasps, it was stitched tightly and uniformly. She touched the strong twine that bound the spine. "A man's hand must have sewn this. I would never have the strength to achieve such tension."

"Father Bernard arranged for the binding in London." His face grew serious. "Since I was a child, I've possessed more emotion than is prudent. My father tried his best to moderate my tendencies, but to no avail. My temper oft overrides my judgment, and I pay dearly for it. But in books," he said, tapping the cover, "in books I find a passion like my own. I've learned there are other men who feel with such intensity and have found happiness with it. Since then I've had hope. Books are my weakness."

She laughed. "Your strength, mean you." She turned the pages. "Giovanni Boccaccio. Francesco Petrarch." She stumbled on the pronunciation. "Where are they from?"

"Italy."

"*King Arthur, Roman de Troie, Rime Sparse.* I've never heard of these stories."

A conspiratorial smile played at the corners of his mouth. "Not from the monks, I am sure. They're stories of romance. Of love."

Her heart fluttered in response. "There are secrets of love in this book? By men? Men write of love?"

He raised a brow. "Think you that only women know of love?"

"Why, no. I'm sure you do. It's just that—"

He pointed to a passage. "Read this."

She looked from his warm brown eyes to the book and swallowed. What would she do if she met an unknown word?

"Go on. If a word is unfamiliar, I'll help you."

She cleared her throat. " 'If it is not love, what then is it that I feel? If it is good, whence comes this bitter mortal effect? If it is evil, why is each torment so sweet?' " She lowered the book and met his eyes. "It's true. All is sweet with you."

"I have these, and other stories. They have intrigued me since I first fell in love, when . . ."

"When you fell in love with Aurora?"

"I know now that it wasn't love. She didn't love me."

"Maybe she did."

"She pitied me. All these years I dared hope that love would come into my life, that I wouldn't be forced to live without it. I'd come to believe it was all a tale, like the Greek myths, but then I found you." His lips touched hers, his kiss a warm caress that reached her heart. "Prithee never leave me. I wish you to never travel again, lest it be with me."

She sighed, nestling in the crook of his arm. "Oh, Tabor, I'm so happy. I've been alone for so long. Not lonely, because I have Kadriya, but," she shrugged, trying to put her feelings into words, "well, alone."

He cupped her face in his hands and kissed her forehead. His eyes shone brown and clear in the firelight. "So long as I breathe air you shall never be alone again, Sharai." His voice rumbled deep with emotion, as if he had just made a sacred vow.

Tabor handed his steward, Edwin, the accounting books. "Your calculations exceed my hopes, Edwin."

Edwin fingered the pockmarks from the illness that almost took him last winter, a frown line creasing between his brows. "But now the harvest. We need men to harvest."

"You posted the notice to London? Many are leaving the city to avoid the plague. We have a place for them here," Tabor said.

"Aye, and sent word to Southampton and Exbury."

Tabor nodded. "Good. Now we wait."

Tabor bade him well and checked the towers and guard stations. Overhead, the skies were clear, the sun unfettered in her morning ascent. He passed the kitchen, filling his lungs with the smell of baking bread for the upcoming dinner. Though he'd just finished breaking his fast, the sweet smell tantalized him, and his mouth watered.

A splash of color moved in the garden, and he looked closer. Sharai was in the garden again, tending the bean plants, just below the wall walk. The wooden walkway hung four feet below the top of the twelve-foot-high stone curtain that protected the bailey. It provided his garrison protection and a strategic place to repel the enemy in times of siege.

He slipped into the gate. She was on all fours in the garden. Her rump, round and firm and accented by her small waist, was poised in front of him, swaying enticingly as she loosened the soil at the base of the plants with a trowel. His body tightened in desire and he dropped to his knees next to her. "Good morn, Sharai." Hidden in the tall bean plants, he nuzzled her neck. "What brings you to the garden every morn?"

She turned to him, the even whiteness of her broad smile dazzling. "Look." She cupped a small blossom on the late bean plant.

Tabor looked closer. "A blossom. Aye, where the pod will grow. And?"

"It's life," she whispered. "What is life, but a promise of tomorrow? And here it is, so white, so tender. Beautiful." She regarded him. "I used to garden with my mother before—" pain pulled at her features, and she paused. "Well, before." She cleared her throat. "I've missed the quiet of a garden." She raised her face to the sky. "See, how the sun filters through the leaves, making them glow light green, and how the darker leaves give it a lace-like pattern? I come here in the mornings to watch the light, to see how the sun falls on the land, on this special place, each day." She scooped a handful of soil and let it sift through her fingers. "This garden, the mushroom tree, the stream where we . . ." She dropped her lashes, suddenly modest, Tabor supposed, at recalling the passion they'd shared there. "This land. It's you. Me. Your family. Your ancestors. All they've ever lived or breathed or bled, it's all here. Always the same, something you can count on." She sighed. "Something of beauty and permanence. I have not felt thus since . . . for years."

She looked so beautiful to him, and the words she spoke united him with William, and with his father, and it breathed color and life into the precise lines Father Bernard had drawn on the heraldic chart that spread across the parchment like so many veins in an ancient rock. That she, who wandered through countries, homeless, could sense his blood investment in the land on which they knelt, amazed him. He wanted to preserve this moment. The dappled sunshine lighting her ebony braids as they fell to the swelling bodice of her gown, her skin, dark bronze in the sunlight, her eyes smiling, no worry, no protective shield barring him from her feelings as she traced his bond to the land and shared the secrets of her heart.

He held her hand. "I missed home in France. I was there for months, and the weather. October, rainy and cold, with illness and death all around. I cannot imagine your traveling, years, without a home." He put his arm around her, pulling her closer. "I'm sorry for the grief you have borne."

"*Chut*," she said, dusting his nose with her braid. "I'm happy for life's gifts. Like Kadriya. Like the priests at St. Giles." Curling tendrils of black hair framed her expressive brown eyes. "Like you."

Rauf stood patiently attentive while Humphrey, Duke of Gloucester and Protector of the Realm, mounted his horse, sitting tall in the saddle to prevent the heavily jeweled collar he wore from chafing his stinking royal neck.

Gloucester seemed to enjoy the view from up there, looking

down at Rauf. The duke's hands sparkled with finger rings of gold, emerald, and ruby, and his eyes held that cool, appraising look that only royalty possesses, a look refined by living for thirty and two years with full license to control others' lives. A look of privilege that Rauf would enjoy changing to terror.

Humphrey swung a final imperious glance at Rauf, then his father. "I shall see you in London then, Lord Hungerford, a fortnight hence."

The old man raised his cane in salute, giving Gloucester a bow and smile, his features brittle and unconvincing. "God-speed, Your Grace."

Gloucester guided his horse through the portcullis, and his small army of knights closed in to protect him. His entourage waddled out of the castle gates, fat on three weeks of feasting and whoring. Forty-five strong, they'd stripped the Hungerford buttery of all but one barrel of its wine and had left the larder bare.

Rauf wiped the sweat from his brow. Just eight bells, yet all traces of dawn's welcome coolness had been burned away by the sun. "Who hosts his hungry household next?"

His father turned to him, his white eyebrows drawn in anger. "The Bishop of Bath, who will undoubtedly be more gracious than you were. You bordered on churlish throughout his visit," he reprimanded him.

Rauf shrugged his shoulders. He didn't want to fight with his father. He wanted to get him to commit their garrison to an attack on Coin Forest, but he couldn't resist sharing his observation. "He is no pillar of grace, himself, though he fancies himself king."

Hungerford stroked his mustache. "He will never be so."

Rauf steeled himself for another story of the continent and his father's glory days.

"Aye, he's not the man his brother was. Henry saved Gloucester's life at Agincourt. Now, Gloucester repays him by stopping at nothing to take control from his son, the legal heir."

" 'Tis no challenge to browbeat a lad of fourteen," Rauf countered, giving a pointed look to his father. "I could trounce Gloucester on any battlefield."

"Keep your eyes open with this one, Rauf. He's killed many men. He's impetuous, but his mind is keen. His days in the field are far from over, and he still fights with the intensity of a hungry wolf. He fights legally, and with that you are as awkward as a horse in church."

"Oh? And how much can you accomplish? You can hardly stand. Your body gets weaker with each day. And don't think Gloucester doesn't know where your loyalties lie." His father was firmly allied with Cardinal Beaufort, Gloucester's enemy. "He knows it, and will never trust you."

"I don't need his trust, nor do I need physical strength, truths you cannot seem to grasp. Use your wits, Rauf. My cousin, Walter, serves at the king's council. We've managed to discredit Tabor and present him, stinking of piss and looking like a swill rat, to Gloucester, who heads the council. Which of us do you suppose will enter that chamber with the advantage? I'm assured of my cousin's vote, and by the time I'm done even Gloucester will want to grant Coin Forest back to our family. When presented with an obstacle, Rauf, one doesn't always have to bash one's head into the wall. Some of the time one can achieve more success by tunneling under it."

"So you mean to ride off to London to meet with a handful of old men when we could hit Tabor hard, now that Marmyl's gone. Let's strike. Avenge your sister Margaret, then call all your old legal owls together for court and make Coin Forest ours again." Rauf took a deep breath. If his father wouldn't go, Rauf would, and while he was there he'd collect the traitorous alehouse whore, Maud. Punish her and that harpy Gypsy woman. "Let's settle it."

"I have a more effective method in mind to sway Gloucester to our cause."

Rauf pounded his fist into his open hand, causing a loud smack.

Hungerford flinched.

"Your mind is old. Feeble. You need to hit an obstacle head-on. No pansy-dancing around it. Slay it."

"You tried once. Not again."

Rauf clenched his right hand, wanting to punch the life out of the old bastard, but Rauf was not prepared to pay the price it would cost if he did it now. He would find a more opportune time.

Tabor held Sharai's hand as they walked along the lazy Poole River that bordered the west fields. Her small fingers laced around his big hand like a soft whisper. Trailing her free hand in the high grasses, she brushed the dew from the tips, creating small rivulets that ran down the blades. She wore a white ribbed gown with an orange and brown striped trim that dropped to reveal the creamy swell of her breasts. She had braided her hair with white ribbons. Her oval face wore a serene expression, and her generous lips, swollen from their night of loving, were turned in a gentle smile.

Mist rose from the river in the early dawn light.

He'd soon meet with Cyrill to work with the squires at quintain, and in a sennight he would leave for London and the royal court, but for now, he would enjoy this time with her.

"It's so beautiful here, Tabor. You have everything you need."

He squeezed her hand. "Now. Now I do."

The sound of soft bleating reached them from the flock of sheep just ahead.

Sharai plucked a stem heavy with grain, twirling it in her

hand. "Your land is rich. Not so where I am from—it's drier."

"In Little Egypt?"

She smiled knowingly. "Nay, as I suspect you're aware, I'm no princess. I'm just a merchant's daughter, and I'm from Wallachia."

"Near Constantinople?"

"Lipscani, on the plains. When we left, we followed the Dunaria River for six days, then we reached the sea. After three days, we saw Constantinople. From a distance." A shadow crossed her features and she looked away.

"Is that the last time you saw your parents?"

"My mother traveled with me."

"But I thought Etti found you, orphaned, in Marseilles."

"During the voyage, plague broke out on the ship. Most died, even the captain, but one sailor remained alive to bring us to port."

An image of the silent ship, and Sharai there, among the dead and dying, made him shudder.

A scream pierced the air. An animal in agony.

Sharai's hand flew to her chest. "What?"

Another scream, unearthly. He'd heard it earlier in the spring. Another lamb. "Not again."

They ran to the source of the screaming, but it stopped. They found a late lamb, convulsing in the grass.

Sharai dropped to the ground, murmuring reassurance to the animal, and felt its stomach. "Full, and hard as stone. He has overeaten."

Tim, the shepherd, hurried toward them and knelt to the animal. He pushed Sharai away and scooped the animal in his arms. "Stay you from it with your dark spells. You've cursed it."

Sharai glared at him. "What foolishness. This lamb has gorged itself. I've seen this happen with our goats, too. Has it been weaned?"

Tim shrank from her. "You curse it with your touch."

Tabor put a hand on Tim's arm. "Quit this nonsense. We lost several lambs in spring from the same sickness. It's not Sharai's doing."

Edwin, the Steward, arrived, winded. "What goes here?"

The lamb gave a weak bleat and closed its eyes, and Tim dropped the animal. The shepherd cast Sharai a haunted, wide-eyed glare. "You killed it. I heard about you and your dark-skinned tribes. You cast evil eyes and spells with frogs. It's the devil's work!" He backed away, then bolted back to his herd.

Sharai knelt and rested her hand on the lamb's neck. "The poor creature has died." She stroked the animal's head. "It's a feeding problem." She met Edwin's accusing eyes. "Or would you believe the shepherd?"

"Be not foolish, Sharai," Tabor said.

Edwin took the lamb and looked to Tabor. "Do you not wonder, just a mite?"

Tabor helped Sharai to her feet and regarded him in reprimand. "Are you daft? Nay. Now apologize to the lady."

Edwin glanced at Sharai, then back at Tabor. "Forgive me," he mumbled, then left them, striding in the shepherd's direction.

Field workers had gathered, staring openly.

Sharai blinked quickly and pulled her hand free from his. Turning away, she ran toward the mill.

Tabor followed, rushing past the wide-eyed peasants. He wished he could have spared her this embarrassment, but it was too late. He caught up with her. "After losing lambs this spring, they're afraid."

She shook her head, an expression of exasperation on her face. "Fear has closed their eyes."

He would explain this to her so she could be spared such embarrassment in the future. Him as well. If Gloucester heard

Tabor was harboring a sorceress, it could weaken his claim to Coin Forest.

"Look at the frog bones and how my mother reacted. People do not take kindly to spells."

"It was naught but good wishes. You know that."

"But it's dangerous, Sharai. Look at the damage it's caused already."

"But what of the young girls who sing 'loves me or not' and pluck the daisy petals? Or those who make a wish on the chicken's breastbone, then break it? They are not accused of sorcery."

Her logic seemed sound, but he shook his head. "You must cease—"

"And what of the floating wishes ceremony on Midsummer's Eve? I have seen this for myself, every summer I have been in England. Nobles and peasants alike float a candle on a piece of wood—"

"I know, I know," he interrupted. "If the float sinks or the flame blows out, you never get your wish. How does that relate to spells?"

"If the candle stays lit, you get your wish. Wishing on a flame. Or with petals, wishing on a flower. Or a chicken's bone. Be it sorcery, or just wishful thinking based on the heart's desires?"

"You were chanting to a dead frog, Sharai. You were seen, and heard. Coin Forest is a dangerous place to practice any kind of sorcery."

"What do you want of me?"

He turned her to face him. "Stop making spells. My father was almost killed with a potion made by Lord Hungerford's sister. She was imprisoned for sorcery. Edwin remembers and it stirs deep fears. That is the one thing from which I cannot protect you."

★　★　★　★　★

The priest's voice droned to conclusion, ending Vespers, and the church grew loud with the shuffling of feet on the rush-strewn stone floor. Lifting his vestments, the priest exited, encouraging all to leave the church and take supper.

Lord Hungerford checked once more for sign of his son. Not sighting Rauf's broad shoulders or bulbous nose, Hungerford breathed easier. Rauf became more impatient every day, and Hungerford had begun taking precautions to avoid being alone, just in case his brash son lost all patience and took a danger-ously rash step, just when victory was within reach.

Today, Hungerford had taken the chance and remained alone after mass. The church grew quiet, and the voices outside faded as people headed to the great hall.

Dank air, heavy with the smell of sweat, manure and ale. hung in the church. High above, near the beam of the clerestory, a trapped bird fluttered, seeking escape it would never find. Its small wings pounded the beam in a muffled frenzy, stirring dust that sprinkled lazily to the floor.

The door opened and a short, stout man entered the church, closing the door behind him. His walk was slow and practiced, as though in ceremony, causing his cape to flow with each step.

A long, straight nose jutted from below keen, dark eyes. His hair, black as night, fell past his shoulders, and his features would probably be considered handsome by the ladies. Not that it mattered, Hungerford reminded himself. This rogue needed only to be properly inspired. And provoked.

The man bowed regally. "Good even, Lord Hungerford. I thank you for lending me your fine horse, and the escorts you sent. I came as quickly as I could."

As he spoke the words, his breath fouled the air. Though faint, it smelled of death, musty and unhealthy. Lord Hunger-ford backed up to avoid it. "I appreciate your speed, and your discretion. You'll find that both will be rewarded." Hungerford gestured to the table he'd prepared with wine and cheeses. "May I offer you refreshments after your ride, Count Aydin?"

CHAPTER FOURTEEN

Hungerford propped his cane on the edge of his chair and engaged the Gypsy in pleasantries, waiting for the wine to hit his gut. He wanted him relaxed and impressionable, ready to consider possibilities.

He was a man of passion and pride, this short foreigner. Hungerford had ample opportunity to observe him at the St. Giles' Fair, when he settled a fight among five members of his tribe. He was quick on his feet, knew how to use those muscular legs of his, to say naught of his quick fists. He kept his people orderly, and with their ready collection of knives and whips, they were the type of men one would not want to offend.

The count was skilled at market, too. He managed to sell Hungerford's knight a string of pearls for seventy shillings, when the poor fool could have bought three strings for the same price, but the clever count had told him it had once belonged to an Egyptian princess, and that the pearls possessed some strange sort of healing powers.

But the man was unhappy. Hungerford had seen Aydin following the Gypsy girl, Sharai, like a puppy, giving her sheep's eyes. The man knew how to face danger, but knew naught about women. Aye, while at the fair the man demonstrated strong passion for women, and horses. Aydin had made such frequent visits to Hungerford's Arabian, Shaker, that Rauf suspected he was planning to steal him.

After a time, the Count leaned his stool back to the wall and propped his feet on the rung. Hungerford organized his thoughts and launched his proposal. "Has the summer been good for you and your tribe?"

"We're thankful for the warm welcome we receive in England," he replied diplomatically, "and we hope to return for the fair weeks next summer. We leave soon to France."

"I've heard your tribe numbers over a hundred."

Aydin's chest rose. "Once we return to France and rejoin the others, yes."

"And your dancers. Will they return with you, too, or stay here?"

He blinked. "The *Gorgios* are from Southampton and Salisbury."

"*Gorgios?*"

"Forgive me. The non-Gypsy dancers."

"And what of the dancer named Sharai? I saw her leave with Lord Tabor, and heard that he bought her from your tribe."

The count's expression became dark. "He is *Gorgio.*" This time he said the word like a curse. "Good Gypsy girls do not go with *Gorgios*. He bought only her services as a seamstress. Her contract will be done soon, and she will be leaving with me."

Hungerford replenished Aydin's goblet. Now he would use the reports he'd received. Embellished, of course. "She will not be returning with you."

His eyes narrowed. "What mean you?"

Hungerford positioned his hand closer to his sword, should he need it. "She is his whore now."

The Gypsy brought his stool upright, the wood thudding onto the stone. "Nay. She is a good Gypsy girl. Unless he—"

"Forced her? She's quite willing, I've heard. They embrace in broad daylight in the middle of the bailey." He picked a piece of lint off his sleeve, letting the silence settle in. "She shares his chamber."

Aydin's face contorted with anger. "Lies. She did not wish to go with him. She went only because Etti committed her to do so. She—"

Hungerford held his hand up. "Forgive me. I think you need to know what's being said about her." By the tension in Aydin's face, worms of suspicion were already crawling in his brain. "Tabor's chambermaid has separate quarters, but she is a curious girl," Hungerford said. "She heard the sound of bells in the night and could not resist peeking into her lord's chamber. She saw Sharai dancing for him. In his chamber."

"But—."

"Wearing the bells." He paused and gave a small smile. "Naught but the bells."

A shadow crossed Aydin's face as the truth stung its way into his brain. "What do you want from me," he growled.

Hungerford gestured to be quiet.

The count lowered his voice, but it still rumbled, dark with suspicion and anger. "Why have you summoned me, only to share foul rumors? And why for do we sit here in the darkness, with just one candle?"

"Tabor has wronged both of us, Count Aydin. He's stolen your woman, and he's stolen Coin Forest from my family. I want you to go there. Visit Sharai in the light of day, as her king. Take her from Tabor and bring her to me."

Aydin raised a dark brow. "Why do you want Sharai?"

"Merely as a diversion. Will she come willingly with you?"

The count sat up even straighter, looking every bit like a passion play puppet about to dance. "Of course."

Good, Hungerford thought. He engaged his pride. Now to engage his greed. "I've hired knights from Southampton to accompany you. My men do not know them, and they wear no livery, of course, so Tabor's men will see no connection to me. If she resists, take her by force. If you arrive peacefully, they will suspect nothing, but however you do it, you must remove her."

"And if I do?"

"Take her to London and wait for my orders."

"Why London?"

"These are my terms. Do it and I will give you an Arabian, a horse like Shaker, the one you rode here." *The one you could not keep your hands off in St. Giles,* Hungerford thought, enjoying the moment. "This horse is from el Maestro, one of the finest bloodlines in Spain." Hungerford stopped, letting that sink in.

The Gypsy's eyes widened in surprise, but just for a wink. He recovered quickly, masking his excitement, but Hungerford had already seen.

"Only the king himself has a horse as fine as this." Hungerford animated his voice, relishing the challenge of gaining this man's services. Admittedly, the price was high, but the prize was higher. "With a horse like Shaker, you can command your price for stud at any horse fair you choose, and hundreds of pounds for every foal. You'll be the envy of all."

Aydin's eyes lit. He was tribal king, and that gave him power. This equestrian gem from Spain would be a fine feather in his cap, giving him prestige, as well.

Aydin examined his fingernails in an effort to conceal his excitement, but he could not mask his quickened breathing. "And?"

Hungerford had heard about the Gypsy greed, and he was prepared. He held out his hand. "Bring me Sharai, and I will also give you this ring." He showed the Gypsy his heirloom ring, holding it close to the flame to reveal the intricate detail and delicate violet stone. The candlelight cast a glow on the thick band of gold crosses. Rauf would be furious, but no matter, it must be done now, and this vainglorious creature was perfectly suited to the task.

The Gypsy's eyes grew keen. "And?"

Hungerford withdrew his hand. "And you get your woman back. Unless it bothers you not that she gives her womanly charms to a *Gorgio* nobleman and not you."

His face darkened and Hungerford worried for a moment that he had pressed too far, but the Gypsy contained his emotions. "I want Shaker."

"Shaker is my horse. I will give you his brother. He'll be delivered to you in London."

"And when do I get the ring?"

"The same time you get the pedigree documents on the horse. When you arrive in London with Sharai. In five days."

Sharai stitched the end of the cording, tucking it invisibly into the seam of the apple-colored seat cushion. Just two more and she would be done. She lifted the next one from the table. Fading twilight filtered weakly into the solar, making it difficult to see.

Fast footsteps sounded and Kadriya appeared from below. Her blue gown was stained at the knees again, and she had weeds in her hair.

Sharai removed most of the weeds and kissed the top of her head. "And what are you so wide-eyed about, Sprig?"

"The village is filled with strange men. Stinky, dirty men. From France. Archers. One lost his eye and half his arm, and a red-haired man has blistered lips, like they were burned in a fire."

"They've been at war, and now they're looking for work." Tabor had sent messages to Southampton and London that the harvest at Coin Forest was excellent, and help was needed. His foresight was paying off.

"And there are some men from London. The plague is back, they say, and they left before they caught it, too."

Sharai crossed herself. "God bless them, and protect us. It

does seem to strike hardest in London."

"Foul air and water, they said. They were all talking at once; then Lady Anne came with Sir Cyrill and they called Lord Tabor out of the church, and I hid behind the tree by the well and listened. She said you were a sorcer."

"Sorcerer," Sharai corrected.

"She wants you to go away. Me, too." Her brows furrowed.

Sharai felt a pang of guilt, and put an arm around her. "Not you, Sprig. Me. Because of Lady Emilyne."

"Lord Tabor defended you. Said he would never let you go."

Sharai stood up, dropping her cushion. "What did Lady Anne say?"

"She said you were a heathen and a sorcerer. She got a post from Lord Marmyl that he canceled the contract."

Sweet Mary. She grabbed Kadriya by the shoulders. "Are you sure? What were her exact words?"

Kadriya looked to the ceiling, thinking. " 'He's canceled the contract,' she said. Then she called him a fool."

Sharai released her, straightening her sleeves. "What did Tabor say then?"

"He said something about duties and he would not send you away. And then Lady Anne started crying, and she hit him in the chest and said he was ruining everything. That without Marmyl he would lose not just this castle but all his holdings."

"She must have been exaggerating."

"Sir Cyrill said he feared she was right."

A vague sense of unease came upon Sharai, but she shook it off. It was just as Maud had said: this ordeal would pass.

And she and Tabor would wed.

Sharai let out a cry, scooped Kadriya up, and spun her in circles. Her fondest dreams were coming true.

A somber atmosphere loomed at the evening meal. Lady Anne

cast Sharai dark looks and sent the minstrels away, and the lower tables hummed with quiet conversation. Sharai felt eyes on her. Growing weary of being watched, she left the table before the final course and took a walk in the bailey. She followed the inner curtain, thinking of the general gloom that had settled since news of the Marmyl contract's demise. People were disappointed, but did they not realize they could prosper without it? The fields were heavy, and after harvest they would see they didn't need the Marmyls, after all.

Returning to the castle, she approached Maud as she swept soiled rushes out the kitchen door.

"Did you hear the good news? About Lady Emilyne," said Sharai.

" 'Tis not good," Maud said.

"But soon they'll bring in the harvest, and—"

"Lord Marmyl is an earl, you know."

"Yes. And wealthy. Britta said he owned several properties. But it did not sway Tabor from his true feelings."

" 'Tis more than money. It was foolish to anger the earl before the council rules on Hungerford's claim to Coin Forest. Did you know that Marmyl serves on the high court?"

"Yes, but it was you who said Lord Tabor can take care of himself. He'll find a way to beat Rauf at his own game."

Maud remained silent.

Sharai looked up, refusing to let Maud evade her eyes. "Maud. Weren't you the one who advised me to stay? You said Tabor needed me."

"But Marmyl serves on the high court. He will be one of the men who decides who gets Coin Forest." Maud untied a bundle of fresh reeds. "I didn't know of this council and trial, and Lord Marmyl's position. This is fearsome, Sharai." Her eyes grew wide. "If Rauf gains hold, he'll kill me, and anyone else who resists him. The lucky ones will be sent away with their lives, but nothing else." She crossed herself and turned away.

Sharai waited for Maud to utter some words of encouragement, but she entered the kitchen with the fresh reeds and never returned.

The bailey fire crackled and the din of kitchen cleanup broke the silence, and Sharai wondered how everything could sound so normal when all was so confusing. It seemed that every development that boded well for her meant trouble for Tabor. How could their love be so right when all else around them seemed so amiss?

A black, short-haired dog approached, looking up at Sharai with eager eyes.

She stooped to pet it and scratch behind its ear. Tabor's life was so much more complex than her own. A sensation of love rushed through her, and she trembled from its strength. She could not lose this man. Maud had been right before. Sharai would be Tabor's strength. She'd help him, and together they'd save Coin Forest. And they would wed and Kadriya and she would finally have a home.

A tear slipped down her cheek, and she pushed it away, willing no more to come. She must be strong.

Later that evening, Sharai and Tabor sat on the bench in his chamber, near the fire. The soft popping of the wood sap provided the only sound. Her thoughts haunted her this eve, and Tabor had seemed distracted, as well. Shadows that had naught to do with firelight lined his face.

His dark eyes regarded her. "What's troubling you?"

"The same thing that disturbs you. Everyone has given up. Why? You can prove your family's claim is valid. Father Bernard is certain, too. You don't need Marmyl's help."

"Mayhap."

"Then what do you fear?"

"The unexpected. This is not like a battle, where a man pits his own strength against another's. It's not like chess, where moves and rules are predictable. I cannot fail. I have obligations. I must prove myself."

"To whom?"

He looked at her as if she had three heads. "To my family. To my peers in Parliament, on the battlefield, in the parish."

"And what about yourself, Tabor?"

"In proving myself to others, I satisfy myself, as well."

"Really? Is that why you were such a contented man when I met you?"

His dark eyes were weary. "I've been carrying a fool's hope, wishing that things would somehow work out, but I can't turn a blind eye to reality. I must retain my holdings. Without the earl, I cannot."

She straightened the ribbon in her braid. "So Marmyl pulls his support, and you admit defeat before even trying? What about us, Tabor?"

He stood. "God's blood, Sharai, must you be so selfish? Everyone here, every knight, every maid, each person stands to lose their home."

"I'm no child. I understand what's at stake. But to just give up like this makes no sense to me." She hesitated, knowing her words would not be well received. "You're afraid."

He stopped his pacing. "You had your sights set from the beginning. Marry a nobleman and live in luxury. Were those not your words to me? And you proceeded with your charm and spells to capture me."

"Well, aren't you full as a tick? 'Twas you who followed my every step, visiting the solar, meeting me at the well every morn."

He ignored her words. "Now you are triumphant, but you hold dust in your hands. If Coin Forest falls to the Hungerfords, you have won nothing."

"I was a child when you met me, Tabor. Hungry and weary of living in a storage tent. You would use the words of a child against me?"

"You must think of other people's needs, too, Sharai, not just your own. You need to stop chasing dreams. Grow up."

"Grow up? Are you talking to me, or yourself?" She rose and stalked to him, glaring up into his eyes. "You chased after money more eagerly than I did. You feigned interest in a woman because of her dowry, and why? To make your struggle less difficult. Then you condemn the plans I had when I was but twelve summers. I love you, Tabor, and it has nothing to do with money. Yes, I wanted it, but at twelve I didn't know it was really security I wanted, not vast wealth. Do you know what I am, Tabor?"

"A Gypsy."

"I am *vatrasi,* of the Gypsies that settle instead of travel. My home and my family were stolen from me when I was but eight, and I have never had either one since. These *corturari* Gypsies I travel with, when time comes to move on, they look forward to new places, adventure, change. For me it's a sense of loss, of going in every direction at once, but never forward. Here, I go to the same church, every day, and I have found a trusted friend in Father Bernard." She touched his hand, welcoming the warmth of his skin and the sense of connection.

"I find joy in sewing, simple things for the solar that will be here tomorrow because the walls are sound, secure. This is the security I seek, not coin.

"And I know responsibility. Kadriya is part of my every decision. But I will never grow up, as you say, if it means I must grow old before my time and surrender my dreams and the love we share. Never."

He exhaled audibly. "What would you have me do? Slay Gloucester and Hungerford, the whole lot of them?"

"Fie! You should neither slay them nor lie down like a wounded puppy and let them slay you. Did you not fight fiercely to regain Coin Forest when Hungerford took it five years ago? Did you not stay in the fray the years since, scheming, gambling, improving your farming and milling practices, all to save your home? You had more spirit before Marmyl waved all those pounds in front of your face."

He turned away from her and leaned on the wall near the window. "I love you. I could not bear to send you away."

She put her hand on his shoulder. "And I love you for it. That was the one thing you did for yourself. Now I would have you fight. Fight for us."

The next morning Tabor mingled at the market, visiting with the retired archers. Bad news from France. More losses, and the Congress at Arras was failing. The French still demanded that Henry drop his claim and title as the King of France. Defeat loomed.

A man shopping the writing booth caught Tabor's eye. Dark-haired and young, he wore a green wool doublet and his long fingers wrapped around the ink vials, shaking the ink to the top of each glass and holding each to the sun to judge its quality.

Something about the man was familiar. He moved to make room for another patron and afforded Tabor a look at his face.

"Will?"

The man turned and looked at Tabor. He cocked his head, trying to place him. "Do I know you?"

Tabor approached him. "You're Will, the scribe from Hungerford."

"Until recently, aye."

"We met in unfortunate circumstances. Hungerford's dungeon."

Recognition lit his eyes. "You. Who would have guessed it?"

he said, taking in Tabor's clothing, then recovered. "Forgive me, I didn't mean to be rude."

"It's understandable."

"You're Richard," he said. "Baron of Tabor. You helped gain our release. I'm in your debt, my lord."

"I'm glad you found justice. Where are you traveling?"

"Anywhere but Hungerford. We proved our innocence, and I, too, left Hungerford quickly."

Tabor laughed. "We have much in common." He noted the tattered state of his doublet. "Are you looking for work?"

"I am, but there are herds of people about from London doing the same."

"But not all of them can write. Come, I wager Father Bernard could use some help, at least temporarily."

They walked, and Will told him of the growing tension between Lord Hungerford and his son, and of the deteriorating civility between Gloucester and Hungerford.

"I was shocked to see Gloucester in Hungerford," Tabor said. "Historically, Hungerford has opposed Gloucester in council." *And supported Gloucester's enemy, Cardinal Beaufort.*

"I handled Lord Hungerford's correspondence," Will volunteered. "He's never wavered in his support for Beaufort, but Hungerford did start offering Gloucester support—financial that is. Secretly, a few years back."

With my treasury, the cur.

"The longer Gloucester stayed, though, the less friendly they became. Remember Ben, my friend?"

"The white-haired man, yes."

"He was there day before yesterday when Gloucester and his party left."

"He left? For where?"

"Bath." He stopped and lowered his voice. "I prepared papers before Gloucester arrived, papers that involve your family, Lord

Tabor, so I know of the issue of servitude."

"Servitude?"

"I copied journals of servitude, records of one of your descendants serving in King Edward's court back in 1270."

So the old fox planned to create a smokescreen from the past to create question of Tabor's bloodline. Tabor grabbed the young scribe by the shoulders. "You've repaid your debt, Will. Wait in the great hall and Father Bernard will come for you." Tabor hurried to the church and found Father Bernard in the scriptorium.

The priest gave Tabor a smile with teeth worn and stained from the years, but his blue eyes were kind and filled with affection. "Tabor."

"Father, I seek your help. Gloucester left two days ago for Bath, where he'll see the bishop and hear cases."

"I see."

"Is my heraldic chart complete?"

"It is."

"How far back does it go?"

"Four generations. Why—"

"Further. Ten generations. Fast as you can get it down. Readable. Forget the embellishments and colors. I need it within the hour."

"Why?" The priest's brows furrowed. "Tabor, your temper. Do nothing rash."

"It's an opportunity, and it requires haste, but it's not rash, Father. I leave this morn for Bath."

"What do you there?"

"See Gloucester. Ask him to hear my case early."

After a moment's hesitation the priest hurried to his writing desk, uncapping his ink. "Will Gloucester hear the case without Hungerford present?"

"He can. The heraldic chart shows all, and Hungerford has

already filed his papers—items of servitude, if you can imagine."

"How did you learn this?"

"Luck, a stroke of pure luck," Tabor said. "All from a good deed. Your chart will refute his slur, which is why I want to present it before the London council."

The priest referred to the original record and copied it to the second parchment. "London's just days away. Why the haste?"

" 'Tis no whim. I spent the night thinking of nothing else. A certain argumentative young woman pointed out to me that I act when I should not, and do nothing when I should act. Gloucester's decision on this claim is vitally important to me, yet I was willing to entrust my fate to Marmyl. Why did I not see it before? No other one will care so much for my affairs as I. I must do it."

"But you've no audience with Gloucester."

"Hungerford likes to play cat-and-mouse, as he did with the dead pigeon, luring me to humiliation in front of Gloucester. He doubtless has more games planned for London. Now it's my turn to surprise him, to act when he least expects it, before he has a chance to surprise me."

"But why would Gloucester see you now?"

"He needs me. Or at the least, he needs an ally in Coin Forest and Parliament. If I wait too long, Marmyl will easily buy Gloucester's attention and sway his judgment to punish me for my treatment of Emilyne. For which I'm sorely regretful."

"If you think Gloucester can be so easily bought, you think little of him."

"I'm not judging him. I just think more of myself." All these years he'd looked up to these men, just as he used to look up to William and his father. They were the competent, powerful nobles, and he was the second-born son who could do nothing right. "I see now what you've tried to tell me these years, that the siege was a huge misfortune that fell on my shoulders. Had

William lived, he would have struggled as much as I have."
Tabor nodded. "It took being insulted to see it."

The priest smiled.

"Gloucester has fallen into financial and political crisis. He
can ill afford to champion causes."

Father Bernard clasped his hands. "But what if you are
wrong, Lord Tabor? Will you not insult Gloucester? Even harm
your cause?"

"He's vain, but fair in his decisions, and he's a patron of
learning, you know. He holds a great interest in books. I trust
his intellect and his reputation."

"And if you're wrong?"

"I may lose all. But if I wait, the full council in London is
heavy with my enemies. It may decide not even to review my
chart. They may arbitrarily decide in Hungerford's favor. If I
wait, I may lose all anyway."

Tabor returned for the chart an hour later. He blew on the
parchment, drying the ink. "Sir Cyrill will accompany me, but
I'm leaving the garrison intact, should Hungerford try anything.
Please give special care to Sharai and Kadriya while I'm gone."

"Of course."

"I'm taking two pigeons. Should I not return or send word
within four days, please move my household to our family
manor in Burley. Take this for Sharai." He handed him a bag of
silver. "If Sharai would rather go elsewhere, please see her there
after you reach Burley."

Tabor covered the heraldic scroll with light paper to protect
the ink and slid it into the wooden box, securing the latches.
"It's a gamble, Father, but not one based on a random roll of
the dice. It's based on knowledge, experience and . . . hope.
Prithee keep this conversation between us and wish me luck."

"Godspeed, Lord Tabor."

Tabor exited the church and looked toward the castle, where

Sharai approached with Kadriya. Her smile was tentative.

His pulse quickened. He smelled the lavender water she used to wash her hair. His gaze lingered on the curve of her cheek, minding the natural way her lashes lowered, adding to her charm.

She could shine warm, awakening the skin and soothing the soul, or she could be dark, like a storm, sapping the warmth with her temper. She was at once exquisite and annoying, and his head pounded with the urgency to make her his own forever. He reached for her hand.

She pulled away from him, her dark eyes holding question.

He lowered his voice. "Please forgive me for judging you. You had ambitious plans, but you were just a child, and they were based on dreams. I had dreams, too, but neither of us found the way, the fair way to make them come true."

She smiled and guided Kadriya by the shoulders. "Into the church, Sprig. I'll meet you inside."

They walked to the side of the church.

"I'm sorry, too, for criticizing you," she said. "You do what you must for your people, and I admire that in you. But—"

"I must needs leave this morn. I'll return in a few days."

Her brows furrowed. "To where?"

"I can't say."

"Why not? I'll say nothing to the others."

She was loyal, he knew. Loyal and brave. But Tabor was risking failure, and he would not risk humiliation on top of it, not in her eyes. "Worry not." He attempted a light smile. "I'm not slaying or fighting."

Not that he didn't want to. He itched to sweep Sharai into his arms and stand at the watchtower and scream his defiance, to Gloucester, to Marmyl, to the royal council.

To live with the passion he so craved, he must first contain it, approach this calmly, and take a calculated risk based on facts and common sense.

He looked down at her hand, where colorful globes of silk peeked out among her fingers. "I would ask to borrow your prayer beads."

CHAPTER FIFTEEN

Kadriya waited while Tommy took his turn. They sat in the bailey, near the well, using a barrel top as their table to play Tali, a dice game Kadriya had learned from Sharai.

Tommy's hair, flattened on the right side from sleep, caught the late morning sunshine. His coarse linen tunic was soiled with grease and sand from cleaning amour. His eyelids drooped, as if he hadn't had enough sleep last night.

Tommy rattled the sheep bones in the wooden cup with a flourish, shaking them near Kadriya's ear.

She laughed and slugged him in the arm. "Just roll them."

He dropped the knucklebones on the rough surface. The Tali bones danced across the wood and settled.

He pointed at the exposed surfaces of the bones and counted. "Three, three, four, five." He mouthed to himself, counting fingers. "Fifteen. I win."

Kadriya leaned closer. "Nay. I rolled vultures. That beats fifteen easily."

"You had vultures of three. That makes only . . ." he paused, counting his fingers again, ". . . only twelve."

"But all vultures beat a regular roll. I told you that."

"Did not." Tommy's face began to redden. "You bend the rules to suit you."

"I don't. Go ask Sharai. She'll tell you."

He raised his brown eyebrows in an expression of superior

annoyance. "Ask a sorceress? She caused all our problems, you know."

"Tommy!"

" 'Tis so. My da told me to stay away from her. Said to stay away from you, too, but you aren't evil. I told him." He smiled proudly, and it seemed to Kadriya that he waited to be praised for his loyalty to her.

Kadriya withdrew. "Sharai is not evil. Take it back."

"Nay. You'll find out soon. Lady Anne will send her on her way."

Fear made it hard for her to breathe. As casually as she could manage, Kadriya collected her Tali bones. "I am not in the mood to play any longer. You spoiled it for me." She dropped the bones in the cup. "Besides, Lord Tabor will not allow Sharai to leave. He wishes her to stay. He knows she's not evil."

"Lord Tabor's gone, so Sharai will be going soon, too. You'll see. You must be good, or you'll go, too."

Kadriya remembered the chatelaine custom. Lady Anne was in charge, and she'd been cruel to Sharai. Kadriya masked her fear with a glare and a harsh voice. "You're a wicked, stupid boy, Tommy. I don't want to play with you anymore."

He flinched from the insult, and his face grew red. "Fine. My da will be glad." He grabbed her wrist. "Listen to me."

She struggled to slip away, but his grip was firm. "Let go of me."

"You're going to be thrown out on your ear and it's just what you need. Go you back to St. Giles, and take your dirty skin with you."

"Dirty skin? You're the one who should bathe, you cur!" She punched him in the hollow of his shoulder hard enough that his fingers lost their grip. Pulling her wrist free, she ran for the castle.

★　★　★　★　★

Sharai and Father Bernard approached the castle, returning from the village market. She stifled a yawn. The implications of Marmyl's contract rejection had caused such tension; she'd hardly slept last night for worrying.

She carried her parcel of herbs by the twine that bound them, its harsh fiber rubbing against her fingers. "I'm sorry you found no black ink."

"I have enough to last until the next market."

They approached the drawbridge, where two knights stood guard. Above, a half-dozen more guards looked down from the muniment tower, and the watchtower flashed with the armor of at least twenty. "Why have they increased the guards?"

The priest's eyes followed her gaze. "Common practice when Lord Tabor's away. Worry not, Sharai."

"Worry?" She laughed. "Father, everyone I saw today held either suspicion or fear in their eyes. There are more guards on duty now than when Lord Marmyl's garrison joined Tabor's."

" 'Tis an uneasy time. It will pass."

She put her hand on his arm, stopping him. "Where is he?"

"He prepares for the meeting to discount, once and for all, Hungerford's claim."

"Why did he not tell me?"

"I don't know."

Though he carried his shoulders high, a deep frown between his white brows belied his words.

"He told you."

The priest averted his eyes for just the smallest moment, but it was enough for her to know. Tabor had told Father Bernard, but not her.

" 'Tis complicated, Sharai."

"So he thinks me too dull-witted to understand."

"He meant no offense."

She gave him a smile, which she hoped covered the disappointment she felt at Tabor's not trusting her. "I know that. Will you tell me?"

He shook his head. "Be patient, Sharai. He'll return soon."

The determination in his eyes made her stop pressing him. Disheartened, she bade him farewell and continued to the castle. Crossing the drawbridge, she met two guards, their eyes cold and mistrustful.

Courtesy conquered them finally, and they nodded to her, but still did not speak. Their manner made it doubtless they wished she would leave, as everyone else seemed to want her to do.

She rubbed her arms, trying to shake away a sudden chill.

Kadriya appeared, running toward the castle, a look of distress pinching her brow, her mouth tense and thin.

"Sprig. What's wrong?"

She continued running past Sharai and disappeared in the main door.

Sharai followed the quick slapping of the girl's feet up the spiral staircase to their chamber.

Once there, Kadriya threw herself on the bed, her shoulders shaking with quiet tears.

"What is it?"

Kadriya grasped the nut necklace Tommy had made for her and tore it off her neck. The small nuts flew in all directions, bouncing on the floor. "That horrid Tommy."

Sharai smiled. Kadriya's friendship with the boy was marked with emotional outbursts and fighting. She'd bloodied his nose as often as he'd bruised her arm, but they were fond of each other. As fond as children of their age could be of the opposite gender. "Punch him back and be on with it, then."

Kadriya rose on one elbow and faced her. "He said his da hates us. That he hates us, that everyone hates us and wants us to leave, and now that Lord Tabor has gone, she'll make you leave Coin Forest."

"She?"

"Lady Anne. And if you go, so will I."

She rubbed Kadriya's back, one of the sure ways to calm her down. "You must have angered him well."

Sprig's neck muscles remained tight. "I know his temper. 'Twas more."

"You play too much with him. You may both be getting on each other's nerves."

"He said we were dirty and should go back to the fair."

Sharai forced a smile. " 'Tis hot today. What say we go down to the river and soak our feet? You can catch some frogs."

"Lady Anne is sending us away, and you want to tarry, catching frogs?"

"Do you believe all you hear, Sprig? Words spoken in anger, 'tis all. Tie up your sandals and we'll go."

"Nay." She fell back onto her pillow, her face turned away. "I would not see his filthy face again."

Sharai patted her back. "Fine then. I shall lie down with you, and we will just rest and think this through."

Sharai settled into the bed and held Kadriya's hand. She would lie here with her until her anger and frustration passed, and then they would talk.

But what comfort could words bring? Sweet saints, the whole village wanted them gone, even those who knew them. Lady Anne, Cyrill, Tommy.

And Maud. Maud didn't tell her to leave, but she'd made it clear that Sharai's presence placed them all in peril.

Tabor had said it himself. Every villager, every knight, peasant, and maid was at risk of losing his or her home. Because of her.

So, all but a priest and the man she loved wanted her to leave.

What could she do? If she had any idea where Tabor might have gone. . . .

A dark thought pierced her brain. Had he gone to Lady Emilyne? Had he become desperate at the thought of losing his lands and gone to her?

Nay. She shook her head. Nay, he was true to her. Tabor's love was true.

Outside, clouds obscured the sun, and the room became dark and gloomy, much like her future. If the Marmyls refused to help, who would? Tabor was one against many. Bloody pox, even though he was more honest and hardworking than his adversaries, her land-wealthy noble had frightful little coin compared to them.

She must be realistic. In all her life, whenever justice battled power, power had won. Her family was innocent, but they had been sold as slaves because the man they befriended had been in a position to trick and betray them. Wealth bought power. Even Tabor had flaunted it, buying her services and bringing her here from St. Giles against her will.

And who had wealth enough to influence this London council?

Marmyl.

Hungerford, still spending the funds he stole from Tabor's treasury.

Only Tabor lacked funds.

Evil. 'Twas so unfair. Merely a simple love spell of frog bones and wishes, no different from their silly customs with bones and flower petals. The shepherd feared her. Lady Anne, too, and all the others. How soon before they condemned her publicly and imprisoned her?

Remembering the cold shackles that gripped her in Lipscani,

she reached instinctively for her ankle. And what of Kadriya?

Tabor would lose everything.

Or she would leave.

She could not bear the thought of either. A sense of defeat overwhelmed her and tears wet her cheeks.

Sleep took her, and Sharai tumbled in the darkness of her dream and landed, walking uncertainly, on high, precarious stilts, soaring above the earth, so exciting, then moving into a field of mud that made the stilts sink all the way to her feet, plunging deeper to her waist, and shoulders, and her chin. The cold, wet darkness engulfed her face, and she was trapped in the grime and drowning in a swamp of suspicious eyes and whispers.

Tabor reined his horse to a stop and gestured to Cyrill. Ahead, the city of Bath nestled in the lush, gentle hills, the spires of St. James and the looming Cathedral of St. Peter rising to disappear in the mists, giving the city a dream-like illusion to match its ancient past.

Next to him Cyrill shuddered and frowned, creasing the collection of wrinkles that framed his eyes. "What did I tell you? Soggy and dismal again." He sniffed, grimacing. "Mired in a fog."

"More mysterious than dismal." Though Tabor would hope for clarity soon, with Gloucester.

Cyrill pushed his elbows backward, stretching. "My back aches, and this moisture makes it worse."

"You whine like an old woman, Cyrill. That 'fog' is from the hot springs. You do covet the healing baths, do you not?"

A smile tugged at the knight's features, and his grey mustache rose. "Aye, that will be welcome."

They crossed over the majestic arches of the Southgate Bridge, the River Avon below reflecting the grey of the skies.

Weaving through the traffic on Stall Street, they neared the abbey, and Tabor fought a growing sense of disquiet. This was the largest gamble of his life, for if he lost, it would not be a purse or pride. It would be Coin Forest and the woman he loved.

Sharai. Her name drifted down from the soaring cathedral towers lost in the haze. He would hold her in his arms in bed and feel the soft curves of her body, see the light of love in her eyes, and he would wonder at the beauty of it, that she had really come to him, that this overpowering gift was real, that it was happening to him. He wanted to spend the rest of his life with her.

But she was a peasant. Suspect, by his own mother's charges, of sorcery. His gut tightened. What if he failed her? What if he angered Gloucester and ruined his chances to save Coin Forest? His stomach knotted with apprehension. He could not endure losing Coin Forest, but he could not live without Sharai. Once he made the commitment, he could not turn back.

He slipped her prayer beads from his travel bag, rolling the silky spheres in his hand. Warm and smooth, they brought him comfort and made him feel closer to her. Though outnumbered, outfinanced, and outmaneuvered, he would fight.

Cyrill leaned forward in the saddle, peering into Tabor's hand. "What do you have there?"

"Tools of persuasion, I hope." He poured the prayer beads in his purse and dismounted. "Wait you here with the horses, Cyrill. I'll leave word for Gloucester, and then we'll see the cellarer for food and lodging."

Tabor walked the well-worn path to the Bishop's Palace.

A stranger bumped into Tabor just outside the gate, a merchant, judging by the fur on his sleeves.

Tabor placed his hand on the stranger's shoulder, stabilizing both of them. "I beg your pardon."

The merchant gave him a curious stare. "My fault. Forgive me." He took slow, uncertain steps away, walking toward Cyrill.

Tabor raised his hand, thinking to ask the man if he knew him, then thought likely he did not, and gave his name and title to the gatekeeper.

Count Aydin and his knights had traveled to a marshy area beyond Hungerford where their horses' hooves pocked noisily in and out of the muck with each step.

A distant shlupping sound came from behind a stand of trees, warning of other riders.

Aydin pulled his sword.

A rider appeared from behind, and others behind him. They closed in on Aydin's men.

The three-quarter moon cast light on the rider, and Aydin lowered his sword to acknowledge him. "Rauf."

Rauf peered closer. "The Gypsy from the fair?" He grimaced, as if to say that Aydin wasn't good enough to be traveling through his land.

Aydin bristled. "I am Count Aydin."

Rauf laughed, a rude, ill-humored bark. "A count from Little Egypt, I know, your land of dreams. What are you doing here?"

Aydin's gut tightened, his hand itching to strike the insolent young dullard, but the fact that Rauf didn't know the nature of Aydin's trip struck Aydin as most curious. He absorbed this significant information. This explained the weak candlelight in the church. Rauf knew naught of his father's plans. This pleased Aydin and eased some of the anger he felt at being laughed at. He searched the shadows, trying to count Rauf's men. They outnumbered Aydin's six, but he could not be sure by how much. Aydin raised his chin in challenge. "I visited your father, and we now pass peacefully on to Owlsbury." He named a village to the east of Coin Forest.

"Whyfore did you visit Lord Hungerford?"

"Horses," Aydin said, volunteering no more.

Rauf rubbed the dark stubble on his chin. "Have you seen the Gypsy woman, Sharai?"

Sharai, the woman who refused his love, his wedding offers. The woman who bedded the wealthy noble for his coin. She, who wouldn't be bought like a horse at auction; he wanted to shove her lofty words down her throat. She, giving herself for wealth like a common whore when she knew Aydin waited for her. Only her.

Aydin swallowed his fury and saw new opportunity. He could tempt Rauf into conscripting Aydin to do the same chore Rauf's father had hired him to do. Double the bounty for the same woman. The count cursed his luck that he was surrounded with Hungerford's hired men and couldn't pursue this potentially lucrative situation.

He shook his head in response to Rauf's question. "Nay. I will see Sharai in two sennights, when we leave England."

"What of my father and horses?"

"He asked me to look for some at the Stourbridge fair."

"That's all?"

"What else could it be? I'm only a Gypsy." If Rauf hadn't annoyed him so much, he might have laughed. He earned much, using that phrase, "only a Gypsy." Foolish Englishmen's vanity.

"Now, if you will excuse us, the night is late, and—"

"It is. Why do you travel so late?"

"I am Gypsy. I travel as well by the light of the moon as the light of the sun."

Rauf hesitated, looking with question at the knights who rode with Aydin. After a moment's hesitation, he nodded. "Good eve, Count Aydin." He uttered the title with disrespect. "And Godspeed."

★ ★ ★ ★ ★

Tabor arrived at Gloucester's quarters at the abbey's manor, a sprawling building made of brownstone quarried from old Roman buildings. He passed the guards at the door and followed the steward inside.

In the solar, the Duchess Eleanor sat near the fire to the left, warding off the chill of the gloomy afternoon. Her green eyes were alert, her features small but sharply formed. Her plucked hair made her forehead fashionably high, and she wore a lace-covered headdress. Her purple brocade gown tucked snugly under her breasts. Sharai would have looked better in it, he thought, but Eleanor wore it well. She was embroidering.

Tabor bowed to her. "Your Grace."

An easy smile pulled at her full lips, and she nodded.

Gloucester sat near the large window to the right, at a table with several books. He wore a cotehardie of stark simplicity, made of simple brown lawn, and one might think England's Councillor was modest, but the collar revealed his vanity and the pleasure he took in his royalty: it stood stiff with pearls and star garnets, and, on each collar tip, a small, exquisitely embroidered red rose.

Curiosity made Tabor wonder what types of books Gloucester read, but he kept his mind on his goal. He must gain Gloucester's concern and understanding. He bowed formally to the handsome prince. "Your Grace."

"Lord Tabor. You look considerably more presentable. The shave and your clothing, they suit you."

Remembering his humiliation in Hungerford, Tabor's face heated. "Thank you, sir."

"I did not expect to see you for a sennight. Why have you come?"

"I apologize for arriving without notice. I brought my armorial chart so you may see the Ellingham lineage, and—"

"I set it for council in London."

Tabor must convince Gloucester of the likely bias of the royal council without casting any shadow on Gloucester, himself. He selected his words with care. "I fear manipulations. Those who would wish to discredit me have political position to do so. I come to you now in hopes to avoid that."

"You think me incapable of hearing facts and judging them?"

"Certainly not. But I cannot be so sure of the rest of the council."

Gloucester shut the book he held and leaned forward. "You suspect the council of being incapable of a fair decision?"

Under his doublet, a trickle of sweat made its way down Tabor's armpit. "There is a Hungerford among them. And an earl whose daughter I refused to wed."

Gloucester laughed.

Tabor waited, desperately searching for a sign that would suggest he should retreat or continue.

The duchess glanced up at Gloucester from her embroidering. She gave Gloucester a knowing smile and returned to her work.

"You do have a way of sabotaging yourself." He crooked a finger to a servant who stood by the stairwell. "Bring Lord Tabor wine," he said, "and for me as well." He gestured to a chair in front of the table. "Sit. Tell me more."

Tabor exhaled. He took his seat, patting the parchment container at his side. "I have brought my letters patent, my family's armorial history dating back ten generations. It was prepared from the heraldic register in London by my scribe, Father Bernard."

"So you wish for me to refuse Hungerford's claim."

"I wish for you to honor King Henry's grant so Coin Forest remains with my family."

"Show me your chart."

Tabor rolled the parchment out on the table.

Gloucester studied it, tapping his finger on the tabletop. "There are claims of servitude."

"The date they mention is March 1270. Physically impossible. Alaric Ellingham died in January of that year," Tabor pointed out.

Gloucester studied the chart. "This looks more than adequate. How could council refute this?"

Tabor thought of the recent defeats Gloucester had suffered. This man knew the dangers, but to protect his pride, Tabor would not refer to them but in the most oblique way. "Politics have been known to rule over fact."

Almost imperceptibly, Gloucester nodded. "That does occur, sometimes."

"You're known to be a fair man, and, as Chief Councillor, only you have the power to decide this."

Gloucester's smile revealed skeptical amusement. "Without council."

Tabor's nerves tensed. He did not want Gloucester to think he was flattering him. Gloucester may be royalty, but what Tabor had come to say was man to man. Tabor looked at him directly, with neither fear nor subservience. "I know your voting record. I know that you champion knowledge and fairness. That is why I'm here."

Gloucester raised his brows and gave a more relaxed smile. "Go on."

Tabor's hopes grew. Gloucester faced intense political pressure from his powerful uncle, Cardinal Beaufort, and lines of loyalty had been drawn in both council and Parliament. Mayhap it would mean something to Gloucester to know that some people appreciated him for his strengths.

"I'll be forever grateful if you help me with this, sir. The people of Coin Forest and Fritham will be beholden, as well."

The last was a not-so-subtle promise that Gloucester could count on future support from Tabor in Parliament.

Gloucester reviewed the armorial chart again, then rolled it up and returned it to its case. He signaled his attendant. "Send my scribe."

Tabor waited in the uncomfortable silence. His future hung on this man's decision. What if Gloucester chose against him? It became difficult to breathe. He sent a prayer to his patron saint Monica and to the Virgin Mary. He thought of Sharai and her frog bones, and the small wish candles. His legs screamed to stand, so he could pace off the pressure, but he could only sit and think about his future and how one man held it all in his hands.

The scribe entered. "Yes, Your Grace?"

"Issue a writ."

The scribe took a chair. His long fingers pulled the wooden stopper from the ink bottle, a smooth movement that reflected experience. He filled his pen and opened his book, looking expectantly to Gloucester.

"Be it recorded that the Ellingham claim to Coin Forest remains valid." He gestured for the scribe to stop.

Gloucester turned to the scribe. "Verify the year of the grant. And note for the record that the Ellingham heirs have passed the test of unfreedom. The alleged servile duty has been proven impossible, in that the claimed incident of servility occurred two months after Alaric Ellingham's death." Gloucester shifted and hoisted his empty goblet, giving a meaningful glance at the servant who stood nearby. "Which, curiously, is the same malady that seems to have afflicted my staff." Responding to Gloucester's allusion, a servant rushed forward to fill his goblet.

Tabor exhaled, his heart lighter by pounds. He thought of his father, and his brother who had died defending Coin Forest. The weight of years of frustration lifted from his shoulders, and relief brought a stinging sensation behind his eyes.

"Here." Gloucester handed the scribe the Ellingham patents and dismissed him.

"Thank you, Your Grace." Coin Forest, his home, the soil of his birthplace, the land of his family would remain with them. The sword and rings banner of their lineage would continue to fly, and his people would finally be safe from the Hungerfords. He, Richard, Baron Tabor, had accomplished this. Feelings assailed him, so strong he almost swooned, and he struggled to keep his voice firm. "My family is indebted to you for your patience and fairness."

"You have proper claim." Business done, Gloucester rose and walked to a food cart, selecting a meat pastry. "Let us finish our wine, and you can tell me why Lady Emilyne is so vile a creature that you cannot bear to wed her."

Tabor pulled himself from his reverie. Another vital issue remained to be resolved. So Marmyl had told Gloucester about the canceled marriage contract. Marmyl would have campaigned for judgment against Tabor. Had Sharai not pressed him . . . Tabor shuddered at the thought of how close he had come to disaster.

Gloucester stopped his pastry in midair. "Well?"

"Lady Emilyne is a lovely young woman, capable and hale."

The duchess paused with her stitches and listened.

Tabor had not thought of having a woman's ear when he met with Gloucester. Eleanor came from a family of no great standing and had married into royalty. Mayhap his story would strike a chord with her. With this, he desperately needed an ally.

"And Emilyne comes from a powerful family," Gloucester said. "What is your objection to her?"

"I have come to love a woman. Very deeply." Tabor glanced at the duke's books. He would use words to convince the duke that his love for Sharai was a noble thing, and marrying Emilyne in the face of that, would be ignoble.

He gestured to the stack of books. "Your library is renowned, as is your patronage of literature. Have you read *A Knight's Tale*, by Geoffrey Chaucer? 'Love is a greater law than any other,' " Tabor quoted.

Gloucester settled in a seat by the fire and rested his chin on his fist. "You fancy romances, do you? Then you'll recall that Chaucer says later in that same work: 'We often desire what brings our own destruction.' "

Undaunted, Tabor continued with his thread of thought. "And your good friend, King James of Scotland, wrote *The Kingis Quair,* about the love of one man for one special woman." While in England the Scottish king met and fell in love with Joan Beaufort, who became his queen.

Eleanor raised a brow. "So you believe in love."

"It has changed me."

The duchess's smile so lighted her face that Tabor's breath caught. 'Twas clear why Gloucester had fallen in love with her.

She set her fabric and hoop aside.

Tabor took the plunge. "The woman I love is a foreigner."

Gloucester crossed his arms. "From where?"

Might as well spill the most damning facts early, Tabor thought. "She's Egyptian."

"From Egypt?"

"Little Egypt, though what difference that is I know not."

"An infidel?"

"Nay. She's a baptized Christian." Tabor presented the silk beads. "I have here the prayer beads she made. She's a talented seamstress."

The Duchess raised her palm. "May I see them?"

Gloucester gave them to her, and she turned the beads over in her hands, studying the invisible seams Sharai had painstakingly stitched.

"Her name is Sharai. The priest at St. Giles taught her letters. My priest at Coin Forest has continued her education, and she is bright and worshipful." Tabor paused. "Lady Emilyne developed a strong dislike for Sharai, and insisted Sharai leave. Much as it pained me to embarrass Lady Emilyne and disappoint Lord Marmyl, for whom I hold great respect, sir, I could not honor her request."

Gloucester leaned back in his chair. "So you seek a wife who will accept your mistress, this Egyptian, Sharai?"

"No, sir."

"You must wed. I shall locate a suitable female, one with tolerance."

Tabor summoned the courage to voice his next request. It would likely anger Gloucester and could endanger the favorable decision Tabor had just won.

He must say it; he must defy the rules of nobility, and, once he spoke, he could not call the words back, and Tabor would be obliged to live with Gloucester's decision.

He swallowed. "I wish to wed Sharai."

The Duchess dropped the prayer beads. They landed with dull thumps on the table.

Gloucester frowned. "You wish to wed a foreigner? From what family comes this Sharai?"

"She has no family."

Gloucester's eyes widened. "An orphan. You wish to wed a commoner?"

"She's no ordinary commoner, sir. She reads and writes, and knows much of commerce with her association with the fair, as capable as any merchant I've met. She could manage the details of a household."

Tabor eased into the next field of thorns. "Lord Marmyl may have told you of sorcery, but 'tis not true. Sharai dabbled in a love spell, but it was innocent. Wishful thinking, as she said, and she has promised to cook no more of such cakes."

The Duchess stood and crossed the room, touching Tabor's arm. "What kind of cakes did she make?" she asked.

"Cherry and walnut, Your Grace."

She raised her thin eyebrows. "And?"

"She says 'tis much like our practice of using a chicken bone to make a wish and break it, hoping to hold the longer end." He took a breath. "She added ground frog bones to the flour. It did not harm me," he added hastily. "She meant only to make me love her. But as I told her, I loved her long before she made that cake."

Eleanor's eyes sparked with interest. "It seems that her love potion has worked quite well. Has she cast any other spells?"

"No spells, truly. She uses herbs for curative purposes. Her people healed me with such when I was seriously wounded during the siege on Coin Forest." Tabor turned to Gloucester. "And that is all, every fact, I swear to you. Might you find to grant me license to—"

"No." Gloucester folded his arms. "This request I must deny you. You are obviously too overwhelmed to think clearly, Tabor."

"Exceptions have been made. Lord Cressener wed his buttery maid, and that was allowed. And Lord Rotherham—"

"Make her your mistress."

"I have considered this carefully, sir. This would be acceptable, and Sharai would be safe, but only when I am with her. Should I leave, her security vanishes. The war with France continues. I want to fight for England, and when I do, I want to leave Sharai in charge of my estates. I do not want to worry about her, leaving her in charge of a wife whose jealousies could lead to mistreatment, even banishment, of the woman I love and the children we will have."

"I will find you a suitable wife who understands this."

"I love Sharai. I will do whatever you wish, sir, but, please—"

"Cease. This Sharai is a foreigner, a commoner, and a sorceress. Have you taken leave of all your senses?"

Anger took hold of Tabor. "I'm neither daft nor wrong. Sharai is a woman, and I love her. Why can it be so right for you but wrong for me?" He strode to the stunned Duchess Eleanor, gesturing with an outstretched arm. "You loved this woman. She was your paramour for years."

The duchess gasped. Gloucester had taken Eleanor, one of Jacqueline of Hainault's ladies in waiting, as his mistress long before Gloucester's first wedding was annulled.

"I mean no insult, Your Grace, just that you were a mistress, and you both loved each other and can understand the limitations and dangers of that position. You both know, yet you refuse to grant this simple request."

Gloucester rose, his face red. "Lord Tabor—"

"She is Christian. She is bright and loving and good."

"Cease." Eyes narrowed, Gloucester signaled to the guards.

They closed in swiftly, pulling Tabor's arms behind his back.

His nostrils flared, Gloucester approached Tabor. "In the future, Lord Tabor, rein your passions before taking audience with me. And speak no more of this foreigner. Is this sufficiently clear?"

Tabor's heart raced. He turned to Eleanor.

"Madam, I meant no insult. What the two of you share is special. Please understand. I know you do."

Gloucester linked Eleanor's arm in his and turned away from him. "Our business is concluded." He nodded to the guards. "Remove him."

CHAPTER SIXTEEN

Outside, the misty rain cooled Tabor's face. He walked the crowded Stall Street, past the cemetery.

From among the tombstones Sir Cyrill emerged. The tension in Cyrill's face showed how tethered he was to the outcome of the meeting. "How was it?"

"It went well."

Cyrill frowned. "Then why do you look like you lost all?"

Tabor sensed he was being followed and glanced behind.

The stranger Tabor had bumped into earlier at the King's Palace walked slowly, about thirty paces behind them.

Coincidence? Mayhap, but Tabor wasn't taking any chances. He made a subtle tip of his head to Cyrill, and they turned left, taking a narrow road between graveyard sections. The high tombstones of long-departed monks and lords seemed to march past them as they walked. "Gloucester ruled in our favor. Coin Forest is no longer at risk."

Cyrill eyes grew misty, and his grey mustache rose above a broad smile. "Splendid, Tabor." He slapped Tabor soundly on the arm. "Well done, my lord. Well done!"

A hollow happiness churned in Tabor, much as it had in France when he had lost three knights in the battle but two had survived. He tried to smile, to stir enthusiasm to match Cyrill's delight, but could muster none.

His mother would react this way, too, Tabor knew. She would dance in relief, as would the townspeople. Father Bernard would sagely nod, eyes twinkling. Sharai's marvelous eyes would be wide with joy, and she would bound into his arms. She loved Coin Forest, and with this decision, she could stay.

Cyrill punched Tabor in the arm. "Be of good cheer, my lord. You've saved Coin Forest, using the very approach through which Hungerford tried to destroy you. You have won." Cyrill's smile faded. "What is it?"

Tabor summoned a smile. "Nothing. We have won."

They returned to Stall Street. Just before the cathedral they reached the King's Bath, the largest of the medicinal hot springs. Steam rose from the walls separating the baths from the dressing rooms. A sharp, metallic smell filled the air, along with the hint of an acrid odor that reminded Tabor of rotten eggs.

Cyrill rubbed the small of his back. "I'll soak until I thaw the cold out of these old bones."

They stated their names and titles at the gate and gained entrance.

In the open-air dressing hall, some dozen men clustered, preparing to enter the baths. Monks circulated among the men, checking for inflamed glands in the groin, armpit, or neck.

One of them approached Tabor. "Have you been in London during the last fortnight?"

"Nay, but I've heard of the deaths."

"Have you been experiencing any headaches, or sickness to the stomach?"

"Nay." Tabor removed his collar, doublet, and hose, lifting his arms to make it easier for the monks to check him for early signs of plague. "Have you found any cases?" He avoided using the dark word, as if not voicing it might somehow keep its horrors from his door.

The monk offered a towel. "No. But we must be alert."

Tabor nodded.

The monk led them past the larger King's Bath to the smaller

Mill bath, closed from public view and reserved for royalty and nobility. Enclosed from the elements, Mill Bath offered comfortable seating and privacy under chambered arches.

Tabor selected a seat in the farthest corner and eased into the hot water. Streams of hot water flowed around his body, bubbling its mysterious blend of healing properties into his skin and lungs.

Cyrill settled in, groaning with pleasure, and moments passed. "What did Gloucester say?"

"That Sharai may be my mistress, but not my wife."

Cyrill's eyes widened. "You asked Gloucester for license to wed her?"

"Aye."

"Sweet saints, Tabor. Why?"

"To spare her the indignity and dangers of being a mistress." Tabor had never thought about the plight of mistresses, but with Sharai the customs seemed unfair and even perilous. Mistresses were required to step aside while the wife socialized with the nobility. Sharai would need to sit at the low tables, subjugated, when in fact her faith was part of the reason he succeeded in saving Coin Forest. She deserved more.

"So her pride will suffer. 'Tis not too high a price to pay for love."

"There are more serious problems. Look at Lady Emilyne's reaction. She would have sent Sharai away. As my wife, she would have the power to do so."

Cyrill laughed. "Against your will, Tabor? I doubt it. Some mistresses hold considerable power. Some of times more power than the wife. Look at Lord Drayton and his mistress."

"Aye, but he's too feeble to fight for the crown. He need not leave for battle. The biggest danger will be when I leave, for then, clearly, Lady Tabor, whoever she may be, can decide Sharai's fate in my absence. She will be superior in church and legal instances."

"So Sharai must learn her place. 'Tis not so bad. Better than living in a tent, eh?"

"In my absence, my wife can imprison Sharai. Send her, and our children, away. This is not the security Sharai needs. Do you know what is so sad, Cyrill?"

"Frankly, no."

"I cannot marry her. A penniless commoner can offer her more than I can."

"It is the way of the world, my lord. Some things you can change, some you cannot."

Silence fell between them. Tabor watched the steam rise, lifting from the water's surface, thinning, then disappearing, along with his hopes.

What choices did he have? Unlike Gloucester, Tabor could not bend the law to suit him. If he defied Gloucester, he would, in effect, turn tenancy of Coin Forest back to the crown and face imprisonment.

He thought of Sharai, her eyes full of hope. He had fulfilled his duty to his family and Coin Forest, and for that he was grateful, but, in what mattered most to him, he had failed.

Lord Hungerford entered the stables, where his favored messenger, George, waited, holding the reins to Shaker's brother, Saran.

Hungerford patted the Arabian, stroking his white, feather-groomed mane. Saran was a magnificent champion, and Hungerford wasn't about to let the seedy Gypsy have him. But he would send him to London to retain the appearance of good faith, just in case the Gypsy had spies.

He nodded to George. "You're ready to travel, then?"

George shifted weight on his long legs, and his Adam's apple bobbed on his skinny neck when he swallowed. "Aye, my lord. I'll take the horse and these papers to your London house. Once there, I'll deliver the letter to your seneschal, and then wait for your further instructions."

Hungerford nodded. The letter outlined his instructions to hire dancers and jongleurs for a party. He slapped George's bony shoulders in affection. He was a good son, better than Rauf, really. A pity he was a bastard, his mother a long-ago chambermaid to his wife, rest her soul. "Go you now with the horses and men to the field house, two miles north. Depart from there an hour before first light on the morrow. Quietly." He did not want George and his party waking Rauf.

George led the stallion away.

Hungerford admired Saran's spirited gait. This would go smoothly. He knew his legal proof was murky, that his chances of ousting Tabor were slim, so Hungerford schemed over an expanded plan. The hired knights with Aydin would keep him informed of the count's progress, and, if the sneaky little man tried to break their agreement any time after he collected Sharai, they were instructed to kill him. The hired knights knew to take only one specific route from Coin Forest to London, one on which Hungerford had planted reinforcements at intervals along the way to surprise Lord Tabor as he pursued her.

If Tabor died, his death would appear to have come at the hand of a Gypsy, angered that Tabor would try to steal his woman from her tribe. And if Tabor survived all obstacles on the way to London, Hungerford had plans for him there, too.

All this was possible because Tabor had been dull enough to refuse Lady Emilyne. But who would have thought Tabor would deny Lord Marmyl over a Gypsy woman? Hungerford shook his head with a smile, appreciating his good fortune.

Count Aydin and his men cleared the hill, and Coin Forest

Castle came into view. The fields were ripe with grain, flax, and beans, still wet from the fitful light rains that fell from a mixed sky. The small castle shone golden in a shaft of afternoon sun, a jewel in the broad meadow, surrounded by gently rolling, forested hills.

Sir Geoffrey, a grizzled man of his late thirties, had assumed the role of spokesman for the muscled bunch of knights Hungerford had lent him. He halted his horse next to Aydin and whistled softly. "Impressive."

Aye, Aydin thought. Sharai has been living in comfort. No wonder she'd scorned his new wagon. Aydin gave a short laugh in response to Geoffrey's admiration. "Land husbandry is fine work if it amuses you to watch grass grow."

They traveled on a path that ran adjacent to a thick hedgerow, on the other side of which a sizeable herd of sheep grazed. Aydin eyed the full shanks and legs, thinking of feasts for his tribe, and then grew embarrassed at his thoughts. He was entering Coin Forest with a fine retinue of knights, not limping in with timeworn wagons behind him. He would not steal from Tabor. He could procure a lamb anywhere, and Sharai was his, not Tabor's.

He thought of her lovely breasts, the silken smoothness of her skin, the demure cast of her eyes. He shifted in his saddle, hungry for the sight of her, for a slim, ragged hope still lingered that the ugly rumors were perhaps, after all, not true. Sir Geoffrey angled his horse to the right. "Follow this path to the left so we can enter more on the village side, out of view of their watchtower."

Aydin hesitated. He wanted to ride in with his knights in full view. He wanted the horns to be sounded, needed Sharai to see him approaching with fine horses and well-equipped, armored men at his command. He sat straight in the saddle, assuming an air of authority. Geoffrey may lead the other knights, but Count

Aydin led the party. "I would approach in full view, not like some thief."

Geoffrey hesitated, glanced toward the castle, then nodded and reigned his horse toward Aydin. " 'Tis better, I agree."

"Do you own such property as this in Little Egypt?"

Aydin nodded. He had told Geoffrey the standard tale, crafted to draw sympathy and support from the Christian nobility. Aydin was, like them, a nobleman, traveling on pilgrimage for seven years by order of the pope. "I miss it dearly, but can't return for two more summers. We leave for the continent soon, and I dread the trip. The weather at Dover is most unpredictable, and many of my people become ill making the crossing." Aydin had been one of the few Gypsies brave enough to take that journey, and he made it a point to keep England's hospitality a secret to any Gypsies in France who might follow him over should he brag. The fewer Gypsies here, the more opportunity and coin for him.

Unlike the French, the English made his people welcome, even gave them alms.

Several hundred yards in front of the village, Geoffrey dismounted under an old oak tree and spread a map on his horse's back.

Aydin dismounted and held one end of the parchment. A map of the castle.

The others joined him.

Sir Geoffrey pointed to the center of the map. "Here's the main entrance. Munitions here, guard tower, another guard tower. Here to the left, a secret tunnel leading from the armory to just past the church. It collapsed from rainfall last year but has recently been repaired. It lets out here, by the church."

Aydin studied the complicated sketch. "Impressive detail."

Geoffrey nodded. "Hungerford is quite familiar with Coin Forest. Rauf was born here."

"How can that be? He's Tabor's enemy," Aydin said.

"The Hungerford family owned the castle at one time," Geoffrey said. "But the king giveth, and the king taketh away."

The knights nodded, sharing smug smiles, likely amused to hear of a nobleman's frustrated fortune.

"And the king gave it to Tabor's family, the Ellinghams," Geoffrey said.

"Why," Aydin asked.

"Because the king said so." The shorter knight nudged Aydin in the ribs. "I hear you're a king in Little Egypt, so you know how these land grants go, don't you, your majesty?"

The knights laughed.

Aydin glared at the shorter knight.

Geoffrey noticed. "All right. That's enough. Point is, there are no secrets in this castle."

Aydin shrugged off their teasing. He would tend to his business. The castle may hold no secrets, but Aydin did. Notwithstanding the tempting Arabian horse or the foolish lord's ring, once he gained possession of Sharai, he would not be letting her go again.

Aydin and his knights entered the village, passed the large market area now quiet in the early evening. People cast Aydin looks of curiosity and respect. Even peasants knew the significance of the fine destrier and the well-armored men who rode with him. Pleasant, well-fed villagers, not emaciated like some he'd seen in France, devastated by the war.

But that war meant no more than the feud between Tabor and the Hungerfords, except where it served his purpose, and Hungerford had certainly done that, enabling him to rescue Sharai.

Guards in the watchtower sounded their horns and Sir Geoffrey, riding just ahead, answered. Aydin sat tall, thrusting his chest out and adjusting his cloak so it flowed smoothly over the saddle. He was within yards of Sharai now, and his pulse quickened. She was skittish but could be softened with the right words. He would claim her before the *Gorgio* Tabor did.

They crossed the drawbridge, stopping at the first watchtower. Four guards blocked their path, and the knights posted above stood ready.

"From whence do you hail, and what brings you?"

Aydin gave an easy smile. "Count Aydin of Little Egypt. We have come from St. Giles to see Sharai the seamstress."

Matching their number, seven knights met them in the bailey and escorted Aydin and his knights inside. "Lady Anne would see you in the great hall," said the head knight.

Aydin glanced at him, certain he had misheard. "Lady Anne?"

"Aye. Lord Tabor's mother, and chatelaine in Lord Tabor's absence."

Sir Geoffrey appeared as surprised as Aydin. Their task had just become simpler. At the worst, they could simply smuggle the young girl, Kadriya, over the curtain and Sharai would willingly follow.

Aydin dismounted and with his men, followed a guard into the great hall, where servants were preparing for supper, unstacking tables, lighting torches and draping the high table in fine ivory and green linen. A large tapestry filled the far wall, its workmanship so fine that Aydin had to force himself to look away lest he appear to be a gaping fool.

Lady Anne approached them, wearing a gown of blue silk, finely pleated under her breasts, the hue of the fabric perfectly matching her eyes. A puffy-faced woman of age, she had plucked the life out of her eyebrows, a queer habit of the nobility, here and on the continent. Her lace headdress covered thick, dark brown hair barely touched with grey. She appraised Aydin from head to foot, clearly noting the quality of his clothes, for her smile widened after her survey. "Welcome, Count Aydin."

Aydin took her hand, kissing it with flourish. "Thank you, Lady Anne. I hope we have not disturbed you."

"Certainly not." She guided him toward a staircase, then stopped and turned to Aydin's knights, stopping them with a gesture. "Please make yourselves comfortable." She signaled to a tall, red-haired woman who was turning the last of the lower tables upright. "Maud, see that our guests get food and drink after their journey."

Maud gave Geoffrey a frank appraisal and winked. "Aye, my Lady. Most specially this green-eyed knight."

Lady Anne's mouth twisted in exasperation. "Food, Maud. Food." She gave a smile to Aydin's knights. "Pray excuse us."

Aydin's confidence waned. Was it a trap? Why would Tabor's mother want to speak with him privately? Aydin was not particularly comfortable with older women. They always seemed taller than him, regardless of their height. And this one was a privileged noblewoman.

Two tall tables lined one wall of the solar, piled high with bolts of fabric. She led Aydin to the other side of the room, took a cushioned chair and gestured for him to take another.

"I am so glad you have come to see Sharai." She straightened her headdress. "I'm concerned for her safety."

Aydin's gut tightened. "Why?"

Her sparse brows furrowed. "How well do you know her?"

Any remnants of comfort fled. "She is a good Gypsy girl."

"She's in danger here. She delves into the black arts and has put a spell on Lord Tabor."

He gritted his teeth. How many times had he told Sharai, and all his tribe members: the English were suspicious of any actions unlike their own. To survive, they must assume the behavior of those among whom they currently lived. *Fie!* "She is but a simple Gypsy girl. She may sings songs, of a sort, but she is no witch, my lady."

"She mixes strange herbs. She put her evil eye on one of our lambs and it died in her arms. And she chanted a frog-bone spell on Lord Tabor. I swear, this is not tongue-wagging. I heard her chanting with my own ears."

Frog bones. Sharai had woven a love spell for the rich *Gorgio.* Aydin's stomach turned. After all he had done for her.

"Did you not hear me, Count Aydin?"

Anger burned, hot, behind his eyes.

"Her work is done, and we've paid handsomely for her services. Can you not take her with you now, back to St. Giles?"

Oh, ho, this was too fine. He could profit from both sides of this coin. He feigned bewilderment. "How can I, without speaking with Lord Tabor?" He paused to make his next question sound casual. "Where is he?"

Lady Anne hesitated, then raised her chin. "I don't know, but I assure you, in his absence I can, and am dismissing her. But she has a sennight more to fulfill."

Lady Anne rose and walked to the window, giving Aydin her back. "Her presence has created serious problems for Tabor." She sighed audibly. "The girl visits his chamber every night, Count Aydin."

Speechless, Aydin blinked. The rumors were true. He would kill both of them.

"My son has become so distracted that he's abandoned his duties to his demesne, to his king."

Lady Anne turned, offering him a weak smile. "I worry for my son, and with her sorcery, I fear for her safety as well." Her smile faded. "Count Aydin? Are you all right?"

She has lain with him. Aydin discarded thoughts of money. She would suffer for wounding him like this, oh, yes. He took a deep breath and shook his head. "I am distressed to hear this, and I apologize for Sharai's behavior. Of course. I will take her. Please bring her to me, now."

CHAPTER SEVENTEEN

Kadriya answered the knock at their chamber door, and Lady Anne entered. "You have a visitor. In the solar."

Sharai noted the smugness in Lady Anne's voice, and alarm tingled up her spine. "Who is it?"

"One of *your* kind, dear. A finely dressed Egyptian. Your king, he said. Count Aydin."

Sharai's heart raced. Was Etti ill? There must be trouble. She hurried with Kadriya, following Lady Anne down the steps.

Lady Anne left them at the base of the stairs leading to the solar.

Count Aydin rose to greet them. "Sharai." He studied her, his eyes cold and flat, chest thrust out, a sweating, glowering image from her past. He reminded her of her vulnerability, of the tenuous security she had held in her old life at the fairs, under the thumb of this needy man, determined to possess her against her will. Her newfound freedom vanished under his cold stare. "Count Aydin."

Aydin glanced at Kadriya. "You will wait downstairs while I talk with Sharai."

"Nay."

His eyes glistened with menace. "Tell her."

"Just go down to the base of the stairs, Sprig. It's all right."

Kadriya tugged at her earring. Did Sharai feel safe?

Sharai tugged her earring in response, telling Kadriya, for the first time, a lie.

Kadriya shuffled down the steps.

Aydin reached a hand out and stroked her face. "You are as lovely as ever. Have they been treating you well?"

Sharai withdrew enough to avoid his touch but not so much as to insult him. "I am fine. You need not worry."

"But I do." He took her arm, and she tried to pull away.

He grabbed the loop of her earring and tore it downward, ripping it out of her ear.

She gasped. Her hand flew to her ear, but it was too late. He held the earring in his hand. She touched her shredded earlobe and tried unsuccessfully to escape his grip.

"You have sewn well for Lady Anne. Unfortunately, she tells me that you've done more than sew. You've been mixing herbs." His face grew dark, and he jerked her toward him. "Baking cakes for Tabor."

He slammed her against his chest. His dank breath reached her, with its dark, unpleasant smell, and she could feel the heat of his fury in the tight muscles of his arm, in the quick pace of his breath. "You've been dancing for him."

Sharai's mind raced. Sweet saints, what could she do? His fury frightened her, but Lady Anne . . . She glanced at the stairwell. Would she help? Certes, Father Bernard would.

She needed time to reach him. She forced her voice to be calm. "Let me go."

Aydin grabbed her braids, jerking her head back. "You sleep with him. You betray me. Lady Anne herself has requested you come with me this night. Back to St. Giles. You are not welcome here."

She must create doubt, delay him. She buckled her knees and fell backward.

Off balance, Aydin released her braids.

Sharai rolled away from him and pulled her dagger, thrusting it toward his face.

Aydin stopped.

She gave him an affronted look. "Must you believe all you hear, Aydin? I thought you smarter than that."

"You are not his whore?"

"I have been honorable," she lied, hoping for a chance to see Father Bernard and avoid the risk of Kadriya falling into Aydin's hands. "Lady Anne hates all *Rom*. I mixed herbs for remedy of pain, and they think the worst."

Aydin straightened, clearly wanting to believe her, blinking in confusion.

She moved quickly to the stairwell before he recovered, then spun around to face him. "I do not stay where I am not welcome. Kadriya and I shall pack our things." She skimmed down the stairwell, her heart banging against her ribs.

Kadriya met her gaze then noticed her bloodied gown. Fear widened her eyes, and she grabbed Sharai's hand.

"Come, Sprig. We must run." They raced to the main door, where some unknown knights gathered. "Move aside," Sharai shouted in her most authoritative voice.

The guards glanced at each other, and, in the confusion, Sharai and Kadriya brushed past them.

"Stop them." Lady Anne's voice sounded, shrill, behind them.

The guards rushed forward but their armor slowed them.

Sharai and Kadriya widened their lead, taking running leaps toward the church. Father Bernard would help them. Sharai would not allow Lady Anne to do this.

Three guards appeared in the growing darkness, stopping Sharai and Kadriya before they could reach Father Bernard. Maud and Britta and a cluster of other maids and servants gathered behind the guards.

Fine, then. I will find the right words.

Lady Anne caught up with them, panting. "The priest cannot help you, Sharai."

She met Lady Anne's eyes. "You defy your son's wishes. And Father Bernard's. He will not permit me to leave. He—"

"He has no say in the matter, you foolish girl. He has been detained for the evening."

"What have you done to him?"

"He is busy in the village with more pressing matters. I will have your trunk sent down to the bailey. You will leave us now."

"You can't do this. I love your son and he loves me."

"You little tart. You would destroy him."

Sharai looked to Maud for support, but Maud's eyes were filled with fear and regret. If Maud defied Lady Anne, her future at Coin Forest would be short-lived.

Lady Anne forged on. "Your presence weakens him in the parish, in the courts, and with the king. You do not grasp the influence of the king's court." Lady Anne tilted her head. "You probably don't even know the parish influence." Her brows arched with a look of superficial pity. "Do you even know what a parish is, dear?"

Sharai's face grew hot. She knew a parish was a division of church, similar to individual tribes within one city, but she didn't know of Lady Anne's reference to influence. Sharai felt diminished under the noblewoman's scrutiny, like that morn standing before Lady Emilyne, being painfully aware of her shortcomings. How could she have ever thought she'd gain acceptance here? "I may not know about the parish, but I know what Tabor feels. You care naught for him, only for your comfort."

Lady Anne's eyes narrowed. " 'Tis you who seek wealth and station. You're a clever girl, Sharai. Do you not see, in your heart, that if you leave, Tabor's woes will end?"

"He loves me. I follow his wishes, not yours."

"And did you promise that you would stay, even if it meant destroying everything he loves? That's right, Sharai, he loves other things besides you. He loves Coin Forest. Do you not see it in his eyes?" Lady Anne scanned the servants behind her. "He loves his family, and he loves the people here. He has worked so hard to save them, and you'll make him lose it all if you stay."

Anne's voice softened. "You're not English. Go back to your Gypsies. Take this." She held out a bag bulging with coins. "Forsooth, it's what you wanted all along. Leave this night. For Tabor's sake."

The purse dangled from Lady Anne's white hand, a red bag Sharai had sewn. It swayed gently, taunting her. It was what had lured her to Tabor initially. What she had wanted so desperately. Security.

It pierced her with guilt, as surely as Lady Anne's words had.

She saw Tabor's face in her mind, the warmth of his brown eyes, the depths of passion and love, and a dull ache of despair overwhelmed her. To save Tabor from ruin, she must leave him.

Her vision became blurred, and Sharai swung her arm at the bag, knocking it out of Lady Anne's hand. It landed with a metallic chink on the bare ground a yard from her feet. "This is not what I want." The words came out in a strangled sob. "You do not know me."

Count Aydin stepped out from behind Lady Anne. "But I do." His mouth was contorted with anger, his eyes raw with pain hardening to contempt.

He had heard all.

Aydin grabbed her arm. "Come."

Kadriya rushed forward, kicking Aydin in the shin. "Let go of her. We don't want to go with you."

"No, Kadriya." Sharai stepped toward her.

Aydin signaled to one of the knights, who picked Kadriya up like a bag of grain.

Kadriya screamed and kicked, trying to free herself.

Too late, too late. We stayed too long. Fear weakened Sharai's legs and she turned in desperation to Tabor's mother. Lady Anne thought her selfish and greedy, but surely she would not force them to leave with Aydin. She swallowed in terror. "Lady Anne, please. I vow we'll leave, but prithee, do not send us with the count." She touched her bleeding ear, proof of Aydin's brutality. "Father Bernard can help me. We can go to a convent."

Lady Anne laughed. "With no dowry?"

Sharai looked at the discarded bag of coins. "Very well. I'll accept your money and give it to the abbess."

"Nay." Count Aydin pulled her along with him and retrieved the bag of money. He lowered his voice. "Resist, and we'll kill Kadriya." He lifted the bag of coins and spoke louder. "Your tribe needs this money, Sharai, and we need you back, with us." He led her toward the drawbridge. "My thanks to you, Lady Anne, for your generosity. Good Eve."

Aydin wiped the rain out of his eyes. Sir Geoffrey said they must ride at least seven more miles to reach the country manor where they'd find shelter and food. He lifted his shoulders, squirming. The fine drizzle had penetrated the collar of his cloak, soaking his neck and upper back.

His hips ached from straddling the wide back of the powerful destrier, and Aydin held wistful thoughts of the compact ponies used by his tribe.

Ahead, Sir Geoffrey held the reins of Sharai's horse. Aydin should be the one to hold them, but Geoffrey mumbled something about convenience in travel and denied him. Another knight carried Kadriya on his horse. Somewhere after the drawbridge at Coin Forest, Aydin had lost control.

He cursed his poor judgment at trusting Hungerford. *The swine.* He'd so enraged Aydin with the chamber dancing rumors that he hadn't thought clearly.

At first Aydin worried they'd try to kill him, but they had

covered a fair distance without attempting to do so. Aydin took it as a new clue: whatever Hungerford's plans were, it benefited him to keep Aydin alive.

This encouraged him. He would pick his time, take Sharai, and go. He'd punish her for whoring with Tabor. She would see her error and come to love him. *Him!*

He noted the smile Sir Geoffrey gave Sharai as he led her horse around a fallen tree on the path. He must escape with her before morn's first light.

Lord Hungerford cut the apple on the stall door and offered Shaker a quarter, being cautious to keep his hand flat.

The Arabian took the treat, lipping the palm of his hand, a snort of hot breath and a soft tickle on his skin that brought back a fleeting joy of childhood, when Hungerford received his first horse.

He laughed and rubbed Shaker's forehead. "Good boy, you be a proud one, you."

The stable boy approached, a question in his eyes. "You wish to ride again so late, my lord?"

"Nay. Just want to spend some time with my champion. 'Tis late. Get yourself some supper, boy, before they give it to the dogs."

The boy nodded with a smile. "Yes, my lord." He hurried into the darkness toward the great hall.

Hungerford walked to the tack repair table in the back of the building and settled into the saddler's chair, waiting. He'd received no word since his hired knights had left with the Gypsy, night before last.

Finally he heard a horse approach, then the footfalls of dismount, then a stall door creaking open.

Carrying a curry brush, Hungerford walked back to Shaker.

The young man who arrived wore a brown leather bag with a

white hawk embroidered on its side. He came from the neighboring village, Cadnam, with a message.

Still, Hungerford exercised caution. He passed him and brushed Shaker for several circles, only then venturing contact. "Dismal evening for travel, eh?"

The stranger's green eyes met his. "Aye, and it has begun to rain. But thankfully the bird arrived."

The homing pigeon Aydin had picked up in Cadnam. "Yes?"

He lowered his voice. "The Gypsy left Coin Forest this even, with the woman and the girl. Traveling east."

Hungerford smiled. "Good, good." The wily Gypsy had proven himself capable. He stored the brush on a shelf and reached in his pocket, producing two groats.

"But there is more."

"What?"

"Lord Tabor is gone."

"What do you mean, gone?"

"He left before your knights arrived. Left word with no one, but was last seen heading north and west."

"That cannot be. You have mistaken the message."

"No, my lord." He pulled a small patch of paper from his bag. "Here it is."

The report confirmed his summary. Hungerford gave the silver coins to the young man. "Thank you," he said, dismissing him.

Hungerford collected his cane and walked swiftly toward the great hall. Turning the corner of the stables, he walked into a large form that appeared seemingly from nowhere. He peered in the darkness and recognized the broad shoulders and angry eyes.

Rauf.

CHAPTER EIGHTEEN

Fury claimed Rauf, tensing his jaw and spreading a rash of heat up his neck. He grabbed his father by the collar and pulled him into the darkness between the stable and farrier stalls. "You lied. You do have plans, and you're hiding them from me."

Hungerford slapped his hands away. "Assault me again and you'll rot in the dungeon." Light from the bonfire in the bailey played across his father's features, showing the hard, determined set to his mouth.

Rauf hesitated. This was no time to challenge the old man, here, among his father's garrison and friends. Rauf shoved his rage aside. "Forgive me. But you lied to me."

"Your temper justifies it. I wanted the plan engaged before you botched it, as you did at St. Giles' Fair, five years ago."

Rauf's face heated. "Where is she now?"

"Stay out of it. She's going to London."

"Why?"

"To snare Tabor. If he reaches her before London, Aydin's men will kill him, and he will have died at the hand of a Gypsy while chasing his heathen whore.

"If Tabor doesn't reach her, she'll arrive in London and we'll use her to disgrace him. Blacken her eyes, break her teeth. Drag her in chains and drop her within steps of royal council. Put people on the streets to curse her as a witch." A thin, deliberate smile softened his features. "Herald her as 'Tabor's Trinket.' "

"You old fool."

"The council will see a filthy, dark-skinned foreigner. With those flashing, defiant eyes of hers, who would defend her? And if Tabor tries to save her?" He laughed softly. "It will strip whatever scraps of respectability he still has. Either way, Tabor falls."

"Ridiculous. Tabor fawns over royalty, and he's a parish puppet. He would never risk his standing over a whore."

"Love can change men. Just you watch. He's already refused the Marmyl dowry. Do not gainsay my plan."

"With Tabor gone, your plan is worth spit." Frustration rang in Rauf's ears. "I wanted to go straight forth to Coin Forest and kill the swine, but you said no. Now he's gone. Where do you suppose he is, wise man?"

"Be patient, Rauf, and you will see how smoothly this runs. Regardless of where Tabor is."

Rauf noted the intensity in the old man's eyes. Arguing would not change his mind, but agreeing might buy Rauf the time he needed to organize his forces. He nodded slowly. "Aye. I can see some wisdom in it."

His father's brittle smile softened slightly. "Shake off your doubts, son, and you will see. Coin Forest will be ours again."

Rauf smoothed his father's cotehardie and gave him a gentle slap on the back. He understood, all right. Tabor was gone, and the castle was vulnerable. While his father had been busy, weaving his complex plans, Rauf had been occupied, too, extracting oaths of loyalty from select knights of the Hungerford garrison. He'd secured oaths from the youngest, strongest knights.

They were hungry for a fight, and so was he. The thrill of contest pulsed hot beneath Rauf's skin, and he shuddered from its power. Before the sun's rays warmed the earth again, his hand-picked knights would be marching with him to Coin Forest.

★ ★ ★ ★ ★

Sharai, Kadriya, Aydin, and the six knights arrived at a small country manor well before dawn's light. Sharai shivered in the damp cold. The manor, a crumbling structure with a great hall a third the size of Coin Forest's and a half-dozen small chambers above-stairs, was covered with an aging thatched roof that in its weakness let water trickle through in steady streams.

A dark, bewhiskered man in a rumpled brown tunic had introduced himself as Samuel and led Sharai, Kadriya, Aydin, and two knights to the last chamber in the upper hall, a mean, grey room with a sagging bed and a gaping, dead fireplace. Samuel left, closing the door behind him.

Aydin took Sharai's hand and nodded to the knight named Geoffrey. "Take Kadriya and leave us." All expression had left Aydin's face.

Kadriya shrank from Geoffrey. "Nay. I stay with Sharai."

Aydin dropped Sharai's hand and grabbed Kadriya by the shoulders. "You will obey your king." His voice ground out, raw as a winter's wind.

Sharai rushed forward to pull him from Kadriya. "Let her go!"

The short knight grabbed Sharai's arm and jerked her back.

Kadriya gasped, her eyes flitting to Sharai in question.

Sharai must grant Aydin his wish to be alone with her, or Kadriya would be hurt defying him. " 'Tis all right, Sprig. We need to talk. About Etti," she finished weakly, trying to find a topic they would reasonably pursue.

Kadriya stopped struggling.

Sharai reached up to pull her earring, but grasped only air. Of course. Aydin had ripped it out of her lobe.

Kadriya saw the gesture, and realization of what they had lost through the course of this night widened her young eyes.

Sharai gave a slight nod. Aydin had stripped her of her dag-

271

ger. Kadriya might still have hers, but they were outnumbered by armed men and could not fight their way out of this. "You must needs obey Count Aydin and leave for a bit, Kadriya. Prithee help in the kitchen. I'll be along."

The look of desperation in Kadriya's eyes tugged at Sharai's heart. "Away with you now, Sprig. Go, and behave." She hoped Kadriya would understand that that meant not using the dagger, if she still had it.

Kadriya allowed herself to be pulled out of the chamber.

Aydin shut the door.

His big chest rose and fell quickly, and all traces of affection were gone from his eyes. Something raw and primitive glowed there.

The air smelled of wet wood, and it filled Sharai's lungs. The years slipped away and she was eight, in Marseilles, being dragged, screaming, as Master Phillip pulled on the ropes that bound her hands together. Her small feet had dragged on the rotted plank of wood that led down from the slave cart, and splinters pierced the soles of her feet. Her footprints, marked with blood, led to the central arena where men placed bids on the Gypsies.

Slave buyers circled the market like hungry hawks. One, a short, thin man with fine clothes and small, mean eyes, approached her. His hands reached for her, and she struggled in vain against the ropes at her wrist and feet, and her throat constricted. Shallow, guttural sounds of terror had escaped from her throat that day.

Now that same sense of helplessness ripped through Sharai. She swallowed the sounds of terror, pushing fear to a place she hoped could hold it. "What did you wish to discuss?"

Aydin traced her cheek with his fingers, then offered her the earring.

She touched her torn earlobe, still throbbing from Kadriya's tentative stitches that mended the torn flesh, and accepted it.

One by one, he lifted her braids from her chest and placed them over her shoulders. "Forgive me, Sharai, for losing my temper."

She cringed. What to say? Neither logic nor honesty had worked before. His eyes were unreadable. "I forgive you."

His fingers curled around her arms, drifting upward.

Her skin crawled.

"I should never have let you go. I missed you so."

In the hall below, Kadriya yelled a curse in Romani, followed by the sounds of a scuffle. Kadriya's young life was threatened by Sharai's failure to leave Coin Forest earlier. Shame weighed on her, but the present held immediate danger. Sharai must pacify him.

Aydin's face drew near and his breath leaked toward her with that familiar odor, hot and tinged with nameless decay.

She forced herself to remain still, just as she had in Marseilles when the mean-eyed slave buyer had touched her. Sweet Lord, she had hoped never to suffer such fear again. She clamped her jaw to keep her arms from pushing him away.

His lips covered hers and he pulled her closer. His lips slid back and forth, and the odor spread, wet, on her mouth.

She fought the dizziness. She would neither encourage nor discourage him, and he might come to his senses. Or be satisfied with a kiss, she thought, panic rising again in her throat, wanting to scream.

He ended the kiss. Warmth had returned to his eyes. His gaze dropped to her breasts and his mouth curved into a smile.

She closed her eyes in a brief prayer. *Saints save me.*

His hands circled her neck, perhaps in warning, then slid to her breasts, kneading them like bread.

The stench from his kiss lingered on her lips, making each breath loathsome. Nausea rose in her throat, and out of necessity she wiped her mouth.

He saw it.

He jerked as if she'd slapped him. Lust left his eyes, and his mouth thinned. He slapped her with the back of his hand. "Whore!"

She backed up two steps, raising her arms in defense.

"You think your noble is better than me? Let us see how he will like you now." He lunged at her.

She put her arms up in defense. "Nay."

He pulled her arms down, pinning them behind her. Pushing his short, wide body against her, he pinned her against the wall. He drew his dagger, shoving the point on her face, just below her cheekbone.

Her heart banged against her chest. Aydin's brother had disfigured his wife, slashed a knife the width of her cheek so that no other man would look at her.

The dagger pricked her skin, and Aydin hovered, dagger poised to slash her flesh, as if undecided.

Immobilized, she could not resist, but she would not give herself to this man. He could scar her, cripple her, kill her, but she would never be his. She was Tabor's. Only. She closed her eyes preparing for the pain.

He made a spitting sound.

Moisture splattered on her face.

Disgusted, she recoiled and banged her head against the wall, wiping the spittle away.

"Harlot! You and your noble. He took you like a bull in the pasture, and you asked for more, didn't you? Whore." He pushed his hips against hers, his hands gripping her neck. "And you refuse to kiss me. I, who gave you bread and mutton. Let you and your orphan ride my ponies. Arranged for your fabrics. Protected you."

His delusion angered her past control. "Wilson protected me, and Etti provided for us. Not you. Etti did it because she loves me."

"Fool. She feeds you because your dancing keeps her in coin. Your rich noble feeds you because he likes to bed you. 'Tis I, only I, who love you." His last words erupted from his gut in a strangled cry. As if cornered, he looked about frantically, then shouted, a loud, guttural release. He pulled her from the wall and grabbed her braids.

She cried out.

He drew his dagger, aiming it just behind her.

Her heart stopped. Her hair! "No!"

"You will learn to obey me, and you . . . will . . . love . . . me!"

Teeth bared, he slashed the dagger against her braids, jerking her hair.

A quick, sharp pain flashed on her scalp, then a sensation of release. "No!"

He was too strong to stop.

He pulled away from her, grasping two shining black braids almost two feet long.

"My hair!" The fantasy of her dance, her liveload. She felt a new wave of sickness. "A pox on you!" She reached behind her neck and grabbed the stump of her hair, just below her ears. "How can I dance like this?"

His lips twisted into a cynical grin. "Indeed." He held out her severed braids.

Knowing more venom could harm Kadriya or herself, she held in the words of hatred, took a deep breath and accepted the braids.

"Now you must help me."

She reeled. "After what you have done? Rot in hell."

A smile played on his mouth then vanished, and he lowered his voice. "If you want to live, you will help us escape."

"Escape? What mean you?"

"Have you not wondered about these knights?"

A chill laced down her spine. "Aye."

"They are Hungerford's."

Rauf. Caught off guard, she froze. "What are you doing with them?"

"I was on my way to Coin Forest when they stopped me. They asked me to come with them to take you from Coin Forest. I know Rauf hates you, and I considered myself fortunate to be able to protect you, so I played along with them, accepting money to lure you away."

His eyes hooded in pain. " 'Twas then that I learned you'd been unfaithful to me. I do everything for you, Sharai. I love you." He paused, waiting for a response from her.

She supposed he did love her, in his own twisted way. "I know that, and I thank you for all you have done."

Her mind raced. If Hungerford wanted her out of Coin Forest, where did he wish her to be? "Where are they taking me?"

"To London. I've saved your life, Sharai. Now we must escape."

Sweet Mary. Aydin was hateful and cruel, but he was trying to protect her from Rauf's knights. "Very well. What do you want me to do?"

Sharai adjusted the scarf that held her shorn hair. The pride she took in her appearance had vanished, replaced with shame and unease.

She sat at one of two tables in the modest great hall. Rain still tormented the old manor, pressing a gloom upon it that the meager fire could not dispel.

Lack of sufficient tapestries made all household sounds echo. From the busy kitchen came noises of the scrape of pots being stirred and exchanged as servants rendered fat in large pots over the fire, and the growl of the tall, wiry dogs she'd seen earlier as they fought for scraps.

Aydin had approached her just before supper. "You must do something to amuse them. Dance."

Sharai's breath caught, and she resisted the impulse to punch him in the eye. Her earlobe festered, hot with pain, and her hair was shorter than most men's. "Cur! I cannot dance without my hair. It would reveal my disgrace."

"Then read their palms."

She glared at him. He was jealous, possessive, and abusive, but he'd saved her life, intercepting these Hungerford knights, putting his own life at risk to save her and Kadriya. She nodded.

He spoke in a whisper. "I'll create a distraction. When I do, react but do not move. Wait until they leave the hall, then run out to the bailey. I'll be waiting."

"What of Kadriya?"

"I have talked with her. She has gone to the Roman highway we passed, a few hundred yards beyond the stable. We'll meet her there."

Caution murmured in her head. "Why should I trust you?"

"These men are Hungerford's knights. I shudder to think what they had planned for you."

Rauf. A flicker of apprehension coursed through her.

"I promised Etti I'd bring you back. I am a Gypsy."

He voiced his last reassuring statement with raw pride. He would insult and abuse her, but he would not kill her. "Aye," she agreed.

And now, her heart beating like a dashing cony in her chest, she entertained these Hungerford knights.

Sharai nodded to Robert, the youngest of Aydin's knights. "Your turn. If you wish to hear your future, that is."

Geoffrey, the oldest knight, gave her a wary glance and

studied his lifeline again, no doubt wondering when he would meet the strange woman Sharai predicted would break his heart. He rose, still inspecting his hand, and gave his seat to Robert.

Robert settled into the chair and offered his hand.

Sharai took it, looked at him through lowered lashes and, working past the bats that flew in her stomach, she assumed the demeanor of her dancing days, distracting him, pulling him from his thoughts of duty. She turned his palm up and brushed it in a light, circular pattern, as if wiping the slate clean to get a better reading, but the touch was intended, too, to create sensations that would fill his mind with things other than duty.

His pulse beat strongly beneath her fingertips. Propped against the stones surrounding the fireplace, two other knights, Jone, a round-faced dumpling of a knight, and Elyas, a leaner one with dented armor, leaned forward, listening. Two others, Alan and Henry, their upper armor stripped off, were settling against the warm stones of the fireplace, drowsy after the heavy supper and ale.

Sharai moved her hands rhythmically in the air, humming lightly, creating an otherworldly atmosphere before the reading to make their hair stand on the backs of their necks in anticipation. She traced her fingernail down his head line, pleased to see him start. She had his full attention. "You hesitate with some decisions, but 'tis because you have strong mental capabilities in battle, and realize a bad decision can be a fatal one."

Robert's eyes warmed and a smile teased at his mouth.

Sharai continued, describing Robert's heart line, lowering her voice so the others leaned in to catch every word, all the while wanting desperately to look up. *Where was Aydin?*

She skimmed her nail on Robert's lifeline. "Unlike the Gypsies, you do not care to travel the world. You must be cautious, because there are shadows."

Robert swallowed audibly. "What kind of shadows?"

" 'Tis a curse that follows you, one that affects your brother and you."

"I have no brother."

"Then one who is close to you, a cousin?"

"Aye, my cousin and I lived in—"

A large clang in the kitchen interrupted him, followed by a splash.

Several women screamed.

Robert jumped up, knocking over his stool.

Geoffrey ran to the kitchen, along with Robert, Jone, and Elyas.

Alan and Henry struggled to their feet, disoriented. "What? What is it?"

A woman broke free from the kitchen, her hair and tunic on fire. Her screams echoed in the hall, and she ran out the door.

Male screams joined the female cries from the kitchen, and fire filled the doorway.

Another woman emerged, her lower gown in flames.

Alan chased her around the room. "Stop running. Stop running!" He caught her and pulled her to the floor, stamping out the flames.

The way was clear. Sharai pushed free from the table and ran.

Henry grabbed her.

Sharai screamed and swung at him, putting her body weight behind it, hitting his unprotected throat.

Releasing her, he grabbed his throat, choking, gasping for air.

Geoffrey appeared from the kitchen, his hair and mustache singed, eyes wide, comprehending Aydin's trick. Seeing Sharai's attempt to flee, he grabbed her skirt.

Sharai fell on the stone floor. Shards of broken reeds punctured her arms. She rolled away. Her skirt ripped, her careful stitches tearing in a loud hiss.

Taken slightly off balance when his grip on her skirt failed, Geoffrey reeled backward.

Sharai grabbed a small footstool and swung it soundly into Geoffrey's groin.

Geoffrey cried out and fell to his knees.

Henry, recovered, closed in.

Sharai flung a handful of mud-soaked reeds in his face and ducked behind the fireplace stonework. She jumped up, her feet slipping on a bare spot of stone, and stumbled out of the hall. Her feet, made nimble by months of dancing, flew down the stairs, giving her a good head start.

She lifted her torn skirt and ran through the bailey, taking earth-swallowing strides.

Enraged, Henry loped behind her, his loose chausses clanging.

Pumping her arms, Sharai took the longest strides she could. Not feeling the muddy earth beneath her feet, she panted for air, sucking it desperately into her lungs, willing her legs to carry her faster.

Other men shouted, and she heard more footfalls behind her.

"*Pen. Pen.*" Aydin's voice, frantic, calling for Sharai in their language. A horse thundered behind her.

Henry grunted, and the sound of a thud and banging armor came from behind.

Aydin's horse must have run into the knight, felling him. Sharai kept running.

Aydin extended his hand.

She slowed and grabbed it, jumping toward him.

Aydin pulled her up in back of him.

She swung her leg over the horse's back, landing with a painful thump behind the saddle. She wrapped her arms around Aydin's torso.

The powerful destrier rushed forward.

"Stop them." Geoffrey cried out from behind. Horses stamped and whinnied loudly, skittish and jumpy from the fire.

Aydin kicked the huge horse beneath them. "Hold on."

She leaned into Aydin and they found the horse's rhythm, flowing with it, absorbing the punishing impacts of its hooves as it galloped.

She glanced behind and saw Sir Geoffrey and two others mounted and taking chase, about two hundred yards behind.

Aydin pushed the destrier with daring and aggression, weaving through groves of trees and taking advantage of the terrain to change direction and remain hidden.

Water splashed in her face. They were following a stream, then a wall of cold air hit her, and the horse slowed. After riding hard for about two miles, they entered a forest.

Aydin stopped and silence fell around them. An occasional plop-plopping of raindrops penetrated the forest canopy. "We lost them." His voice came, breathless.

Sharai straightened, her own breath coming hard. "Now Sprig." She glanced around, trying to find her bearings in the darkness. "Which way is the Roman road where we are to meet her?"

Aydin motioned the horse forward and said nothing.

He continued, deeper into the forest, away from the manor.

She grabbed the collar of his cloak. "What about Kadriya?"

Tabor and Cyrill rode side by side, following the road that lined the outlying fields of his demesne. They had made good time from Bath and would be home before nightfall. Tabor loosed his armor, relieved to be finally free of the Hungerford shadow. He nodded toward the shrubs. "Look at those hedgerows."

"Aye, well trimmed and healthy."

"William the hayward tends them well. I shall give him a

bounty to reward his faithful service."

The fields were thick, the air sweet with ripening grain that promised a great harvest.

It all meant hope. The future, no matter how uncertain, would include Coin Forest, his home.

And Sharai.

Coming closer, the green banners Sharai had sewn came into view, and his heart beat faster. He would see her soon. An image of her enchanting eyes and her stunning hair, curling past her waist, swept over him, and his body responded with a pulse of desire.

Horns sounded from the watchtowers, and Cyrill answered them. Tabor tapped his horse's flanks, pressing him to a run.

They crossed the drawbridge, and Tabor searched for Sharai. Her presence worked magic on him, and the touch of her skin on his kindled a hot, smooth hunger that he minded not suffering.

Lady Anne appeared from the castle entrance and ran to meet him, reaching up to grab his arm. "Tabor. Thank the saints. Where did you go?"

Tabor dismounted. "Bath." He saw no sign of Sharai's dark skin and shining braids. Nor any sign of Kadriya.

Lady Anne's eyes became wide. "You saw Gloucester?"

"Aye." Tabor dropped all pretenses of their conversation and scanned the bailey. "Where's Sharai?"

CHAPTER NINETEEN

Sharai stood in the forest clearing, glaring at Aydin and regretting she'd trusted him. "We can't leave Kadriya!"

Ignoring her, he stepped onto a fallen tree, using it as a step, and mounted the destrier. From the saddle he looked down at her.

"She's a Gypsy—well, at least half. Let her find her own way back to the fair."

A blade of panic sliced Sharai's heart. "She's only seven summers."

Aydin motioned in front of him and offered his hand. "Let's go."

From beyond them came the sound of pounding hooves. Sir Geoffrey and his knights.

Sharai jumped up, mounting in back of Aydin, and he spurred the horse to a run.

She and Aydin burst from the forest, branches whipping at their faces, and their horse churned through a muddy, fallow field. They dodged under a copse of willows, and the ground sloped to a wide, fast-flowing river.

Aydin uttered a string of Romani curses and reined to a stop.

Geoffrey and the others followed, just fifty yards behind. Sharai shook him. "What are you doing? Let's go."

Aydin's face blanched. "I cannot swim."

"The horse can." Sharai kicked the horse, sending it plunging down the steep bank into the racing water. "Hold on."

The river, swollen from the long rains, rushed through her skirts, taking her breath away.

In front of her, Aydin gasped and tensed.

The horse waded to its chest and lost touch with the bottom and they bobbed in the swift-running current that carried them downstream.

Some thirty yards ahead the river made a sharp turn, churning white with unknown obstacles.

Aydin gasped and clung to the saddle.

"Those logs," Sharai shouted. "Kick them away."

On shore, racing hooves splashed along the left bank. Sir Geoffrey and the others in pursuit.

"They'll trap us at a peaceful stretch." Desperate, Sharai scanned the right riverbank, looking for an easier exit. "There, Aydin." She jabbed him on the shoulder to stir him from fear. "Hold on."

They completed the turn and new portions of the river came into view. The river turned again, falling several feet, tumbling over unseen debris below. "Sweet Mary. Hold on."

A sickening thrill whirled in her stomach. They tossed in the churning water.

The horse ran into a rock. Air rushed out of his lungs, and he squealed.

A huge log bumped Sharai, smashing her leg between the log and the horse.

They dropped into a whirlpool, and the horse lurched onto his left side. Nostrils spewing water, the horse twisted frantically to right itself.

They went under water. Clutching desperately to the saddle, Sharai stayed connected.

The horse righted itself, and Sharai clung to its slippery saddle.

It was empty. "Aydin?"

No answer.

She glanced behind her.

Snared on a gnarly log, Aydin's elegant red cloak rippled silently on the water's surface. Its owner was nowhere to be seen.

Kadriya huddled in a grassy ditch under an arch of the old Roman road. It was quiet now. She inched her head out, searching in all directions for the knights who had been thundering down the road. Not a soul in sight. Absence of the knights was a relief. No sign of Sharai brought shivers of fear.

The fields were untended and sorry with tall weeds amid struggling patches of grain. Overhead, the sun had risen to half its height. In two more bells it would be dinnertime. She pushed her stomach to stop the growling. *No, Kadriya. Think of anything but food.*

The grasses stirred, their dry seedpods chattering secrets and danger. What if Aydin had lied? What if he was escaping from the knights only to have his way with Sharai? He'd hurt her already, and Kadriya did not believe he was protecting them, as he said. Still, Kadriya had relied on him because she had trusted the desperation in his eyes. Better to trust a Gypsy than a bunch of unknown *Gorgio* knights. Even if she was wrong, getting rid of the knights would make it easier for her and Sharai to escape from Aydin later.

She wanted to be safe in her bed at Coin Forest, with the big stone walls and a warm fire. She wanted to hold her dove, stroke its soft feathers, hear it coo. She wanted Sharai to wrap her arms around her and tell her everything was going to be all right.

She had been reassured when she heard all the shouting and saw Sharai and Aydin in his red cloak, racing away from the knights. But they had never come for her, and none of the knights had returned. Had Sharai and Aydin been caught? Or killed?

Kadriya swallowed her panic and blinked her tears away. Something had gone terribly wrong. She must find Sharai.

Emerging from her cool hiding place, Kadriya found her bearings. East and south she would find the fair, but it was at least a whole day's journey from here. She looked west, whence they had come. Tabor and Father Bernard would know what to do. She would make her way to Coin Forest.

Rauf lifted the armor that chafed the skin above his left armpit. Inept armorer. He was supposed to have adjusted it for the weight Rauf had gained. He moved through the bailey in the predawn grey, nodding to the knights on guard, those who, before dawn, would leave their posts and depart with him for Coin Forest. The rains had stopped just after midnight, and the sky had cleared. If the weather held, travel would be easier.

He entered the armory, a small, cluttered building fifty yards from the manor house.

Inside, Joseph the swordsmith waited with a collection of weapons. His brown hair was combed neatly off his face, his beard full and well groomed. "Good morn, my lord."

Rauf nodded, but looked past him to the worktable where two grey flannel wrapped bundles lay. "Are they ready?"

"Aye, and they will please you." He unwrapped a combat sword.

Rauf held the sword, swinging it to test balance, then lunged, striking the target. The blade flexed on impact and penetrated deeply.

Joseph grinned. "See? Look at that flex. Did you even feel a shock?"

"None. Show me the new dagger."

Joseph unrolled the dagger with a flourish. "I thought long

about what you wanted, a dagger capable of causing a double wound with each strike." He offered it to Rauf.

The fifteen-inch dagger had a round pommel and thick handle with a thick cross guard. Nothing worth comment, but the blades—two deadly-looking blades—erupted from the single grip and, two inches from each blade tip, they fanned out to create an inverted V. Rauf whistled. "Very fine."

Joseph beamed. "Aye. See the slight burrs here, and the way the blade begins single at the tip, then triple, with the side blades, like wings? Short, but effective. The burrs are curved to allow easy entry, then here," he indicated a point where the blade joined the cross guard, "here, the blade will not only puncture the flesh but spread it outward, and the burrs will grind the flesh like sausage when you jerk it back out. Here. Try it." He motioned to the right, where he had mounted a squash on the wall, painted with crude eyes, a nose and mouth.

Rauf lifted the clever new weapon, cool and smooth in his hand, and faced the painted squash. "That looks a bit like Tabor's face, does it not?"

Joseph laughed. "Indeed."

A thrill ran through Rauf, the thrill of power, which made the only sense in this world. All else—friendships, love, alliances—would betray or disappoint, but power granted all. Bracing his legs, he thrust the dagger into the squash. It entered smoothly, then spread the flesh of the vegetable, causing it to crack up the forehead. "Aye." Rauf jerked the dagger out, and ragged fragments of the flesh came out with the dagger. "Better than tongue slitting." He plunged the dagger in again. "Die, devil!" The squash splayed, ruptured, and dripped on the floor. Rauf laughed. "Well done." He handed the clever weapon to Joseph.

Swirling the dripping dagger in a bucket of water, Joseph dried it, slid it in a leather sheath, and handed it to Rauf.

Rauf unwrapped it, turning it over repeatedly in his hand.

His eagerness to get to Coin Forest had just increased tenfold.

Lord Hungerford lifted his head off his pillow. His temples throbbed, and his muscles, though always weak, shook from the small effort.

Cook had prepared a special meal yester eve, galantined chicken, with an exotically seasoned stuffing. In a fine mood, Rauf had entertained more than the minstrels, telling tales of Rouen and miming in lewd fashion the Maid of Orleans, the woman who dared to wear armor when he helped deliver her for trial.

Swept away by the feast and good wine, Hungerford enjoyed Rauf's lighter mood, and celebrated far more than he should have.

He could feel it now. Hungerford pulled his bed curtain back and blinked in the harsh sunlight. His legs responded like dead logs, but with the help of his cane, he pulled himself up and opened the shutters all the way. The sun was high. Too high. Guards were at their posts, but the garrison was not on the field. He listened. Nor were they in the hall below-stairs.

Out in the bailey, Lucas, his seneschal, hurried from the stables.

"Lucas," Hungerford called down. "Why are the men not practicing?"

Lucas stopped, holding his palms up in question. "Do you not remember, my lord? You sent Rauf to Fritham."

"God's blood. I did no such thing. Get Sir John to my chamber, posthaste."

Sir John arrived. "My lord?"

"What the devil is Rauf doing at Fritham? Did you approve this?"

"Nay, my lord. 'Twas your decision, I heard."

Hungerford studied his knight. His brown hair was disheveled, and his eyes were bloodshot. "You look terrible."

John nodded. "I feel poorly. My head is pounding."

"So is mine. Did you have trouble rising this morn?"

"Aye, forgive me."

Hungerford waved the apology aside. "I know nothing of Fritham."

"But Rauf said it was your request."

"And you thought not to ask me about it?"

John's brow furrowed. "I overslept, my lord. From the others, I learned that Rauf did not want to wake you."

"Indeed not. He kept the butler busy filling my goblet last night. Yours as well. And all the while he was scheming. Damn." Hungerford banged his cane in frustration.

He called forth a half-dozen wives of the absent knights. After some carefully worded threats, a pretty brown-haired lass revealed Rauf's true purpose, and the others confirmed it.

Coin Forest.

Hungerford ordered them out. *Damnation.* He checked the sky. "How late is it?"

"Nine bells."

"When did they leave?"

"Just before dawn."

"We must stop him. Have the stable boys saddle Shaker, and get the messenger to ride."

Later in the great hall, Hungerford gathered his most trusted knights. "The messenger will reach Rauf by midday."

"But what if he defies you?"

Disappointment lodged in Hungerford's heart. "He will."

Somewhere in his aching head it became clear to him that Rauf, his strongest son, would never inherit. Though brave and fierce and the picture of Hungerford's proud father, Rauf's uncontrollable temper and limited wits made him incapable of fulfilling his destiny. "If he continues to Coin Forest, I vow, I will disinherit him."

John grimaced. "That won't set well with him."

"Aye, but if he attacks Tabor after Gloucester set council to solve this peacefully, Gloucester will have Rauf's head." A new thought chilled him. "Sweet saints, he may have mine, as well."

James, another of his long-loyal knights, shook his head. "Nay. You've shown Gloucester your loyalty and restraint."

"Not so at last council. I supported Beaufort." Sweat rolled down Hungerford's back. Rauf's attack could be catastrophic.

Sinking in the growing muck of the crisis, Hungerford returned to his chamber. With each step he took to pull his tired body up the staircase, one thought repeated itself like a dull throb in his aching temples: *What if Gloucester thinks I'm responsible?*

Hungerford released a long sigh and smoothed the two small squares of parchment. Filling the reservoir with ink, he held the pen, poised, over the paper. Was he saving his skin? He thought of George, his faithful bastard son, and his sister, Margaret. *Margaret, I tried my best,* he said silently to his sister. *Now I must save what's left of our holdings for the Hungerford line.*

He folded the paper and touched pen to it. "To be delivered posthaste to His Grace the Duke of Gloucester, in Bath." Hungerford had no Bath pigeons, so he would send this to his cousin's husband, Burton, assistant mayor of Bristol, just twelve miles from Bath.

He pulled the second square of parchment to him, and his hand shook. He was not long for this world, and he had so hoped that Rauf . . . He dismissed the thought. Within the framework of their birth, all men made their fortunes, and Rauf had rebelled in spite of Hungerford's best efforts. Now Rauf must live with the consequences. "Your Grace," he began, "It grieves me to advise that Rauf, angered at Lord Tabor's insults, left, armed, this morn for Coin Forest. Please be advised he does so without my leave."

He sealed the messages, took a weary swipe at the moisture in his eyes, and worked up the energy to walk to the pigeon cotes and send the message that would doom his son.

Sharai directed Aydin's horse into the shelter of a sprawling old oak tree. Pursued by Hungerford's knights, she had said a quick prayer for Aydin's soul and run the destrier full speed. Following Aydin's example, she took a northerly direction while they might see her, then turned south in the protection of the trees.

Destined for the place they were supposed to have met Kadriya, Sharai had ridden for four miles, following the smoke that lingered from the kitchen fire. The little manor came into view, its thatched roof collapsed over the kitchen. The fire had spread to the small cottages circling the manor. Peasants solemnly scoured the remainders of their homes for valuables, and some dozen men hacked away at the charred timbers, cleaning up.

The destrier balked at approaching the still-smoldering ashes.

Sharai patted its neck to soothe him and then reined him away to the Roman road. The land dipped in a pronounced, narrow valley, cut by a swift-running stream. Over the years, the stream must have changed its direction, for there on the right was an ancient streambed, now overgrown with weeds, over which an arched bridge remained, along with an old road leading south.

She scanned the weed-infested field, looking for a glimpse of the small-framed child she thought of as her own sister. Her heart beat faster of its own accord. She must find her.

After a cautious check to be certain no one had followed her from the manor, she tethered the horse and searched through the high weeds.

"Sprig," she whispered, then became more bold. "Sprig? V*es' tacha,* it's safe. Come out."

She walked cautiously toward the bridge. Mayhap Kadriya had taken shelter there and fallen asleep. Stepping into the dry streambed, she bent down and looked under the arched bridge. 'Twas empty, but the long grasses had been trounced and laid flat, as if someone had been sleeping there. She felt the earth. Cold.

"Who are you?"

A man's even-toned voice sounded behind her.

Startled, Sharai straightened, bumping her head on the low bridge. She scrambled out and up.

A short man dressed in oiled linen from head to toe stood before her. His upper body buzzed with thousands of bees.

Sharai gasped.

From somewhere behind the layer of bees, he regarded her. "What are you doing here?"

Sharai stepped back. "I am no enemy. I'm searching for my sister. My name is Sharai."

"Your skin is dark, like the man who set fire to the manor."

"He held me against my will. Me, and my sister Kadriya. We were to meet here, but I was delayed. Have you seen her? She is this tall," she gestured, indicating Kadriya's height, "And her hair is lighter than mine." She reached for her braids and touched her shorn hair. Her scarf had fallen off and lodged under the saddle. She covered her hair, trying to recover some dignity. "Have you seen her?" she repeated.

"A girl was here."

Sharai's heart skipped. "Curly, brown hair?"

Something had startled the bees, and a few thousand flew away, revealing the man's thin arm.

Sharai gasped and backed away.

"Stay still. I have the queen. They will settle." His voice held a soothing quality. "A young girl was here. She left shortly after dawn."

"Which way?"

"I cannot say. She was clever in her movements. Like you." He moved to a large wicker skep five yards away. He lifted the lid and put his right arm inside, keeping it there.

"Please. Her life is in danger."

He removed his arm from the skep. All but one or two of the bees had left his sleeve. "The fire burned two of our women, one to the point of blindness. Go, before I sound the alarm and they kill you." He emptied his left arm of the remaining bees and closed the skep. Carrying his net and tools, he left her, heading for the burned manor house.

Sharai wanted to cry out, to stop him, to force him to remember which direction Kadriya had gone, but his threat rang in her ears.

She rode out of the small valley to the top of a hill. Gentle hills rolled before her for untold miles, dotted with wildflowers and patches of yellow grain, and bordered with dark hedgerows.

A white bird flew by, and Sharai was reminded of Kadriya's dove. Kadriya. Somewhere out there she wandered, her soul strong with courage but likely scared, right down to her teeth. Muffling a cry, she blinked to clear her vision and pulled from the strength of her vow to Kadriya: *it will be all right.*

"Kadriya. Kadriya," she shouted, trying to purge the panic rising in her chest. She rode the hills, crying out Kadriya's name. "Sprig. Sprig, answer me!"

Gloucester tucked Eleanor's arm more snugly into the crook of his own. Her skin glistened from the moisture of Bath on a hot summer's afternoon. She wore a pale green silk gown that bared her shoulders, right at the point where she liked him to nibble. Her skin was fair and smooth as a pearl. She'd caught his eye when first they met in Hainault, when he was newly wed to Jacqueline—an arranged marriage to a pleasant woman, but a political disaster he was still working through.

After years of calamity, the pope finally annulled the marriage, freeing Gloucester to wed Eleanor and legitimize their children. Now, riding with her in the whirlicote down Stall Street after a midday church service, he noted with pride the admiring glances his lovely wife drew from everyone they passed, not only for her physical beauty but also for her unique mixture of inner strength and charm.

He nudged her. "Elaborate services, weren't they?"

"Aye, though I dare say the monks need more voices. Well, melodic voices, at least."

They both laughed.

She touched her brow. "Will we be staying much longer here? I miss the sun, and an occasional breeze."

Gloucester stroked the special spot on her neck.

The corner of her mouth turned sensually.

He felt himself tighten in response. "A few more days, dear one." However the peace mission at the Congress of Arras turns out, he must gird himself for Bedford's return. His older brother had chafed at Gloucester's power when last he returned home from France, and Gloucester had been busy garnering support to fend off another political attack.

The char stopped with a small jolt at their manor house, and Gloucester helped Eleanor out.

A messenger approached, and Gloucester's knights intercepted.

"Urgent message from Harry, Baron of Hungerford."

Gloucester extended his hand. "Thank you."

He had written Hungerford of his decision to verify Tabor's claim to Coin Forest, but the messenger had not left until late this morn, so Hungerford could not have received it yet. What was he wanting?

He read the message, scrawled in the old schemer's distinctive handwriting. Rauf was attacking Coin Forest.

So the arrogant young sod had defied Gloucester's position as the realm's keeper of the peace. Could it be a plot to embarrass Gloucester at council? Damn the Hungerfords. Angered, he crumpled the note. "Paul, prepare my garrison, all sixty. We ride before dawn to Coin Forest."

Tabor eased his horse closer to his mother and repeated his question. "Where's Sharai?" The afternoon sunlight turned the keep's stones golden, but the tight expressions on the faces of Maud, the buttery maids, and his mother drained the pleasure of his return home.

Lady Anne worried her fingers. "I knew not where you had gone, Tabor. I could not get word to you—"

Tabor dismounted. "Where's is she?"

His mother avoided his eyes. "She returned to her people."

"Her people? What people?"

"The Gypsies. At St. Giles' Fair. Count Aydin came for her."

"Aydin." Cold settled in his gut. "She'd never go with him."

"But she did. Kadriya, too. Her contract was almost complete, so I released her. She really did wish to leave, Tabor."

Panic chewed at Tabor's gut, and he shook his head. "This is wrong. All wrong."

Distress pulled at Maud's features, and she bit her lip.

Tabor strode to Maud. "Did Sharai wish to leave?"

"Aye."

He studied her eyes for a sign. "Forsooth?"

Maud nodded.

Tabor noted her thin lips. She might say more, but not, it seemed, in front of Lady Anne. He turned away from her and handed his reins to the stable boy.

Tabor strode to the church, where Father Bernard waited. "I trust you to tell me the truth, Father. What happened?"

"I was not here. I was called to the village for last rites for the ale master's wife. Childbirth. Both died, bless their souls. By the time I returned, she had gone."

"What did you learn?"

"I've sent word to the priest at St. Giles. He'll let me know when she arrives there."

"Did she leave willingly?"

"From what I was told, she said she wanted to leave, but not with Count Aydin. She wanted to go to a monastery."

"But why? She promised she would wait for me."

"She may have been forced. The count brought knights with him."

"Knights? Whose livery?"

"None, my lord."

"What would a Gypsy be doing with knights?" Alarm coursed through him. "Did they hurt her?"

"Sharai was bleeding, but there are several different stories of how. One said her head had been struck, another swore it was her arm, and Maud says it was her earlobe."

Tabor strode to the kitchen, armor clanging.

Maud was lifting a large kettle to a higher hook above the fire.

He helped her gain the hook and took her shoulders. "What happened last night? The truth, Maud."

Her eyes filled with worry. "Count Aydin arrived, with six knights."

"Armored?"

"Aye."

"Aydin is a Gypsy. He has no knights. Did you recognize any of them?"

"Nay. Strangers, all. The count had words with Sharai in the solar. When she came down, she was hurt. Her ear. She and Kadriya ran to the bailey, where guards stopped them." She lowered her voice. "Lady Anne told her to leave and gave her some money. The count took her coins and they left."

Maud laid her hand on his arm. "She said she loved you and she followed your will, not Lady Anne's or the count's." Her blue eyes were direct. "She did not leave of her own free will."

He imagined Sharai, the fear in her eyes and the stiff set of her spine to disguise it. If only he'd taken her with him. Afraid that her dark skin and bracelets would shout her foreign background, he'd thought it best not to bring her. Worried about appearances, he'd failed to protected her. He spotted a mill bag of flour and punched it. The white stuff fluffed into the air, but did nothing to quell his concern for her safety. Where had Aydin taken her?

He tore through the kitchen, out into the bailey, into the great hall. Ripping his armor loose from the shoulder, he discarded the sleeves as he rushed through, up the stairs to the Lady Anne's chamber. He kicked the door open.

Lady Anne was standing at the window. Her hand went to her throat. "Tabor."

"Spare me the trembling." Tabor opened the trunk at the base of his mother's bed and stripped the chest clean, throwing linen in a wild flurry.

"By the light of heaven. What are you doing, Tabor?"

"Packing for you, Mother. For a long trip."

"Where? Why?"

"You defied my wishes and put the woman I love in danger. You're off to Fritham, posthaste."

"Fritham? 'Tis cramped and humid there. I cannot—"

"You will." Tabor pulled gowns from her wardrobe, stuffing them in the chest. "I'll visit you from time to time to see if you've learned compassion and honesty."

"How dare you? I have done all for you."

"For yourself, mean you. You care more for your social standing than your son. At least your living son."

Lady Anne opened her mouth to speak, but held whatever words she thought of saying. She toyed with the pin on her gown. "I am your mother."

"You're cold, untrustworthy, and care not a jot for me."

"But you leave for London. Who'll watch over Coin Forest?"

"The Hungerford claim is settled. Gloucester ruled in my favor. That surprises you, doesn't it, because William didn't do it. I did. Richard, your worthless son. And I didn't need to sell myself or sacrifice others to do it."

"Oh, Tabor, that is good news. I never thought—"

"Forsooth, you never thought. You released a trusting young woman and an innocent child to a man you knew to be ruthless, all to please Marmyl." Tabor strode to the door.

"Where are you going?"

"To find Sharai, and hope she forgives me for leaving her under your 'care.' "

CHAPTER TWENTY

Maud waited at the door of the mill while Sarah, the miller's wife, collected the flour. The last weak rays of sunlight sifted through the door in soft sprays of gold, making the large grinding wheel glimmer.

Sarah appeared from the storage room, dragging two twenty-pound bags forward, huffing from the effort. "So Lady Anne lied," Sarah said. "Sharai was forced to leave. Does Tabor know the truth?"

"Aye." Maud lowered her eyes. "I can still see Sharai's smile, hear her kind words when I first arrived here. No one's ever done that for me. I should have helped her, but I just stood there with my heart in my shoes."

Sarah patted Maud's arm, her worn face drawn in sympathy. "By rights you were scared. Seven men, and Lady Anne all but pushing them out the gate."

Two tawny kittens scampered in front of Maud, chasing a string that blew in the slight breeze.

Maud picked up the smaller kitten and held it to her breast, stroking its whisper-soft fur, feeling its fragile ribs beneath her fingertips. "I only pray he finds Sharai, and little Kadriya."

Sarah wiped a damp curl from her forehead. "You've seen Tabor in the lists."

"Aye, fierce. Those knights are good as dead."

The kitten watched Maud, his eyes a pale blue, clear as the new world it had entered. New and free, like Maud's second chance in Coin Forest. "I must find a way to help Tabor."

"Small deeds count, Maud. If cook has an empty pantry, this flour will help."

Maud released the kitten and hoisted the bags of flour over her shoulder. "Aye. I can help with the travel breads and pack the cheese."

Sarah made a clucking sound. "What's best, I wonder? That he find Sharai, or not?"

"What mean you. She's a good person."

"But the dead lamb, and the spells—"

"Bite your tongue, Sarah, and pray he finds her unharmed."

Maud spun away, leaving Sarah with her small thoughts, and loaded the cart, pulling it through the village. The tanner had closed his boards for the day, and the butcher had left as well. Dogs combed the area, scratching for dropped morsels, and flies crowded on the blood-drenched ropes that hung from the slaughtering beam, their wings and motion creating the illusion of glistening black poles.

Mary and Libby, alehouse whores Maud had worked with when she first arrived, leaned against a weighing table at the market, currently deserted due to the villagers' scurry to provision Tabor and his knights for their travel. The women waved as she passed.

"Hello, Maudie."

"Good eve, Maud."

Kindness. Generosity. Tabor had brought her to this fine place, and now in his time of trouble Maud could do naught but haul flour. She pushed the cart with renewed vigor. She would deliver her goods swiftly to cook and make a special bundle of dried beef and figs for Tabor. At the least, he would not suffer hunger during his search.

Just past the alehouse, a wavering light caught Maud's eye. Flames licked the corner of the large storage building used to store wool and shelter the horses during storms. "Fire!" she called, dropping the cart handles and running down the street between the alehouse and market shop. "Fire!"

Mary and Libby peeked around the corner, open-mouthed.

The storage building door was open, no animals inside. Where was everyone? The flames grew, racing up the side of the structure. From behind the other closed door a man appeared, hoisting a torch, touching it to the old wood.

Maud pulled a dagger from her thigh. "You there. Stop."

He turned to her, his face calm and deliberate.

The door swung open, revealing three more men. Armored. Dressed in black and white livery.

The tall one cast a sharp, assessing look at Maud.

She hesitated. *Sweet misery. Gurvis Cooper, from Hungerford.* Fear clenched her stomach. *Rauf is here.*

She flung the dagger at Gurvis, piercing his arm.

He cried out and removed the dagger, examining the wound. "Foul wench." He started for Maud.

To the left a dozen archers drew bows, aiming at the top of the north castle wall.

Maud lifted her skirts and ran. Mary and Libby had disappeared.

Maud's heels pounded on the cobblestones, sending shocks up her spine. *Must warn Tabor.* Atop the castle curtain were wall walks where the guards stood watch. They leaned over the top, looking toward the burning storage barn.

"Get down," Maud screamed. "Duck!"

From behind the fishmonger's stall a rain of arrows sprung with a loud whang. Their metal heads pierced the guards' armor and the men fell like broken bottles over the edge, one dropping so far as the moat.

Hungerford's mounted knights rushed out from the market stalls, thundering toward the drawbridge.

Maud shrank back, dreading a glimpse of Rauf.

"An attack. Draw the bridge." A chorus of alarm rang from within the castle curtain.

From the gatehouse, another guard pulled the drawbridge. Its mighty chains rattled and the bridge rose. With a loud clank it stopped abruptly, the bridge poised a foot above the road.

Merchants bringing provisions to the castle dropped their goods and carts, and scattered for cover.

"The portcullis," another guard screamed. The iron gate screeched, then stuttered to a halt half way down.

A guard shouted a string of curses. "They jammed it, too."

A roar filled the air, and a large, burly knight led the charge into the bailey. His big head was armored and decorated with a black and white emblem, his horse's armor colored the same. His bulbous nose poked out of the helmet, and his powerful legs resembled tree trunks as they hugged his destrier.

The legs that had kicked her poor brother as he begged for warmth. *Rauf.* Maud's heart seized. She hid behind a palisade until he passed the curtain, then fought her way through the confused crowd, jumping onto the slightly raised drawbridge and running into the bailey as if the devil himself pursued her. She bounded for the church, hoping to find Father Bernard and learn where Tabor was.

Above her, Tabor's guards filled the wall walks, pumping arrows into Rauf's men. "Stop them." One cried, and another clutched his chest and fell.

Below, several of Rauf's men fell, clasping the arrows that doomed them.

More Hungerford men rushed in. Flames burst from the stable. "The horses. Release them," men cried out. Stable boys opened the gate to the fence that enclosed them. Horses thundered out, eyes bulging, hooves pounding.

Tabor's knights poured down the steps from the great hall.

Yellow hair streaming from his helmet, John led the defense, hacking at the enemy with his sword.

Maud reached the church and pushed through the door. "Father Bernard. Father!" She ran past the rood screen, checking the sacristy. It was empty.

Outside again, Maud stumbled past the pigs, now loosed from the sty. Excited dogs nipped at the pigs' heels. A short mongrel bit a horse's leg in error and paid dearly, filling the air with his cry of pain.

Maud ran toward the kitchen. *Run.*

A warhorse thundered in front of her. Rauf. His sword was bloodied, and he clutched a strange, two-bladed dagger that dripped with blood and human flesh.

Rauf spied her and turned the evil-looking dagger in his hand. "Maud. Time to pay for your treason."

She screamed and pulled another dagger from her calf. *If he tries to take my tongue, I will kill him.*

A Hungerford knight grabbed Maud, stopping her.

Maud turned to Rauf. "What," she taunted. "Be you so cowardly that you need help to down a woman?"

Rauf scowled at his knight. "Let her go."

The knight released Maud.

Rauf pursued, his huge horse pounding the earth.

Maud ran in a rabbit pattern, rushing for the kitchen.

He cut her off.

Desperate, Maud headed for the chicken coop, steering clear of the warhorse before it trampled her.

Rauf jumped on Maud. She crumpled to the ground. The earth punched the air from her lungs, and she lost grip of her dagger.

Rauf rolled with her.

Her dagger lost, Maud screamed, punching his breastplate,

hurting her hands but not Rauf. "Let me go."

The stream water cooled Sharai's throat. She splashed some on her face to cool her bruised cheek and gingerly wet the scrape on her leg. Rising, she wiped her hands on her skirt, then approached the tall warhorse, reaching up to rub his neck. "You've been good to me, Valiant," she soothed in the melodic tone she had learned from her mother, using the name she'd given him in honor of his swim through danger. "Just a jot farther, then it's rest and oats for you." Stepping up on a large fallen log, she slipped her foot into the stirrup and used the pommel to pull herself up onto the saddle.

Her throat was hoarse from calling for Kadriya, but she had never found a trace of her. Mayhap she had found her way safely back to the fair. Sharai would hold that hope for now.

The land had changed in character. Here the fields were more defined, the hedgerows healthy and well trimmed. The golden grain, not yet harvested, stood tall, brushing Sharai's legs as she rode. Her heart beat stronger. *Coin Forest is not far.*

To the west the sun dropped, shooting her last quiver of rays, so weak that the vibrant colors in the hills faded to grey.

"Tabor." Memories of him brought warmth to her heart. The burning interest in his eyes when he saw her on stage, the playful teasing when he pretended to choke on the frog bone. The intoxicating excitement when he told her he needed no cake, and his gentle touch when he found her in the garden. She remembered the passion when he loved her, the joy of their bodies united in love, and heat flashed in her belly, leaving her weak and empty.

Her soul ached, as if a golden thread of love connected them, but the thread had frayed and her wound, neither bleeding nor healing, remained.

Her decision to leave was right, but the harshness of living with it hurt all the way to her bones.

To warn Tabor, she must risk seeing him and summoning her will to leave him again. She could not stay and destroy him.

A breeze swept through the tall grasses, curving them gently in the wind. He loved this land, and she had come to love it, too. Hungerford must not take it. She must warn him and seek Father Bernard's help, one last time, to help her find Kadriya and get them safely to an abbey.

At the top of the next hill she saw the castle, rising high behind the village.

Flames leapt above the buildings, some two hundred yards distant. The bailey fires, would they be so tall so early? A thorn of anxiety pricked her. She urged Valiant into a breathless run down the hill.

Closer, it became clear that there were two fires, one in the village and another in the bailey, where the flames cleared the curtain. Coin Forest was under siege. She was too late.

Sharai raced toward the drawbridge. A group of knights wearing black and white livery clustered there, blocking entry to the castle. She reined the horse to a stop and backed away to avoid being seen.

To her right, several buildings burned, and more Hungerford knights roamed, along with several archers. She picked the opposite way, moving toward the darkness and an uneven collection of small roofs to her left. Peasants' cottages. Sharai urged Valiant away from the fires and the mill. She entered the humble section of the village.

People rushed by, wide-eyed, carrying chickens, tools, babies, and squealing pigs, running from the village. Sharai pulled Valiant in front of a fishmonger's cottage. "Have you seen Father Bernard?"

The lean man slung nets over his back and dragged a bag from the door. "Prayers won't help you. Run." He swerved around her horse, hurrying toward the fields.

A young boy scurried nearby, chasing chickens. He caught a tan cockerel and stuffed it into a large burlap bag. He turned his head while knotting the top of the sack and his unruly hair and profile became visible.

"Tommy."

Tommy turned and recognizing her, his nostrils flared in anger. "You're back, too?"

"What do you mean, 'too'?"

"You and Kadriya." He spat the words out. "You two did this."

Sharai's heart stuttered. "Where is she?"

"She's going to hell, where you'll soon join her." He lifted the throbbing, squawking bag of chickens and turned his back on her and his home.

Sharai placed her hand over her heart. Sweet saints, Kadriya was here. But where? She couldn't pass the enemy knights at the drawbridge. How could she get in? Long planks of wood stored under Tommy's roof caught her eye. The stilts. She remembered walking on them, so high that on the hill she could see over the castle curtain. She jumped off the horse and grabbed two pairs of them. Balancing them awkwardly across the saddle, she headed to the left, guiding Valiant along the shoreline of the moat.

She reached the south side and then slowed, trying desperately to remember that day, the thrill of balancing on the stilts. They had been near the garden, far from the great hall and kitchen, close to the pigsty. The knights would likely storm the great hall and take the keep, but they would not fight over beans or pigs.

Follow the smell. She closed her eyes, searching past the smoke and burning pitch for the scent of pig manure.

At the next curtain section, she caught a strong whiff of it.

Just a little farther. *Here.*

Valiant slid into the deep moat, head bobbing as he swam. He struggled, then found his footing and they reached the curtain. She slid off the destrier and lay the stilts on the ground, facing them together to form two H's. Resting the top two stilts on the footboard of the lower two stilts, she ripped strips from her skirt, tying them together, then propped the improvised ladder against the wall.

A quick glance at the height of the curtain dissuaded her for a moment. She could never climb that high. Even if she could, she had no dagger to defend herself. But Kadriya was there, maybe Tabor, too. She pushed her doubts away.

She checked her silk headscarf, making certain it concealed her hair. To cover her disgrace, she had looped the bottom so it dangled as if her hair were still long. The color worried her, bright orange and red that might draw unwanted attention, but inside the walls chaos reigned, and she would, with luck, land in the shadows of the garden.

Curling her toes around two chipped stones on the wall, she gripped the wooden poles and gained the first high step. A splinter drove into her hand. She balanced herself, pulled it out, and grabbed fistfuls of her skirt to protect her fingers. The next step was too high to reach. She wobbled on the stilts. She would have to step on a stone to get high enough to reach it. Leaning her torso toward the wall, she felt for a stone large enough that she could gain footing. She found one. Pain shot through her back from the awkward angle, but she maintained the stance to avoid swinging away from the wall on the stilts.

Taking a deep breath, she committed herself and curled her toes around a stone. She strained upward and found the top footboard with her left foot. She slipped off, and found it again.

From the other side of the curtain, horses whinnied and cried, pigs screamed, and the clash of metal was joined by grunts and moans of death.

Sharai's muscles burned. She gritted her teeth, lifting herself even higher.

Her second foot found the board, and her leg muscles relieved her shaking arms. She pulled herself up slowly, gaining enough height that she could grasp the top of the wall and see over.

To the far right the front face of the stables had collapsed into the fire. To the distant left the church burned, consuming the roof and cross. *Poor Father Bernard.* Flames shot high from the knights' housing, too, illuminating the Hungerford knights, who rammed the gate some sixty yards distant. Defending knights squared off, fighting the invaders, and servants and children hid in the shadows.

Sharai spied the wall walk with relief. The wooden walkway would allow her to move freely, high above the danger below. Rolling over the top, she landed on the high platform.

By the entrance to the keep, a tall woman broke free from the snarl of people, running in Sharai's direction. As she neared the south wall, the color of her hair became apparent. Red. *Maud.* A mounted knight pursued her, weaving in an attempt to cut her off. Maud veered away at the last minute, running for the chicken coop, yelling curses at him.

They came closer and the big knight jumped from his horse, tackling her. She punched him with the heel of her hand, sending his helmet flying and revealing a beefy face with a bulbous nose.

Rauf.

He grabbed Maud's arm, but she kicked free and scrambled toward the garden, just below Sharai.

Sir John rode up, his yellow hair dripping with sweat and plastered against his head. He angled his horse close to Rauf, and swung his sword, striking Rauf on his back. Slightly off balance, John recovered and raised his sword again.

Rauf spun, well balanced on his thick, muscular legs. He pulled a sleek sword and ran John through.

Sweet Mary.

John fell.

Rauf caught up with Maud, and they struggled, twisting, pulling. "Take your punishment, Maud."

Maud grunted and kicked, trying to reach for the weapons she wore on her legs. When that failed she splattered something in his face. "Dog-hearted whoreson! Go you to hell," she shouted.

Rauf wiped his face, looking at his hand. "Shit." He twisted her arm and grabbed her hair, jerking her head back.

Sharai glanced about frantically for a weapon. A bow and arrows rested at the southeast corner, too distant, and she was unskilled at archery. A stack of stones caught her eye. She grabbed a large one, throwing it at Rauf's head. It landed too far left. She hurled a second and hit her target, his big head lurching from the impact.

Eyes slit in anger, Rauf looked up at Sharai. "Ah, the Gypsy."

Responding to the diversion, Maud kicked him, wrenching herself free. She pulled a dagger and drove it toward his neck.

Rauf blocked it with his armored forearm. "Whore." With a primeval growl he swung his fist into her face.

Maud's knees buckled from the impact, and she fell, silent.

Horrified, Sharai sought to distract him. "Coward. White-feathered coward. So easy to fight a woman, eh?" She forced a taunting laugh. "But remember me, Rauf?" she taunted, "the little girl at St. Giles' Fair? I can fight you."

Huffing like a cornered boar, Rauf left Maud sprawled on the ground and strode toward Sharai.

From the east wall came the sound of wood splitting. An arrow burdened with pitch spattered its fiery fuel onto the wood at the southeast corner of the wall walk. Other fire arrows followed, and the walkway disappeared in a cloud of black smoke and orange flames. To her left, the wall walk ended abruptly where it led to a bolted, locked door.

She was trapped.

Directly below her in the garden, the healthy bean plants grew on their stakes. The raw ends of wood pointed at her in challenge. Sweet saints, she would impale herself if she jumped there.

Rauf ran under the walkway, glaring up at her with murder in his eyes. "Gypsy dung. I remember your dagger, and I have a special one for you." He slung a metal ball at her. It flashed in the air as it flew toward her face.

Sharai hurled herself on the floor of the walkway.

The grapnel hook caught in the wood, just an inch from her ankle.

Below, Rauf dug his heels into the knotted steps on the rope attached to the hook and started climbing.

Sweet saints. Sharai grabbed the hooks, trying to wrest them free from the wood, but Rauf's weight only made the hooks bite deeper into the wood.

"Come, Gypsy whore. Show me that pretty face." Rauf climbed with surprising agility to the walkway. "Come here, and I'll show you how I fight." He drew a dagger with two vicious-looking blades.

Sharai struggled to swallow. She had no dagger, no weapon of any sort. She edged backward toward the flame-filled corner, the acrid smell of burning pitch and her own terror filling her lungs.

CHAPTER TWENTY-ONE

Tabor joined his knights at the southwest tower of the curtain. Kadriya had arrived with her warning at almost the same time as Rauf, giving Tabor only enough time to don neck and breastplate armor, but he and his men had been able to settle Kadriya and the women safely with Cyrill above the solar, and they had heated pitch and distributed a good supply of stones and arrows about the inner curtain walkways.

Rauf's men had breached the main gate, but they would not take the castle. Not this time.

Straight ahead a narrow wooden walkway hugged the stone curtain that circled the perimeter of the bailey and led straight ahead eighty yards, where enemy knights held the exterior southeast tower. Tabor turned to his knight, Walter. "How many are there?"

Walter looked from Tabor to Henry then Wilson, counting. "Twice our number."

"From their position they threaten the solar. Drive them out of the tower."

Tabor shot an arrow, piercing a knight in the chest. He fell. The others rushed back to the safety of the tower.

Arrows whizzed back in reply, and Tabor and his men took cover.

Tabor grabbed a handful of pitch-soaked arrows and positioned himself behind a loophole. "Burn them out." Flames engulfed the walkway and the Hungerford knights spilled out, hurrying down the stairwell.

Tabor and his knights picked them off as they exited. Shooting his last arrow, Tabor felled another.

The pitch fire illuminated the previously dark south walk. There, twenty yards from where the walkway ceased, stood Rauf. He'd removed his helm and was advancing on a short woman dressed in a patchwork skirt and a long, orange scarf. She was trapped between the knight and the fire. She backed away from him, then climbed up on the handrail. If she jumped, she would fall on the wooden stakes below.

In the flickering light of the fire, Tabor saw her oval face and dark eyes.

Sharai. Her name stuck in his throat. Afraid to distract her and cause her to fall, he held his tongue. Tabor grabbed Walter's shoulder. "Look."

Walter sucked in a breath. "God's bones."

Rauf grabbed Sharai by the hips and pulled her back, throwing her on the walkway floor. He pounced on her and pulled a dagger. He shoved his beefy face in front of hers and held the dagger high above her, menacing her with it.

God's nails, and my arrows are spent. Must save her. He felt for his short war sword and dagger, then stepped up onto the handrail.

Wil blocked his way. "Nay, Tabor. There's seven feet of air between here and the south walkway. Your armor."

Tabor waved the warning away, but couldn't dismiss the danger. The walkway was twenty feet off the ground. Hungerford's knights swarmed below. If Tabor survived the fall he'd be run through several times over. Could he gain a foothold when he landed and if he did, could he keep his balance? He shrugged off the needling questions. There was but one answer: Sharai.

Concern for her cooled his fear and determination settled in his veins, tensing his muscles, clearing his mind. He saw his path and added a foot for good measure. He crouched low and committed himself.

A cry ripped from his throat and he sprang from the safety of the tower, toward the walkway.

He cleared the handrail and landed on his shoulder, crashing into Rauf, metal on metal, punching the wind out of him.

Pain shot through Tabor's knees from the impact. He grabbed Rauf by the back of the neck.

Rauf choked, then turned his dagger backward and stabbed.

Tabor ducked and released him.

Pivoting, Rauf faced him, and Tabor scrambled upright unsheathing his short sword.

"Tabor." Sharai cried out his name like an oath, her voice strangled with emotion. Her face was bruised, and tears filled her eyes.

She was alive, and she had returned. Joy flowed through him. "Get down and stay back." If Rauf killed him, so be it, but Tabor would die saving her.

Rauf's eyes widened in surprise, as if he had flushed out a boar, only to find himself facing two.

Rauf forced a laugh and drew his sword. "Well, my father was right about something. Chase the stench and you find the pig." He gestured, curling his fat fingers toward himself. "Come on, peasant."

Tabor stepped forward. "You seal your fate."

Rauf's lips thinned. "A pox on you, Tabor, though you'll not live long enough to grow a blister."

Tabor took the first step forward. The wall rose to Tabor's right, dangerous because it meant his right arm would be restricted, unlike Rauf, whose right arm would be free. Tabor must overcome the disadvantage with thrusts and footwork. And pray for an opening.

Tabor plunged forward. His sword slid the length of Rauf's

blade, making a jarring stop at the crossbar, sending a jolt all the way to Tabor's skull.

"I'll kill your Gypsy whore." Rauf whipped his sword, striking Tabor's left shoulder. "And feed her bones to the dogs."

Arcs of hot pain shot into Tabor's shoulder. He retreated, and then advanced again. His sword struck Rauf's armor solidly just below his ribs.

Rauf bared his teeth and rushed forward, clashing his blade against Tabor's. Rauf hovered with his sword and the evil-looking dagger, looking for his chance. "Lord of the castle, are you," he said through teeth clenched in pain. "Let's see if your blood runs thin as William's."

"This day," Tabor panted, "you go to hell."

Rauf advanced again, and their swords clanged.

Sweat blurred Tabor's vision, and his arm grew weary.

Sensing Tabor's weakness, Rauf lunged, his weapon reflecting the surrounding flames. His dagger sank beneath the plates of armor covering Tabor's left arm.

Tabor's arm spasmed in pain. He pushed Rauf's bulk away from him, extracting the blade and giving himself room.

He swung his sword high to low, crashing it into Rauf's neck.

Rauf stabbed his lethal dagger at Tabor, but Tabor's armor served him well, stopping it. Rauf advanced, kicking Tabor in the knee.

Tabor's leg buckled and he fell.

Rauf dropped heavily on Tabor, his knees on Tabor's chest.

"Now, you scum peasant. Now." He raised his dagger and plunged.

Tabor stopped his wrist and struggled against Rauf's massive weight, the burden almost breaking Tabor's arm. Two deadly blades curved from substantial chunks of steel into small fangs hovered, inches from his face

Rauf smelled his fear and leaned more of his weight on Tabor.

Sweat blurred Tabor's vision, but an image trickled into his consciousness. Rauf's armor was fractured, a visible break from under his left pouldron to mid-chest on his breastplate.

If he could create a diversion . . . *Sharai.* She had no weapon. Couldn't fight, but she had proven her courage in the past with Rauf, and her mere presence now could help him. Gambling, he opened his eyes wide and lifted his left hand gesturing to stop, looking behind Rauf, not at him. "No, Sharai. Nay!"

Rauf had been bested before by the courage and speed of the slight woman standing behind him. Would he respond?

He did. Rauf spun and raised the dagger, preparing to stab her. His movement lifted his pouldron, revealing the broken breastplate and exposing his upper chest.

Tabor pounced. He hacked at Rauf's wrist and Rauf lost his grip on the handle.

Tabor punched him in the face and claimed the dual-bladed dagger. Tabor lunged toward the spot in the broken breastplate and drove the strange dagger deep into Rauf's chest.

A slight grunt escaped Rauf's lips. His mouth flew open and he rolled sideways.

Tabor kicked him, and Rauf slammed into the handrail, splitting the wood in a series of loud cracks.

Power coursed through Tabor's veins, a blinding intensity that brought the blade out and back in again. "This is for William." His brother's arrogant grin flashed before him. "For Aurora." The pain in her eyes. Tabor withdrew the dagger and stabbed once more. "And Maud's brother."

The broken rail gave way from their combined weight. Sharai grabbed Tabor's arm from behind, steadying him, and Rauf, still speared by the strange dagger, fell onto the garden spikes below. Tabor held Sharai close to him with his good arm, and her trembling subsided. He lifted her face to his. Angry bruises marred her lovely face, swelling the skin at her left cheekbone, and her earlobe was swollen and bloody. But her eyes, her eyes. She lifted her veil of dark lashes, sparkling with tears, and the love shone through.

"Sharai, forgive me."

She kissed him, hard, as if dispelling their separation. "I love you." Her eyes filled with worry. "Kadriya?"

"She's safe."

The blazing timber behind Sharai collapsed, and the walkway just twenty yards distant sagged to the stone wall.

Tabor dropped to Rauf's rope ladder, extending his hand. "Hurry, before it collapses."

The bailey was tainted with smoke, spent arrows, and the smell of death. The injured moaned, pleading for help, and Father Bernard hurried among them, offering wine and encouragement.

"Father," said Sharai. "Maud, is she . . ."

"Alive, yes. In the kitchen," he nodded, moving on to another wounded man.

Tabor led Sharai past the, smoking ruins of the church.

Kadriya burst from the keep, her skinny legs flying. "*Sharai!*" With a shriek of joy, the young girl threw herself on Sharai, wrapping her legs around her waist.

Sharai released a strangled cry of relief and kissed the top of Kadriya's head, hugging her tightly. "I searched for hours, Sprig. I feared . . ." She trailed off.

"I knew you wouldn't leave me," Kadriya said.

"And here you are, you smart girl."

Kadriya touched Sharai's hair. "Where's that dog, Aydin?"

"He drowned, I fear."

"Fear my eye," Kadriya said. "Hooray!"

Cyrill approached, his eyes haunted. "Sir John," he said, misery in his voice. He shook his head.

Sharai's heart ached for Tabor as he followed Cyrill to confirm his friend's death.

They hurried to the kitchen and found Maud, bruised, bloodied, and making a feeble protest to a blood-letter who held his knife and basin at the ready.

Sharai nudged between them, protecting Maud. "Leave her be." She poured ale from the cask and moistened a cloth from the table, waving it to cool, and placed it gently on Maud's swollen eyes. "Thank heaven you're all right."

"You've a good aim," Maud said, laughing weakly, her red hair caked with blood at her temples. "Rauf, that fatheaded sod," she murmured, too weak to move her head. "He could not tame my tongue."

"Oh, Maud." Sharai's voice wavered and she patted Maud's hand. "It's a joy to hear your voice."

Sharai looked around. "Where's Lady Anne?"

"Fritham," Sprig said. "Lord Tabor found out she paid Aydin to take us, and he sent her away."

Hours later, Father Bernard had brought villagers to clear the bailey and bury the dead on the other side of the curtain, behind the church.

Sharai explained her escape, how Lord Hungerford had supplied Aydin with horses and knights, and how she found her way back to Coin Forest.

Then Tabor surrendered to treatment. Sharai helped him out of his armor, bathed him, and cleansed his wounds, working with herbs and knowing hands, applying the treatments Etti had taught her.

Sharai had returned to his chamber and stood before him now in the flickering candlelight, hesitating.

"We have a few hours before dawn," he said. "Come. Rest with me."

She shrank from the light. "I cannot." She avoided his eyes.

Tabor thought she must be disappointed in him for leaving her in Lady Anne's care. He rose from the bed, protecting his arm, and approached her.

She held out her hand to stay his advance.

He stopped four steps from her. If he had damaged her love for him, he would never forgive himself. "I knew not the depth of my mother's fear, Sharai. Please forgive me. Had I thought for a moment she'd send you away—"

She waved his apology aside. "Of course you didn't know."

He shook his head. "I should have brought you with me."

Her eyes welled with tears. " 'Tis not that."

"I was on an important errand, and I thought your appearance would work against my petition. Yet it came to naught after all. You could have represented yourself better than I."

She stepped forward and tugged at the orange scarf, and it slipped from her head and fell to the floor. Her gaze followed the scarf's descent, the downward movement loosing two tears that had welled in her eyes. The delicate globes of moisture sparkled in the candlelight and streaked silently down her skin, leaving two dark, wavering trails.

Her hair hung ragged just below her earlobes.

His stomach turned. Her hair was shorter than Tommy's.

A vision came of her, dancing for him, here in this chamber, just days ago, her long, ebony curls falling to her waist. The count. Tabor's hands fisted. Her grace. Her dignity. He moved toward her.

She pulled away.

"Aydin did this."

"He said he would make me love him."

"I'll kill him."

"He's already dead."

"Then I'll kill him twice and again." Fury choked him, making it difficult to speak.

She tucked her ragged hair behind her ears, trying to hide it.

His heart ached for her. "Your beauty shines through. 'Tis no matter."

"You know better."

He pulled her toward him and kissed her, running his fingers through her short hair.

She cried out and pulled away. "My hair is only part of it. I am a peasant, Tabor, and always will be." She held his gaze. "Seven pounds."

"What?"

"I was sold at market for seven pounds."

"Sharai."

Her voice broke in defeat. "I can wear the silks and dress like one, but I'll never be a noble—"

"You're noble inside, Sharai. Inside."

"—and your villagers suspect me of sorcery. Now Rauf is dead; Lord Hungerford will be even more determined to steal your land. Lady Anne is right. You'll lose all if I stay." She hovered at the door.

Not wanting to press her, Tabor retreated to the chest and sat. "I went to Bath, and—"

"Aydin took me from here, but I was going to leave, anyway. This love we found." She hesitated. "What we *shared*," she corrected, "was more than I ever dreamed of, but," she choked, "it's not possible."

"I saw Gloucester there."

She looked out the darkened window. "From that time I first saw you from the stage, my life changed. I wanted you, but I could never hope for someone like you. I am unworthy, and I should have looked the other way. I even tried, but stubborn you. You made that contract with Etti, and I came here and—"

"Sharai, I love you."

She studied the palms of her hands as if to find an answer there. "You weren't at all what I thought you would be. You were kind and responsible, and your people cared for you. And so did I."

"I love you for loving me, Sharai. Don't stop."

"I never will." She came to him. "But we fooled ourselves, Tabor. It can never be for us."

What had happened to her fiery spirit? What had become of her fierce conviction that they could triumph if they believed in the power of their love? "You've changed. I'll strangle Aydin for killing your spirit."

"He didn't. I came back to fight for you, and fight for Kadriya. But I will not fight for us, because it's hopeless."

"I will."

She bent down for her scarf.

Tabor grabbed it, flipping it out of her hands.

She nodded slowly. "You're right. I cannot hide." She turned to leave.

Tabor grabbed her wrist and pulled her toward him. "Listen to me. Gloucester ruled in my favor. Rauf is dead; his father has no claim to Coin Forest. The castle, my family, the village— everyone's safe."

Her brown eyes watered again, and a weary smile softened her face, but it couldn't hide her pain. "I knew you were capable, of that and so much more. I'm happy for you, Tabor."

She turned from him, and when she met his gaze again, her eyes were dry. "Did Gloucester give his blessing for our union?"

Tabor swallowed hard.

"I thought not. You see, I cannot stay."

He dropped the scarf and held her hand, running his fingers lightly between hers, savoring her velvet skin and warmth, and the exquisite sensation of her closeness. "I know." He met her eyes and put voice to what he had been considering since Bath.

"Which is why I am leaving with you."

"What? You can never leave Coin Forest. 'Tis your home."

"In my heart, I am tied to you, not the land." He gestured to the bed. "Come, rest with me. I've missed you so much. I want to hold you close."

"I must leave." She shut her eyes, and another tear escaped.

He rushed to her and kissed her gently on her lips and her cheeks.

She put her arms around him and they stood together. He felt her fear and tried to hold her closely enough to give her the strength to believe in their future, in spite of Gloucester's decision that they could not wed.

She followed him to the bed and lay with him.

He held her hand. "Coin Forest is safe from the Hungerfords. It can revert to the crown, and it can be granted to a deserving noble. I can leave with a clear conscience, and we can wed."

"You would defy your king? Abandon Coin Forest?"

Aye, there were still problems he had not worked out. "You ask too many questions. Can you find it in your heart to love a simple knight?"

"Your family, Tabor."

"I love you more than my family," he answered.

"More than your liege?"

"I'm a skilled knight, though I'll never fight against England. We'll build a home, small, but in a fertile valley. You can have your garden. We'll have horses. You and Kadriya can ride. We'll have our own family, our own children."

"But at the cost of your honor."

"My honor is not tied to Coin Forest. I know that now. I also know if we stay here, I must wed another woman of the king's choosing. Would you rather that?"

"I would rather you love me, one last time." She met his

gaze, and she seemed to slip into his soul, her large brown eyes darkening, filling him with an aching joy and need. She stroked his lips lightly with her finger, then kissed him, her mouth warm and thrilling, sliding wet against his lips, stirring his body to response.

She ended the kiss and slipped out of her clothes. Poised above him, she lowered herself onto him, gently, as if concerned her weight would hurt him. Sooth, she felt light as a fairy, but every curve all deliciously woman. She took him inside her.

He gasped from the pleasure, and stroked her, returning the pleasure.

She moved slowly, delicately, and the gentleness of it wrapped around him, warm and loving.

Hope and desire flooded him, and he held her tight, responding to a new urgency.

He moved deep and fast.

Her breasts pressed into his chest, her mouth on his. She answered his movements, withholding nothing.

They clung to each other, steadfast against all else or others. His heart pounded insistently and he tumbled out of control, bursting inside, releasing his seed. He held her bottom tight to him for a moment, savoring their union, then moved again, stroking her with his body and fingers, bringing her closer.

She trembled against him, her sharp cry of release filling the chamber, and then she lay still, snuggling.

Her heart raced, beating strongly against his chest.

His heart hurried in answer. Tabor smoothed his hands over her soft curves, relishing the sensation of skin on skin. Their hearts slowed, along with their breathing.

He stroked her hair, playing with the ends. "It will grow."

"I know." She kissed him, and then closed her eyes.

He gazed at her features, memorizing her high cheekbones, strong, straight nose, and small chin. Her face was serene now, but it could be so lively and expressive. Like the time she saw her bean plants blossom. He smiled, remembering the breathless anticipation in her eyes when he ate the frog-bone cake. And her concern when she first read his palm, and saw something so dark she had yet to tell him of it. And the joy when he told her how much he liked the pennants she sewed for him.

He pushed a ragged strand of hair from her face. She was so full of love and life.

Dawn lit her face, overpowering the candle.

His thoughts grew grim. Neither king nor duty will keep her from me. *I will die before I give her up.*

Could he forfeit his honor and abandon his family? Was there any hope left to petition Gloucester again, annoy him into granting him the right to wed her? His chances would be slim, nay, disastrous, if he took the issue before the royal council.

A shuddering sickness overwhelmed him. He had but two choices. Stay on Gloucester's terms or leave and give Coin Forest back to the crown.

A distant sound awoke him. The sun still shone low to the east; he must have drifted off for a short time. He listened for more. Had he dreamt it?

A horn blew.

Another answered from the watchtowers.

Tabor bolted from bed, grimacing with pain.

Sharai rose. "What is it?"

A single name came to his mind.

Hungerford.

CHAPTER TWENTY-TWO

Tabor left Sharai in the safety of the solar and hurried through the demolished gate door, down the steps and into the bailey. Cyrill joined him, along with what was left of their garrison.

In spite of his orders, Sharai appeared with Kadriya, peeking out of the stone way.

A large party advanced, a dozen knights wearing royal livery and carrying a banner: three fleurs-de-lis on azure and three lions passant guardant.

"The king," said Cyrill.

"They're royal arms," agreed Tabor, "but note the white border around the shield." He nodded. "It's Gloucester."

Confident, Tabor stood ready to receive him. He had not provoked the attack and had only defended himself and Coin Forest.

Horns sounded, and the herald announced His Grace, Humphrey, Duke of Gloucester, Chief Councillor and Keeper of the Peace during the king's minority.

Gloucester approached, draped in a purple velvet cloak with white ermine trim.

Tabor bowed. "Your Grace."

Gloucester surveyed the damaged bailey with a frown. "I see Rauf has been here."

"How did you know?"

"Lord Hungerford wrote, warning me. It was not his wish that his son attack."

"Too civilized for that, is he?"

Gloucester searched among those gathered in the bailey. "Is Rauf here?"

"He has expired," Tabor said.

"Are his knights here?"

"Twenty dead and eight detained in the tower," Tabor answered.

"The Lady Anne?" inquired Gloucester.

"Safe in Fritham."

"Your priest?"

Tabor looked toward the burned shell of the nave. "His church lies wasted, but he's alive."

Gloucester leaned forward. "And the Gypsy, Sharai?"

"Safe and well, in spite of Rauf's best efforts. Please, Your Grace," Tabor said, recovering enough to observe protocol. "The hall is damaged, but we can offer food and the comfort of the solar after your travels."

In the solar, Gloucester approached Sharai and Kadriya.

Sharai had covered her hair in a headdress and veil, which also discreetly covered her torn earlobe. All her clothes had been lost because of Aydin, and her skirt badly torn during her struggle with Rauf. She had changed into the green silk gown she had sewn for Lady Emilyne, inches too wide and a foot too long.

The length made her steps uncertain, and in the presence of royalty her usual confidence seemed to have wavered. Her back was stiff with apprehension, and anxiety flickered in her eyes, but her beauty shone through it all, and Tabor thought his heart would burst with love for her.

Gloucester's mouth curved in a gentle smile, and his keen eyes watched her. "I've heard much about you, Sharai," he said.

She said nothing, giving only a slight nod and a tentative smile.

He scanned the solar and raised his voice. "You will excuse Lord Tabor and me," he commanded smoothly to all in earshot. "We have private matters to discuss."

Tabor led the way to his private chambers. Inside, Gloucester took a position by the fireplace and Tabor, too nervous to sit, stood by the window.

"At Eleanor's insistence I have reconsidered your petition." Tabor's stomach pitched. He waited.

"The duchess thinks me inconstant that I should be forceful in my own selection of a wife, and then admonish you for like conduct."

Tabor gripped the frame of the window. Could it be possible?

Shaking his head, Gloucester continued. "On the other hand, you must see the awkward position this puts me in. Should you wed this peasant girl, the crown forfeits any favorable alliances it could draw from your union."

Tabor steeled himself. "What are you thinking?"

"A long memory of this boon, Lord Tabor, and a considerable marriage fine to rectify the crown for lost alliances."

Relief rushed through Tabor's veins. "Of course."

"I will rely on your political support."

Tabor fought the urge to shout for joy. Though Gloucester's statesmanship was marred by the long-running power feud with his brother and his unfortunate trait of carrying grudges, he was a fair man, a hero at war, and a long-standing patron of books and scholars. "I will be pleased to provide my support, Your Grace. I vow you shall have it."

Gloucester nodded. "I remember your loyalty in Paris." He pulled a sealed envelope from a pocket in his cloak. "And I wish you happiness. Please hand deliver this to Sharai."

Wearing a self-satisfied smile, Gloucester returned to the solar.

The moment rang loud in Tabor's ears. He pounded the table

and fought the urge to run to Sharai like a raw squire and twirl her around in circles.

He slipped Sharai's envelope in the pocket of his cotehardie. No, that would not do. He had something else in mind.

The next morning Sharai sat with Tabor at high table. Gloucester had left as quickly as he had come, and Tabor had been distant. Likely the prince had laughed at Sharai, wearing ill-fitting clothes that matched her ill-fitting presence in this castle. He was no doubt relieved at his decision to refuse their union. Marriages were based on station and political advantage, not love. Tabor's security depended on his alliance with Gloucester, and she simply had nothing to offer.

Lady Anne's chair was empty. Sharai would never forget her condemnation, but she felt sorry for her. The woman lived in constant fear of other people's judgment, and she didn't realize the many fine qualities her son possessed. Sharai fingered the hem of the linen tablecloth, turning the smooth fabric in her fingertips. No matter. The Hungerford problem was solved, and mother and son would eventually work out their problems.

Father Bernard was at table, his blue eyes haunted from the deaths and burials. Once his work was done, Sharai would ask him again about the monastery. She had no dowry, but certes the nuns could make use of her skills, and they in turn could offer education for Kadriya and safety behind the abbey's high, thick walls.

Tabor, freshly shaven and handsome in spite of his bruises and wounds, gave her that special look, taking her breath away, and he squeezed her hand. "I must see you now, in the solar." He looked pleased. Sharai supposed he should be. The morning sunshine reached into her heart, a quiet joy for him, yet she would not be here to share in his life. She pushed the thought away and forced a smile. "Of course."

In the solar, he directed her to sit in one of the chairs

clustered by the window. She fluffed the apple-colored cushions she had sewn and did so.

With a look of childlike anticipation on his face, he placed a small white casket on her lap. A hand length long and half wide, it was a rectangular box with a truncated triangular lid. Carvings of roses ran the length of the box. On the front of the lid, two cherubs danced with scarves, while two others played a drum and flute. Sharai traced them with her fingertips. "Ivory. I have seen such art, but only from afar. I have never touched it." She ran her fingertips lightly over the sides, where soldiers stood guard, holding spears, swords and shields. Age darkened the exquisite detail of each face, each hand, and the hinges shone golden in the sunlight.

Tabor sat opposite her, watching her every movement. "Open it." His voice rang with excitement, and her heart danced like a stone skipping over water.

What could be inside such a treasure?

She pulled the latch gently and lifted the lid. She stared at the contents, then met his gaze. There was no mischief in his face. She resisted a frown and tried to read his mood.

"Dirt." She nodded slowly. "You're giving me a box of dirt."

"But look inside."

Her disappointment and weariness from the last several days threatened to draw tears. She swallowed, trying to show some interest. "Look inside the dirt?"

"Aye. All is not always as it seems."

He was enjoying himself to excess. She gave him a "watch-yourself" look and plunged her pointer finger in the dirt, stirring it around. She found a small object and pulled it out, holding it between them, in front of his mischievous face. "You gave me a bean."

Love shone in his eyes.

Her skin tingled from her face, down her neck and to her

chest. Her heart jumped two wild hops in her chest. "Do not tease me," she choked on her words, terrified to believe if it were not so.

He pulled her to her feet. "Come with me."

He pulled her down the stairs, out to the bailey. Holding her hand, he pulled her so fast she had to run. He stopped at the garden. "There. See, I had Hungerford's knights till it for you."

He looked to the end of the garden, or where it used to end. A new, five-foot square section near the chicken coop had been dug and turned. " 'Tis yours, Sharai. Ready to plant with beans, herbs, whatever you want, because you—and Kadriya—will be with me, season after season, year after year. If you will have me." He took her into his arms. "What say you? Will you be my wife, bear my children, and make frog-bone cakes for me till the end of our days?" He kissed her, a quick, hard kiss, as if he was too excited to linger because he must go on. "Gloucester has granted us license to wed."

Sharai jumped up into his arms, swinging her legs around his hips. She cried out in joy, kissing his face, his eyes, his bruised cheek.

He cradled her head in his big hands and covered her mouth with his, and his kiss melted her.

But then she thought about the box and the dirt, and she pulled away. "We're free to wed? Fie!" She punched his good arm. "You knew yesterday, and you didn't tell me. You left me to suffer while you filled a box with dirt."

He laughed, then sobered. "I hope you forgive me. But I needed a betrothal present, and I couldn't wait." He lowered her to the ground, and his voice became hushed. "When we first met, I thought you cared more for coin and earthly riches than you could ever care for me. When Gloucester finally gave us license, I thought of giving you an exquisite gem that would shine for all to see, so they might know how much I treasure you. But your needs are deeper. You explained that you are *vatrasi,* of the Gypsies who settle. I wanted to give you what you love most—not gems, but a home."

His eyes had become moist, and he pulled away. "I almost forgot, I have this for you, from Gloucester's wife, the duchess, Eleanor." He stopped, envelope midair, and looked around the bailey.

Cyrill, Kadriya, Maud, and servants and knights alike had gathered, pretending to sweep, scrub, or visit, but all sounds had died, and many curious eyes focused on them.

Tabor cleared his throat loudly.

Heads turned away, and everyone returned to their feigned activities.

Sharai grew lightheaded. "I must sit." They settled by the well, leaning against the old stones in the shade of the rising sun, and she opened Eleanor's letter.

Sharai,

I wish you happiness. Be always true to England, and remember my husband's kindness. He will need your loyalty in the upcoming parliament.

We share an interest in love charms, you and I. I am most curious about your love-spell cake. Not since my own husband have I seen a man so smitten. Mayhap at your wedding you will share your secrets with me, and I will share a secret spell of mine own, one of bay leaves and rooster's feathers to help you conceive a son.

E.

Tabor nudged her. "Well? What did she say?"

"You told her about the frog bones?"

"I had heard she dabbled with spells, so I thought it safe." His eyebrow lifted in curiosity. "What about the frog bones?"

"She thinks me a sorceress."

He rubbed his chin like a wizened sage. "These things happen. At one time I thought you a simple dancer."

She leaned in to him and smiled. "Aye, and I thought you a selfish noble."

"And now?" His eyes captured her.

"Why, Lord Tabor," she said, joy catching in her throat. "Might you be fishing for a compliment?"

He widened his brown eyes ever so slightly, as if startled at the thought.

She laughed and gestured him closer. "Come and let me do so with a kiss."

AUTHOR'S NOTE

Over the centuries, Gypsies (Romani) have been romanticized, feared, tortured, and expelled. Yet these nomadic people for a brief time enjoyed a social honeymoon in Europe. In a time span of several decades, royalty, the church, and nobles in many countries not only welcomed the Gypsies but also willingly financed their journeys through their lands.

Records of their travels suggest that India is their land of origin, but these nomadic people more often claimed Egypt as their homeland. During their exodus through western Europe, the clever Gypsies ascertained that nobility had its privileges. Always adaptable, they assumed titles such as "Count" and "Duke." Harnessing the popularity of pilgrimages, their story evolved: they claimed to be of noble blood, ejected from their lands in Little Egypt. They traveled on a pilgrimage of penitence by order of the pope himself, who directed them to roam the earth for seven years without sleeping in a bed.

Dark-skinned and handsome, riding choice steeds and dressed in exotic clothes, the Gypsies dazzled peasants and royalty alike. Gypsies gained papers ensuring safe conduct from such dignitaries as King James IV of Scotland and Sigismund, Holy Roman Emperor (1411–37) and King of Hungary (1387–1437).

While the first written evidence of Gypsies in the British Isles is dated April, 1505, it's probable that the Gypsies arrived at an earlier time. Official documents exist, along with stories which tell of Gypsies arriving in Paris in 1427, last seen heading toward England, likely enticed by the rich, powerful country that seemed to be finally winning the Hundred Years War.

During this time Gypsies were sold and traded, along with their bears and monkeys, in Bulgaria and Wallachia, and shipped to southern France. Thirteenth-century records reveal that a young Gypsy girl was sold in Marseilles for nine pounds and fifteen solidi.

Tens of thousands of Gypsies were confined in slavery, and yet, with the right clothes and a convincing story, they could become noble pilgrims, receiving respect and sustenance during their travels. One would be hard put to imagine better incentive to escape.

It is in this atmosphere of early social honeymoon that my fictional heroine, Sharai, appears in *Tabor's Trinket*. She was shipped as a slave from Wallachia to Marseilles, fled France and ferried to England with a small band of fellow Gypsies, seeking freedom from slavery and a new beginning.

Also during this time Humphrey, Duke of Gloucester, periodically ruled England in his child nephew, King Henry VI's stead. He met his future wife, Eleanor, when she was but a lady-in-waiting for Gloucester's new wife, Jacqueline of Hainault. That marriage, conceived in politics, died in politics and was annulled. This freed Gloucester to wed Eleanor, his paramour from a considerably more humble background than his, and one who was known to dabble in sorcery.

Gloucester often traveled the far reaches of the realm, settling feuds between nobility. An intelligent, quick-tempered man, Gloucester savored power but was destined to live on the fringe of it, first as the king's brother (Henry V) then, at his brother's death, grasping what power he could as the child king's uncle.

ABOUT THE AUTHOR

Janet Lane, Nebraska/Iowa native and Colorado transplant, graduated with distinction from the University of Colorado at Denver. Her words have appeared in newspaper, television, radio, magazines, songs, outdoor billboards, on a paperweight, a Frisbee, and even on a puzzle during her ad agency days. She's been a promotion director, a television reporter, a crude oil buyer, a waitress, ad agency owner, elevator operator, director of her community's annual musical production, a bar maid, tennis captain, and a special sections editor for a women's magazine. No, not in that order. Yes, she's a Gemini. She currently pens a monthly column on writing, and her fiction work has won several national awards. She lives in the Denver area with her husband, their two daughters, two Labs, and a Don Juan cat. She invites you to write to her at P.O. Box 1070, Littleton, CO 80160 or visit her web site at www.janetlane.net.